MONSIEUR MAL

Also by Daniel Pennac in English translation

Previous volumes in the Belleville Quintet

THE FAIRY GUNMOTHER

THE SCAPEGOAT

WRITE TO KILL

PASSION FRUIT

Essay

READS LIKE A NOVEL

Daniel Pennac

MONSIEUR MALAUSSÈNE

Translated from the French by
Ian Monk

THE HARVILL PRESS
LONDON

First published by The Harvill Press, 2003

2 4 6 8 10 9 7 5 3

Oirignally published with the title *Monsieur Malaussène*
by Editions Gallimard, Paris, 1995

This book is supported by the French Ministry of Foreign
Affairs, as part of the Burgess Programme headed for the
French Embassy in London by the
Institut Français du Royaume-Uni

Liberté • Égalité • Fraternité
RÉPUBLIQUE FRANÇAISE

First published in Great Britain in 2003 by
The Harvill Press
Random House, 20 Vauxhall Bridge Road,
London SW1V 2SA

Random House Australia (Pty) Limited
20 Alfred Street, Milsons Point, Sydney,
New South Wales 2061, Australia

Random House New Zealand Limited
18 Poland Road, Glenfield,
Auckland 10, New Zealand

Random House South Africa (Pty) Limited
Endulini, 5A Jubilee Road, Parktown 2193, South Africa

The Random House Group Limited Reg. No. 954009
www.randomhouse.co.uk

A CIP catalogue record for this book is available from the
British Library

ISBN 1 84343 020 7

Typeset by SX Composing DTP, Rayleigh, Essex
Printed and bound in Great Britain by
Mackays of Chatham Plc, Chatham, Kent

For Odile Lagay-Préaux
and Christian Mounier

To Belleville
(or what's left of it)

In the vanished smile
of Robert Doisneau

May a shower of thanks fall on Françoise Dousset and Jean-Philippe Postel; if they do not know why, the author does. As for Roger Grenier, Jean-Marie Laclavetine and Didier Lamaison, thanks be to their iiiiiiiiiiimmense patience.

Faites vos yeux, rien ne voit plus.
Christian Mounier

I
IN HONOUR OF LIFE

*Can you write, Malaussène? Well, can you? Of course you can't . . .
then do something meaty instead, a baby for instance, a beautiful,
chubby little baby!*

Chapter 1

THE CHILD HAD been nailed to the door like a bird of ill omen. Its full-moon eyes were those of a screech-owl.

Meanwhile, seven people were bounding up the stairs. Of course, they did not realise that this time a kid had been nailed to the door. They thought they'd seen it all, so they were in for a surprise. A couple more landings and a little Jesus aged six or seven would be barring their way: a baby God nailed up live on a door. Who could have imagined such a thing?

Belleville had already thrown everything it had at them, so what more could it now do? They had been welcomed by lumps of dead meat and potato peel, hordes of ululating women had scratched at their faces, once they had had to shoo their way through a herd of sheep which was taking up the entire six floors, with hundreds of amorous ewes flanked by jealously polygamous rams, on another occasion they had found the whole building was empty, deserted by a human tidal wave which, in its flow of eviction, had relieved itself on each step. Such a brown-carpet welcome did make a change from those dawn raids when it rained shit on their neat official heads.

Everything, Belleville had tried it all – but not once, not one single time, had they retreated from a property without opening the door they had come to open, repossessing the furniture they had come to repossess, and evicting the undesirables they had come to evict. There were seven of them and they had never failed. They had the Law on their side. Even better, they embodied the Law, they were the Law's pseudopods, the lords of the pre-emptive strike, the guardians of the sacred threshold of the tolerable. They had studied hard to get where they were, they had cultivated their minds and learnt to control their emotions. What did last-ditch stands or thoughts of despair matter to them? But they still had their souls, which were well protected by their muscles. They handed out blows or words of consolation, the customer was always right, but they always did what they had to do. They were human, in fact, splendid social animals.

They even had names. The bailiff was called La Herse, whose offices stood on Rue Saint-Maur, his trainee assistant was called Clément, the four removal men also had names and, last but not least, the locksmith had a nickname that everyone in Belleville pronounced while spitting on the ground: Cissou the Snow. Cissou the Snow, the Open Sesame of repossession, the housebreaker of evictions, La Herse Ltd's favourite skeleton key.

It sometimes occurred to La Herse to wonder how Cissou could go on living in Belleville while taking part in all these evictions, but La Herse lost no sleep on that score. There would always be cops to be jeered at, teachers to be harassed, tenors to be booed at and bailiffs to relish the hatred they inspired. So why not a locksmith-cum-bouncer on the streets of the homeless? Cissou must really get a kick out of strong emotions. Such was La Herse's wisely realistic conclusion.

So up they went towards the little crucifix, their souls at peace and their wits alert. The silence should have worried them, but then events in the buildings of Belleville always started silently. They were used to working as a team and trusted one another's reflexes. They were running up. That was their trademark. They worked fast and unflinchingly. Clément the trainee was leading the way, followed by his boss and the four removal men. Behind them, even Cissou was running, despite his sixty-odd years of infamy.

The first thing La Herse saw was not the child, but the face of Clément, his trainee.

Who had frozen on the landing of the fourth floor.

Who had spun round then doubled over, like a boxer who had been hit in the liver.

Whose eyes had rotated through 180 degrees.

Whose mouth suddenly opened like a crater.

From which burst an arching walnut-brown spray of quite extraordinary acidity and considerable nutritional value.

Monsieur La Herse had no more time to protect himself than his trainee had had time to block the deluge. His own croissant resurfaced too, followed by the eight coffee and liqueurs which the removal men had knocked back while awaiting the legal time for the eviction.

Only the locksmith escaped this friendly fire.

"What the fuck's going on?"

This was the sole question with which his deep compassion inspired him. Far from thinking of running away, he elbowed his way through the others' convulsions. On the landing of the fourth floor, the trainee bailiff was now curled

4

up against the wall, producing staccato bursts, which for the most part hit his employer's shoes.

Only then did Cissou spot the child.

"Jesus Christ!"

He turned round and pointed.

"Have you seen that?"

La Herse's answering stare informed him that he had eyes only for *that*. Revelation was written all over his face. The removal men, too, had seraphic gleams about them. They were medieval angels, horrified by the dark side of creation.

Everyone was now looking at the child. And, even from between the trainee's sticky fingers, the kid was not a pretty picture. Six-inch nails with triangular heads – real biblical stuff in the imagery of Hollywood – had apparently crushed their way through his bones, causing his feet to explode around them. The child did not look nailed up as much as squashed flat right in front of them, there on that door, with a violence of a bygone age.

"It's all over the place."

Thus do we speak of the dead, when our living souls tell us that someone is now nothing but inanimate matter. And this particular matter was sticky and forming into clots right across the floor of the landing.

"They didn't even take his glasses off."

Indeed they had not and, as usual, this touching detail added greatly to the scene's horror. The child's dilated eyes were staring at the gang through the double ring of its rose-tinted glasses. The look of a sacrificed owl.

"How . . . how could they?"

La Herse was suddenly against all forms of violence.

"Look, he . . . he's still breathing."

If you could call that wheezing of tormented lungs a breath. If you could call that pink froth bubbling up at the child's lips respiration.

"His hands . . . his feet . . ."

There were no hands or feet . . . they must have been crushed inside the jellaba by the nails. The worst thing of all, in fact, was the jellaba, which had once been so white, and had now been amputated four times over.

"The police . . . call the police at once!" La Herse chanted out his order without taking his eyes off the slaughtered child.

"No, not the police!" This was one point on which Cissou never conceded. "Since when have we been calling in the police?"

And it was indeed one of their guiding principles: never call in the forces of order. Since when had a qualified, governmental official, duly sworn in and ably assisted, needed help from the up-keepers of Law and Order?

The old locksmith then scrutinised the little martyr's face calmly. And the child spoke. Clearly, but like a soul that had already taken wing.

The child said:

"You're not going in there."

Cissou raised his eyebrows.

"And may I ask why not?"

The child said:

"Because it's even worse inside."

It was hard to think of a more off-putting answer. But it didn't trouble the locksmith. He just looked carefully over that gory mess and asked:

"Can I have a taste?"

Without waiting for permission, he plunged his forefinger into the wound which ripped into the jellaba on the child's right side. He then licked it lingeringly, smacked his tongue and observed:

"Chilli sauce."

His eyes raised, he analysed the composition.

"Chilli sauce . . . Ketchup . . ."

He licked his lips like a real connoisseur.

"With a hint of raspberry jam . . ."

It was as if he had spent his entire life savouring martyrs.

"But why the onions?"

"It's for the skin," the child replied at once. "The bits of skin on the door. They make a good likeness."

Cissou was now staring at him tenderly.

"You little bugger . . ."

Then his voice rose up from the depths of his guts:

"You're in for a lovely descent from the cross, take my word for it."

His smile had gone and he was now booming, thundering even. Holy Jesus, he was going to un-nail that little fucker in less time than it takes to convert to the true faith! He thundered and raised his hands, like hooks of vengeance.

It was then that the miracle happened.

The locksmith's hands smashed down on a jellaba which had just given up its ghost.

The child was no longer there.

The rest of the gang did not immediately understand why Cissou had collapsed, clutching at his guts, nor did they recognise a child in that gleaming pink naked thing which leapt over the body of Clément the trainee, before bombing downstairs without even slipping on the remains of their breakfasts. By the time they realised that the little ghost was wearing trainers and had identified the dancing peach as the arse of a quicksilver kid, it was too late. The doors of the lower storeys opened to reveal a clamorous multi-coloured crowd of street Arabs who were escorting their resurrected god.

Chapter 2

"AND THEN? WHAT happened next? Tell us how they got into the flat!"

"I've already told you a hundred times. No more nonsense with a locksmith, they kicked the door down to work off their tempers."

"Breaking and entering! But La Herse is a qualified bailiff! He should know better!"

"And then? And then?"

"And then they all came to a halt again. Because of the stench, of course."

"Two thousand six hundred and sixty-seven nappies! Me and Nourdine and Leila went round collecting. The whole of Belleville chipped in: 2,667 nappies all full to the brim!"

"Did you put them in all the rooms?"

"Even one in the butter dish."

"A lovely slice of bread and shit in old Widow Griffard's butter dish, can you just imagine it?"

"But there's worse to come . . ."

"Really? Then tell us the worst bit, Cissou!"

"Come on, Cissou, we want to hear the worst bit!"

∗

Sorry, but it's high time that I, Benjamin Malaussène, as the highly responsible big brother that I am, interrupt this yarn to point out that I thoroughly disapprove of my brothers and sisters taking part in such orchestrated attempts to push La Herse the bailiff into serious professional misconduct.

Serious professional misconduct, you say?

Yes indeed. For the flat whose furnishings he was supposed to seize was not the flat on whose door my youngest brother was playing crucifixions, but the one upstairs. That's right, on the next floor. The door on which they discovered our prophetic martyr with rose-tinted glasses belonged to Widow Griffard, the owner of the entire block. And so it was that, in the throes of deep emotion, our bailiff made off with the plaintiff's furniture, while supposing that it belonged to the tenant about whom she had lodged a complaint with the forces of justice; that it was the landlady's door which was kicked to matchwood; and, even more seriously, that it was the widow's nest egg which vanished into La Herse's incorruptible pockets because he believed he was making off with the ill-gotten gains of some supposedly skint tenant from the wrong side of the Mediterranean. At the sight of such a terrible travesty, I, Benjamin Malaussène, protest most solemnly . . .

*

"Stop getting into a sulk, Ben. Don't you want Cissou to tell us the worst bit?"

Whether I wanted him to or not, the damage had already been done, and my authority had upped and gone.

"Come on, Cissou, tell us the rest. But before you do, give us a sip of the Sidi-Brahim. I feel like I'm fading away."

This was all going on at The Zebra, Belleville's last cinema, around a table which had been set up on the stage, with eighteen of us sharing Yasmina's couscous. My tribe: Clara, Thérèse, Louna, Jeremy, Half Pint, Verdun, What An Angel, Julius my dog and Julie my Julie, to whom we must add Cissou the Snow, of course, plus our old friend Suzanne, who ran The Zebra, along with the entirety of the Ben Tayeb clan, who, if things had run their legal course, would have slept that night in a flat devoid of furniture.

Eighteen guests implicated in some highly serious goings-on, who were probably enjoying their last couscous as free men and women in Belleville's last living cinema.

"The worst bit . . ." Cissou began.

(I'll have a word or two to add about this particular guest.)

"The worst bit was the flies."

"Was the flies or were the flies?" Half Pint asked.

"Who cares?" Cissou went on. "Forget the grammar and let's see what you're like at mental arithmetic. Right, so how much does 2,667 multiplied by an average content of 300 grams make?"

"Eight hundred kilos of shit!" Jeremy yelled.

"Jeremy, we *are* eating, you know," Thérèse moaned, putting down her laden fork.

"Spot on! Eight hundred kilos plus another hundred grams for the butter dish."

I must say Thérèse was right. All of this was in the worst possible taste. Doing a bit of light-hearted law-breaking was one thing, but such awful taste, such a denial of all things civilised, was more than I could take! So we shall ignore Cissou the Snow's long calculations which led to the conclusion that one gram of shit produces a swarm of bluebottles every six hours, so 800 kilos of the same substance, stocked for three weeks during a particularly hot July in a flat in Belleville (facing south with its windows closed) produced a quantity of muscidae which defied all forms of mental arithmetic – unless you wanted to measure the *depth* of the living pattern which was covering the entire surface of the walls.

The little prophet had been right: it was definitely worse inside.

*

"You see, Benjamin, you're laughing now too!"

"It isn't the tale that's making me laugh, it's the teller. Which isn't the same thing at all."

"It's what you call 'style'," Suzanne added, as rosy and as spot on as ever.

"We know, we know," the kids groaned. "He's been bending our ears about style since the year dot!"

(A complete lack of authority! Not the slightest cultural influence! I was no longer holding the reins. It was time I let life just get on with it.)

"Now, when a fly wakes up, it takes wing. And so do its sisters."

"Did they all take off at the same time?"

"When the bouncers opened the shutters they did!"

"And then?"

"Then they all showed what they still had in their guts."

"You mean they started puking all over the place again?"

"For goodness' sake, Jeremy, *we are eating*!"

*

This tale is all the sorrier in that it has little to do with what was to happen later. But it is certainly true that the sudden arrival of sunlight, the flash of life in Widow Griffard's flat, woke up its teeming wallpaper and night fell again, a sunlit, paradoxical night, a night with wings of black velvet, a hairy spinning night, a night of a thousand eyes, the screaming night of everyman's vision of a hell in which La Herse was paying a heavy price for the existence during which he had intentionally confused justice and intimidation, duty and torture, morality and the law.

Amen.

*

"Go on!"

"Go on, Cissou, what happened then?"

Cissou looked round at me sadly.

"Go on . . . go on . . . the tragic thing about kids is they think that things always do go on."

Ecce Cissou the Snow. Anyone would think that he had stainless-steel humour, was a laugh a minute, ever bent on pulling a fast one on the boys in blue, then suddenly he cracks open to reveal some "unfathomable sorrow", as they say in upmarket books.

"Did poor old Thian's story go on, Benjamin? And what about Stojil? Do you think his story's still going on up in cloud-cuckoo land?"

It was at Thian's funeral that we'd met Cissou. And Suzanne, too. Thian, Cissou and Suzanne were neighbourhood friends, apparently, all from a generation which does not believe that anything goes on for very long any more. Cissou had been standing in for Gervaise, Sister Gervaise, old Thian's daughter, who was too busy saving whores' souls to come and drop a flower on her father's grave. "You spend so long with your whores that you're neglecting your old dad." "And would my old dad prefer me to neglect my whores?"

Three months later, Suzanne and Cissou had come back to bury Stojil, for he had died too, before finishing his Serbo-Croatian translation of Virgil. Yes, Uncle Stojil had deserted us, just before the Serbs, Croats and Muslims started ripping each other apart.

After the funeral, Suzanne had taken us back to The Zebra. She'd treated us to a showing of a short film she had made at the time when Stojil used to take Belleville's old dears out for drives in his vintage imperial coach, which had been annexed by his superb imagination.

"Suzanne O'Blue Eyes," was how Jeremy had baptised her.

This capital O and its apostrophe seemed to Jeremy to epitomise an incorruptible joy devoid of illusions – which was typically Irish, according to him, and which beamed from Suzanne's eyes and monolithic personality. Jeremy had added:

"She hasn't just got eyes that see. She's got eyes that show."

"Very well," Cissou sighed. "Let's go for what happened next."

*

So far as I was concerned, the continuation did not concern La Herse's astonishment upon discovering a fortune in period furniture beneath layers of shite-besmirched flies . . . No, what interested me, Benjamin Malaussène, was right there on the stage of The Zebra, where the table had been set, under the spotlights, facing the darkness of the auditorium: the next thing that mattered to me was the little me waiting in Julie's belly to take my place. How beautiful women are in the first few months, when they honour you with a double presence! But, honestly speaking, Julie, do you really think we're being reasonable? Do you? Really? And you, shit-for-brains, do you really think you've picked the right world, family and epoch? You're not even here yet, and you're already hanging out with the wrong crowd! You've got no sense at all, apparently, just like your mother, our "reality journalist" . . .

*

Come on, now, cheer up. Cheer up. We are supposed to be enjoying ourselves. And, as ever at such times, what happened next led to a new beginning: the despair of Amar and Yasmina when they showed up last week with the bailiff's letter; the strategy worked out by Cissou; the staging which Jeremy then came up with; then every afternoon on the stage of The Zebra the training of Half Pint, whose feet are still bent double ("Just hold on for four minutes, Half Pint, not a second more, then, when Cissou raises his hands, you drop down, got that, have you Half Pint? And we'll rub you down with olive oil. That way, they won't be able to grab you."); the choice of props from Suzanne's cinematographic memory; the cooking-up of the human mush thanks to Yasmina's and Clara's culinary skills; doubts, more doubts and the appeals for optimism.

"Course it'll fucking work!" Jeremy bellowed. "It's just got to!"

"But they know that our flat's on the fifth floor."

"Don't forget the psychological shock, Amar, it's crucial! Thérèse, tell him about the importance of the psychological shock!"

And Thérèse made her usual psychobiblical contribution:

"That will be the door they open, Amar, because it will be the forbidden door."

What happened next was Jeremy rising in senatorial dignity, clambering up on to a chair and raising high a drop of Sidi-Brahim.

"Ladies and gentlemen, brothers and sisters, Julius the Dog, friends, Romans and countrymen, lend me your ears. You shut it too, Benjamin, and stop muttering away with Cissou."

Silence fell. Solemnity, too.

"Dear family, dear friends, I would first like to pay tribute to two of you, without whom this victory would not be what it is. I'm talking about . . ."

(The speaker turned towards the two babies seated at the end of the table, between Julie and Clara, a bright blond beaming angel, and his devilish neighbour full of congenital fury.)

"I'm talking about Verdun and What An Angel, who, of all their contemporaries in Belleville who took part in this glorious struggle, produced by far the runniest, smelliest shit, packed with fly larvae . . ."

Then, Thérèse leapt to her feet.

"Jeremy!"

Thérèse's chair tipped over.

"Jeremy, stop it!"

Suzanne's crystal laughter.

"The little bugger's going to succeed in making us all puke!"

Then knocking on the door of The Zebra.

A new beginning and the end.

Knocking.

It's terrible to see laughter frozen in mid-grin . . . all those gaping mouths, then more knocking, with Suzanne's projector aimed at the door at the back, the door everyone was looking at, just like at the cinema in fact. Not a move. A gaggle of geese which had taken the wrong turning. Slap bang in the middle of a hunting ground with no way out.

A third volley of knocks.

Only cops and insurance salesmen are that persistent. But insurers had now learnt that they would get no joy from us.

Mourners of all sexual persuasions, you're right, everything does end badly, especially victories.

Now now, calm down. After all, what was the risk for us? Trespassing, voluntary degradation of property, obstruction of justice, inciting a minor to commit crucifixion . . . you can't get much for that.

While our minds were swirling with such considerations, and as no-one had thought of going over and opening that sodding door, it opened all on its own. The door of The Zebra, Belleville's last living cinema, opened.

And Mum appeared in its frame.

Chapter 3

A ND YOUR FUTURE grandmother appeared in the frame. She's another person I'm going to have to introduce you to. Your future grandmother has a responsive heart and generous guts. Benjamin, my good self, Louna, Clara, Thérèse, Jeremy, Half Pint and Verdun are all fruit of those guts. Even Julius the Dog looks up to her like a son.

So what do you say to that, you who are the product of so much procreative hesitation: Should we bring children into this world where we live? Does the Great Paranoiac deserve having his labours added to? Do I have the right to start a destiny? Don't I realise that beginning a life is setting death at its heels? Will I be a good father and will Julie make a good mother? Can someone take the risk of taking after us?'

Do you reckon your grandmother ever wondered anything of the sort? Course not! A child each time she's smitten, that's her approach. Every try is converted and the father totally forgotten.

Some people might call your grandmother a whore. Don't believe a word of it. It's just them bitching. Your grandmother's actually a perpetual virgin, which is completely different. An eternity in each of her loves, that's what, and we're the sum of those eternal moments.

From which she emerges as virginal as before.

I mean, did the person in the frame that evening in The Zebra look the slightest bit like a whore? I mean, did she? Did she even look like a grandmother? Was it an old dear with a shady past who was coming towards us, shimmering with sequins and carrying a little girl's suitcase? But you can't judge her, little one, not from your iridescent dwelling place. Apparently, you can't see further than your nose in there, and you're bathed in a bluish light. Lucky bugger . . . The only thing I'll ever be envious of is your nine-month stay in Julie's belly.

But you might still notice the quality of the silence. Did you feel how our silence changed? A silence of clenched buttocks switching to pure delight.

When a door opens, your grandmother doesn't enter, she *appears as a vision*. When she wakes up in the morning, your grandmother doesn't show up in the kitchen with glassy eyes and fumbling hands, she *descends as a vision*. Your grandmother isn't just a woman, and she doesn't content herself with being a *vision*, your grandmother is a *vision of womanhood* (it might sound stupid put this way, but when you see her, you'll see just how much she beggars description).

*

So, Mother appeared in the luminous doorframe of The Zebra. *We're at The Zebra*, that's what Jeremy had pinned up on our door. He had been pinning up notes for the past twenty-eight months just in case Mum came home and found no-one in the nest.

Twenty-eight months.

Twenty-eight months of absence, without a single "hello", or "it's me" or "hi there" or "how are things?" . . . She clambered up on to the stage, spotted What An Angel at once and said:

"Ah! I see there's a new addition!"

She put down her suitcase and went over to What An Angel. While picking up Verdun and running her fingers through Half Pint's hair she said:

"Well, what an angel you are."

Then she looked at Clara:

"Was it you who produced this blond masterpiece?"

What An Angel smiled, Verdun looked a bit less sulky, Half Pint climbed up on to the other side of her lap, Jeremy who was still standing on his chair with his wine glass in hand couldn't force his mouth shut, Julius the Dog was walking on his tongue, Louna's stare seemed to be saying that she found Mum too good to be true, Clara brightened up for the first time since Saint-Hiver's death and Thérèse looked at me.

As ever, truth was glittering in her eyes.

Something was wrong.

It was Mum, and yet it wasn't.

Mum without her insides.

Normally, she never came back alone.

Normally, she arrived belly first in a declaration of imminent motherhood.

This time, no belly.

Twenty-eight months on the run with Pastor, and empty on return.

No future.

Just Verdun's and Half Pint's bare legs clamped round her slim waist, the better to perch on her hips.

Thérèse looked at me. It was the first time we had seen Mum carrying her children *on the outside.*

So we looked back at our mother's face, then Thérèse turned away and I thought I glimpsed a tear in her eye.

Thérèse, Thérèse . . . why does she always have to think a shade faster than the others?

*

There is no point trying to do otherwise, little one, you're going to have to learn to take Thérèse's tears seriously. The truth of the matter is that this family is bound up with tragedy. In fact, you're not so much heading for a family as a massacre. Your future grandma shacked up with Inspector Pastor, a cool killer who's got more than a couple of stiffs to his credit, then came back empty. Your aunt Clara was widowed before she got married and What An Angel was orphaned on his father's side before being born, thanks to a murderer. Verdun was born at the very moment that her grandpa, the other Verdun, gave up the ghost. What An Angel appeared because, as Thérèse put it, Thian's time had come. Uncle Stojil got sent down for trying to protect Belleville's old dears against dishonest drug dealers and honest property developers, and he died in prison. Your mother Julie nearly copped it during this business as well; they tried to drown her, they burnt her with cigarettes and turned your mum into a leopard woman. In the subsequent episode, I got shot through the head. That's right, little one, your dad rings hollow, with a fontanelle of lead and doubt everywhere.

And so, foolhardy son of the goat and leopardess, I really wouldn't blame you if you decided to cash in your chips before touching down. As for Julie, she would comfort herself with great swathes of reality. Reality is what Julie likes. Lots of reality with a twist of me in it. Your mother has always got reality boiling away somewhere in her head.

"But Father," I can hear you say, "since you seem to be such a pessimistic so-and-so, and have yourself escaped, albeit provisionally, from such tragedies, why oh why did you give the green light to that wee spermatozoid and its genetic cargo?"

What am I supposed to say to that? The entire world lies in that question. Let's just say that, in life, optimism nearly always triumphs over the wisdom of oblivion. This is one of the secrets of our species, even though ours is better informed than most. And then . . . and then we're never alone when we decide.

You can't imagine how many people attend the great symposium of existence! There was your mother Julie, of course, your mother's eyes, the hunger in your mother's eyes when I emerged from the seeming death into which I'd been plunged by a .22-calibre long-rifle high-penetration bullet. There was family lobbying, orchestrated by Jeremy and Half Pint: "A little brother! A little brother! A little sister! A little sister! A baby! A baby!" and encouragement from such friends as Amar, Yasmina, Loussa, Theo, Marty, Cissou and so on in French, Chinese and Arabic, if you don't mind: "*wawa! wawa!*", "*r ada^e! r ada^e!*" it's enough to make you think that you were the product of a multinational board! All the sexes and sexual persuasions managed to make their different lifestyle attitudes, as they say, heard. Even Queen Zabo, that dried husk, my boss at the Vendetta Press, put her oar in: "Can you write, Malaussène? Well, can you? Of course you can't . . . then do something meaty instead, a baby for instance, a beautiful chubby little baby!" And Theo, my friend Theo, who prefers e-less blonds: "Benjamin, you should realise that the worst thing about being a queen is never to have any princes and princesses. So, my brother, give me a nephew!" And Berthold, the surgeon to whom I owe my renewed existence: "I resurrected you, Malaussène, so now you owe me a bit of procreation, for Christ's sake! Go on! Get to work! Stop firing off blanks! Get a bit of live ammo up into your breach!" But the one who topped it all was Stojil, your uncle Stojilkovic whom you will never know, which is the first of the sorrows you're in for.

I went to see him in his cell, two days before he died. He had lost a bit of weight, but I thought that was down to Virgil, all that toing and froing between Latin and Cyrillic . . . His face was drawn and there were dictionaries everywhere. He gave himself a break. We unfolded the chessboard and set up the pieces. He drew white and we started to play. I'll reproduce our conversation word for word for you:

HIM: . . . (e4)

ME: . . . (e5)

HIM: . . . (lights a Gitane)

ME: Julie wants a baby.

HIM: . . . (knight to f3)

ME: . . . (knight to c7)

HIM: Do you like Australia?

ME: Australia?

HIM: . . . (bishop to c4)

ME: . . . (chin in hand)

HIM: The bush, the Australian outback, do you like that?

ME: Dunno.

HIM: Well read up on it fast. Because even the Australian outback isn't deep enough a place to flee a woman who wants to have children with you.

ME: . . . (f6)

HIM: . . . (reflection)

ME: . . . (meditation)

HIM: Nor is the Sierra Madre vertical enough.

That's the way it goes: you're going to appear in the world and never will I hear Stojilkovic's voice again. Uncle Stojil's voice which was so deep it was like Big Ben chiming through our personal smog. A sonorous lighthouse. A hunting horn of sorrow. It rose up from the depths and filled our space so richly that we no longer feared our shadows . . .

No more Stojil.

He said:

"Follow my advice, because it's the last you'll get from me. Let Julie get on with it."

Then he quite simply informed me that the end of the road was approaching.

"It's my lungs."

When, after the fatal X-ray, the doctor told him to stop smoking (you'll see, death is always announced from afar by the gradual prohibition of life), he just replied:

"But, doctor, how could I do such a thing to my Gitanes?"

And he started dying slowly, a smoke in his lips, leaning over his dictionaries.

"But Uncle Stojil," I said dumbly, "Stojil, oh Stojil, you swore to me that you were immortal!"

HIM: True, but I never swore to you that I was infallible.

ME : . . .

HIM: . . .

ME : . . .

HIM: Anyway, I'm not dying, I'm castling.

*

There you are, so you're the product of headstrong sperm and a greedy egg; you were born from that final visit to my uncle Stojil.

Who was the honour of life.

II

CISSOU THE SNOW

Since when have we been calling in the police?

Chapter 4

CLÉMENT THE TRAINEE bailiff kept his eyes down. His Biro was panting for breath. He was absorbed in the letter he was writing in a calm, blue hand whose spontaneity had been carefully thought out.

21 July of my first year

Dear Parents,

I have some good news and some excellent news for you. So let's start with the good news: I passed my constitutional law, statistics and accountancy exams with flying colours. And now for the excellent news: I'm giving up constitutional law, statistics and accountancy; or, in more general terms, all of the ambitions you have nurtured for me since the day I was born.

You will certainly find this rather direct, but I have been beating about the bush for the past twenty-three years and it is high time I spoke my mind.

It goes without saying that I shall also be abandoning your friend La Herse. Father was quite right when he said that a training course in July with the right bailiff would be a formative experience. It certainly has been. I have followed his paternal advice and "taken a good hard look at the real world", I have "seen the world as it really is". A little comedian aged about seven or eight greatly assisted me. Hence this letter.

Talking of comedy, and to reassure you about my future, I have decided to devote myself henceforward to the cinema. In what capacity, you might ask? I do not have the faintest idea. Everything about it interests me – I could be a script writer, an editor, an actor, a sound engineer, a property man, a sound-effects man, an archivist, a pundit, an usher or a critic. I even think that I could strip naked in front of a camera, get a monstrous hard-on and screw a young office girl senseless, until my sperm erupted and something like peace settled down.

But that's all rather vulgar, isn't it?

With this letter you will also find enclosed (along with the keys to your bedsit and my career as a model son) the only three words your up-bringing has provided me with as critical terms: "vulgar", "mediocre" and "remaaarkable".

There. I don't think I owe you anything else, except life itself, for which I have never been indelicate enough to reproach you.

Clément

Without rereading it, Clément slipped the letter into an envelope, added his savings book, went out, locked the door of the paternal bedsit, put the key in with the rest, addressed it, stamped it, then strode off towards Châtelet Métro station. A small Super-8 camera was bouncing off his hip, faithful as a service automatic.

Direction Porte des Lilas.

His old life just had to be dispatched from the Belleville post office and nowhere else. Belleville where, the day before, a Lilliputian with rose-tinted glasses had plunged him quite unexpectedly into a Tod Browning movie. When that tiny naked being had leapt over him, uttering its war cry, trainee bailiff Clément realised at once that he had just puked up twenty-three years of fear and submission. What he saw running down those stairs was not a child, but one of Tod Browning's crazed dwarfs. And, when the door below released the rest of the troop, Clément's only desire was to join them, to melt into them, to become one of those fey goblins, whose fiery imagination alone was capable of giving reality back its true colours. (Purplish prose which had been cooked up during the sleepless night he had just had.)

He had not gone into the flat with the others. The dwarf had warned them: it was worse inside. And Clément had taken him at his word. Lon Chaney's ghost was probably waiting for the removal men behind that forbidden entrance. Instead, Clément set off in pursuit of Tod Browning's mad midgets. He skidded over the pool of regurgitated breakfasts, slid down a flight of stairs on his stomach and, when he got to his feet, found himself face to face with a black giant and a red-head as broad as the lift shaft. It was too beautiful to be true.

The black asked:

"Where do you think you're going, Sunny Jim?"

"With them! With them!"

The red-head grinned. He had the teeth of the Prophet: a wind blew between his incisors.

"Are you a member of the club?"

Two hands twisted him round.

"Go back up and play with the big boys."

They kicked his arse so hard that he shot halfway up the stairs.

Further up, Lon Chaney's ghost was in fine fettle. For the purposes of his film, Tod Browning had trained every fly under the sun.

When Clément turned round again, the stairwell was empty. The building silent.

He was now walking through Belleville. His head was back on his shoulders. It was children he was looking for, and not escaped dwarfs from a demented circus. And, among them, a kid aged about seven or eight with rose-tinted glasses. If need be, he would spend the rest of his life looking. The kid might grow up, turn into a grandfather, but still he would find him. Once he had got rid of his letter at the post office on Rue Ramponeau, he started to feel infinitely light. He did not have a penny to his name, but his camera was bouncing off his hip. A camera, plus three extra films. He was being borne along by the scents of Belleville. It was the first time that he had really taken them in. He felt at home here, with a new existence beneath his feet. A destiny! He finally had a destiny! His own world and a destiny! He did not even find it particularly funny that he was mumbling such inanities.

He let his camera feast on peppers, dates, watermelons, red chillies and aubergines. If he could, he would have filmed the smell of coriander and the sizzling of merguez.

People were tapping their temples.

Most of them just thought he was wasting good film.

Along the groceries and hardware stores, the lacquered ducks and cheap rags, he arrived on Boulevard de Belleville.

And spotted him.

Right in front, about twenty yards away.

The child with rose-tinted glasses.

Coming out of a cinema called The Zebra.

With another boy. And a girl.

Clément drew and, walking backwards, started to film them.

The three kids took up the width of the pavement.

They were coming towards him, feet splayed and bellies out.

They were laughing, chin up, necks stretched.

When they realised that they were being filmed, they exaggerated the swing of their hips and their gooselike swagger.

It looked as if they were all eight months pregnant.

Chapter 5

O YOU WHO DON the spectacles of prejudice, ever prone to forbid delight and summon up scandal, if you spot three skinny children – one of them wearing rose-tinted glasses – hanging about on Boulevard de Belleville, with hunched backs, hands on hips and splayed feet, in that painfully full posture of a carrying woman, do not for a moment imagine that Belleville impregnates its young.

Indeed not!

Look instead at the pavement opposite.

I'm the one the little blighters are imitating.

I'm the one they're taking the piss out of.

If I get my hands on them . . .

*

It's true. Those first few weeks of Julie's pregnancy made Benjamin Malaussène, the goat with the steel bonce, go completely loopy. He wandered about, far from his first-person singular, with his belly out and his feet like quotation marks. Leila, Nourdine and Half Pint imitated him. Julius the Dog seemed to have lost the plot.

Julie laughed:

"Is this an empathy crisis, Benjamin?"

Malaussène was preggers. Unfit for work. That expected existence was too much for the Vendetta Press. He even talked about it to the authors who had spent their own writing the manuscripts he turned down. He wondered out loud if it wasn't vain to create and criminal to procreate. He considered that he had a large number of aggravating circumstances.

"Scapegoats should have their balls cut off."

He got various silly ideas into his head.

"Lousy luck like mine must be hereditary . . . Just wait and see what the kid gets blamed for as soon as it pokes its nose outside!"

He was wearing out his most faithful friends.

"You're exaggerating, Benjamin."

"If I'm exaggerating, Loussa, then I must be basically right. Thanks a lot. You've really cheered me up. The truth is far darker than I ever imagined."

For the first time in his life, he became the accuser:

"It's all your fault, Your Majesty! You sent me off to procreate from behind the defences of your virginity!"

Queen Zabo agreed:

"It's my job to pack people off to the front."

He looked for others to talk to:

"How are things with you, Macon?"

Macon the secretary felt sorry for him:

"I've been through my books carefully, Monsieur Malaussène, and I think I can say that I've never experienced a single moment of happiness in my entire life. Not one."

Calignac the sales director butted in:

"Stop getting Macon down, Benjamin. You're starting to get on everyone's tits."

"You've got a rugby ball instead of a heart, Calignac, thick leather full of air."

He was depressing his colleagues so much that people were beginning to wonder where they had found enough energy to be born.

They went on sick leave.

The company started to go down the drain.

Finally, Queen Zabo made up her mind:

"OK, Malaussène, I'm putting you on maternity leave. How does nine months on full pay sound?"

*

As soon as he was free from his obligations at work, Malaussène turned against medicine. He went to see Marty, the family doctor who had saved all of them from certain death on two or three occasions, and laid into him. He did not even talk about the coming child. He just bawled him out:

"I mean, all this crap about saving people! For Christ's sake, can't you even think about the future sometimes?"

Professor Marty listened to Malaussène improvise around this theme. Professor Marty showed patience with his patients. For him, it was not a virtue, but more the essence of clinical investigation. His first thought was that someone must have discreetly popped another bullet into Malaussène's goat skull, but he then rejected the hypothesis, searched elsewhere, and interrupted only when his diagnosis was ready:

"Really, Malaussène, you're not bending my ear like this just because you're going to be a father, are you?"

"Absolutely."

"Fine. There are probably about five hundred million Hindus going through the same thing right now. What is it that you want to know exactly?"

"The name of the best obstetrician in the world. Is that clear? The best one in the entire world!"

"Fraenkhel."

"Never heard of him."

"That's because he's not only the best, he's also the most retiring. You'll never see him on TV, like Berthold. And yet he's delivered the babies of more celebs, monarchs and other individuals than you've talked pounds of bullshit since Julie got pregnant."

"Fraenkhel?"

"Matthias Fraenkhel."

*

That evening, Malaussène headed home as if wild dogs were at his heels, grabbed Julie by the elbow, and dragged her upstairs into their bedroom faster than if they'd been going to set about producing a twin.

"Julie," he said. "Drop your usual gynaecologist and go and see Doctor Fraenkhel."

"That's my business, Benjamin. But it so happens that we want the same thing. Faenkhel's been taking care of me ever since my periods started."

"You know him?"

"So do you. You recall the anti-abortion lecture a few years back, with Leonard the Ogre? I was going to write an article about it, remember? You came with me . . . it was the first time we went out together. Fraenkhel was there, too."

Malaussène released her, as though she had given him an electric shock. He could clearly picture Fraenkhel sitting behind the conference table: an unfinished lanky git, a human construction of bones and tendons, hair like sparklers and a lost look in his eyes, as though he had gulped down the Holy Ghost all in one go. Not only could Malaussène picture him, he could also hear him. He could hardly believe his own memory.

"And you, Julie? Do you remember what that creep came out with at that lecture?"

26

Julie was journalistic memory made flesh.

"Perfectly. Like all of those gentlemen, he was against abortion. He quoted one of the Church Fathers, Saint Thomas I think it was: *It is better to be born unhealthy and deformed than never to be born at all.* Then he was interrupted when that tall girl flung a lump of red meat into his face while yelling that it was her foetus. Is that what you mean?"

Malaussène paused to draw in all of the air in the bedroom.

"And you're giving the responsibility of our delivery to *him*?"

"Didn't Marty tell you he was the best?"

"The best? But he's a closet ogre! Someone capable of forcing kids with six heads to live!"

"I think the best thing would be if you met Matthias, Benjamin, and had a chat."

"Matthias? You're on first-name terms are you?"

And then, for those who know Julie, she came up with rather a surprising reply:

"We are what might be called friends."

*

And so there was the visit to Matthias Fraenkhel, obstetrician to stars and crowned heads. Sure enough, he had a massive surgery in the upmarket sixteenth *arrondissement*, with Aubusson tapestries (from the sixteenth, too) on the walls. Carpaccio's *Saint George Slaying the Dragon* (early sixteenth) hung up above the patients. Even Fraenkhel's head looked like it went back to the sixteenth century. A face of Grünewald dried bark. As scrawny as the Inquisition. A blaze in his eyes fit to light the stakes. And a conflagration of white hair on his weary skull.

"That's really what you said, isn't it? I really did hear that Saint Thomas quote, didn't I?"

"And unfortunately that is just what I believe . . . It's an old bone of contention between your wife and me."

(My wife? What wife? Julie isn't "my wife", my good sir. But what to call one's wife if you don't like business terms?)

"Excuse me . . . I was forgetting that you and Julie . . . live in sin . . . you poor souls."

The looks of a root-eating anchorite and then, all of a sudden, a change of style – the grin of a Marx (Harpo)!

"Seriously, Monsieur Malaussène . . . do you really think that I would deliver you a child with six heads? Or twelve, in the case of twins?"

"That's what you said at the lecture!"

"It's what Saint Thomas said . . . As for me . . . I was cut short by a lump of bloody offal . . . I was going to add something."

Fraenkhel fell silent. As though resting after a long talk. His delivery came in fits and starts. An asthmatic rhythm. He peered at the backs of his hands and apologised:

"I've always been very slow . . . Even when speaking, I have to make a rough draft first . . . I was looking for the right words when that young lady sent me her . . . point of view . . . What I was going to say was . . . was . . ."

Very slow indeed. A salamander's long fingers settling so gingerly on the inches of future space. A dubious smile.

"I was going to add . . . that I personally agree with what Saint Thomas said . . . but this is a matter of individual choice . . . Because there is no greater crime than to assume the place of another person's conscience."

(OK there.)

"I believe that it is the only important lesson that we can learn from history."

(Please develop.)

"This obsession about trying to impose one's point of view . . . it's caused so many deaths down the ages, don't you agree? All those convictions, those murderous *identities* . . . See what I mean?"

Of course, of course. The numbers had been piling up even recently. So, in the end, I was starting to take a liking to Fraenkhel. It wasn't only the right words he had to look for.

A smile.

"In other words, Monsieur Malaussène . . . in a few weeks' time, Julie will know all there is to know about her little guest . . . How many heads and limbs it has got . . . its sex . . . weight . . . its blood group . . . it will then be up to her whether to keep it or not."

Fine.

"And, in any case, who has ever pushed Julie into doing something against her will?"

How true.

There then followed a long silence, during which I realised that this character with his asthmatic voice and soft hands was bringing me slowly back down to earth. My anxiety level dropped sharply.

He went on:

"Julie appreciates me because she is interested in everything . . . and I know all there is to know about obstetrics . . . everything that has been dreamt up since time immemorial when it comes to being or not being born . . . everything that is being cooked up today . . . everything that will be invented tomorrow . . . And, believe me, Saint Thomas was not the maddest one of the bunch."

"But why are you interested in Julie?"

My question just slipped out.

As did the reply:

"You mean she didn't tell you? I was the doctor who presided at her birth, Monsieur Malaussène."

(Oh! Right then!)

That's life for you . . . You reckon you're off to see the monster that delivers monsters, you're stuffed full of principles as though you're going to cross swords with Torquemada in person, and you find yourself face to face with the man responsible for the light of your life.

"Her father, the Governor, was a friend of mine . . . Our children used to play together during their summer holidays in the Vercors . . . That's where Julie was born. To be perfectly precise, on the kitchen table in Les Rochas farmhouse . . . It was a very big table . . . A real farmer's wife's table."

A little out of breath, slightly astonished at such a long speech, and rather embarrassed too, perhaps, he stared at me.

To stay on his patch, I asked:

"How many children have you got?"

"Just one son. Barnaby. He lives in England now."

He stood up.

His body of bark and rope seemed to be endlessly unfolding itself.

Standing beside his desk, he plunged back into his thoughts. With one word in each pan of the scales:

"Tolerance, Monsieur Malaussène . . . it's . . . how can I put it? . . . it's . . . prudence raised to a metaphysical level."

A turn round his desk. He walked stiffly. A long, rheumatic vine stalk.

"I have an old father, too, Monsieur Malaussène, who's still with us . . . Julie knows him well . . . An extremely aged father with wanderlust . . . far more vigorous than I am . . . an industrialist dealing in spools of cinema film . . . (hence my clientele) . . . always travelling . . . but who is scared to death of flying."

A hand on my arm, our footsteps towards the door.

"Every time he has to take the plane, he says a rosary at church, a psalm in the temple, a brief sura at the mosque, not to forget the synagogue, of course . . ."

Hand on the door handle.

"And do you know what he does then?"

I didn't.

"He phones the airline to make sure that the pilot doesn't believe in God!"

Shy smile, extended hand, door open.

"Goodbye, Monsieur Malaussène, you were right to come and see me. You should never hand over a baby casually to a captain who believes in eternal life."

*

Well, this character certainly brought me back to my senses. Not the slightest worry about the pregnancy now. Julie was in the right hands. There was just the question of what would happen next, in what we call life . . .

That's what I was chewing over along Boulevard de Belleville, with my feet unconsciously splayed and my belly empathetically jutting out, when Black Mo and Simon the Berber suddenly loomed up in front of me. The dark giant and his ginger shadow. My friend Hadouch Ben Tayeb's two henchmen.

"Give the grey matter a rest, Ben, we've got something to show you."

"Something important."

Chapter 6

THE IMPORTANT SOMETHING was in the cellar at the Koutoubia, Amar's restaurant, where Cissou was downing his pastis while playing dominoes with the boss.

("Hello, Benjamin, my son. How are you?" – "Fine, Amar, and you?" – "Fine, thanks be to Allah. And your mother, how is she since yesterday?" – "Fine, Amar, she's moved back in, and Yasmina, how is she?" – "Fine, my boy, there's a little something for you in the cellar . . .")

The something was strapped up amid the boxes of Sidi-Brahim and looked in quite a state. A young lad tethered in his light grey suit. An upper-middle-class student who had been caught in a whirlwind. He was creased all over.

"We caught him filming Half Pint."

"With this."

Hadouch handed me a Super-8 camera.

My noble brow wrinkled.

"What's so surprising about that? Half Pint's a cute kid, isn't he?"

Hadouch, Mo and Simon stared round at one another in a triangular take.

"You got him play-acting on your door yesterday, so why can't he do a bit of street cinema today?"

(Just a passing reminder that I hadn't been too keen on their crucifixion routine. There are symbols best left alone.)

"But that depends who's doing the filming, Ben."

With the tip of his finger, Simon hiked up the student and stuck him in front of me.

"This is La Herse's apprentice . . ."

"A budding bayleaf . . ."

(If he survives this adventure, I can't help thinking that this is a nickname which will stick.)

"He was there yesterday morning with his boss's gang."

"He was trying to follow the kids, but we dissuaded him."

"With a kick up the arse."

"Apparently, it wasn't hard enough."

"He's a tough nut."

The "tough nut" was now dangling on the end of Simon's finger like a limp dishcloth. He didn't budge an inch. He wanted to say something, but terror was clamping his lexicon shut.

"All we have to decide now is what to do with him."

"Because you must get a nice long stretch for false imprisonment of an officer of the law."

"I don't want to risk getting banged up for twenty years for a budding bayleaf."

Simon bent his finger and Budding Bayleaf fell back on to his arse between the bottles.

Mo grinned. An explosion of white teeth.

"Maybe he doesn't know what goes into a Belleville couscous?"

Simon crouched down and put the question his way:

"Well, Budding Bayleaf? Do you know what the Arabs put in their merguez?"

From a safe distance, this may all sound grotesque, but right there, in the cellar, in the gleam of Simon's incisors, under Mo's ravenous stare and in the aloof silence of Hadouch, who was busy cleaning his nails with the tip of his knife, it must have sounded perfectly plausible to such a well-brought-up young fellow.

"Everything goes into merguez."

"Which means, there are no remains."

"And today's rumi eats yesterday's rumi."

I know, I know, I should have intervened, but I was curious to see just how far they would go. Benjamin Malaussène, delver into credulity, potholer into terror . . . Not nice at all, really. But then I don't have much of a soft spot for bailiffs, either.

"What do you reckon, Ben?"

"Have you taken the film?"

"No, we were going to give it to Clara to develop, that way we'll find out what the cunt was filming exactly."

I looked at the cunt.

I fell silent.

Everyone fell silent.

And I put a stop to it. After all, real torturers probably start by playing at torture.

"Hadouch, untie him."

And Hadouch did. But without cutting the rope, by simply undoing the knot.

"What's your name?"

He stayed there, frozen, as if we hadn't undone the parcel.

I said:

"Calm down, it's all over now. Relax. We were only joking. What's your name?"

"Clément."

"Clément what?"

"Clément Clément."

It was probably true. He looked like someone whose dad is proud enough of his own seed to turn it into a tautology.

"Why were you filming my brother?"

"Because he changed my life."

And he who had been muted, so terribly scared, suddenly launched into an express-train monologue, that seeing Half Pint's bare butt bowling down the stairs had brought about a 180-degree existential turnabout, that ever since this road-to-Damascus-like revelation he was no longer the person he used to be, or else had become, either way, he'd handed in his spurs to his family and his uniform to his boss, and all he wanted to do now was live in Belleville and work in the cinema, just the cinema and nothing but the cinema . . .

He stopped for a second to get his breath back.

Pop! Hadouch handed him a bottle of Sidi.

"Here, have a drink. Autobiographies are thirsty work."

He knocked it down fast enough to explode a breathalyser. Then he wiped his mouth with the back of his hand and said:

"Phew, that's better."

"Where do you live?"

For the first time, he smiled.

"Since this morning, I don't live anywhere."

Simon gave him a paternal shake of the head.

"All this business about the cinema is all very well, but how are you going to live?"

"That's right," said Mo. "Bottles of Sidi-Brahim don't grow on trees, you know!"

Hadouch added:

"Do you know the unemployment rate in the movie business?"

What I really like about my friends is the way they make me no longer believe my own eyes. We start off with a standard beating, you're expecting them to get out the hardware any minute, then suddenly it all turns into a nice family debate: "It's high time you thought seriously about your career, young fellow my lad, and from our considerable experience, we can tell you that any successful career requires forethought and planning . . ."

But these were telling arguments, all the same. Budding Bayleaf frowned.

"I dunno. Maybe you could find me some work?"

And there we are!

There we are again!

The Malaussène tribe has another kid on its hands. I expressed my reservations loudly:

"Can't you lot leave him alone? Just let him film away then piss off! Don't you think my family's big enough already? That I haven't got enough mouths to feed? That there aren't enough of us crammed into the flat? That we really need to worry about another person's future? What with Julie, who's probably going to have quins!"

I was off now. A Clément-like launch, a harangue to follow his soliloquy. It could have gone on for an entire chapter if Hadouch hadn't immediately stuffed a bottle of Sidi into my hands and said:

"There is one possibility."

Then:

"Simon, go and get Cissou."

And, to me:

"Cissou can't manage on his own any more. And we're not always there to help him out. He needs an assistant."

*

I really thought Budding Bayleaf was going to drop dead in terror when he saw the huge form of the locksmith loom up in the cellar. It was a terrifying leap backwards in space-time.

After we'd brought the kid round again, and explained the new distribution of roles, Cissou asked his first question:

"Know anything about carpentry?"

Budding Bayleaf stared round at us, but we were of no help.

"Never mind. What about locks? Know anything about them?"

How terrible it is to see lost panic in the eyes of a kid who's been primed for success since his birth.

"All right. Nothing doing with carpentry. Bugger all about locks. What about electricity? You look like a bright spark."

No matter how hard you plug in the gaps, the extent of your ignorance is always astonishing.

"Fine . . ."

Cissou took the bottle from my hands and said:

"I'll take him on."

As he headed back up to his game of dominoes, someone asked him:

"Where will he sleep?"

Without turning round, Cissou replied:

"At The Zebra. The Zebra will make a perfect squat for a film buff."

Sure enough, the idea of Budding Bayleaf sleeping in a Belleville squat did seem rather appropriate. And given that the squat in question was Belleville's last living cinema, then it would be a heavenly gaff for Clément son of Clément.

Chapter 7

W HAT I'M TELLING you now is your prehistory. The papers in your file, so
to speak. This way, when the parcel finally arrives, it will be correctly
addressed. Some might say that I'm wrong to talk to you like this, that you're too
young to get to know the cast, that this is all adults' business . . . but according to
Doctor Fraenkhel, your own personal stork, age is a decidedly complex matter:

"Did you know that, from a genetic point of view, our children are older than
we are? . . . I mean, in terms of the age of the species . . . genetically speaking,
they're our seniors . . ."

To which Fraenkhel added:

"I've always thought that birth announcements in newspapers should include
the child's age."

Absolutely: *Madame and Monsieur Bustamentalo are delighted to announce the
birth of their son, Basil, aged 3,797,832 years old . . .*

*

So it was that Budding Bayleaf was taken on by Cissou and lodged in the belly of
The Zebra.

Cissou got him doing exactly what he used to do with La Herse. It was quite a
surprise for the young lad. The same visits to the same inhabitants of Belleville.
The same evaluations of fixtures and fittings. The same removals. But no-one put
up any resistance to Cissou's repossessions. There was no need for a skeleton key
– the Belleville which Cissou pillaged was wide open. It was willing. It was
thankful. Old Habib's TV set in Cissou's arms; "How about some coffee, Cissou
my brother, let me make you a nice cup of coffee." Or Selim Sayeb's fridge on
Cissou's back; "My mother's made you some tea, Cissou, with pine nuts, just as
you like it." Cissou emptied flats like he was shelling peas, but was then invited
back for a mechoui the next day. People helped him. "Moktar's going to give you
a hand getting the cooker downstairs, Cissou. Hey, Moktar! Help Cissou with the

cooker!" Yes, it was exactly the same work as with La Herse the bailiff, which only goes to show how much the atmosphere can change a job. But it all happened at night. Every night that Allah gave, Cissou pillaged the goods of the Just. And, while he was spat on in the morning, at night he was welcomed with hands on hearts and open doors: "*Salaam' alaykum*, my brother Cissou." To which Cissou replied simply: "*Alaykum salaam*, has Idris packed the crockery?" And Budding Bayleaf went back downstairs bent double under the weight of tajine dishes. With all these flights of stairs, Budding Bayleaf was acquiring the calves of a ballet dancer, a smattering of Arabic and a camel-like placidity. "Your lad's no Mister Universe, Cissou, but he's strong. Doesn't he ever sleep?" Clément was living out a dream which kept him awake: taking new fridges down to Cissou's van, and bringing back up wrecked old hulks, swapping beaten-up old mattresses for four-poster beds, replacing gleaming crockery with chipped porcelain. This was free-market thinking pushed to its perfection: pure profit. In the early hours, Belleville's goods were stashed backstage at The Zebra. Everything shone as in Ali Baba's cave. Budding Bayleaf slumped down on to a mattress. Suzanne O'Blue Eyes tucked him in. And Budding Bayleaf dozed straight off with stars in his eyes. The Zebra watched over the camel's repose.

*

Once back home, Cissou snorted a long line of coke (you can't do much about either your health or your nicknames). The entirety of Siberia shot up into Cissou the Snow's nostrils, sending him straight off. On the far side of the boulevard, a zebra was bounding along with him across the early-morning sky. Keeping one eye on the beast, Cissou picked up the phone. He rang Gervaise, the recently orphaned daughter of Inspector Van Thian.

"Rise and shine, sis, it's the time when zebras take wing."

His "sister" lived on Rue des Abbesses. She was a nun in a home for repentant streetwalkers. Every morning, she replied with a few sleepy words.

He answered:

"You should be like me, sis. Don't go to bed in the first place. It makes life easier."

This phone call to Gervaise was Cissou the Snow's one real pleasure in life. It probably meant more to him than his Siberian flurries. On this occasion, it seemed to Gervaise that he had a strange tone of voice:

"Got a bunged-up nose, Cissou?"

He confessed:

"It's as clear as the driven snow."

Gervaise told him off.

Cissou stuck up for himself.

"There's them as take Communion every morning."

Gervaise started into an argument about the mystical body, but Cissou butted in at once:

"Amen, sister, amen . . . How are the whores? Sorted yet?"

For the past few months, Gervaise had been worried about her whores. One by one, they kept disappearing.

"I have a lead."

"Watch out for yourself, sis. When one whore vanishes, she's found a new life, when it's two, there's been a moral crisis, but three or more points to murder most foul . . ."

"I've been given two guardian angels, Cissou, two special-branch Inspectors have been assigned to protect me. They're called Titus and Silistri. They're really good. Then there's also Pescatore's dark angels."

Such was her name for the penitent pimps who, under the leadership of Pescatore, a Tuscan tattooed with the arms of Saint Michael, watched over her at night. Inspectors Titus and Silistri then went on day duty.

"How's the family, Cissou?"

This was her way of asking after the Malaussènes. The Malaussène tribe had adopted Inspector Van Thian at a time when she had been so taken up with her whores that she had neglected her old father. She was grateful to them. Cissou was Gervaise's spy in the Malaussène household.

He gave her his daily report. He spoke about the mother, who still was not eating, about Julius, who was eating too much, about Thérèse, who was still stargazing, about the entire tribe, who felt so-so, even though they were far better than many an ancient family. He gave her news of Benjamin, of Julie, and then of Doctor Fraenkhel.

"Doctor Fraenkhel?"

"The mother hen on Julie's belly and the celebs' delivery man, apparently. He's an old mate of the Corrençon family. He comes round to dinner some evenings. They've become friends."

"What about the rest of the family?"

Cissou hid nothing. Even when he should have. The crucifixion of Half Pint, for instance. Half Pint's crucifixion really did not go down well at all.

"No offence, sister! It was only a joke. It even shot a good dose of God into La Herse's skull. You know how it is . . . the Lord moves in mysterious ways."

Then, finally, she asked for his news.

38

"What about you, Cissou?"

She became extremely attentive. Every morning, it was as though they spoke once a year.

"I'm fine, sister, just fine . . . They keep on smashing up my dear old Belleville, and I keep on organising the resistance. Our Budding Bayleaf's turning into a good little worker. Meanwhile, the Malaussènes have taken Suzanne and her Zebra under their wing."

He heard her smile. That's right, *he heard her smile*. He said:

"I'll have some more pictures for you soon, if you're a good girl."

Her laughter was like a rush of cool water over his face. She thanked him in advance for the pictures and promised to put them away in her "favourite album".

"Whenever you want, sister."

She was now wide awake. She wondered how she would have managed to emerge from that night, and all of the preceding ones, without him. And how she would emerge from her future sleep if he ever stopped phoning her. He pretended to believe her. She said: "Speak to you tomorrow, Cissou." Then she added: "Don't forget, now, will you?" She suddenly sounded like a little girl. This time he really did believe her.

He hung up feeling important.

In the end, maybe he really was her guardian angel.

Sitting in his solitary armchair, and watching the fly-away zebra, he knocked back a good half-pint of apple brandy in order to come down again from those snowy peaks. And, while the zebra continued to mount, Cissou slowly descended towards the day he had in store.

Which was soon announced by La Herse's ring on the door.

*

La Herse the bailiff rang twice. Cissou went out, with his set of keys on his belt. Cissou was going back to work. To his day job. The honest labour of a worthy citizen. At cockcrow, Cissou the Snow turned into a housebreaker. He and La Herse strode through Belleville, flanked by four removal men. In the name of the law, they were about to repossess a batch of dead fridges, blind TVs, rickety beds, chipped plates and three-pronged forks. It was terrible to see how Belleville clung on to its junk. The women sprouted claws and the oldsters tore their hair out. Herds of sheep were released in apartment blocks and kids with rose-tinted glasses were nailed to doors. Cissou did not even stop to wipe off the spittle. He had lost count of how many eternities he would rot thanks to Arabic curses.

"You'll end up as a merguez, Cissou, with the Prophet's skewer up your arse!"
"May evil sprout inside you, Cissou, may you piss your own blood!" "Fuck your
mother and eat your own shit!" "Eternal shame on your children's children!"
"Cursed be the turd you have for a name!" All this never stopped Cissou from
opening the doors and raising his troops' morale: "The police? Since when have
we been calling in the police?" And, sure enough, nothing untoward happened.
Belleville did not murder Cissou the Snow, and this fact was summed up by La
Herse in a phrase he used to trot out at dinner parties: "Arabs are just a lot of hot
air." The gang went back down again, leaving the flat as desolate as Job's dwelling
place. Cissou photographed every building that had been struck by the housing
office's curse. One day, La Herse was curious enough to ask: "Are you the
nostalgic sort, Cissou?" To which Cissou replied: "No, they're for a sister who's
into memories."

Then they laid into the next block of flats. And so the day passed by. And night
returned. And Budding Bayleaf took up the yoke once again. They now had to put
all the furniture back. Selim's fridge in Selim's kitchen, Idris's cutlery in Idris's
hands. So that Belleville could become Belleville again. So that La Herse would
never be anything more than Belleville's dustbin.

*

There we are. That's exactly how things were.

Before setting off, Cissou and Budding Bayleaf came to dinner in the ex-
hardware store where we live.

Cissou ate silently, his peasant shirt buttoned up to his neck and around his
wrists. From time to time, he gave Clara a film:

"Thirteen-by-eighteen format, as usual."

Clément the Budding Bayleaf spoke instead of eating. As he had experienced
only the other side of Cissou, and thought that he was up against Eric Campbell,
the huge bad guy in Charlie Chaplin movies with wild staring eyes and bushy
eyebrows, he was amazed to find himself in fact in the presence of Willard Louis,
Robin Hood's jovial friar, in the Douglas Fairbanks version.

Budding Bayleaf knew a thing or two, his family had seen to that, but his real
knowledge lay in films. He was an unwearying coiner of celluloid metaphors.
Even Suzanne O'Blue Eyes, who was still sometimes recognised in buses for being
the "Madame Cinema" of the 1960s, was astonished.

Every evening, at bedtime, the kids in their bunks, with the creases in their
pyjamas leading straight down to their furry slippers, would listen to Budding
Bayleaf rolling out his reels and, believe me, their ears opened their eyes for them!

This lad was the death of literature, his words rushed out like pictures.

All of which was far from unappealing to Clara, my little photographer, who seemed to be paying attention to a masculine presence for the first time since Saint-Hiver's death. And my Clarinette even went so far as to indulge in a bit of film-buff duelling.

"OK, Errol Flynn was Robin Hood, that's easy. But who played Richard the Lionheart?"

"Wallace Beery in the Allan Dwan version and Ian Hunter in the one by Michael Curtiz."

"And what about the Ken Annakin?"

"Annakin doesn't even deserve to be remembered!" Clément answered, with that categorically brutal certainty which is to be found only among film buffs.

Love has never been fussy about its initial nourishment. Love's early conversations are like baby food. The ingredients are irrelevant, what's being discussed lies elsewhere. Love defies dietary laws, it feeds off anything and needs nothing to feed it. True passions have been born of conversations so low in protein that they scarcely had the strength to stand.

And it was just such an amorous nibbling that we were witnessing between Clara and Clément. Neither of them yet knew what he or she was talking about exactly, but Mum realised that everything which emerged from Clément's mouth – be it addressed to Cissou, Jeremy, Thérèse, Julius the Dog, the kids or me – was in reality aimed at Clara, like brightly coloured kites with little messages of love which, without batting an eyelid, Clara caught as they flew towards her.

She was catching them in full flight.

Mum realised that, approved and said nothing.

Mum, whose plate remained full.

My eyes met Thérèse's stare.

She looked away.

Pastor, Pastor . . . what have you done to our mother?

Chapter 8

O I! ARE YOU listening to me? Come on, concentrate will you, for Christ's sake! Stop snoring in your mother's belly! I'm only trying to introduce you to your future tribe. So you'll know who you're dealing with when the day of your arrival comes. So that you won't be able to say I didn't warn you. I'm fed up with Verdun pulling a face from dawn to dusk as though we'd broken the trade description act. I've only got about eight months left to describe them all to you . . . If you reckon that thirty-two weeks will be enough to define such "contrasting" personalities (as they say in lecture speak), then you've got another think coming. I've got a few decades' lead on you and I'm not sure if I really know a single one of them deep down. Take Jeremy for instance, your uncle Jeremy . . . or else Half Pint, the one with the rose-tinted glasses . . . or both of them together . . .

Jeremy and Half Pint

Before dinner the other day, your uncle Jeremy showed up in our bedroom. He knocked, which is unusual for him. Then he waited for us to ask him to come in, which is even less like him. He then came in and said nothing, which is utterly original.

So I said:

"Yes, Jeremy?"

He said:

"Benjamin . . ."

I was lying on our bed, my knees getting a good basting from Julius's tongue, while contemplating your mother sitting at her desk, her golden features lit up by the ray from the lamp. Meanwhile, I was redistributing your future traits (whether you're a girl or a boy, I really hope that you pick up as many pieces as you can from her identikit jigsaw, and leave mine to one side – I've seen enough of myself already).

"Yes, Jeremy?"

I felt a slight suspicion.

Despite his exterior immobility, Jeremy was squirming on the inside. So the lad had been hoist by his own petard again. I knew that look on his face. He was about to announce the fuck-up of the century.

"Ben, this is a bit embarrassing."

I was right.

"I don't know how to put it, Ben."

Julie put down her pen and stood up. She looked down at Julius and pointed towards the door.

"Confidences between men aren't for doggies' ears, Julius. It's the secret of the confessional."

They left us on our own.

"So?"

"So, I want to ask you something."

"Which means you think I know the answer. The child raiser in me is deeply honoured."

"Stop playing silly buggers, Ben. This really isn't easy."

"It isn't easy for any of us, Jeremy."

(I love this kind of answer. It's practically meaningless, but it warms the cockles of the heart of the person who pronounces it. I'll have a few ready for you when you tell me your troubles. You'll see, it will do me the world of good.)

Jeremy stared hard at his pumps.

"Ben, tell me how to do it."

"To do what?"

"For fuck's sake! You know what I mean!"

His toes were dying to escape the inferno inside his shoes and his ears were ablaze. To put out such a fire, he had to dive, so dive he did.

"Babies, Ben. Tell me how you make babies."

Surprise is the mother of all silences. Immediately after a slight explosion of astonishment came the hesitancy of disbelief . . . No, no, no, Jeremy as he stood there, corseted in embarrassment, was definitely not taking the piss. Then followed the dumb silence of stupor. How was such a thing possible? How could a child at the turn of this pornophilic century, in this highly sexual country, in this capital reputed for its voluptuousness, in this highly sexed neighbourhood and in a family where newborn babies rain down like a meteor shower, how, I wonder, can a teenager – my own brother! – not know about the basic mechanisms of sexual reproduction? Jeremy! Jeremy, who was making bombs when he was barely twelve! Jeremy who, only last year, was planning the collective killing of all my employers! Jeremy who goes to a school where "mothers" are "fucked" at the slightest disagreement! Jeremy who greets Thérèse's bad moods by asking if she's having "a hard end of the month"! Jeremy who witnessed live the arrival of What An Angel from between Clara's thighs! Third silence: the pit of consternation. I hadn't done my job as an upbringer properly, that was all there was to it. I'd let the epoch have its say. Like everyone else I thought that childhood no longer existed, that everyone was born in the know, I'd believed in the punch of words and the shock of images, I hadn't given innocence its due. Shame on me! So let's make amends. Let's make amends straight away, for goodness' sake!

"OK, Jeremy. Take a seat."

He sat.

I stood up.

"Jeremy . . ."

This was the most unpleasant of all silences: educational embarrassment.

I went at it softly-softly. I started at the beginning. I told him about male gametes and female gametes, about haploid and diploid cells, about DNA and Léon Blum ("who was the first person, Jeremy, to give us the possibility to procreate when and if we want"), ovulation, flaccidity, spongy tissue, vestibules, Fallopian tubes and cones . . . I was starting to feel really proud of myself when Jeremy leapt to his feet.

"Are you taking the piss?"

Tears of rage were welling up in his eyes.

"I didn't ask you for a sex-education lesson, for fuck's sake! I asked you how you make babies!"

The door opened and Half Pint appeared.

"Dinner's ready and Matthias is here."

And, as he saw us both frozen in the same iceberg:

"Babies, is it? I know! It's easy, just look."

He grabbed a sheet of paper and Julie's pen, then handed the result to Jeremy.

"Here, that's how to do it!"

Two seconds later, they were bombing downstairs and giggling like they were in the school playground. Half Pint's rough sketch had left little room for doubt. It was exactly like that.

*

When I got downstairs, the conversation around the table was already in full swing. Clément the Budding Bayleaf was singing our praises to Matthias Fraenkhel, who still had much to learn about the Malaussène tribe.

According to Clément, I was the hero of Belleville, the Malaussène house was something like Sherwood Forest, La Herse the bailiff was the Sheriff of Nottingham, the evil henchman of wicked King John who had pinched the throne of good old Richard the Lionheart. Belleville and its inhabitants stood in for the nice Saxon people, under Norman domination, but the troops of Robin the My-good-self were on the warpath, so John Lackland had better watch his arse!

"A present-day Robin . . . what a good subject for a film," Matthias observed.

"A play more like it!" yelled Jeremy, in the throes of sudden inspiration. "Making a film's dead complicated, but a play would be a piece of cake."

"And then I could video it," Budding Bayleaf nodded, seizing the chance to shoot his first masterpiece.

"What do you reckon, Suzanne? Would you lend us the stage in The Zebra?"

"And who's going to write this play, then?" Thérèse asked, sceptical as ever about anything that did not concern the stars.

"I am!" Jeremy exclaimed. "I am! We've got plenty of material what with everything we've been through over the last three or four years!"

"Can I act in it?" Half Pint asked.

"You'll be in it, and so will Clara, Leila, Nourdine, Verdun, What An Angel and everyone else. Even I'll be in it! I'm a really good actor, I am! Ain't that right, Benjamin? Aren't me and Half Pint excellent actors?"

My fork stopped in mid-air.

Diplomatic as ever, Jeremy added:

"And you make a pretty good procreation teacher, too. Really at ease . . . with your male and female gametes . . . and your cone of attraction . . . You'll be in it too, Ben, I promise you that!"

And off he and Half Pint went again in their private giggling fit.

"Which day of the week would you perform it?" asked Suzanne O'Blue Eyes, sprouting the wings of sponsorship.

"So you agree?"

Jeremy's laughter turned into a gargling noise.

"You'd agree to lend us The Zebra?"

"When do you want to perform?"

"To start off with, on Sunday afternoons when everyone's bored to death. And then . . ."

"Take it easy to start off with. When you've written your play, I'll free up Sunday afternoon, then, if it goes down well, we'll see about the evenings."

"Suzanne!"

Jeremy was positively screaming.

"Suzanne! Suzanne! Jesus Christ, Suuuuuzaaaaane!"

And off he rushed to the kids' room, bellowing:

"I'll get started straight away. The Malaussène Saga! Robin Hood in the concrete jungle! And with Belleville's furniture as well! We'll bring the house down!"

A law of family physics: any child leaving the dinner table in a rush unleashes a flood. A second later, only the adults were left.

Mum said:

"That's very nice of you, Suzanne . . ."

Suzanne cut her off with a tinkle of clear laughter.

"Given the state The Zebra's in now, one more turkey won't make much odds . . ."

When I say "clear", Suzanne's laughter quite literally is. When she laughs, light passes through her without meeting the slightest vested interest, the smallest mood or the tiniest regret. The result is a chorus of pure notes, a morning peal of bells in a country church (if I may go so far) which lifts you heavenward.

"Are things that bad?" Julie asked. "Is The Zebra in real danger?"

"No more or less than the rest of Belleville," Suzanne replied solemnly.

"The key's in La Herse's pocket, as with everything else," remarked Cissou, who had remained silent until then.

A round of anticipatory commiserations.

Which Matthias Fraenkhel interrupted with his confused stammering:

"Excuse me, Suzanne . . . but if The Zebra became . . . I don't know . . . a kind of . . . historic monument . . . a temple raised to cinematography, for example . . . that would be some sort of protection, would it not?"

(Thus spoke Matthias Fraenkhel: "cinematography", "gramophone", "wireless set", "would it not?", a little lexicon of obsolete words in which time had stood still for many a long year.)

"A temple to the glory of cinematography, Doctor Fraenkhel?"

Suzanne's smile was awaiting further clarification.

Matthias turned to Julie:

"I think the time has come . . . to sell your nest egg . . . my little Juliette."

That's right, Matthias had his own pet name for Julie.

"Well," Julie announced, "Old Job, Matthias's father, has named me as sole legatee when it comes to his film property. And, you see Suzanne, it's probably the largest private collection of films in the world. So it seems to Matthias and me that you are probably the person who's best placed to deal with the heritage, by turning The Zebra into what Matthias calls a temple to cinematography. The films will belong to you. We will transfer ownership to you for one symbolic franc. Then it will be up to you to draw up the programme. What do you say?"

Suzanne, who had spent her life teaching Latin and Greek in those schools that still offered such subjects in order to support her cinematographic passion, was pretty much in agreement. It was quite obvious that she could not believe her ears.

"And there's more to come," Matthias went on. "Tell her . . . about The Only Begotten Film, Julie . . . about Job's and Liesl's masterpiece."

"Old Job was ninety-five years old this year, and his wife Liesl, Matthias's mother, who is ninety-four, is slowly passing away in Saint-Louis Hospital. For the past seventy-five years, they've been making a film together, with Job taking care of the pictures and Liesl recording the soundtrack. Seventy-five years of secret footage, Suzanne! They don't want it to be shown until after they're both dead and only then to a limited audience, who Job has asked me to choose now that he knows Liesl won't recover. We could show it at The Zebra, and start picking the spectators right away. How does that sound?"

It clearly sounded absolutely fine to Suzanne.

"Job will impose just one condition," Julie continued. "He wants the reel *and the negative* to be publicly destroyed after the showing. This is his essential concept of a 'cinematographic event'. Only one showing for The Only Begotten Film. *Events aren't repeatable.* Job never stopped bending my ear about that all through my childhood."

"But isn't that in complete contradiction with having a film collection? Such a collection is based on the idea of repeatability, surely?"

Suzanne's amazement led straight into one of Matthias's smiles.

"My father hates practically all the films in his collection. In his eyes, they aren't so much works of art as . . . pieces of evidence."

"Pieces of evidence?"

"Proof of the decline of the cinema since it became a public medium . . . He's a fountain of knowledge on the subject."

Suzanne listened, Suzanne appreciated, Suzanne was highly grateful, but Suzanne O'Blue Eyes couldn't really see herself making off with the family jewels.

"What about your son? You did say you had a son, didn't you?"

"Barnaby?"

The angel of melancholy fluttered around the table.

"Well, Barnaby goes even further than his grandfather in his hatred of the cinema . . . While my father has devoted his life to the making of The Only

Begotten Film, Barnaby has spent his doing what might called . . . the opposite of cinema."

"The *opposite* of cinema?" Suzanne exclaimed, with her brightest laugh. "What in heaven's name is the *opposite* of cinema?"

"Maybe he'll show you some time . . . I do believe he's supposed to be coming to Paris . . . one of these days."

("Maybe" . . . "I do believe" . . . "One of these days" . . . the dubious syntax of dysfunctional families.) Embarrassment would have settled once more if the kids' door hadn't flown open.

"Suzanne, could we all sleep at The Zebra with Clément?" Jeremy asked, indicating his brothers and sisters, who were standing behind him. "To bond with the theatre, see what I mean? It'll make our spatial relationship easier to manage."

"Spatial relationship", "To bond with the theatre", here we go . . . The little bugger hadn't even written the thing yet and he was already developing a luvvie's jargon. Suzanne caught on at once:

"Personally, I can see no reason why you shouldn't manage your spatial relationships in this way, Jeremy, but if you really do want to bond with The Zebra, I'm not the one you should be asking."

Jeremy looked at me. I looked at Jeremy. Jeremy pressed the point. I didn't say a word. Then, Jeremy caught on. He turned towards Mum.

Who said:

"If you want to sleep at The Zebra to get the show ready more easily, and if Suzanne doesn't mind, then why ever not?"

*

And thus, with a few smiling words spoken over her untouched dinner, Mum decided to separate herself from the rest of the family and live alone in her tribe's house, with a broken heart she refused to tell us anything about.

I turned round to look at Thérèse.

Who was looking away.

I thought of Mum.

Then of Clara.

While my eyes can still shed their load of tears . . .

Clara working on that poem a few years back for her oral French exam . . .

While my eyes can still shed their load of tears . . .

Louise Labé . . . how did the next line go?

While my eyes . . . While my eyes . . .

Each line sang its own love song.

While my eyes can still shed their load of tears
And I regret past joys with you
Yes, that's right . . .
And then? . . . And then what? Speak, damn you, memory . . .
The verse ended with a suspended decasyllable:
I do not yet have a desire to die.
Not yet, Mother . . .
Not yet . . .

III
SON OF JOB

I was born out of curiosity.

Chapter 9

So it was during those evenings before your arrival. And when it was time to part, Julius the Dog and I kept Matthias company while he was looking for a taxi.

"So, Benjamin . . . How's your paternity coming on?"

Parting conversations of this sort . . .

"OK, Matthias, I'm having full and frank discussions with myself, as they say."

"And, at the end of the day, have you reached an agreement?"

We chuckled. Words in their new clothes are always good for a laugh.

"We're in arbitration. Julie's little squatter and I are having a good chat. With him mostly listening, of course. I'm warning him about what he's in for. You know, like in 1940, the final briefing of the hero before he gets dropped into occupied France. Only yesterday, I advised him to get the bees out of his bonnet as soon as he touches down . . . Whether in war or in peace, they never let you get by with your bees."

(This sort of crap was doing me the world of good.)

"You are a strange man all the same, Benjamin . . ."

We weren't in that much of a hurry to find a cab.

"When it comes to strangeness, Matthias, you're no shirker either."

We even let a few taxis go by. With their yellow lights, they drove their emptiness around. They were paying for all the ones that don't stop when you want them to.

"But seriously, Benjamin . . . someone shoots you through the head . . . a surgeon removes all your vital organs . . . you get killed two or three times . . . and it doesn't seem to bother you one bit. Then you get Julie pregnant . . . and you get into a terrible state! A rather odd preconception, wouldn't you say?"

"A preconception?"

"Yes, in favour of nothingness. The idea that nothingness must necessarily be more agreeable than life is nothing if not a preconception."

A thought which required a few moments' thought.

"And what about you and your eternity, Matthias?"

"Ah, but I have no preconceptions about eternity!"

A few steps more, then he added:

"That's precisely why I'm in no hurry to pack it full of babies."

*

Julie spent some of our nights filling me in on the Fraenkhel period of her childhood.

"It was during my early teens. My father the Governor had packed me off to boarding school in Grenoble. And I exchanged letters with the Fraenkhels. They lived in the Loscence valley in the Vercors."

While awaiting the surprise of your own childhood, I was delighted to discover Julie's. That's life for you. On one side you're on rewind, while on the other you're slipping in a new cassette. Ready for the show to go on.

"So Old Job plastered the world with celluloid while holed up in the middle of nowhere?"

"No, the house in the Vercors is his little secret. A hidden, intimate place which doesn't even have a phone! Just a fax machine, and he's the only one who knows the number. Job's headquarters are a flat in Paris. What's more, he also used to travel a lot, Rome, Berlin, Vienna (his wife, Liesl, comes from Austria), Tokyo, New York, and so on . . . And yet, in all my memories Job, Liesl and Matthias are there in Loscence, just as though they never left the place. I suppose they arranged to be there while Barnaby and I were on holiday."

"While we're on the subject, what's all this business about a private film collection? Are you really Old Job's legatee?"

"Yes, and it's one of my most amusing memories from the period."

In our shared night, it made her laugh all over again. She laughed softly against my shoulder.

She was about thirteen. She was in her third year at secondary school. One day, during the Easter holidays, she went to the Fraenkhels' place in Loscence with an essay to write, whose title had been set by a teacher who clearly considered himself to be advanced for his time.

Imagine the tragedy of a silent-movie star eliminated by the invention of the talkies.

"It's the opposite which would create a tragedy!" Old Job exclaimed. "All of today's actors would be eliminated if the cinema went silent again! All they're good for is gesticulating with their mouths and the music takes care of the rest!

54

Their chatter . . . their music . . . their sound effects . . . It's simple, Juliette (all the family called her Juliette), these days, no-one acts any more, they just talk. Their bodies are expressionless . . . all we have left are their lips, and the words don't even follow the right rhythm! If you want my opinion, Juliette, silent films were already empty, and talkies are just the wrapping round the vacuum! Don't laugh, try it out for yourself, shut all those chatterboxes up, stuff your ears full of chewing gum and then you'll see how they vanish from the screen! They vanish completely!"

Old Job had gone on about the subject all morning. He and Julie went down into the old barn which housed his film collection and watched a couple of spaghetti westerns to see. As a result, Julie's essay was perfectly symmetrical to the original title.

Julie Corrençon   24 March

Essay

Imagine the tragedy of a movie star in the talkies eliminated by the invention of silent films.

A lovely little essay:

It's the story of a big Hollywood heart-throb, a living legend in the world of the talkies, who is abruptly confronted by the upsurge of silence. All his fellow actors rail against such a step backwards, but he, the great actor-cum-crooner says no, no, not a bit of it, long live the silent movie, a true art form once more, finally free of the chatter of Tinseltown, and he declares himself ready to offer his services to silence. They take him at his word and take him on in a super production costing megabucks. And there he is in front of the eye of the camera, like the first Christian before the lions. (This was, by the way, what the film was about.) Action. They shoot, he postures a bit, they cut and develop. (On celluloid supplied by Old Job's lab.) Nothing. A total blank. Not the slightest trace of the heart-throb. The rest is there: the set, the lions, the other actors . . . but not him. They check the camera, remix the emulsions, top the producer up with Valium and have another go. Same thing: not a glimpse of the crooner. After a good dozen attempts, they have to face facts: a star of the talkies doesn't impress silent celluloid. Maybe it's something to do with chromosomes. Anyway, no matter how much they film, he remains as invisible as a vampire in a mirror. Things turn tragic. They annul the contract. The producer picks up

55

his chips, sues the crooner and sets off to hunt down the descendants of Chaplin
and Keaton. The heart-throb splashes out what's left of his dosh on a trick
cyclist, who relieves him of his finances but fails to get a single word out of him,
for, not only has the silent cinema struck him off, it has also struck him dumb.
So he commits suicide. Reduced to nothing, the former legend drowns in a vat
of developer which, of course, once developed reveals nothing at all.

Silence . . .

Oh, those gorgeous silences of sleepless nights . . .

The amount of delicious insomnia your mother and I have shared since we
met . . .

Sleep is a separation . . .

I finally said:

"Not bad."

"No, not at all bad considering how old I was."

"And what did you get for it?"

"Four hours' detention. The teacher turned out to be not that ahead of his time
after all. But Old Job was delighted."

Old Job read the essay with tears of laughter. Then, without any transition, he
started really sobbing. He hugged Julie and cried his eyes out. She knew he was a
bit emotional, like all good industrial killers, but this did rather take her by
surprise.

"What's the matter Job?"

"Nothing's the matter. On the contrary, I've just found myself an heir."

*

"But what about Barnaby?"

For there was also Barnaby, Matthias's son, and Old Job's grandson. He
intrigued me.

"Were you at boarding school together?"

"Yes, but not in the same dormitory."

"What was he like?"

A childhood friend, they'd shared their first steps, a blood brother, a kissing
cousin, the sort of person who, when you see them thirty years later in the family
album, you say: "Look, it's Barnaby!" Except that Barnaby never let himself be
photographed.

"What do you mean?"

"As soon as he was old enough to understand the symbolic dimension of words, he refused to allow himself to be *taken*. He has a primitive hostility against photography."

"Why?"

"A fascinated hatred for Old Job, and a radical rejection of his celluloid world. A fierce opposition against the grandfather. Barnaby's a special case."

While Job and Liesl were working on their Only Begotten Film, Barnaby was destroying his baby photos.

"In terms of family iconography, Barnaby's a black hole in the albums. There isn't a single picture of him."

"The opposite of cinema?"

"Its total negation."

Julie and Barnaby had a little game. When Julie went to the cinema in Grenoble, Barnaby never went with her. He just looked at the stills pinned up in the lobby. By using this fallout, he then reconstructed the story of the film being shown.

"What?"

"I'm not kidding. If you show Barnaby ten stills from any film you want, and in any order, he'll piece the storyline together right in front of you, beginning, middle and end, without missing a single sequence. He even used to guess what sort of music was used to underscore the vital moments."

This strange talent turned out to be a good little earner. Their school friends did not believe it possible. So Julie bet with them for increasingly large sums. They stuck Barnaby in front of the stills, went to see the film to check, then pocketed their winnings.

"He needed money to buy his potholing equipment."

Because, every summer, when the rest of France was exposing its acres of flesh to the sun, Barnaby used to go underground in the caves of the Vercors, stubbornly depriving his skin of its pigmentation in the attempt to become transparent. When school started again, he was as limpid as a salamander. The autumn light shone through him.

"And did you go potholing with him?"

A vital question, indeed.

"Yes, and without a lamp! Barnaby's greatest ambition was to move around in total darkness. To cancel out shapes. Of course I went potholing with him! That's how I spent my holidays. When I wasn't in front of a screen with Old Job, I was in darkness with Barnaby."

Barnaby and Julie, aged fifteen, in a black abyss.

"And did he take your cherry?"

That one just slipped out. It isn't even an expression I use. It was the delicate metaphor Jeremy used on the evening when Clara left us for Saint-Hiver's bed.

Julie laughed.

"You could put it that way. Though it would be more historically accurate to say that it was me who made his tulip blossom."

When you ask questions, you lay yourself open to replies.

Silence.

"Don't take on like that, Benjamin. And don't forget: it was in total darkness. He never saw me naked!"

That's exactly what was bugging me. Just imagine it, it's completely dark, he's got your mother who's totally starkers in his arms, and it doesn't even occur to him to light a match . . . if you want my opinion, this Barnaby must have a screw loose . . .

Chapter 10

A ND SO THE tribe moved into The Zebra. Meanwhile, Julie and I kept our bedroom and Mum stayed alone downstairs in the former hardware store. We took it in turns to try and make her eat. Jeremy called these fruitless sessions of comforting our "nasty turns". Mum preferred solitude to us. She blessed The Zebra for returning her to her absence.

"No, honestly, Benjamin, things are just fine as they are. And just look how much fun the kids are having with their play!"

The fact of the matter was that Jeremy had cast a glamorous glitter over their departure, like a famous company setting off on a world tour, Molière and his harem, medieval strolling players . . . I could just picture them harnessing their rickety carts to their scrawny horses and heading off in their worn-out cloaks and feathered hats. I could just hear the jolting of the wagon train over the cobblestones at dawn. Clara found it all rather amusing, but she did not miss out on this official opportunity to get closer to Clément. What An Angel on one hip and Verdun at her heels added to the realism of the picture. Thérèse was perfect in her role of resigned disapproval and Julius the Dog's woeful stare seemed to confirm her worst suspicions: they were both horrified at having to follow such a band of excommunicated wastrels.

Even though The Zebra is precisely 624 yards from the home, Jeremy even put on a scene of tearful farewells!

Suzanne found it all hilarious.

"I don't know what Jeremy's play will be like, but I wouldn't have missed his staging of Exodus for the world!"

Half Pint had a more realistic viewpoint:

"We're an army. We're going to defend The Zebra."

He could probably already see himself being burnt at the stake on stage so as to throw La Herse and his men into a state of mystical terror.

Even Matthias put his oar in:

"Don't take on like this, Benjamin . . . after all, this is a holiday . . . and theatre courses are all the rage right now . . . corporal expression . . . you can even find such goings-on in the Vercors . . . summer schools . . . so move with the times, for heaven's sake!"

And then Matthias Fraenkhel left as well.

"To bury my mother."

*

Because, as you will see, we die. We die a hell of a lot, as I think I've already told you. So don't come to me on some adolescent dark night of the soul and tell me that death is an excellent reason for not being born, it's too late for that now!

So Liesl, Old Job's wife, Matthias's mother and Barnaby's grandmother, died. At Saint-Louis Hospital, where Julie had sent her to see Professor Marty.

"What's the matter with her?" Marty asked.

"She's ninety-four, she's got a bullet in the tip of her femur and a lump of shrapnel in her left shoulder blade," Julie replied.

"I would expect nothing less from a patient sent in by you. Her case will interest Berthold. Where did the ammo come from?"

"Sarajevo."

"What the hell was an old dear her age doing in Sarajevo? Had her package-tour flight broken down?"

"No, doctor, she was wandering round the streets with a tape recorder slung over her shoulder and brandishing a mike."

Which is exactly what Julie had told me. In the Fraenkhel couple, Old Job took care of the pictures, Liesl of the soundtrack. An entire life spent garnering the world's noises. If Julie could be believed, Liesl was the very birth of the radio. Her sole passion was having people in one place hear what was going on elsewhere. Miss Ubiquity in person.

"She's put the whole world on tape."

We went to visit her in hospital. Liesl wanted to meet Suzanne, and Julie dragged me along too.

"She's my godmother, you see. My model as a footloose woman. I'd like her to meet you."

In her hospital bed, the footloose model had now been reduced to a small plaster sarcophagus with a frizzy head, suspended from a complex system of straps and pulleys. Only her lips and eyes still moved. Her hands were lying on the sheet, but her speech was so lively that you could almost see her fingers fluttering around like hummingbirds.

"And so, it's you, is it?"

She looked at Suzanne.

"That's right."

Standing in the sunlight at the end of the bed, Suzanne smiled at Liesl. On the bedside table, in full view, a little tape recorder was running. Liesl recorded life, indiscriminately.

She raised her voice:

"Did you hear that, Job? This is Suzanne, Julie's chosen one. She's the one we've been working for all these years. She's the one who's going to show The Only Begotten Film!"

Slightly deaf, Old Job was as small as his wife, but without a single hair on his scalp. As his youth had faded away, it had drawn a map of the five continents across his head.

He looked up, stared long and hard at Suzanne with his tiny sparkling eyes, and said:

"She has the right look."

He then added, for Suzanne's benefit:

"Not a word before the showing, agreed? Nobody else knows anything about this work."

Suzanne promised that there wouldn't be a word.

"And not a word afterwards, either," Old Job added. "This is a film, not a subject of conversation. So keep your comments to yourself."

Suzanne's peal of laughter was a clear refusal.

"Is that all? Aren't we allowed to think about it, either? Are we supposed to commit collective hara-kiri when the house lights come back on?"

During the ninety-five years of his multinational existence, nobody had ever laughed off one of Old Job's orders. He looked round at Julie. She simply shrugged to signify that this was Suzanne's way, take it or leave it.

"We'll talk about it if we want to talk about it," Suzanne insisted. "And I'll answer for the quality of what's said."

"Don't you think it would be easier to guarantee silence?"

"That depends on the choice of the audience."

Old Job's eyes were weighing her up. Where had Juliette unearthed such a bundle of cheek? But Old Job also knew Juliette extremely well.

"And no more than a dozen in the audience. This isn't because I'm interested in symbolic numbers, it's simply because, given the height of your ambitions, you won't find any more than that in today's cinema."

"I quite agree with you."

"And don't forget my instructions," Old Job went on. "It must be destroyed after the showing. Events are not repeatable."

Suzanne agreed to the auto-da-fé.

"The reel and the negative," Old Job insisted.

"The reel and the negative."

"Fine," Old Job said.

This brought the business to a close. The official appointment had now taken place. Suzanne had just inherited the couple's Only Begotten Film. Two whole lifetimes spent making the same film – which made almost two centuries! – and not another word about it.

Liesl changed the subject.

"What about him over there, the one who waddles like a duck . . . who's he?"

It was me.

Which Julie then confirmed in her purring savannah laughter.

"This is my Job, Liesl, so show a bit of respect."

"It looks like he takes things to heart."

"Yes, that is one of his characteristics."

End of me.

There was a silence. Which was recorded on the tiny tape. As ever at moments like this, the decor became more visible. The hospital room, the emergency buttons, the personal record of the patient's temperature changes, noises in the corridor, cold wafts of ether, iodised smells of survival, a dry cough in the next room . . . Good God, how many hospital beds had I visited? And how many of their occupants had escaped? It was at this very moment that Liesl chose to stare at Julie's belly.

"When is it due?"

"Next spring," Julie answered.

"That's not necessarily the best time. I had mine in springtime, and he's spent his life blossoming all over."

This was a delicate allusion to Matthias's chronic eczema and rheumatism.

He replied stoically:

"What matters is the obstetrician, Mother. If I had been delivered by myself, I would have arrived in a better condition. But you've always had your own way when it comes to obstetrics."

The mini-sarcophagus burst into a fit of laughter, which sent its suspension system into panic stations.

"What did he say?" Job asked.

"For crying out loud, don't make her laugh! Don't you think she's in enough of a mess as it is?"

Everyone turned round.

Berthold was standing in the doorway, his gloomy looks perched high above his professional skills. Berthold! Professor Berthold! My saviour! The genius of the human plumbing system! He turned me from being permanently bedridden into a visitor to hospitals! Liesl greeted him joyfully.

"Come to look at your favourite toy, doctor?"

She indicated the tiny recorder on the bedside table.

"Would you be so good as to turn the cassette over? It's like me, almost run to a stop."

Scowling at her, Berthold obeyed. After that, he pointed us all towards the door. It was time to count Liesl's bones.

Once we were exiled in the corridor, Job brought us up to date.

"You know Liesl, Julie. She must be in absolute agony, but she refuses to take any morphine because she finds her condition *interesting*. She doesn't want to miss a moment of her death throes."

"Are things really that bad?"

"According to Marty, she should have died in Sarajevo, or while she was being flown back . . ."

"But that would be to overlook her curiosity," Matthias intervened. "Sudden death just doesn't suit Liesl's temperament."

"And Matthias knows what he's talking about. He's the fruit of our curiosity."

Matthias agreed:

"That's correct. I was born out of curiosity. But is there a better reason to be alive?"

This fascinating conversation was then cut short by a bunch of exotic flowers.

"For goodness' sake, Job, what on earth was Liesl doing in Sarajevo?"

The flowers were blooming. It was clearly a family bunch.

"She was doing some recording, Ronald," Job answered. "She was walking round with her microphone."

"Recording at her age!" the bouquet roared. "Don't the two of you ever stop?"

"I'm afraid not," Job replied.

Silence. An embarrassed head emerged from the flowers.

"Is it really that bad?"

The head was white, and devastated. Aged, but with a flowing mane of hair. Straight out of one of those American soaps devoted to the longevity of Texan oilmen.

"She's had it," Job replied.

And then introduced us.

"This is Ronald de Florentis, my distributor. He's a fake aristocrat, but a true friend. A sower of images before eternity. He's distributed the best and the worst the film world has to offer. Especially the worst."

"Which you allowed to be placed on your celluloid."

"Celluloid always starts life blank."

"Like machine guns before they've been fired."

"That's right, and it's the distributor who presses the trigger."

The two of them had been carping at each other like this for decades. They finally ran out of breath and Job named Julie and me in no uncertain terms:

"This is my goddaughter, Juliette. And this is her rapscallion. He's got her with child."

"I remember her, Job. I knew her when she was little. She never left your projection room."

"The baby is due next spring."

"And Matthias is taking care of the birth? Your child couldn't find a better doorman, Juliette. It will slide down a velvet carpet . . . And Matthias, how are you?"

And so on.

Until Professor Berthold's next bark.

"And why not a baobab while you're at it? Are you trying to take away the little air she has left?"

The bouquet was wrenched out of Ronald's grasp and vanished in a shower of petals, while Berthold banged on about families' "floral incontinence".

"Don't hold it against him," Liesl said in a whisper. "Professor Berthold is in a bad mood because I sent him packing. He'd got it into his head that he was going to bone half a dozen teenagers in order to rebuild my infrastructure and launch me afresh into the new century. Apparently, he doesn't have much time for the young people of today."

Florentis interrupted her.

"Liesl, would you tell us what the hell you were doing in Sarajevo?

"Sarajevo, Vukovar, Karlova, Biograd and Mostar," Liesl corrected him.

And then asked:

"Do I ask you how much you paid for your latest Van Gogh, Ronald? Do I ask you what things you get up to in order to enlarge your collections? If there's one person here who's incapable of writing the words 'The End' then it's definitely you, Florentis! Just look at yourself. Aren't you ashamed of being so young? At your age?"

*

No, there was no need of us to keep up the atmosphere. We left them to pick over their old passions. Matthias later told us Liesl's last words. When the time had come for him to leave as well, he promised to see her again the next day.

Liesl replied:

"No way. Tomorrow, I'm dying."

"What time?" Matthias asked, being little used to criticising his mother's plans.

"With the sun, my boy, and don't come along and spoil the moment. I've been waiting for it so long."

Her only emotion – almost a tear – was when she said:

"If you see Barnaby, tell him . . ."

She searched for the right words.

"Nobody sees Barnaby any more, Mother . . ."

Matthias realised, too late, that this was no consolation. He stammered:

"But he should be coming to Paris, I think . . . I'll write to him . . . I'll . . ."

She died the next day at the appointed time.

On the bedside table, the little tape recorder had picked up her last sigh.

Matthias left to bury her in Vienna, Austria, in the land where she had been born.

"She was Karl Kraus's niece," he explained.

Then added, while smiling to himself:

"Monomania is a family tradition . . ."

We let him spill out his grief in his usual stuttering, concentrated manner:

"Getting herself buried in Austria . . . the poor thing . . . she devoted her life to ubiquity . . . in Austria . . . the only country that has no doors or windows . . . Europe's cave . . ."

Then he added:

"I'm leaving tomorrow. You'll receive the results of your tests by post, my little Juliette."

(They were your tests, in fact. You were no bigger than a kidney bean, and you were already doing tests. You might as well get used to it from the word go, because they test you all your life. You have to get your grades from the start to the finish. And good ones, at that. The pathologist adds up your final score.)

65

Chapter 11

E XIT MATTHIAS.

Just Julie and me, then. Or rather, the three of us, as it were. A love holiday. That's the way it had always been for Mum, but for Julie and me it was a first. The tribe had never given us much chance to live our lives in private.

We spent the first week in bed. This was far from being a record. At the time when your aunt Louna and uncle Laurent's love fed off itself, they spent an entire year without touching the ground. A year between the sheets! We took them up delicate meals and fat books. From the way they sent us packing, it was clear that they would have preferred to love on a drip and in radio silence . . . But, what with their families waiting for them, a mob of admirers, the two-faced buggers who envy them and the stars looking down on them, even the most solitary of navigators has plenty of company.

A week alone, then.

A week spent diving one into the other, then come up gasping for air, before diving again to explore our submarine geography for so long that sometimes we dozed off on the other's seabed, letting sleep separate us and slowly float us up to the surface along the curves of our dreams . . .

Don't press the point, don't act up like Jeremy, all you will get in this chapter are metaphors. Everything in this sublunar world begins with an image and then proceeds with metaphors. You need to grasp this point. It is then up to you to use your neurons to seize the meaning! Which is just as well, because if the wonderful "book of life" (sic) revealed its meaning straight away, you would probably snap it back shut again and leave us to meander alone through the great metaphorical maze.

All I can add is that, during those odd moments when love left your mother and me lying on our sides, we used the little breath we had left to pick your name from one of the catalogues at our disposal. Since we did not have a television, cathode-tube commemorations were clearly out. You had no chance of being called Apollo, just because a couple of loonies had put mankind on the moon, or Sue Ellen either, you shouldn't worry about that. Among the more usual Christian martyrs' names, we wanted one which would be easily borne, not age too quickly, and not go off like a firecracker when yelled out in the playground. But, there's nothing I can do about it, whenever I hear a martyr's name, I can't help but go over the circumstances of their removal from human affections.

"How about Blandine if it's a girl?" your mother said. "Blandine's nice."

"Thrown to wild creatures. A bull bearing down on Blandine, Julie, the frothing bull charging with its might horns at our little Blandine . . ."

"Stéphane, then . . . I really like Stéphane. A soft name . . ."

"Stoned to death on the road to Jerusalem. The first martyr. He started the whole thing off. Do you have any idea what it must be like to be stoned? When your skull cracks open, for instance? Why not Sébastien while you're at it? I can just hear the whistle of the arrows and the creaking of the painters' easels . . . No, Julie, let's try looking among the prophets and patriarchs instead. They knew how to take the right place in their time. They just announced disasters, they weren't victims of them . . . Or not so much."

"Isaac?"

"What? So the Great Paranoiac can tell me to send him back to limbo with a penknife? No way."

"Job?"

"Already taken."

"Daniel . . . from Babylon."

At this point, something weird happened, which I can't really explain. I went pale, I think, it felt as if all my cogs and wheels had seized up, as if an icy blast had frozen what remained, and, in a blank voice, I murmured:

"No!"

"But why on earth not? He did tame the lions, after all!"

Without batting an eyelid, I said:

"No Daniels in the family, Julie, promise me that. If we have just one Daniel, then all the shit in the world's going to land on our heads, I can feel it, I just know it. Don't you think we've been through enough as it is?"

My voice must have worried her, because she hiked herself up on to an elbow to look at me.

"What's all this about? Have you taken to reciting Thérèse's part now?"

I just replied:

"No Daniels."

She was too tired to insist. She slumped back again and, with a sigh which foretold sleep, she said:

"Anyway, it's always Jeremy who does the forenaming round here, and I don't know if our kid's going to escape that . . ."

True enough. Jeremy had the gift of baptising at first sight. Half Pint, Verdun, What An Angel all owed their handles to him. And when he wasn't forenaming, he was nicknaming: Cissou the Snow, Suzanne O'Blue Eyes . . .

IV
SUZANNE AND THE FILM BUFFS

JEREMY: *She hasn't just got eyes that see, she's got eyes that show.*

Chapter 12

O N   T H E   M O R N I N G of the eighth day, Suzanne O'Blue Eyes knocked on their door.

"It's open!"

Suzanne came in and nearly fainted. Airless love. Julie leapt to her feet, opened a window and drew up a chair.

"Sit down and breathe deeply."

She then dived back between the sheets. Suzanne noticed the old traces of burns on Julie's skin. And the splendour of her breasts, so admired by the children of the tribe.

Malaussène went straight for the worst scenario:

"Jeremy's burnt down The Zebra."

Suzanne let out three notes of her laughter.

"Jeremy's got everything under control. I've been laid off. The show's coming along and the Big Boss is beating them all into shape. Meanwhile Clara's smoothing the rough edges and taking the stills. Clément's working like a slave so he can buy her real professional equipment. He wants to give her a brand-new state-of-the-art camera. This is love with a capital L."

"Coffee?"

Benjamin staggered over to the cupboard which functioned as their kitchen. Love had dug out trenches under his eyes and made his hair stand up on end. A thin scar marked the borderline of his scalp. Suzanne was touched: a lobotomised Captain Nemo.

"I'd love one."

"Turkish?"

"Sure."

"What day is it?"

Suzanne told them the time and the day. While Malaussène was boiling the sweetened water, she explained her intrusion.

"We've got to pick the audience for the projection of Old Job's Only Begotten Film. I've let a week go by. By now, all of cinema's corrupted classes will have left Paris for Saint-Tropez, the Luberon, Belle-Île, Cadaqués or Saint-Paul-de-Vence . . . Only the pure of heart remain."

The brown foam flirted with the narrow rim of the coffee pot three times while Suzanne was attempting to define her notion of purity in cinematographic terms. From inside his cupboard, Malaussène seemed to understand that this involved a love of images which was never dazzled by sunlight, refused marriages of convenience and swore only by style.

"Style is their code of honour."

Malaussène reappeared in his woolly slippers and gandoura, with the tray on one hand and a Chinese dressing gown in the other, which then fluttered over Julie's shoulders.

"Coffee is served."

In the tribe, coffee was always drunk in silence. Once the cups were empty, Suzanne got down to business: there was no way she was going to recruit all on her own. She needed Old Job's approval and she could get that only through Julie. But she insisted on one point:

"It will be a crowd of terrorists."

She explained:

"Terrorists with morals. If Old Job's film ruffles their ethics, then they will probably destroy the reel before the end of the projection."

"How many of them will there be?" Julie asked.

"In my day, there were about two hundred of them. But there's only about a dozen left. Honour has worn them out. Job was right about that."

Julie smiled. She thought of the world of cinema as it is portrayed in magazines. And how a dozen good men and true still remained in this teeming Babylon . . .

"Fine. So how can I help you?"

"By testing them."

*

Two hours later, the iron door Julie opened revealed a devil's workshop. Hellfire was rising off white-hot sheet metal. In the courtyard, a slagheap of written-off cars was blocking off the sky. Julie advanced through a shadowy jungle of greasy chains and pulleys. She screwed up her eyes.

"Anyone there?"

A stench of saturated oil and melting rubber.

"Monsieur Avernon?"

The iron roof was creaking beneath the searing sunlight.

When nothing moves, play dead. Julie owed her life to this law of nature. She froze. The heat closed in around her.

She did not have to wait long. Just by her ear, a voice growled:

"Quite a wildcat we've got here."

She turned round.

"A journalist are you?"

He was now staring into her face.

"And a gutsy one at that."

A hirsute sixty-year-old. A sneering moustache and judgemental eyebrows.

"Just let me guess . . . We're on to a big scoop. We want to get our Range Rover bulletproofed before setting off. We're going to risk our skin for the moral good of the species. Is that it?"

She let him get on with it.

But he did not go much farther.

"Shove off. I don't pack pregnant women off to the killing fields."

He turned on his heels and headed off into his shed.

Julie stayed put. The fact that he had guessed she was a journalist was one thing. The fact that he supposed she was on to a big scoop was merely a chronological error. But the fact that he had spotted the chick pea she was carrying without Matthias's scanner was something else . . .

He was swaggering like a bear and gliding between the chains and winches. It was his forest. He vanished into it while Julie was taking root.

Her nostrils flared.

"I'll track him down by the smell of his hooch."

She was reproaching herself for this unpleasant observation when a blinding, muted explosion made the shadows cast by the chains dance. Then came the crackle of soldering.

This time it was Julie who stood behind him. He was soldering a roll bar on to the side of a 604, against which someone had apparently had a serious grudge. Julie's finger tapped him on his arched back.

"You're wrong, Monsieur Avernon. I'm here to ask you a question."

He turned, blowtorch in hand.

She reassured him:

"Just one."

He raised his visor of iron and mica.

"What, a big girl like you still has things to learn? Not likely!"

A fleeting thought crossed her mind: No, but I'd willingly chop your bollocks off from under your overalls.

73

But that was not what she was doing there. She asked the question she had come to ask:

"Monsieur Avernon, what, in your opinion, is the basest form of immorality?"

He glanced round at her in disbelief, then at least half his bristles vanished into gulfs of deep thought. He thought so hard that the flame on his blowtorch burnt itself out. The silence lengthened into a series of detailed examinations. Then he shook his head and said:

"Dollying sideways."

At which point Suzanne emerged from the shadows to invite Pierre Avernon to dinner at The Zebra that very evening.

*

The second candidate worked for France Telecom. He helped out those in ignorance or distress. Directory enquiries were his daily bread.

"He works from two to ten p.m. and covers our district, along with three colleagues," Suzanne explained. "So we have a twenty-five per cent chance of getting him. Put on the loudspeaker, Benjamin. If I recognise his voice, I'll give you the nod."

"What's his name?"

"That's irrelevant. You're just a member of the public and he'll be expecting you to ask for a phone number. You call, hit him with the question, then wait for the answer. That's all."

"Remind me of the question again, Suzanne."

Suzanne repeated, slowly and distinctly:

"*That Delannoy fellow, what was his name again, Jules or Jean?*"

Benjamin dialled 12 while muttering the question over to himself. It rang a couple of times then there was a click. France Telecom. A recording confirmed this while singing the praises of the company and of patience. Then a male voice announced that help was at hand.

"Directory enquiries, can I help you?"

Suzanne nodded rapidly to Malaussène, who asked his question:

"Hello, what I want to know is . . . *That Delannoy fellow, what was his name again, Jules or Jean?*"

The pause which preceded the reply was not born of hesitation but of delighted surprise. This was then confirmed by the cheerful lilt of the voice:

"It's Truffaut in a film by Jacques Rivette, *Le Coup du berger*. Truffaut had a walk-on part. He was rhubarbing in a party and slipped the line in just as the camera was passing by. *That Delannoy fellow, what was his name again, Jules or*

74

Jean? The gag can't have gone down very well with Delannoy, but we never cared much for his films. Have you seen *L'Eternal Retour,* or *La Symphonie pastorale?* They're just rehashed psychology . . . No, they were really nothing to write home about, in fact . . ."

Suzanne took the receiver and cut short this lecture:

"Armand Lekaëdec? This is Suzanne. Come and have dinner tonight at The Zebra. It's important."

*

So, one by one, Suzanne recruited them by setting them such unexpected tests that only a true buff would have the reflexes to respond.

"It's the *Seven Samurai* method," Malaussène observed.

"Though God knows Kurosawa isn't my cup of tea," said Suzanne, with her usual way of killing by euphemism.

She belonged to the Mizoguchi school and could not believe that any so-called film lover would ever deign to glance at a single Kurosawa image.

Malaussène had been a lifelong Akira fan, and restated his admiration.

"Your what? Your admiration?" Suzanne roared. "How could you? Or do you admire him with your eyes closed? Do you close your eyes when you go to the cinema, Benjamin? Otherwise, how could you fail to *see* that that fraud is the king of redundancy?"

Suzanne's cheeks had gone purple and Malaussène thought it wise to beat a retreat. His tiny conceptual extinguisher would never put out such a sudden and knowledgeable inferno.

That evening, the apostles Suzanne had summoned all had cheeks of the same colour: film-buff crimson. After only a couple of drinks, the tone had risen, their voices had hit the high ground of moral certainty and statements of principle were fluttering around like party streamers. They wasted few words on civilities and went straight to the heart of the matter. They recognised themselves for what they had always been: children of the cinema and of nothing else, born of celluloid in clinics whose names they fervently repeated: some were from Rue de Messine, others from Studio Parnasse, others still from Mac-Mahon . . . Suzanne had called them in from various horizons and now they were seated around the table at The Zebra, as zealous as ever, bellowing out their favourites, which were far more than mere preferences, Parnassians and Mac-Mahonians bawling one another out, countering this article in *Positif* with that one in *Les Cahiers du cinéma* as if they still held those faded pages in their pock-marked fingers, after the forty years which had taken away their hair, wrecked their marriages, scattered their families, broken up empires, shattered the eastern bloc and in which History had so thoroughly garbled the TV's daily script that the word *memory* was on everyone's lips.

Except theirs.

Their memories were infallible. Completely intact. Their passion still entire.

A glance from Julie to Benjamin. An uncertain smile from Benjamin to Julie.

In fact, Julie and Benjamin had never in their lives before been surrounded by such a crowd of sectarian loonies, never heard so many categorical judgements, nor witnessed such apoplectic opinions being uttered. (Avernon was hammering on the table, projecting a bottle into Suzanne's hands, which she then emptied into the glasses which were immediately reached out. To his thunderous condemnation of sideways dollying, Lekaëdec added the cutting smile of a Robespierre aware of the fate in store for adepts of static shots.)

Extremely well informed, extremely loud and extremely film-buff crimson, they were perfectly sincere in the exercise of their wild exaggerations and, most of all, were utterly joyful in their fury in such a way that each death sentence was greeted with howls of laughter.

They argued about anything, about the subjects dealt with during a century of celluloid, about the techniques used to make them visible, and of course about the people who had been imprudent enough to place themselves at one end or the other of the camera.

"Films matter more than people, and each film more than its maker. Cinema is life. We're quite simply sitting in judgement over life . . ."

And this was why Suzanne had called them in: to judge the life Job and Liesl had shared. To judge the life's work of a couple who had devoted their lives to the cinema.

They all knew Old Job. He was the one who had been providing everyone with celluloid for almost a century, for better and for worse. The impartial provider. A sort of God the Father leaving men free to choose . . .

They all accepted.

They all wanted to see God the Father through his film.

"When will you be showing it?" someone asked.

"Old Job's wife died last week," Julie explained. "And Job considers that this is the natural end of their project. I'm going to fetch the film and his entire movie collection as soon as Matthias comes back."

Chapter 13

Y OU SEE, NOTHING much was happening. Clément the Budding Bayleaf and
Cissou the Snow were giving Belleville back to Belleville, Jeremy Malaussène
was staging the Malaussènes, Suzanne was setting up a film museum in a cinema
forsaken by film makers, and your innocent form was waxing in Julie's womb.
Alliterations, imitative harmonies, the ticking over of life, not the slightest hint of
destiny . . . The aimless charm of a novel which just won't get started.

If ever you ask me what happiness is – and I am sure you will – then I shall tell
you that it is just like this.

Your mother and I get up long after the sun, have a bite to eat, then stroll down
Boulevard de Belleville towards the rampant sign of The Zebra.

One way or the other – no man is watertight – word of the showing of Old Job's
film had got round. The place was crawling with wannabe viewers, but Suzanne
stuck to her initial selection – not one more was taken.

"Only this morning, I threw five of them out. If I listened to them, I'd have to
hire the Grand Rex."

She booted them out with smiling firmness.

"But where are they crawling out from?" I asked. "I thought they'd all left
Paris."

"They're crawling out from under themselves, Benjamin, or from a grave, if
you don't mind my saying so. They're giving us a remake of *The Return of the
Living Dead*. They spent their lives making pseudo-cinema, they tainted their
hands with false images, they lied, they lied to themselves, but there's one thing
you can't take away from them: at the beginning, they all had the cinema in their
guts. They're like fallen angels. Lost souls, who'd give anything to see The Only
Begotten Film of a unique existence." There was a dreamy look in the blue of her
eyes. "All the same . . . it's incredible how fast word gets round in the celluloid
universe."

"At the speed of light?"

She nodded.

"Multiplied by the power of greed."

A smile.

"Now you're here, stay a while. You're going to witness the arrival of the most frustrated one of the lot. Their king! He's so up to his neck in all the industry's deceptions and so vociferous about his own original purity that in the trade he's baptised himself the King of the Living Dead."

The King of the Living Dead

We don't have a TV, the tribe doesn't give us much time for going to the cinema and yet, when the King of the Living Dead came through Suzanne's door, it was as if all the screens in the world had flickered into life. (There's no escape these days, as you'll see, even the blind have a screen fitted into their eyes. No-one sees any more, you just spend your life recognising.)

He was so like his image and his image was so familiar that I was surprised to hear the floorboards creak as he advanced towards Suzanne with his arms open.

"Suzon!"

So, he wasn't just an image. He also had a body with its associated weight, width, depth, density, aftershave, hair . . . a third dimension, maybe an age as well . . . maybe even a life . . .

"Suzon, my darling!"

If he had just risen from the tomb, then it must have been fitted with one hell of an ultra-violet lamp.

"It's been so long . . ."

He pressed Suzanne against his bull-like frame. His amber flesh, his gold trinkets, his greying blond mane, his healthy teeth and the sparkling frankness of his stare freely gave back to the world all the light he had lapped up while filming.

"Just let me look at you . . ."

He held Suzanne at arm's length. His fleshy lips had a childish grin.

"Still as much of a pain in the arse as ever?"

He broke out into the sort of laughter which asks itself no questions, gave Suzanne another big hug, though this time against his shoulder, then turned to Julie and me.

"Ladies and gentlemen, whoever you are, may I introduce you to the conscience of the movie business!"

Then, to Suzanne:

"No, honestly, only last night I was looking through my notebooks from the good old days of the Studio Parnasse, and, goodness me, you really did lay into us something rotten during our debates! You'll see! I've held on to everything, I'll show you if you like!"

And back to us:

"No kidding. She's the conscience of a generation! You probably don't realise it, but you owe her everything of any worth that French cinema has produced since the 1960s."

A sudden glimpse of a crack:

"And as a result nothing that I've done personally . . . I have, so to speak, rather let the side down . . ."

It was at this precise moment that Suzanne's laughter pealed out.

"And to what do I owe the honour of this visit, o letter-down of sides?"

He finally released his grip, his hand slapped his thighs, he shrugged and said, as if it was obvious:

"Why . . . remorse!"

Suzanne apparently thought that this deserved looking into, because she then offered him a seat, some whiskey and introduced us.

"Corrençon?" he exclaimed. "Julie Corrençon? The journalist?"

Julie butted in:

"Yes, but Benjamin writes all my articles."

He wasted no time on my vital statistics and instead went straight to the point:

"Now, you see Suzon, a fortnight ago I heard from Doctor Fraenkhel that Old Job, his father, was handing over his film collection to you."

I knew from the look in Julie's eyes that I ought to have shut up, but my astonishment had already slipped out of my mouth:

"What? You know Matthias Fraenkhel?"

"He was the gynaecologist of my first four wives, and the fifth one is now in his capable hands."

A small aside which did not distract him from the matter in hand.

"But you know our good doctor, Suzon. He doesn't have an ounce of common sense when it comes to budgeting a business."

("Budgeting a business" . . . the ring of those words . . . the wring of those words . . . smile, please, Matthias.)

"Gifts are all well and good, but the state is going to take its pennyworth too! How much is Old Job's collection worth, do you think? He quite simply has everything! Or everything of any worth. All the reels and the negatives . . ."

Suzanne didn't get out her pocket calculator. She was having a ball. But her delight was invisible to eyes blinded by their own light.

"OK. Well, apart from death duties, there's also the question of storage and conservation. Conservation, Suzon. Not to mention the restoration of a good many reels. How are you going to cope with it all?"

"From the box office, I suppose."

"The box office is scarcely going to cover your community charges, my dear. Don't imagine that there will be a full house every night. Not for the first few years, at any rate. The cinema's a dying art. I should know, I'm the one who buried it!"

And to us, opening his spectral arms:

"Yes, me, the King of the Living Dead!"

Back to Suzanne:

"And so, this is what I suggested to Matthias."

He marked a pregnant pause.

"Yes?" Suzanne asked sweetly.

"I'll take everything in hand."

"You'll take everything in hand?" Suzanne was smiling genially.

"Everything. Even the renovation of your hovel, which is apparently falling down around your ears. As a matter of fact, haven't you received an eviction order?"

"I'm only the manager . . . We're still discussing terms . . ."

"You'll be the owner and have no more terms to discuss, I'll make that my business."

"And what did Matthias Fraenkhel say to that?" Suzanne asked diplomatically.

"He was delighted, of course. He leapt at the chance."

"He leapt . . ."

Suzanne relished the word, slowly repeating it beneath the blue brazier of his stare.

"You'll make it *your business* and Matthias *leapt* . . . Is that it?"

This time, he finally heard the italics in Suzanne's smiling voice. And what Julie and I then saw was like an eclipse: he was extinguished.

That's exactly what happened. The King of the Living Dead was extinguished. All of a sudden, he went a basement grey. Not the slightest sparkle! Bracelet in mourning, signet-ring dead, a past-it smell. The high-pitched voice of an eternal adolescent sank down to an earthy, shaky ruggedness. The crackly breath of an ancient vinyl disc. A morphing into old age.

"Very well, Suzanne . . ."

A moment's hesitation.

"I knew I'd find you just as I'd left you."

"As *I* left *you*," Suzanne corrected him politely.

You'll see, no person in the world is more polite than Suzanne O'Blue Eyes. Nor merrier. Nor more incorruptible in her merry politeness.

"OK. As *you* left *me*."

That's right. Truth isn't to be found at a great height. It lies low. You have to bend down and dig it out.

Julie, sensing that things were getting private, tapped me on the arm and motioned to me to leave. Suzanne glanced at her and waggled her finger. We sat back down. We did not really exist any more. It was to Suzanne that the King was speaking.

"Very well, Suzanne, now listen to me. I admit that I've become the King of the Living Dead, that I've wasted my footage and never sent you reeling. And I'm not going to try to do so now."

He was staring at his shoes. His fat stubby fingers were grappling after words.

"This isn't a *business* deal I'm offering you, nor some chance to be *leapt* at . . . I want to pay. That's all there is to it. I'll pay and you'll keep your freedom."

"And what do you imagine Old Job's reaction will be?" Suzanne asked, before adding: "Let me freshen your glass."

He shook his head.

"Old Job isn't Matthias. He lacks his innocence. If I went to see him and offered to look after his heritage, then he'd send me packing, just like you." A bitter smile. "Though God knows how much celluloid the bugger sold me!"

"So why did you come here?"

"To tell you that I'm not doing this for myself."

He stared at the ceiling. He wanted to get it over with.

"Look, I'll say it again Suzanne. I'll come up with the finances, and there's an end to it. Old Job chose you, and he was right so to do. You'll buy The Zebra, you'll set up a company, in the way you want, it will be watched over by the lawyers of your choice, my name won't appear anywhere, you'll owe me nothing, I'll have no rights, I'll quite simply finance the operation for as long as you live, with a renewable lease for the person of your choice after your death and mine. This really is a massive project, Suzanne. You won't be able to manage without backing."

"I'll find other investors . . ."

". . . Who will give you complete freedom? Oh no you won't. They'll want their share of the profits and their slice of the kudos. You know that as well as I do. You've spent your entire life running away from sponsors, bankers, TV channels and in-house stooges who want to grab all the limelight and leave you in the dark."

"What if Old Job paid for it himself?"

"Through a foundation? I've thought about that. It would cost too much money. He shut up shop twenty years ago. As you know, neither his son nor his grandson has followed in his footsteps. The old boy flogged off his laboratories at a price that amazed everyone . . . barely more than a peppercorn. He has just about enough to live on. All he has left is his Paris office."

"What about the Ministry of Culture?"

"It doesn't exist. Only ministers exist. And do you want to be in a minister's clutches? For how long?"

Suzanne smiled and shrugged. "In other words, there's no one but you."

"Just my money. I repeat: I'm not going to be directly involved."

He suddenly got to his feet.

"Look, Suzanne, if a hack asks me if I'm really the king of France's soft-porn industry, then I'll say yes, even though it isn't true, just to maintain my image of being a glorious scoundrel; and if someone sticks pieces of bamboo under my fingernails to find out if I'm financing The Zebra, one of the world's finest film collections, I'll say no, even though it is true . . ."

"Why? To save your soul?"

"For the young man I would have remained if you had stayed in command."

This came from afar. Thirty years accelerated by. He was falling from a great height. He was going to hurt himself very badly. But Suzanne raised her bright eyes.

"I'm not one for commanding people."

The King's head fell on to his shrunken breast. Another sniff of death. Beneath his aftershave protection, he stank something rotten.

"I know," he murmured. "I know all about your respect for my freedom . . ."

He was now powerless. He tried to raise his cumbersome arms, but they flopped back down beside his thighs.

"And I came here in a spirit of freedom."

Suzanne stared hard at him.

"With nothing in exchange?"

"Nothing."

But she had sensed a moment's hesitation. She waited until he added:

"Just one thing."

She didn't give him the chance to go any further.

"You want to see Old Job's film, don't you?"

Then went on, before he had time to reply.

"It's out of the question."

Her tone was apologetic.

"And that isn't just down to me. You know perfectly well that the others would all run a mile as soon as they set eyes on you. And the others have Old Job's blessing."

"Then hide me! Stuff me behind a pillar up in the balcony!"

He was squirming.

"I want to see it, Suzanne. Kneel me down on a ruler with a dictionary on my head if you want, but I've *got* to see that film!"

There was a sudden gleam of panic in his eyes. He stretched out his open hands.

"But don't take this for an exclusive condition. You'll get the subsidy for The Zebra anyway. You'll still get it, even if you don't let me join the audience! That's not what matters . . . this showing, Suzanne . . . for me, it's . . ."

He did not have time to explain what Old Job's Only Begotten Film meant to him, because Suzanne's door blew open to reveal a crimson Jeremy and a panting Clément.

"Suzanne, some wanker's parked his big shit heap of a motor in the front of The Zebra's door . . . it's a Rolls, or something, and we can't unload."

The King of the Living Dead turned round heavily and his sparkle returned somewhat.

"The wanker's me, kid. As for the Rolls, it's a Bentley."

Jeremy treated him to a suitable kiddish smirk.

"Sorry, I didn't recognise it! I know more about crap than I do about motors."

Then to me, in great excitement:

"You must come and see the rehearsal tomorrow afternoon, Benjamin. There'll be a surprise for you! Be there at five, all right? And not a minute before, promise?"

Then, to Clément, who was paralysed by the King of the Living Dead's presence:

"Come on, Budding Bayleaf, we've got to get unloaded."

As they thundered downstairs, Clément's voice drifted up to us.

"Don't you even know who that was?"

And Jeremy's reply:

"All I'm interested in is the theatre!"

Then silence. Which the King, as a good loser, broke:

"Quite a lad."

To Julie and me:

"Is he your son?"

Then, without waiting for an answer:

83

"Keep him under your command."

Silence.

"Too bad for freedom."

The King was now wilting, marinating in his stench of death. The bottoms of his trousers exposed his ankles, which were thin and red in his leather moccasins.

"Well, I suppose I'd better shift my shit-heap of a motor."

Suzanne had not closed the door of her flat.

The King looked at us as if he was waking up. His brows creased.

"So . . . goodbye, then."

He was swaying slightly. A big teenager leaving the surprise party he had not been invited to.

Suzanne followed him out on to the landing.

Gripping the doorframe, he half turned round.

"You will call, Suzanne, won't you? You will keep in touch?"

"Of course. Don't call us, we'll call you."

V

THE CAVERN OF EPILEPSY

It's the devil's rags, or something like that?

Chapter 14

B Y INVITING ME to a rehearsal, the renowned spatial director Jeremy Malaussène was doing me no small honour. And such honours must be honoured. It keeps everyone happy. So off I went to hire a tuxedo from Boudiouf and Company, the paradise of the snappy dresser.

"Are you getting married, Ben, my brother?"

"No, I'm getting commemorated."

After all, wasn't it the demiurge in person that Jeremy had invited? The Object and the Subject? He without Whom nothing is accomplished? Nothing is writ? Nor put into a spatial relationship with itself? Malaussène in flesh and in myth!

What's more, I reckoned on giving the little bugger a start. Since he'd never seen me dressed up in so much as a tie, I was going to show up at his rehearsal in tails, like the maestro on the icing of the cake.

I was feeling good, in fact.

You were a pleasant perspective.

And real happiness plays the fool, that's its way of being discreet. We're happy, that's all there is to it, so stop preaching and go for a bit of good pointless fun!

"As for the shoes, Ben, my brother, what would you say to these nice shiny jobs?"

"I've got the necessary, thanks."

*

In tailcoat and furry slippers, I turned up at The Zebra at the appointed time with Julie on my arm.

Not quite the appointed time, in fact, as a cool bouncer – thirty kilos of bone and measuring at least one metre thirty – pointed out:

"The boss said five o'clock, sir. And you're six minutes early."

Nourdine was tapping the face of a watch which looked strangely adult on his scrawny wrist.

"Six minutes", said I, "ain't much."

"Sorry, sir, but it'd be more than my job's worth," said a second bouncer, arms crossed beneath his rose-tinted glasses.

(Today, as all belligerents will tell you, negotiating means giving war the time it needs to cut History's cloth.)

"Look," I said, "I'm known here. And the shit will hit the fan if they find out that you've kept Madame and me outside waiting. Madame who is, by the by, in the family way . . ."

"Sorry, sir, but six minutes is six minutes," Nourdine said.

"Sorry, madam," Half Pint confirmed.

"And with this?" I said, shoving a ten-franc piece under Nourdine's nose. "How long does six minutes last now?"

"Six minutes," said Nourdine, pocketing the coin.

Julie and Half Pint sniggered.

"And what if I picked up this little rumi with his rose-tinted glasses and bounced him off the head of this street Arab?"

"You'd only crease your nice suit," Half Pint said.

"And be buggered by the Prophet in person, Monsieur," Nourdine observed, then added . . . "Monsieur . . . what was the name again?"

And so the six minutes went by.

*

You should never play at surprises with Jeremy. When it comes to surprises, he has always had several lengths' lead over life itself. Take his birth, for example. Mum was expecting two girls, all the oracles agreed, the clinic was adamant and the quacks unanimous. Twin girls! But what popped out was Jeremy, just Jeremy, all on his own and joyfully loud. He must have scoffed his sisters.

When the doors of The Zebra finally opened, I went in dressed in tails and slippers, with my favourite star on my arm, so sure of the effect I was going to produce, only to be stopped in our tracks by a dazzling blast of spotlights which hit us right in the face, blinding us with glory, as though we were on the top step of the Cannes staircase. Light and nothing but light, then a tide of applause that rose up in waves from the belly of the cinema.

Then glory dimmed and the house lights came up.

They were all there.

Giving us a standing ovation.

The people in my life.

All of them.

The Malaussènes and the Ben Tayeb tribe, of course, Suzanne, Cissou and all that Belleville had offered me in terms of friendship, those immutable oldsters Soul, Kidney and Merlan, the entire staff of the Vendetta Press, obviously, but also all my old mates from the Store, where I used to work, Theo and his little old men in grey smocks, Lehmann in person, that innocent old bastard of a Lehmann, and the magicians of Saint-Louis Hospital, Marty who had saved me from a thousand deaths, Berthold the brilliant surgeon who had emptied my poor body before refilling it with another and who, by applauding me, was acclaiming his own masterpiece, but there were other, less expected presences too: none other than Chief Superintendent Coudrier, Napoleonic lock on his forehead and on his belly a waistcoat embroidered with bees; beside him, Inspector Caregga in his fur-collared World War II fighter pilot's jacket; they were all there, all of them, so much so that it raised the presence of those who were not there, who were no longer here, Stojil presumably perched somewhere up in the flies, staring down at us with his grim watchman's gaze, Thian, poor old Thian, who died to save me, and Pastor's face floating in Mum's transparent stare . . . What have you done to mother, Pastor? What have you done to her? And is Mum there, too? You came as well, did you Mum?

I did tell you that Jeremy was a one for surprises!

They had now stopped clapping and were brandishing champagne glasses, while Jeremy was heading up the central aisle with two more glasses, which he handed to Julie and me after treating us to one of his innocent grins.

"Happy birthday, shithead. You look great in your whistle!"

Then, with his innate sense of occasion, Jeremy beckoned to us to follow him and, while the crowd was booming out their happies and their birthdays, led us to the place of honour: two seats awaiting us in the front row, between Queen Zabo, my boss at the Vendetta Press, and Coudrier, my very own personal Chief Superintendent.

"Happy birthday, Malaussène," the boss repeated. "How did you like the surprise?"

Yes, quite a surprise . . .

A real surprise . . .

A Jeremy-style surprise . . .

Because *it was not my birthday*!

I had forbidden any twelve-monthly celebration of my damned birth so firmly that I was no longer even sure if I could remember the date. A total ban. On pain of a good hiding. And so it was that the tribe celebrated it whenever they felt like it, and if possible several times a year, so that each time was a real surprise.

"Yes, I know!" Jeremy confirmed, after a spotlight had pinned him against the stage curtain and he had faced the audience and waggled an accusing finger at me. "I know that you're going to bawl me out *again*, because you'd *forbidden* us to celebrate your birthday, I know you're going to wait for me down some dark alley and you'll have your own celebration by giving me the hiding of a lifetime, but then that's the story of my life!"

(There were real tears in the little bugger's eyes and a genuine quiver in his voice, thus thrusting the entire audience into a state of deep compassion . . .)

Then, he barked in a tone of furious accusation:

"But just look at the honourable assembly here around you, Benjamin Malaussène! Do you really think they're all here just to celebrate your appearance? An event which, I must say, does not merit the slightest plaque on the meanest vespasienne!"

At that, he crouched down and got all technical, talking only to me as if we were alone in the place.

"In my first draft, I put 'urinal', but your neighbour –" he indicated Queen Zabo with his thumb – "replaced it with 'vespasienne'. I negotiated, I suggested 'public convenience', she turned up her nose at that, so I proposed 'amenities', but she reckoned that sounded too modern, she stuck out for sodding vespasienne, and you know as well as I do what a stubborn cow she is, so there was nothing doing. 'Go for vespasienne,' she said. 'It has a splendid, Roman ring to it. Montherlant would have loved it!'"

Upon which he stood up again, wrapping his imaginary toga around his shoulders and launching back into his harangue:

"No, no, no, Benjamin Malaussène, if on this high day and holiday we have all come together around your insignificant personage, if we have drained these cups of fartwater to your health, o brother, so forgetful of what you owe us all, it is not to honour the day which witnessed your birth, o smuggest of all mugs, *it's because you had to be born*, you old sod, *if you were to be resurrected!*"

A silence long enough for him to refill his lungs. Then, in thunderous tones:

"It isn't your birth we're celebrating here, Benjamin Malaussène, it's your *countless resurrections!*"

Brasses trumpeted out. The same ones that welcome Caesar on to the screen.

"Splendid, don't you think?" Queen Zabo bellowed.

"For, while staring into the shiftiest haze of your eyes," the orator went on, once the horn section had calmed down, "I want to ask you if you'd still be here today, Benjamin, if he –" (pointing at Inspector Caregga) – "had not dragged you from the murderous clutches of your rabid colleagues, or if he –" (indicating

Chief Superintendent Coudrier) – "hadn't saved you from the Store bomber and if the other two here –" (designating Berthold and Marty) – "hadn't pulled you back from the idle comfort of brain death?"

He named each of my saviours, and each name set off a storm of applause, with Stojil and Thian getting the best slice of it, a standing ovation with their names being chanted out, lights flashing on and off with every handclap, while I was making the most of this carry-on by crying my eyes out with just one thought buzzing round my mind, looking for the way out:

Friends, friends, why do you die? Thian, Stojil, I'm on my way! I'm coming! Death is just a passing delay . . . on, off, on, off . . . Jesus, what a silly bugger that Jeremy is . . . dry your eyes, Benjamin, don't be a party pooper . . . Stojil, Thian, why oh why? . . . STOP IT, Benjamin . . . I'm coming, my friends, I'm here, I'm on my way . . . OK, Benjamin, OK, we're here too, we're expecting you, you'll be very welcome, we're not going any place, so why not try and enjoy yourself a bit in the meantime . . .

The Play's the Thing

Once silence and darkness had returned, and I had dried my eyes, I saw the curtain go up to reveal an empty stage hung with a huge painting.

Another surprise. Jeremy was taking me back a few years, into Half Pint's early childhood. The picture depicted one of the "Xmas Ogres" that Half Pint used to draw when his temperature was raging, and which used to worry his school-teachers so. From the quality of the silence in the auditorium, it was clear that the Xmas Ogre had lost none of its power of suggestion.

QUEEN ZABO (whispering): Not a pretty picture, eh?

ME (between my teeth, eyes fixed on the stage): So you're in on this too, are you, Your Majesty?

Her massive head wagged on the thin stalk of her neck.

"It's brilliant, Malaussène. As you're about to see."

She fell silent for a moment.

"Of course, I'm not talking about the actual staging," she went on. "Productions such as this . . . with their inevitable pleonasms are always rather . . . childish."

At either side of the ogre, the sleeves of its greatcoat stretched down to the floor, and on them were depicted the alleyways of a department store. They were overflowing with merchandise, which tumbled down as far as the stage until only a tiny space was left empty where the actors, as prisoners of commerce, were flailing around. The monster seemed ever more bug-eyed.

"No," Queen Zabo resumed. "I'm talking about the script."

She patted the manuscript she had on her lap.

"He's really talented, Benjamin!"

She called me Benjamin only on those rare occasions when her literary enthusiasm mistook itself for affection.

I was now staring at her intently.

"You're not going to tell me that . . ."

"I'm afraid so. There's a drastic shortage of young authors, Benjamin . . . and your Jeremy is so terribly talented! You know how it is, each to his own profession . . . creation or procreation, and you've made your choice I believe. You'll make an excellent father. How's the pregnancy coming on, by the way? Like a house on fire?"

I'd have loved to wring her neck there and then, but yelling drew my attention back to the stage. Amid the circle of goods, one man was shouting at another, threatening him with lifelong unemployment, ruin, decay, prison, even an asylum. The other was on his knees, begging for pardon, swearing that he'd never do it again, imploring him for a second chance. The one on his knees was Hadouch. Hadouch was playing me! My old mate Hadouch, my one and only childhood brother was in my goat's skin! ("You see," Jeremy explained later, "an Arab makes for a far more credible scapegoat in this day and age. That said, I could always give you a minor role if you want . . .")

But, once again, the real surprise lay elsewhere. Standing above Hadouch and bawling with all his evil glee, Lehmann was doing a perfect performance of himself as head of customer complaints at the Store. I found this so incredible that I turned round to check. Sure enough, Lehmann's seat was empty. Lehmann who had *really* tormented me at the Store was now tormenting Hadouch on the stage! ("Retirement was boring him witless," Jeremy explained. "Apart from his neighbours, he didn't have anyone to bollock any more, which was really getting him down. I've made his life worth living again . . . He's brilliant, isn't he?")

Gripped by a terrible doubt, I leant over Julie and asked Chief Superintendent Coudrier:

"Don't tell me you're in it too!"

"I resisted, Monsieur Malaussène. He pressed me hard, but I resisted."

Then, leaning over to me:

"But I cannot say the same for Inspector Caregga."

Sure enough, Caregga's place was empty. ("His girlfriend had dumped him, Benjamin, the silly bitch is a beautician and she couldn't stand his life as a copper any more. He was starting to go downhill, wandering about with a rosary, you know, those things priests have to say prayers, can you just imagine it? The theatre's just what he needed . . . The best way to mop up your sorrows! I'll give you a lead role when Julie chucks you!")

*

The Xmas Ogre of the second act opened its arms above a bedroom containing two facing rows of bunk-beds. Sitting in their pyjamas, half a dozen kids of all ages and appearances were dangling their carpet slippers down into a central space occupied by a storyteller and his dog. The central idea was still the same, with the beds hanging down from the Xmas Ogre's arms revealed by its rolled-up sleeves, and the whole scene seemed to be focused on the little bedside lamp, which was illuminating Hadouch's face and Julius the Dog's attentive bulk. The ogre was still just as bug-eyed, but he now seemed gently curious, with a yearning for fantasy, soothed by that filtered light. Hadouch was reading part of *War and Peace*.

"What happened next?" the Xmas Ogre insisted. "What happened next?"

But there wasn't much next. Jeremy had so far scripted only the first two acts of his play.

"But in just two weeks," Queen Zabo observed. "Which isn't bad going. He wants to call it *The Christmas Ogres* . . . But I'd go for something simpler such as *The Scapegoat*. What do you reckon?"

I didn't reckon anything. I was being hypnotised by the ogre's sleeves, which were silently unrolling and gradually swamping the bunks. Fast asleep, the children were vanishing one by one into an abyss of black-lined red silk.

"Neat, isn't it?" Queen Zabo murmured. "And rather impressive in its slow unrolling, on two violin notes . . . All very Bob Wilson . . ."

Hadouch and Julius the Dog were now sleeping in a sinister bedroom draped in crimson. Above them, the ogre was dozing, with his fluorescent eyelids closed above his satisfied pout. A knock at the door. Julius the Dog raised his drowsy head, emerging from deepest slumber.

"What a trooper!" Queen Zabo exclaimed.

The knocking got louder. Hadouch finally got up and felt for the door, which stood at the back of the stage in the midst of the ogre's beard. With the final series of knocks, the ogre's eyes suddenly opened with a flash of murderous glee.

The audience jumped.

"Real Punch and Judy stuff," Queen Zabo sighed.

Hadouch opened the door, revealing four men in black standing around a white coffin.

"It's for the corpse," yelled the sturdiest one of them. (It was Cissou the Snow!

Cissou the Snow in person! "Just a little role, a one-liner, he's got enough on his plate with La Herse, but I just had to have him. He's got quite a presence, hasn't he?")

Hadouch was wearing a pair of my pyjamas. He was scratching his head and right buttock in an unmistakably me-like way.

"Pop back in about fifty years," he said in a sleepy voice. "I'm not quite ready yet."

He slowly closed the door.

And I leapt up from my seat.

As soon as the Xmas Ogre had opened his eyes, Julius the Dog's slumbering fur had stood up on end over every inch of his body, his legs and neck had gone stiff, his lips curled up over his nightmarish fangs, his eyes rolled over white and he was now starting to lament, softly at first, like a moan coming from the depths of time, but which then expanded, filling itself with all the pain that had been experienced down the centuries, a massive scream, full of a terribly familiar humanity, the cries of my dog in the throes of an epileptic fit! For Christ's sake, Jeremy, he's having a fit! I thought as I jumped up on to the stage.

But Jeremy blocked my path.

"Stop, Ben, he's *acting*."

Hadouch held me back.

"That's right, Ben, he's acting! He's putting it on! Jeremy taught him! Look, he's acting out an epileptic fit!"

As stiff as a park lion on its stone butt, his eyes staring wildly and his lips frothing, Julius was now holding his note more steadily than I'd ever heard before.

"Good, isn't he? Just look at the effect on the audience!"

They were all on their feet. But this was no longer standing-ovation stuff, it was terrified hesitation, the doubtful immobility that precedes a panicked stampede.

"He's acting!" Jeremy repeated for the audience's benefit, while making soothing gestures. "This isn't a real fit. He's *mimicking* epilepsy."

While Jeremy was sounding off, Julius modulated into the bass register, in an increasingly disturbing oscillation, like a statue about to topple over – which is exactly what happened, he began by flopping on to his back, his head hitting the boards with a cavernous thump, then he twisted over towards me, still screaming out his one note around a tongue which was as dry and as quivering as a flame. His eyes had now gone right round, and had not brought back any good news from their introspection. They were staring at me with a weight of terror and fury I had never seen before, even during his most violent attacks.

"He's never done that before . . ." said Jeremy, suddenly breaking off into doubt.

Then Julius's tongue folded back into the depths of his throat like a whiplash, and the screaming stopped abruptly. A sudden cutting of sound. Silence in the house.

"Julius . . ." said Jeremy, now worried. "Don't you think you're hamming it up a bit."

This time, I rushed over to my dog.

"He's choking!"

I stuck my arm down his throat.

"Help me, for Christ's sake!"

Hadouch and Jeremy held Julius's jaws open while my fingers desperately fumbled around in the depths.

"I don't understand it," Jeremy was stammering. "It all went off fine during the other rehearsals . . ."

"Give me your tongue, Julius, come on!"

I yanked at that damn tongue with all my strength. Like I was trying to pull out all of Julius the Dog's innards and reveal once and for all the unmentionable secrets that so terrified him in the cavern of epilepsy.

The tongue finally gave way and I fell on to my arse.

"Sweet Jesus . . ."

I grabbed my dog's head.

His eyes were still just as crazed.

"Watch out Ben!"

Too late. A flashing of teeth. Julius's mouth opened and closed. On my throat.

In the audience, Julie screamed. She was by my side at once, pushing aside Hadouch and Jeremy, and bending over Julius's jaws. Then with my neck stretched out, I said:

"It's nothing, Julie. Just my bow-tie and collar."

I pushed as hard as I could against Julius's chest. I heard a long ripping noise, then fell once more on to the stage, my hand clutching at my bare throat.

Julius stayed there, bow-tie in his mouth, a shirt front for a bib, and still as tripped out as ever.

"He's going to bite his tongue."

Julie tried to open his mouth again. Nothing doing.

People were now standing all around us.

"All right, Malaussène?"

Marty was examining my neck, while Berthold produced a syringe from a small bag.

I stopped his hand as it rose towards me.

"What are you doing?"

"I'm going to get you back your bow-tie."

As soon as he approached Julius with the needle, the dog's jaws opened and the tie fell to the floor.

"See?" said Berthold, putting his kit away.

"If he is play-acting, then it's one hell of a performance," mumbled Marty, who was now raising one of Julius's eyelids.

"Careful, doctor . . ."

Marty announced his diagnosis.

"An absolutely authentic epileptic fit."

"It was bound to happen," Thérèse muttered.

The flash of Clara's camera crackled.

Chapter 15

"It all went off fine during the other rehearsals . . ." Couldn't the little twat think of anything better to say? Kids!

Julie and I were heading home with an upturned Julius in my arms, his head against my chest and his snout stuck in my armpit as though trying to escape his own stench. He weighed no more than the shell of a teddy bear in the attic of oblivion, but he still reeked as much as ever. His fit had drained him of his substance, which was now adding an odoriferous extra layer to Boudiouf's tailcoat.

"Are you sure your throat's OK?"

"Fucking kids, can you imagine it? Getting him to *act out* an epileptic fit! And that dickhead Hadouch going along with it!"

"Watch out!" Julie yelled.

Too late again. This time Julius's jaws had closed round my shoulder.

"Jesus Christ!"

"Hang on!"

Julie started yanking at the vice once more.

"Never mind," I said.

"What do you mean 'never mind'?"

"Boudiouf decided to flesh me out a bit. He gave me shoulder pads. Julius's teeth are pinching me, but they aren't making contact."

Then, softly into Julius's ear:

"It's the tuxedo you've got it in for, is it? It's the devil's rags, or something like that? You're right, this is the last time you'll see me in uniform, promise! We'll take it back to Boudiouf. And won't the king of the snappy dressers be pleased when he sees his suit!"

The news must have been a relief for Julius, because he promptly released my shoulder. But this was only to attack the lapels three minutes later. It was once again impossible to prise open his jaws. I tore off the strip of black silk and let him keep it.

"I reckon it's some sort of spasm," Julie said.

"A spasm?"

"Like hiccups. Every three minutes he snaps his teeth, that's all. He's done it several times now."

Watch in hand, we found this to be true. Three minutes later, Julius's jaws snapped at thin air; every three minutes he took a bite out of destiny. Then, thirty seconds later, they automatically opened again. Obvious once you knew.

"We could always use him as a punch to make holes in belts," I said.

*

Once we were back in our bedroom, I set up the hammock we had taken to using for Julius when he had his fits, and laid him down on it with all the delicacy of a bomb-disposal expert.

"A hammock's ideal, because it supports every part of the body," Julie had explained. She had clearly been supported by many a hammock before meeting me.

Julius's jaws snapped.

"It'll be handy for timing boiled eggs."

I took off the remaining scraps of the tuxedo. It was as if I was extracting myself, still steaming, from my dog's hide.

"Benjamin! Just look at your shoulder!"

His fangs had not bitten into my flesh, but my shoulder was now black. A complex, violet-tinged darkness, reminiscent of a peacock's tail.

"Yes, he's got quite a bite."

No-one is more pain-resistant than Julie, but she is also quite capable of swooning away if I so much as catch a finger between two pillows. I drew her against me.

"I'll take a shower, then we'll have a nice quiet couscous, OK?"

She kissed my shoulder.

"Go on, I'll check my mail in the meantime."

Julie's mail was always ministerial in its bulk. All I ever get are gas bills, phone bills and attempted confidence tricks from the landlord. A correspondence of numbers.

I was attempting to balance the freezing against the boiling when Julie's voice was heard above the downpour:

"Barnaby's arriving on Sunday!"

"Barnaby?"

"Barnaby, Matthias's son, he's arriving on Sunday and says we'll be in for a surprise!"

What have you done to my shoulder, Julius? I can barely wash my hair.

I let the scalding water wash away the worst of the pain and dissolve my plots of vengeance against Jeremy. The little bugger must be sweating it out right now, waiting for my return, with Thérèse's stare fixed on the nape of his neck. There's nothing more depressing than bollocking a kid who knows he's in for a bollocking. Clara had summed that up nicely when she was a little girl; one day she said: "Stop telling me off, Ben, *can't you see I'm crying*?" Clara, my Clarinette, my little velvet sister whose redeeming flashbulb captured Julius's madness . . . Julius . . . we were going to have to clamp something between his jaws until the fit was over. Even if he didn't bite through his tongue, he was certainly going to wear his teeth out at this rate. A clacking of the jaws every three minutes for, let's say . . . two or three months . . . like so many slips in the ballot box. We'd have to come up with some way to protect his fangs. That Jeremy though, getting an epileptic to act out a fit! Why not get a cancer patient to play at a new tumour, or someone with rabies to froth at the mouth? Jeremy, the director of realism . . . take a good dose of reality, confront the world with itself, and never mind about the fallout! A behaviourist! Shock treatment. The silly bugger . . . that's the kids of today for you! Hotter please, there on my shoulder, there . . . Jesus Christ, Jeremy, "Stop telling me off, Ben, *can't you see I'm crying*?" OK, OK . . . I wonder if Jeremy realises how many beatings Clara's existence has saved him from? . . . If Clara hadn't been around, you little bugger, then you'd be no more than a mass of bruised and rotting flesh . . . and I'd have ended up inside, as a child beater, handed over to the long arms of justice, which is still a child at heart, or so it seems . . . All the same, getting Julius to act out a fit . . .

Even the best of showers does not wash away all of our moods.

I turned off the water. I unplugged my brains. When I went into the bedroom, the steam from the shower had settled into a London smog.

"How can you read your mail in this?"

I went round Julius – a suspended rock in a Magritte painting – and opened the window.

"Julie?"

She wasn't at her desk.

"Julie?"

Nor was she on the bed.

I leant over Julius.

"Has she gone out?"

Julius snapped his teeth.

"Fog eater!"

An empty bedroom. Shower door open.

"My love," I hummed. "My wandering love . . ."

I closed the shower and opened the cupboard.

And that's when I found her.

"Julie . . ."

Crouching between the two doors. Doubled up. Even stiller than Julius, if that was possible. Her gaze just as fixed. With a letter in her hand.

"Julie?"

Other pages had tumbled down around her.

"Julie, my darling . . ."

Then I caught on.

Balls in a vice. That's fear in a man: balls in a vice, terror crushed into the tiniest blood vessels, blood turned to sand, legs gone to jelly and saliva sickly sweet . . .

The headed paper of the lab, the columns, with percentages of this and that . . .

God knows I didn't want to understand . . . but understand I did.

The results of your tests were lying at her feet.

The tests you'd failed.

The precise account of what you were lacking and so would never reach us.

The announcement that you were giving up.

Oh . . .

I'd like to say that I bent down over Julie, but I just collapsed, I'd like to say that I took her in my arms and comforted her, but I just collapsed and sat there next to her, wedged between the shower and the cupboard door.

And time did not make it go by. Time quite simply stopped dead. No matter how often Julius did his three-minute timer routine, the present remained the present.

I thought it wiser to keep my suspicions to myself . . . but unfortunately they now have been confirmed . . .

Matthias's handwriting. Matthias's quivering loops and curls . . .

Perhaps I should not have given you so much hope . . .

Oh . . .

. . . this is such a rare condition . . .

Julie . . .

. . . we shall terminate the pregnancy next week.

Next week.

I know how empty words of comfort are, but . . .

Motionless, both of us, like Julius the Dog in his net of pain.

She laid her head on my shoulder.

Time passed . . .

She finally said:

"Let's try not to be too pathetic, OK?"

She pressed down on my knee.

"Matthias had his doubts."

What an effort just to stand up.

"He had the results sent to him in Vienna, before sending them on to me . . . with this letter, poor sod."

The letter she now dropped on to our bed.

We were now standing. Back on our feet. Wobbly, but on our feet. Life . . . what an obsession!

"And there's no . . ."

"None. It's over Benjamin. It'd be too . . . technical to explain . . . Later . . . if you really want . . ."

Then the final blow.

"I'll go and see Berthold tomorrow."

She insisted.

"Berthold, Benjamin, and no-one else. He may not be very pleasant, but he did save you."

A pause.

"And you're all I've got."

She pieced together a smile.

"All I've got. I'll not say it again."

Upon which she asked me to go and get Yasmina.

Chapter 16

I RAN TO THE Koutoubia, I ran so that thought would not have enough time to catch up with me, but thought came in any case, just as though I were running on the spot, in motionless thought, a sleeve which did not unravel, a knot of bug-eyed thoughts seething in the hammock suspended across my brains . . . so this was the news Julius had announced . . . your departure . . . this was the yawning gulf he wanted to warn us about.

You giving up!

And I'd been warning you about your arrival for weeks on end! What a dickhead! Playing the big shot! As if you ever really had a choice: "This is the reality you're heading for, kid, so forget it if you don't feel up to it, unfold your wings and ascend, no-one here will blame you if you do . . ." As if I hadn't measured, from the very first moment, the depth of the hole you would dig out if you did ascend . . . the depression of your ascension . . . the abyss which would gobble up Julie and me alive, this gulf, this cloak of absence slipping down on to our shoulders at the bottom of our pit, the icy cloak of your absence on our naked shoulders . . . Be brave, now, Malaussène! You're good at playing Godfather when there's no danger, "Go on, leave us alone, if only you knew the shit we were in, return to the bliss of limbo," even though my life was already so full of you, my little listener, you had curled up inside me, as we strolled merrily along the boulevard of my put-on anger . . . But you took me literally . . . You believed my blethering . . . You shouldn't have! It was nothing! Just words, just the pure irony of words! A knee-jerk reaction of language, playing with fire so long as the flames don't flare up . . . rolling your muscles before the mirror of fantasies . . . What a dickhead! I was warding off evil, and you took me at my word . . . You took me at my word! So, was it life you ran away from, or *this father* in this particular life? Because if it's just this particular father, you can still change your mind! Come back! For Julie! Fathers don't mean a thing. They just supply the magic bullets! After that, you can easily get by without one! They're a modern invention! A working hypothesis! Part of a Greek tragedy! Pure histrionics! An instinct that crept in from the cold! A lovely earner for trick cyclists! A literary commonplace! Fathers have been done to death! Just one equation among others . . . a nexus of unknowns . . . irrelevant! Totally irrelevant! Do I have a father, for example? What about Louna, and Thérèse, and Clara, and Jeremy, and Half Pint, and Verdun, and What An Angel? Where are their fathers? What about Queen Zabo? And Loussa? It isn't the father that matters, it's what happens next! It's you! You're the one that matters! Come back! I'll be a shadow father, a micro-dad, scarcely a pilot-fish, tiny, not much of a pilot in fact, just enough to guide you through your steps . . . not exactly absent, more discreet, you'll see . . . a father of the most respectful discretion, I swear to you, hand on my heart . . . a father's mere Plasticine! Are you listening to me or what? Are you coming back? Come back you little bugger! For the love of Julie, come back!

"Monsieur Malaussène?"

All the strength she'll need if you don't come back!

"Monsieur Malaussène . . ."

I want to see her lean over you . . . like a typical mum . . . a pause in her heroics . . . a few years with nature in command. So she'll lean over you and let the rest of the world get on with it . . . The world never leans over, it just goes on spinning on its axis, going nowhere . . . in orbit . . . the world needs no-one . . .

"Monsieur Malaussène, are you talking to yourself?"

Let's try not to be too pathetic, OK . . . Did you hear that as well as I did? *Let's try not to be too pathetic, OK?* Doesn't that rip right into you? Doesn't it clip your wings? What kind of a sodding angel are you? And what kind of a murderer am I?

*

"Monsieur Malaussène!"

Wake up, Benjamin, stop running in your head, someone's speaking to you.

"Monsieur Malaussène?"

There he was in front of me. He put his hands on my shoulders. He shook me. I told him I was walking my dog.

"I'm walking my dog."

(Where's Julius?)

"Don't you recognise me?"

(Where's my dog?)

"OK, Ben?"

And up came Hadouch.

Hadouch's eyes already? And the Koutoubia's terrace? And Julius the Dog still in his hammock? And you vanishing into the clouds? Everyone in their places, in fact . . . So that's all right, then . . . just fine.

"Fine, just fine."

"The name's Sainclair. Remember me?"

"Who?"

"Sainclair, from the Store. Sit down, Monsieur Malaussène."

Hadouch and this Sainclair I didn't know stuck a chair under my butt. They pressed down on my shoulders. They sat me down.

"OK, Ben?"

Now it was Mo and Simon.

"Hey, Ben, OK?"

Mo very black. Simon very red. Hadouch, Mo and Simon very worried.

"What's up?"

"Wanna drink?"

"A drop of Sidi?"

The order echoed off the back wall of the Koutoubia:

"One Sidi for Benjamin!"

"You're very kind."

"You were talking to yourself, Monsieur Malaussène."

But who was this person talking to me? I got him into focus. Someone young, fair, clean, still impeccable even though trying to appear casual, with a three-day growth, pony tail, threadbare jeans above shiny shoes . . . like something off the cover of every lifestyle magazine . . .

"Sainclair, Monsieur Malaussène. Sainclair, from the Store . . . Are you with me?"

"Not any more I'm not."

Though I once was. Years back. In his Store. But the lovely manager had fired me with such force that he had shot right out of my memory.

"I'm no longer there either, for that matter! It's all ancient history, water under the bridge . . . can I get you something to drink?"

But I was already drink in hand. And Hadouch's hand around mine was lifting the drink to my lips.

"Drink."

I drank.

I drank it down.

"Better? What's happening, Ben?"

"Julie wants to see your mother, Hadouch."

I repeated:

"Julie wants to see Yasmina. At once."

*

"You were talking to yourself, Monsieur Malaussène . . ."

Hadouch, Mo and Simon had gone back to work. Sainclair was looking at me and smiling. I was looking at him and not smiling. And the sky broke above our heads. It was evening. It was summer. It was a thunderstorm. It was in Paris. To the north-north-east. In Belleville. It was one of those diluvial atmospheres in which post-war Yankees clambered up lampposts to sing of the world's beauty to cinemagoers.

"Who were you talking to?"

Drops exploded around us. There was a heavy drumming on the Koutoubia's lowered blind.

"You were talking to someone. You were asking them what kind of a murderer you were."

I would like to know who conducts thunderstorms. How swiftly he handles the downpour of water . . . from the roar of cataracts to the tinkling of fountains.

"Do you often soliloquise?"

And the rumour from the pavements, like mounting violins . . .

"It's since your operation, I suppose?"

Belleville was now draining away. Sainclair was looking at me, his moustache attentively dipping into his golden beer.

My operation?

It was perhaps time I took part in the conversation.

"Which operation's that?"

"The one that brought you back to life. The miracle Professor Berthold performed on you last year."

A smile of complicity.

"Professor Berthold is a real card. But he's also peerless, as I'm sure you'd agree . . . Our finest surgeon, perhaps even the world's finest . . . Nobel material I should say."

My smile vanished. "A real card", "peerless", "Nobel material" . . . Yes, this was definitely Sainclair. You may have changed your look, Sainclair, but I still recognise you. From your three-piece style . . . The understated superlatives . . . The elegant ecstasy . . .

"Sorry, I do apologise . . . I owe you a word or two of explanation."

So he explained. He explained how he had left the Store a few years back,

105

shortly after my own departure ("your departure being, Monsieur Malaussène, not totally unrelated to my resignation, but that's a company secret . . ."), to set up a weekly medical magazine called *Affection*.

"Ever read it? It's a weekly magazine which is not aimed at doctors, as the rest of them are, but at their patients . . . The ill are dying for information and they adore their illnesses . . . It's a solid-gold opening, and the title's perfect. *Affection*. Don't you agree?"

This was clearly no time to ask what a "solid gold opening" looked like.

"And from this perspective . . ." a brief hesitation, "I mean, in terms of medical news . . . you must agree that your case is of particular interest."

How the hell had word of *my case* got to his ears?

"Some time ago, your brother Jeremy came to see me."

Oh . . .

"Incredibly enough, he was trying to talk me into taking up the theatre . . . into acting in a play of his conception."

A play of his conception, I see . . .

"I had him tell me the plot . . . And I seemed to recognise certain items which are common to our respective biographies . . ."

All we have in common, Sainclair, is mutual indifference and the need to forget each other.

"He explained how it was the first part of a tetralogy, and so I asked him to tell me about the other three episodes . . . And, my word, when he reached your brain death and all those transplants, and when he sketched in a truly hilarious portrait of a 'dickhead surgeon with a golden touch', to quote his very words, then light dawned! I had despaired of ever discovering on whom Professor Berthold had exercised his skills, but now thanks to your brother Jeremy . . ."

While listening to Sainclair I said to myself that Jeremy never made just one balls-up at a time. Or rather, each of Jeremy's balls-ups is like a nuclear reactor, setting off a series of fission. Jeremy didn't just baptise, he liberated the energy of destinies.

"And did Jeremy take you on?"

You bet he didn't. Despite the three-days' growth and the hitchhiker's jeans, Sainclair was still a squeaky-clean arsehole and as cold as fish shit. Even limelight couldn't warm him up.

"No . . . he found me a little too . . . reserved, I think . . ."

(What did I say?)

"In any case, I have little time for the theatre."

(Just as well.)

"But I have plenty of time for you, Monsieur Malaussène."

Or more exactly, for *me as reconstituted by Berthold*. The result of those operations, in fact. Me and the Other, who Berthold had filled me up with . . . the Other within who sees to it that my life goes on . . . our shared life goes on . . . the common mental ground beneath my trepanned skull.

"I just have a few questions for you."

Here we go . . . Monsieur Sainclair, editor of *Affection*, was planning a special issue on transplants and their psychological side effects. His readers were in need of my words of wisdom, "in desperate need, Monsieur Malaussène . . ." OK, I was with him at last.

"Who were you talking to just now?"

And, for the first time, I understood the question. The plonker thought Krämer and I were doing a double act, having regular little chats, weighing up our respective numbers of cells and measuring our varying influence . . . we were, in fact, concerned about our body share . . . and we wanted it to last . . .

"It was *him* you were talking to, wasn't it?"

His eyes so hungered for a yes, that I almost gave it to him . . . Yes, my dear Sainclair, that's right, my donor and I have were having a discussion . . . as we so often do . . . it's Jekyll and Hyde negotiating their rota . . . you know how it is when you live with someone, we all have our little ways . . . so everyone has to make concessions . . .

But, right then, I was in no laughing mood.

Really not.

I stood up, dying to get home.

"Go fuck yourself, Sainclair."

And off I went.

At high speed.

" . . . "

"What kind of a murderer are you, Monsieur Malaussène?"

" . . . "

" . . . "

I stopped.

I turned back.

At slow speed.

I sat down.

He smiled.

" . . . "

" . . . "

"Do you often nail children to doors?"

"..."

"Symbolically, I mean . . . But, all the same . . . would such an idea have occurred to you *before* the operation?"

"..."

"While, if Professor Berthold is to be believed, such forms of recreation were right up your donor's street, were they not? Krämer was quite a vicious killer."

"..."

"So one can legitimately wonder . . ."

"..."

Right. So what he wants is a remake of *The Return of Frankenstein*.

He raised his beer to his lips.

So if he wants to play at resurrected murderers . . .

Let's play.

My fist shot out. As it was in such a hurry, it made no distinction between the glass of beer and Sainclair's face. Explosion of froth and glass. Sainclair tumbled backwards into the nearest puddle. I shoved the table to one side, leapt on top of him and picked him up by his jacket collar. My head then followed the same trajectory as my fist. My steel bonce made a bass-gong note against his nose, which was flattened. My left hand was holding him up with the strength of two men (thus giving credence to his article and his police statement: "There were two of them, officer!") while my right was busy slapping him around as though applauding an artiste.

"Stop, Ben, stop! You're going to kill him!"

It took all three of them to remove him from my *Affection*.

Hadouch held me back, while Mo and Simon dragged him into the Koutoubia.

"For fuck's sake, Ben, what's up with you?"

Hadouch, my eternal brother . . . what's up is that I suddenly feel a bit lonely . . . and it's time for me to slaughter a scapegoat for a change.

In the bar, old Amar was sponging down a mess of beer and blood which looked vaguely like Sainclair.

Whose finger pointed at me.

"You all saw him hit me, didn't you? You're witnesses!"

Simon disagreed.

"No, no, no, I was the one who hit you."

And Simon's fist, head and claws redid the whole thing, only more so.

"See? It was me! Simon's what they call me, Simon the Berber. Remember that?"

Old Amar had to change towels for a second hosing down.

*

At home, Yasmina greeted me with her finger on her lips.

"She's asleep, my son . . ."

Then she took me in her arms, sat me on her lap, put my head against her breasts and rocked me, too.

"Soon, you'll be asleep as well, my son . . ."

VI

BARNABOOTH

Oedipus squared.

Chapter 17

That same Saturday, Cissou the Snow fell asleep, too, with a dog's crazy stare in his mind's eye. Of those who had witnessed Julius's fit during the rehearsal, he had not been the most terrified, but rather, shall we say, the best *informed*. The dog's screams announced something irreparable. And his stare was confirmation. Not that Cissou the Snow was the slightest bit superstitious, he had just learnt about certainties over the previous few years. The dog was bearing terrible tidings. Cissou wasted the first few hours of his slumbers by trying to work out how the terrible tidings were going to hit us. Then he gave up. If prophets started making clear predictions, they would turn into politicians. And, as Cissou knew only too well, politicians are never prophets and nothing can ever be avoided. This dog was making an accurate prediction, but in ignorance, blinded by the truth, as with all prophets. Cissou's last thought before dozing off was that Julius the Dog may well have announced his death that day . . . So he thought it prudent to have a little "review of his existence" before going to sleep. The expression made him smile.

∗

All the Arabs knew him by name, but they still asked: "*Esmak-eh?*" ("What's your name?") for the pleasure of hearing the answer:

"Cissou the Snow."

Cissou, from his native Auvergne, where *cinq sous* have never made *six sous*, and *the Snow* because it was an open secret that Ramon of Belleville had sold him his eternal snows.

But Cissou the Snow had really stuck because Jeremy Malaussène had so decided. Jeremy Malaussène had thus baptised him, and the older of the Arabs called the kid *Jeremy m^eammed*, Jeremy the Baptist, no less.

"*Esmak-eh?*"

"Cissou the Snow."

"*Nín guìxìng?*" asked the Chinese, who always used polite forms of address when talking to him.

"Cissou the Snow."

"*Liù fen Xue*," the Chinese translated.

The Arabs and Chinese like names which sum up a life. And Jeremy *m^cammed* was good at such CVs.

*

Cissou the Snow was a ghost from Place des Fêtes. Not even a survivor, but a ghost. For over thirty years, he had been the traditional charcoal dealer (bar-coal-hardware-locksmith) of a small circular village perched up above the roofs of Paris. Then the peace criminals descended on Place des Fêtes. What they had done to his village is done by men in uniform in other parts of the world. Bombings or pre-emption, machine guns or pneumatic drills create the same results in terms of exodus and suicides. "Peace criminals" was what Cissou called them. Peace criminals destroying homes, creating exiles, promoting crime. Cissou, who never participated in large-scale public debates, inwardly declared that the sole defence against the spread of inner-city lawlessness would be the public execution of half the architects, two-thirds of the promoters and as many mayors and town councillors as was necessary until they finally came round to his way of thinking.

For a long time, Cissou had defended his premises on Place des Fêtes. He had fought red tape with red tape and the law with the law. His background as a stubborn Auvergnat had taught him how to survive in such a jungle. And, for a long time, he won. The entire place fell down in ruins, but his bar remained. He photographed each house and building before it was demolished. Threats fell on deaf ears, and offers become enticing. When all that was left was a set of photos, Cissou resigned himself to the inevitable. He decided to sell. He talked up the price. He talked it up as high as the cliff of concrete which was obscuring the view from the windows of his bar. The slaying of the last café on Place des Fêtes was paid for dearly. The law had taught him that denials of justice can be haggled over at dizzy heights. They thought he was a money grabber and admired him for it: "Ah, the crafty Auvergnat rustic!" It was this misunderstanding that led to his first encounter with La Herse the bailiff. When he was told to negotiate the departure of the café owner, La Herse went even further. He asked for his hand in marriage. What if you become my very own official locksmith? Full time! With a monopoly! And an under-the-table bonus for each door you open . . . how about that, eh? And a commission as a percentage of the goods seized . . . how does that sound?

Great.

Deal concluded, and a thirty-storey skyscraper crushed Cissou's bar.

Cissou would die rich.

His ghost went to see Ramon of Belleville, the snowman, where he changed his profits into powder. Cissou did not want to frequent the small-time dealers, so he bought his Mont Blanc all in one go. "Talg abadi", as the Arabs put it, "the eternal snows". Enough to keep his nose happy until his second death and even beyond. (Other people put banknotes under mattresses . . .)

"It'll be dangerous to keep all the coke in your place," Ramon remarked.

"You're the only person I can think of who'd try to rob me," Cissou replied. Then added:

"Just try. The door's always open."

Ramon just smirked.

"A charcoal man, ending up as white as snow . . ."

*

Since he pillaged by day and refunded by night, Cissou slept only on Sundays. This was merely a bodily requirement, because sleep did not relax him. His soul woke up again just as lucid. He was fighting a rearguard action, and he knew it. Houses continued to be pulled down around him, he went on taking even more photos, and could now envision the day when there would be no more photos to be taken. Belleville and Ménilmontant were dying. How could he get any rest when he knew that? Do dying men sleep? Ever since he had ceased to be, Cissou slept sitting upright in an armchair, facing a gambolling zebra.

Cissou had rented a one-room flat in the least attractive building on Boulevard de Belleville. Spanking new, it looked like a metallic, plastic toy, with its prow in the form of an aircraft carrier's turret, which must have warmed the infantile cockles of its architect's heart. After a few months' navigation, rust had started to eat into its sides, and the aircraft carrier looked as if it had run aground there on the pavement, as though in a harbour which had been abandoned by the sea.

From his window, he could see the gambolling zebra. His second life was clasped around that zebra's neck.

If he hadn't already died once, Cissou would have set out to win Suzanne, the beast's stable keeper, but what consolation can a ghost give to a woman whose zebra has been condemned? He'd dropped the project. He loved Suzanne from a distance, in silence. Suzanne whom Jeremy had baptised Suzanne O'Blue Eyes. And sure enough, all of Ireland would have recognised itself in those eyes.

Cissou kept his hopeless love secret. He'd mentioned it to no-one. Not even to

115

Gervaise, old Thian's daughter, whom he woke up every morning with an alarm call. Gervaise put Cissou's memories in order. Once a month, he gave her his photos of Belleville as a corpse. Gervaise then turned them into an album of living images, which Cissou kept with him and never tired of examining. His friendship with Gervaise was so secret that he mentioned it to no-one either. Not even to Suzanne.

These were the two women of his second life. The only woman of his first life, his wife Odette, had died so poor that the only thing she'd left him was a small mirror in a copper frame, and so young that this pool of light retained no recollection of what she looked like. For years now, the only thing that Odette's mirror reflected were Cissou's nostrils bending down over their morning snow.

*

The first three things Cissou the Snow did after waking were:
1) Snort Siberia from his blind looking glass;
2) Hail the gambolling zebra;
3) Call Gervaise.
A ritual sequence which was as immutable as a religious rite.

*

It was with no small surprise that Cissou woke up that Sunday morning at the stroke of eleven.

Alive.

So, the dog had foreseen something else.

So be it.

Cissou poured out a chain of white mountains on the mottled face of the mirror. Triple density for Sunday, his day off. His hand did not shake, there were no peaks or troughs, just a fine high-altitude cordillera. Which he would demolish in four snorts, just as he did every Sunday.

With the mirror at nose's reach, he sniffed once. While his right nostril was whipping up flurries on the ridge of the cordillera, his left eye noticed a sort of *absence* on the far side of the boulevard. Cissou looked up. The zebra had lost its head.

Oh well.

The mad dog had robbed him of a few hours' sleep. Cissou supposed he must be overtired.

But, during the second snort, as the white line started to vanish from the surface of the mirror, the zebra also lost its neck, its torso and legs as far as its rear hoofs.

No more zebra.

This time, Cissou reckoned it must be his age. And the terrible effects of the snow. The cordillera got ever higher and the caverns ever more insatiable, no-one could resist that, least of all him. But he also knew that he was lying to himself. He knew that he was calling himself senile from love for that zebra. From the depths of his anxiety, he swore that the third snort would bring the zebra back in the full motionless splendour of its gambolling.

Not only did the zebra not reappear, but the pediment of the cinema started to vanish too, followed by its façade, which disintegrated noiselessly.

His balls in a vice, Cissou recognised that fear a man experiences two or three times in a lifetime which signals that something has gone for good.

He forced the rest of his strength into his legs. The armchair rocked on to its back and slid over to the middle of the room. Standing by the window, Cissou now understood what the mad dog had been trying to tell them.

The destruction of The Zebra.

Belleville's last cinema no longer existed.

A police cordon was protecting the gap which the building had left behind it, and keeping back the Belleville crowd. Cissou recognised the Ben Tayeb tribe, and everyone Belleville had introduced him to. Arabs and blacks from all over Africa, Armenians and Jews in all sorts of exile, Chinese from the multitudes of China, Greeks, Turks, Serbs and Croats from a united Europe, the young and the old, men and women, believers in Judaism, Christianity and Islam, dogs and pigeons, such was their silence, and the planet was so still, that the only thing now existing was the hole left between those buildings by a Zebra which had been there only the night before. And this hole did not seem to believe in itself. It was quivering with amazement at its own absence.

Cissou looked for Suzanne in the crowd of statues. He found her between Malaussène and Julie, with the rest of the tribe gathered around them.

At the edge of the crowd, a man carrying an official briefcase was standing staring, beside La Herse the bailiff and his wife, in her Sunday best.

Cissou the Snow reached out his hands. A second later, the curtains were drawn and, in his flat, it was as if the day had never come up.

He switched on his little desk lamp, picked up the phone, dialled Gervaise's number and waited. There was a click. A voice then announced that no-one was home.

Cissou was not surprised.

"When there's no answer any more, you put on the answering machine."

So it was that his life's last message was deposited in a plastic box, with an endlessly turning tape loop.

He said:

"Well, sister, it's all over. They had the law on their side, and when they didn't, they used arson. They've now come up with a new method. It's clean. It's quick. There isn't even time to take a photo. They've just made off with our Zebra. So, as for me . . ."

He hesitated. He fumbled for his words. But the tape was turning, so he had to think quickly. He wanted to say something nice to her, something she would be the only person to understand, a truly personal farewell.

He said:

"As for me, my little Gervaise, it's the Universal Exhibition."

He did not hang up.

Engaged.

For ever.

He opened the desk drawer, took out an envelope he had sealed long ago and placed it there in full view.

He took off his trousers, slippers, socks and carefully unbuttoned his waistcoat and charcoal dealer's long johns which, from his wrists to his ankles, had never revealed a single inch of his flesh.

When he was completely naked, he stood the chair in the middle of the room in front of the mirrored wardrobe and beneath the droplets of the chandelier, which he then unhooked. He stepped down and placed it on the floor, before removing the rope from the bottom drawer of the wardrobe. He had kept this rope with him ever since the massacre of Place des Fêtes. Some ropes can sense their destinies at the very moment they are made.

He got back on to the chair.

He attached the rope to where the chandelier had been. He tested the strength of the hook. He hoped that the architects of today were at least capable of providing hooks capable of bearing the despair their flats produced. He tied the slip-knot which his father's father had taught him to slide over cows' horns when it was milking time. He placed his neck in the loop, which he then tightened around his throat, slowly and carefully like a Sunday-best tie.

He stared intensely at his reflection in the wardrobe's mirror.

"Just to hang on to one memory."

Then he kicked away the chair.

The hook remained in place.

The rope went taut.

Chapter 18

THE MOST IMPRESSIVE part was the silence. Even Jeremy shut up. Stripe after stripe, the zebra vanished completely. Until a sky-grey gap had been left on the cinema's pediment. All of Belleville had seen the animal dissolve into thin air.

But then, the zebra was only a wooden effigy, a flat drawing. It would be different when they got to stone. They could not *make an entire cinema disappear*, could they? A cinema's a building! It is not just a façade, it also has its innards, its hall, balcony, stage, seats, Belleville's furniture in its wings . . . its intestines of cables and plumbing . . . the volume of the whole thing . . . it could not just vanish like that!

Between the two cops barring his way, Jeremy was staring intensely at the space left on the pediment by the disappearance of the zebra.

The crowd's silence deepened.

And now the blue of the pediment started to fade! The colour had been diluted! It looked as if bare stone or brick were about to appear behind it. But there was neither brick nor stone. The whole lot went. No more pediment. Just a square of cloudy sky in its place. The top of the cinema had quite simply disappeared. *Wiped out*! A building had been *wiped out*! With no more difficulty than a chalk drawing on a blackboard.

Such a silent fading was far more impressive than a collapse. Jeremy had seen several buildings collapse, becoming twisted in their flames, he had seen skyscrapers fold into themselves, blown apart by the centrifugal explosives they had been stuffed with. Whatever the result, there was always one hell of a din. The earth drew back its stones to its breast and the stones were making waves. Buildings shrieked out in agony. Clouds of dust or ashes fell down on to the neighbouring houses, which wore mourning clothes until next it rained.

But this . . .

This was the worst of all.

"Jesus Christ," someone muttered.

Like a boat sinking *top first*, Jeremy thought. Swallowed by the sky! Absorbed into the void! A backwards shipwreck. The Zebra was going down with all hands. As a matter of fact, with its small lateral balconies with their rounded turrets, and its iron ladders apparently leading up to the bridge, The Zebra had always been rather reminiscent of an old disarmed World War I battleship. ("More like the gunboat on the Yangtze," Clément the Budding Bayleaf objected. "You know, Steve McQueen's one in Wise's *The Sand Pebbles* . . .")

"It's the first time I'm really *seeing* it," Jeremy said to himself and, lacking the strength to turn around, he thought of Cissou's block, the aircraft carrier moored just opposite, on the other side of the boulevard.

One day, Cissou had told him:

"Nothing is forgotten more quickly than an old building you've walked in front of without paying any attention to for the past fifty years. One day, a gap appears and you wonder what used to be there. That's even worse than a memory! Who *really* remembers Place des Fêtes? Ask your brother."

"Place des Fêtes?" Benjamin had replied. "A round village . . ."

"Was it nice?"

"It was lively."

And that was all Jeremy had got out of him.

The void was nibbling into the posters stuck up on The Zebra's façade. The void attacked them one by one, then dissolved the walls. The void was slowly crawling along the pavement, wiping out each stone, until all that was left was a black iron gate standing at the foot of the vanished building.

A black iron gate.

All on its own.

With emptiness padlocked behind it.

And not a single sound.

Then the whole crowd went crazy.

Cries, clapping, flashing cameras, camcorders, journalistic superlatives! Three or four thousand snaps of the gate to be splashed over the front pages the next day.

Only the police remained impassive. They were facing the crowd, with their backs to the miracle.

"Hey!" Jeremy called out to the officer directly in front of him. "A cinema's just been stolen right behind you!"

Clara's camera now flashed.

But she had photographed the cop's expression.

"Someone's just half-inched a cinema, and you couldn't care less?" Jeremy pressed the point.

Order had just enough force not to respond.

"A cinema and a theatre all in one go!"

The force remained silent.

"Shame," said Jeremy. "Because, even while we speak, a sly little bugger is pinching your TV set."

The eyes in the helmet stared down at him. Above the jugular, a mouth opened . . .

Too late.

The crowd had quietened down.

Silence.

All their eyes were now fixed on the gate.

The black iron gate was now losing its bars.

One by one.

They were being wiped out from top to bottom.

Every single one of them.

The gate had gone.

All that was left was the golden padlock, floating alone in mid-air.

For some reason which was beyond Jeremy's understanding, this incongruous sight of a padlock, this hint of gold just barely visible in the electric atmosphere, brought the house down.

"Brilliant!"

Then the laughter died once more.

Silence again.

Something unexpected was happening. Jeremy caught on thanks to the furious glances the officer was exchanging with his neighbour. Someone had forced their way through between them. A momentary loss of concentration. The officer had probably been thinking about his TV set.

Then Jeremy recognised Thérèse's back.

Absolutely alone, Thérèse was crossing the no man's land between the crowd and the cinema, as straight as justice, as stiff as the truncheons which should have blocked her way. Her step was as confident as one who separates seas. She was heading straight towards the floating padlock. Even the boys in blue forgot about their orders and were now peering round at that gawky girl as she walked on through the silence.

Then, when she reached the gap, she produced a key from her pocket and opened the lock. The effort could be seen in her arm muscles and everyone could hear the familiar squeaking of the invisible gate.

Thérèse stepped forwards and vanished too.

Swallowed up by the void.

A deathly hush.

One second.

Two.

Three.

And the cinema reappeared.

So abruptly that the crowd started.

With its open gate, bright posters, blue pediment and bounding zebra, it was The Zebra all right, back safe again, Suzanne O'Blue Eyes' cinema, Belleville's last living cinema, brought back to reality by the illusionist's handkerchief!

Another roar from the crowd. Applause, yells, children's screams, running dogs, flocks of pigeons . . . they all ran to touch the walls, to talk to their neighbours, to stock up on future subjects for conversation, and started discussing the disappearance as if it were already a distant memory . . .

"Fuck me! Did you see what I saw?" Jeremy yelled. "One minute it's gone, the next it's back."

"We all saw it," the cop replied. "Who was the girl?"

"My sister," Jeremy answered.

*

JULIE: I did tell you Barnaby had a surprise in store for us.

SUZANNE: Quite a surprise . . .

JULIE: So now you understand what Matthias meant when he said that his son had devoted his life to what might be called *the opposite of cinema.*

SUZANNE: An eraser . . .

JULIE: Yes, Barnabooth the illusionist . . .

SUZANNE: . . .

JULIE: No-one's going to forget your Zebra now. It's become a national monument.

*

Now everyone was trying to get hold of Barnabooth the illusionist; radio hacks, TV hackettes, photographers and columnists, cultural attachés sent out by the Mayor of mayors, admen and theatre directors, everyone wanted him for themselves, with official invitations, contracts in their pockets or mikes in hand, the photographers dashing off to develop their films, to bend over their fluid baths to rediscover the appearance of this disappearance, the gate standing in front of nothing, the floating lock, they straddled their powerful motorbikes, kicked off with horns blaring, in a terrible whirl of greed, the yearning for a scoop, but at the same time, here and there, the drawling of sceptical brains could already be heard.

"Nothing to write home about, really. All he's doing in fact is the opposite of the hologram."

"The same principle as Christo, in fact. By concealing, you reveal. Not that original at all."

"And there's work still left to be done on it. Didn't you see that quivering where the building was? Like vapour . . ."

"Liquid Christo . . ."

"Very well put, Georges. Liquid Christo . . ."

"All the same, he really has made progress. I saw his first show in London . . ."

"If you can call it a show . . ."

"And do you remember his production of *Hamlet* in New York?"

"All hell let loose!"

"It's *where* the technique can be applied that is most interesting, don't you think?"

"Erasing my wife's family, for instance."

Meanwhile the apprentices were struggling.

"What's his name again? It's slipped my mind."

"Barnabooth."

"Barnabooth? Is that his real name?"

"It's probably a pseudonym."

"So he's conjured away his name?"

"He's conjured himself away completely. Never gives interviews. Won't be photographed. Never shows himself. To anyone. Hasn't been seen for years. No-one knows what he looks like. Which is logical, when it comes down to it."

The facts were there. Those who looked for the illusionist ran into a silent props man busy unhooking a projector, who pointed with his thumb over to the head of the technical team, tangled up in his cables. All of them ended up facing the tightly buttoned blouse of a press attachée, who was sworn to secrecy and wearing a severely tailored suit. "No, Monsieur Barnabooth cannot be seen at present, you can leave a list of questions, and no, unfortunately Monsieur Barnabooth's diary is too full for him to accept your invitation . . ."

As she spoke, the press attachée's eyes were hunting out someone, for if Monsieur Barnabooth didn't want to be seen, if he wanted to avoid being photographed and buttonholed, he was *absolutely* insistent on seeing one and only one person, the very person for whom he had crossed the Channel, chosen this awful neighbourhood and its run-down cinema, even though the Ministry of Culture, the Mayor of Paris and even the President himself had spent the last few years graciously inviting him to erase historical monuments and to wipe out memories, by knocking a hole in the façade of the Louvre, for instance, or by evaporating the Eiffel Tower, but no, he had chosen Belleville and its Zebra, for heaven's sake, what a disastrous career move, and all for the sake of some woman, apparently . . .

"Madame Corrençon? Julie Corrençon?"

"In person."

The press attachée's breath was quite taken away. She had to admit that this really was quite some woman.

"Monsieur Barnabooth would like to see you. I have a message for you."

The press attachée gave Julie a little headset, helped her to put the earphones on, then vanished into the crowd.

Julie could not help but smile.

"Barnaby the mysterious . . ." she muttered.

Upon which, Barnaby spoke straight into her skull.

"See you tomorrow morning, Juliette, at eight on the dot."

Barnaby the early bird, thought Julie.

Then the address followed: Old Job's Paris office on the Champs Élysées.

"Not a word to a single soul, Juliette. I'm counting on you."

Then, a final precaution.

"Come alone, otherwise I won't be there."

His voice had not changed.

And neither had he.

He's wearing me out already, thought Julie, who really did not need this added wear and tear.

VII
GERVAISE

It's not your fault, Gervaise.

Chapter 19

S HE HAD NOT been there.
   While Cissou the Snow was dictating his last words to her answering machine, Gervaise was already out. She would blame herself for ever for that, even though she knew she was blameless. But *culpa* was her trademark, as Thian her father would have put it.

"It's not your fault, Gervaise."

Of all the sweet expressions with which Thian had nurtured her childhood, this was the one that came back most often.

"Not your fault, Gervaise."

"So whose fault is it?"

Inspector Van Thian had never managed to answer this question. He had spent his entire life searching for a reply.

"Whose fault, Thianie?"

"Good coppers don't judge, Gervaise, they look for *the one that did it*. Judging's the judge's job."

"So why do coppers look?"

"Normally speaking, it's a matter of damage limitation."

But by attempting to limit the damage, Inspector Van Thian had in turn been damaged beyond repair.

*

That Sunday morning, at exactly eleven o'clock, while The Zebra was being conjured away, the nun-cum-cop that Gervaise had become since Thian's death was looking for *the one who was doing it*.

The one who was abducting her whores.

And then killing them.

The one who was abducting her whores then slicing them up alive.

"Her whores". Another one of Thian's expressions.

"By coddling your whores, you're neglecting your old dad."

"And would my old dad prefer me to neglect my whores?"

But Thian was now dead and she was looking for the one who was doing it, abducting her whores, slicing them up alive and filming their death throes.

A killer-voyeur, a snuff merchant.

"Another example of American cultural imperialism," Thian would have said.

That morning, Gervaise had been counting on nabbing the killer-voyeur.

Inspectors Adrien Titus and Joseph Silistri were sharing her impatience.

"Your snuffer's had it, Gervaise. We're going to get him."

"Red-handed!"

"He won't even have time to put his dick away."

Inspectors Titus and Silistri were keeping up Gervaise's morale.

"What about Mondine?" she asked.

"Mondine will get out of this alive."

"She'll just be leaving a rather hotter customer than usual, that's all."

Thanks to Mondine, Gervaise's finest grass, Inspectors Titus and Silistri had located the snuffer's studios, put them under surveillance for weeks, studied the various points of entry, settled for the sewers, marked out the route, timed their approach and sealed off the exits. They had followed Mondine, who not only gave them most of the information but also had bravely volunteered to be the fall girl. They had admired all her performances as an artist whore, from public soliciting to private stripteases. They had recorded her telephone come-ons, bugged her bed, envied her visitors' ecstasies and been taken away by the warmth of her sighs. Their faithful-hubby hearts had fluttered as they filed away all this information. Mondine had really made a name for herself. Finally, Inspectors Titus and Silistri had witnessed her abduction by the snuffer's team. It had been discreet, rapid and violent. Mission accomplished.

And, that morning, all three of them were in a cellar with the intention of preventing her murder.

Gervaise, back to the wall, to the right of the door, unarmed.

Silistri to the left.

Titus facing.

Titus and Silistri telling their beads.

A dose of geli stuck on the lock.

No walkie-talkies. Radio silence. Not the slightest detectable airwave. Complete reliance on timing. Hope that Inspector Caregga and Chief Superintendent Coudrier's men were covering the exits from the lair. Hope that the coppers fade into the lampposts and that the ambulance does not look like an ambulance. Running through such parameters sounds the death knell of all hope. Nothing can possibly work out if you think of everything that is required for it to work. They were now by the door, at the fatal moment when thought must stop. They could not hear what was going on in the room, which had been thoroughly soundproofed because of the screams. They were simply hoping that they had timed everything right, that they would not get there too late and find Mondine in little pieces. They told their beads and mumbled prayers of timing. As planned, the lock would explode after the third paternoster, "Deliver us from evil."

"Amen!"

Explosion, smoke, the door falling, Titus and Silistri rushed inside, guns held out.

"Police!"

Then in went Gervaise.

Everyone froze in their various degrees of nakedness and various positions, arse out and eyes agog.

"Stay just where you are!"

"Keep your dicks out!"

"Stay away from the doors!"

"On the floor!"

"One move and you're dead!"

Titus and Silistri were walking among them, dishing out slaps, shoving their bodies to the floor and desperately looking for Mondine, whom they did not find immediately, put off as they were by the video screen on the wall in front of them: Mondine being skinned alive, a rectangle of her flesh already in the surgeon's left hand. For a moment, they thought that the torture must be going on in another room, or that Mondine was already dead and they were merely watching a rerun.

"Hey you, dickhead, keep your camera going!"

Titus and Silistri then spun round simultaneously to look in the direction the camera was pointing in, towards the far left-hand corner of the room, while the performance was being broadcast live on the screen at the other end.

Silistri's breath was taken away.

"And you, there, the surgeon . . ."

The "surgeon" was still working away, as though nothing was wrong, skinning Mondine's shoulder, while she was strapped naked to a bloodstained slab, either unconscious or dead, with Gervaise now running towards him, suddenly getting into Silistri's line of fire. The surgeon must have had eyes in the back of his head, because this was the very moment he chose to turn round, throw his scalpel at Gervaise and leap towards the light switch.

Total darkness, doors opening, a patter of bare feet, limp dicks, Titus and Silistri rushing together to Gervaise, who had doubled up under the scalpel's impact.

"Get the fucking lights on!"

"Let them leave first."

"You OK, Gervaise?"

And the lights came back on in the empty room, revealing Mondine on the gory slab, and Gervaise with a sort of steel-hafted knife sticking into the middle of her chest.

"Fuck, fuck, fuck, are you OK, Gervaise?"

"Fine . . ."

"Let's have a look."

Silistri took off Gervaise's coat and undid the straps of her bulletproof jacket.

"Sure you're OK?"

"It didn't go through."

"The point has ripped it, all the same."

"What about Mondine?"

"She's alive."

Meanwhile, Titus was sticking the skin back on to Mondine's shoulder, as though he were making a bed, amazed at what he was doing, but determined to hold that rectangle of flesh in place until the medics turned up and stitched it straight back on for her. Mondine was still breathing. Apparently, there were no other wounds, but she was so deeply out of it that she must have been swimming many fathoms away from what she was going through, without any desire to return. If it had been me . . . Titus thought.

Then he saw the other girl.

Between the slab and the wall. Dumped there, in bloodless lumps, like leftover meat. Inspector Titus did not faint, he did not vomit as he should have done, he ran out into the corridor, from where the patter of bare feet could still be heard, he rushed out with a drumming in his head and his gun in his hand, determined to shoot the first one he found, then the second, then the third, until the human race was extinct.

Chapter 20

AFTER THE ARRIVAL of Chief Superintendent Coudrier, the stretcher bearers, Postel-Wagner the forensic surgeon with his burettes, and specialists from the lab who could sniff out the slightest trace of absolutely anything, science took over, so Inspectors Titus and Silistri went home, with Gervaise's blessing.

In the same block of flats in Ménilmontant, where Silistri lived just above Titus, they threw themselves on to their wives, Hélène and Tanita, as though amazed to find them still in one piece after such butchery. It was the same convulsive lovemaking, which both Hélène and Tanita knew so well as a sign of those days when their men had experienced fear – or, perhaps, even worse. Ever since they had been taken off the special branch and been appointed Gervaise's guardian angels, every time Titus and Silistri came home, it was from a far-off distant place, and they plunged into their wives, merging with them, vanishing away, impregnating them with themselves, as though needing rebirth.

"It's exactly like that."

Hélène and Tanita had discussed the matter that Saturday at about one o'clock, while having their customary drink in the Envierges bar, their shopping bags at their feet and their noses in their port.

"It's exactly like that. He comes back from *somewhere else*, diving down from some great height. And if you want my opinion, I don't even think he knows what he's diving into at times like that, or what he's got in his hands. Last time, I couldn't even put the homework I was marking to one side. He went straight in like he was returning to his earth."

Hélène the schoolteacher underwent the assault while correcting philosophical essays, while Tanita, the dressmaker from the Antilles, was thrown back amid her multi-coloured fabrics.

"My one's running away from a werewolf, a *quimbois* which is out to get him. He runs up the stairs like a thing possessed with its jaws snapping just behind him.

I swear to you, he dashes up the stairs looking for air, then runs into the flat with his arms stretched out."

"They must be really up to their ears in it."

They were worried, but without really complaining. They were quite capable of giving rebirth to their men every time they came home. They were not the sort of coppers' wives who make a melodrama of their tragedies. They knew that their men were even less immortal than others and that they would make widows who are less easy to comfort than others. For the past few months, some sort of holy woman had been taking Titus and Silistri down into the basements of hell, then packing them off home, lovelorn and with mad staring eyes, Titus making up lies to lessen the horror, and Silistri as silent as the grave he seemed to have just crept out from.

"Joseph only recovers the use of speech *afterwards*," Hélène said.

"My one starts talking *during*, just like at the beginning, when he was still finding out what was what. And then he calls to me . . ."

"He calls to you?"

Titus called to Tanita. He kept on calling out to her. Tanita, my cream! My heart! Light of my life! My bedmate! My joy! My lace! My toffee apple! My inkwell! My smooth madras! My white slip! My sweetness! My sleekness! My flesh! My liver! My spliff! My riff! My glans! My cup of tea! My ladies' fingers! My little lump of chocolate! My life! My life! My life! My life!

Sometimes, Hélène or Tanita dreamily asked:

"Just who is this Gervaise?"

But they did not have much to go on. Titus and Silistri never talked shop at home, Silistri because of the children, and Titus so that Tanita would still see him as "the only poet cop in two thousand years of coppery and poetry".

"What does she *do* to them to put them in such a state?"

They sniggered valiantly into their port.

"Make them tell their beads?"

Because when the rosaries had appeared, both wives had been utterly speechless.

"What, yours too?"

"Yes, he's got a rosary strapped on his belt, just beside his handcuffs."

Right at that moment – with Titus still inside her but slowly regaining his wits – Tanita was gently stroking away the pain. Someone had hit her man. A lump by his temple was quite literally doubling the size of his head.

"I slipped on a parking ticket."

"I'll buy you a hat for two heads, my love."

He got up and staggered into the bathroom.

She fetched two glasses, some rum, lemons, ice, absinthe, skins and a nice lump of hash – his "little lump of chocolate".

Still steaming from the shower, Titus declared:

"We'll throw this lot out."

He was pointing at his bloodstained clothes, lying dead in a heap on the floor.

"Right now. Then we'll get in some nice new threads, OK?"

She had decided to calm him down by placing clothes worth three months' pay on his shoulders. Not that he was a particularly snappy dresser, but fabrics with Japanese names which fitted like a second skin eased Titus's troubles.

Upstairs, as Sunday had not yet turned into Monday, and the kids were at their grandparents', Hélène suggested going out to the movies. They would walk down to the Bastille with Titus and Tanita, then see one of the latest Resnais films, *Smoking/No Smoking*, then back up for a bite to eat at Nadine's place, the Envierges, how did that sound?

"What are the films about?"

"What would have happened if I'd chosen Titus and if Tanita had gone out with my Silistri."

"Tanita would be the happiest woman alive, and you'd be skinning up. I want to see it."

"And then eat at Nadine's?"

"Fine."

But then the phone rang.

It was Gervaise.

*

Instead of a film, they got a hanged man.

A man hanging naked in front of a mirrored wardrobe.

A hanged man gently illumined by a bedside lamp.

A hanged man Gervaise knew. She sobbed.

"O . . . Cissou."

What a lovely Sunday.

Titus and Silistri would have certainly agreed, but amazement was stifling them. The hanged man was tattooed from the base of his neck to the soles of his feet. A circular village around his waist, in which Joseph Silistri recognised the former Place des Fêtes, a tight network of old streets covered the hanged man's torso, back, arms and legs, tracing out their paths amid a hoard of vanished buildings. While Gervaise was softly repeating "Cissou . . . Cissou . . .", Silistri could not help but reel off the names of the streets which the tattoos brought back to him: Rue Bisson, Rue Vilin, Rue Piat, Rue de la Mare, Rue Ramponeau, Rue du Pressoir and Rue des Maronites, Rue de Tourtille and Rue de Palikao. The stairway in Passage Julien-Lacroix, which went up the spinal chord, was overflowing with lilac at the base of the neck, at the upper crossroads with Rue Piat, Rue du Transvaal and Rue des Envierges, just a couple of yards from Nadine's bar, where Titus and Silistri should have been dining out with Hélène and Tanita that very evening. The pictures stopped right there, cut off by the rope.

Then Joseph Silistri saw the hanged man's face.

"Oh, Jesus . . ."

Titus saw him blanch.

"You know him?"

Silistri's voice came out unbroken.

"It's Monsieur Beaujeu."

A rediscovered voice. From thirty years back.

Oh no . . . it was old Monsieur Beaujeu!

Monsieur Beaujeu who used to take in the Silistris when their father had been beating them, old Beaujeu's bar, where Joseph dried up the glasses after finishing his homework, Beaujeu, the coal merchant of Place des Fêtes, who was not too fussy about topping up people's supplies for nothing and who, for next to nothing, changed the locks and windows old man Silistri smashed, Beaujeu the barman, with his last furlong of vines, whose grapes Joseph and his mates ran to pick after school, Beaujeu who had bankrupted himself by spoiling the neighbourhood's street Arabs, but who never smiled and used to warn them against wastage. "Never lose your money, kids, and never lose your marbles."

"Cissou . . ." Gervaise murmured. "O Cissou . . ."

Titus noticed that the phone on the table was off the hook.

(You shouldn't have switched on your nasty-phone, he thought. There's nothing worse when you need a real voice. Silence did have its advantages . . .)

Titus hung it up.

"He left a note."

A few words on an envelope.

"It's for you, Gervaise."

Gervaise put out her hand. The envelope when open gave her everything. She was his heiress.

"The chandelier," Gervaise said.

Titus and Silistri glanced round at each other.

"Take down the crystals."

In fact, they were not the crystals of a chandelier, but instead a set of tiny salt cellars. Almost all of them were exactly half full of powder. Titus sprinkled some on the back of his hand.

"Fuck me," he declared, after a cautious lick.

Then, passing the salt cellar to Silistri:

"Gervaise has inherited a mountain of coke."

Gervaise was not listening. She stood up. She had also inherited a little mirror, which she slipped into her pocket. She was now in front of the window. She looked at the zebra gambolling across the night sky between two lampposts. Beneath the zebra's hoofs stood the neighbourhood's last living cinema. The mirror in the pocket of her robes was communicating its chill to her thigh.

"What did you *see*, Cissou?"

Chapter 21

W HAT CISSOU THE Snow had seen was splashed all over the front pages of the next day's papers. An unprecedented cultural event. Julie was reading them out to Barnaby, somewhere on the Champs Élysées, in Old Job's Paris offices.

"*Barnabooth, or the ultimate paradox of plastic expression.* It's all here in black and white. So, Barnaby, how does that make you feel?"

"Read on."

Barnaby was speaking to Julie, but had refused to show himself. She was sitting on a settee and talking to a mirrored cupboard. The mirror reflected back everything: the settee, the far side of the room; the corridor leading to the front door, everything except Julie herself. A mirror which rejected the human image. A return to Barnaby's early attempts at childish illusions, painted looking glasses which reflected someone's surroundings down to the slightest detail, but not the person's image.

The cupboard was speaking with Barnaby's voice, which had hardly changed over the years:

"Please, read on . . ."

Julie continued with her press cuttings. A flurry of headlines. Universally superlative commentaries.

Barnaby was not taken in.

"The trivialisation machine is in full swing."

Julie quite agreed. So much media enthusiasm would soon overwhelm a moment of pure delight. Soon the same pens would be setting the illusionist up against the aesthetic limits of his illusions. The steam would drop and then nothing would seem more trite or "hidebound" than this "non-work", which was now being hailed as the "ultimate paradox of plastic expression".

"*The ultimate paradox of plastic expression . . .* again!"

Julie looked for the journalist's name.

"Typical," she murmured. "Do you want to see the photos?"

She held up the paper in front of the false mirror.

"No," the mirror answered irritably. "You know that photos and I don't agree . . ."

"Don't piss me about, Barnaby."

For a moment, Julie stared thoughtfully at the photos. The same emptiness surrounded the black iron gate and its padlock. Emptiness, filling up an entire front page . . .

"This emptiness is really weird . . . like pages full of silence."

"Go on. Keep reading."

"Is it your press attachée who usually reads them out to you?"

"Just read."

Julie smiled.

"So it does interest you, after all?"

Some politicians had been interviewed. They claimed all the credit for themselves. The Town Hall said it was responsible for the coming of Barnabooth, who was supposed never to leave his studios – but this version was then gently corrected by the Ministry of Culture, who claimed that it had set up the entire operation. Meanwhile, an aesthete close to the President was preening himself because he had discovered Barnabooth during his staging of *Hamlet* in New York. Backstage squabbling. Barnabooth the invisible illusionist belonged to one and all.

"The Holy Ghost, in fact . . . So, is becoming the Holy Ghost your ambition now, Barnaby? You want to fall down on our heads in the form of omniscient flames?"

"Stop taking the piss, Juliette."

Another headline caught Julie's eye. *The Immortal Zebra*. The title was not great, but the article raised an issue which would interest Suzanne: "*We will now look twice before demolishing a building if it has been made invisible for a few seconds . . . In the same way that Pont Neuf has been made new since Christo wrapped it up, the Town Hall will leave unscathed this small white plaster cinema, which has experienced ten seconds of oblivion in front of the cameras . . .*"

"Well put," Barnaby admitted. "After all, saving The Zebra was the entire point of the show."

"Saving The Zebra? You want to save The Zebra now, do you?"

"Because Old Job has chosen it as his tomb . . ."

"And you're interested in Old Job's tomb?"

"As a gravedigger, yes I am."

Julie put the stack of papers down on to the settee.

"Stop messing around, Barnaby . . . Come out of there, so we can talk properly."

"No way."

"You refuse to show yourself? Even to me?"

"Especially to you. You didn't come here alone. You brought the journalist with you."

(The journalist . . . journalism . . . this is like having a row with Benjamin, Julie thought.)

Suddenly, she was no longer there. She could not give a damn any more about the mystery of Barnabooth. A hangover from her adolescence . . . A bygone era when they had played at being Valery Larbaud lovers. Right now, she was carrying a dead child, and the child was Benjamin's. A Benjamin who was trying pathetically not to be pathetic with his infuriating Malaussènian empathy. (Their second minefield, after the evils of journalism.) One day, when she had bawled him out for his empathy, he had promised to change, to sweep the world and its woes under the carpet and to *change*. She had then started waving her hands in the air madly: "No, not at all, I don't want you to change, what really gets on my tits is that I want you to stay just as you are!" He had replied: "Great, because I want you to stay just as I am, too." They had laughed. She loved him. As soon as she was through with Barnaby, she was going to see Berthold the surgeon, then she would stick a towel between her thighs and head straight home. She did not give a damn about Barnaby. She stood up.

"Julie, I don't want you to show Old Job's film!"

It was not so much what he said that stopped her, as how he said it. A blast of hatred coming from thirty years before. Barnaby insisted:

"You just can't do it!"

OK, so this was a start.

"So why save The Zebra, given that the film's going to be shown there?"

"There won't be any showing, trust me on that score! I saved The Zebra so you can use it to house Old Job's film collection. I promised Matthias that I'd help you. So help you I did. And God knows, I have plenty of other things I could be doing! It's fine with me if Old Job leaves his films to whomever he wants . . . even though, as his heir, I could block the move! In return, all I want is for The Only Begotten Film not to be shown. It just cannot happen!"

Julie did not respond.

He went on:

"Fair's fair!"

She remained silent.

"If you show the film, Julie, you'll regret it as soon as it starts."

She looked at the mirror.

"Come out of there Barnaby, and let's talk."

"No, I'm staying where I am, and you're going to listen to me."

She sighed and sat down on one of the arms of the settee. She listened. They had not seen each other for years, but she was already getting fed up of hearing him being himself. Barnaby the grandfather hater. That palpable hatred in eternal adolescents . . . Underwriting an entire life on the detested elder's budget, living out the exact opposite of his love of images, squatting in his Paris offices when everyone thinks you're in a five-star hotel . . . spending all your life chained to a loathed old man . . . reduced to nothingness without the *cordon insanitaire* of that hatred . . . The hatred of the grandfather! Oedipus squared . . . no doubt an object of analytical curiosity . . . but a source of profound indifference so far as Julie was concerned.

All of which she then summed up in her own manner:

"It's twenty years since I last saw you, Barnabooth, and twenty years since you last surprised me."

"But you have seen me, Juliette! Only yesterday, you saw me in front of The Zebra, and you saw me in the hospital when you visited Liesl . . . you've seen me several times, but you never recognise me."

Well, well, well . . .

"See, I can still surprise you!"

She fell silent.

"Liesl saw me, too, just a few minutes before she died. And so did Job! And Ronald de Florentis, the bulimic collector with his bunches of flowers! And so did you! As clearly as I can see you! But your eyes glided over me . . . I was nobody. The same for poor Liesl! That's right, I was there when she decided to let go! I was there the day you were there, and I was there the day she died! Poor old Liesl went without recognising me, and regretting that I wasn't there at the end!"

(This is starting to get out of hand, Julie thought.)

But he was off:

"My ideal is not the Holy Ghost, Juliette. It's *nobody*."

He repeated:

"Nobody, *personne, ninguém, nessuno, niemand, không ai* . . . the *persona*, Juliette, the mask! By no longer seeing me, you've all lost sight of me. But I'm there, perfectly visible, walking in the street, going into a theatre, going into a hospital . . . and looking!"

"What about Matthias?"

"Matthias lost sight of me when I was three months old! All Matthias ever sees are newborn babies. The only viable baby Matthias has ever had in the placenta of his mind is little Job-the-father! What a delightful tumour!"

She stood up.

"Don't show that film, Juliette!"

"That's up to Suzanne now."

"No, it's up to you. It's up to you and me. And I'm going to stop it from happening!"

(He's expecting me to ask what the damned film's about, Julie thought. Just so he can tell me that it's none of my business . . . But I don't give a fuck, Barnaby . . . I really don't give a fuck!)

She headed towards the door.

"I'll talk to Suzanne and the others," she said. "If you want to listen to the discussion, come along."

She turned around.

"Come by this evening. With or without your optic tomfoolery. I couldn't give a toss."

When she reached the threshold, he called after her:

"Where are you going?"

"To have an abortion."

Chapter 22

IN THE RISING dawn of his Napoleonic office, Chief Superintendent Coudrier was thinking about Guernica. Not, of course, about the bombing of the small Basque town and the 2,000 casualties, but about the painting. And not about the canvas in its entirety, just about the crazy horse. In the middle of Chief Superintendent Coudrier's mind was the image of a horse with its *tongue agog*. Even though Coudrier was in no laughing mood, he thought the expression would probably have appealed to old Pablo Picasso. In the Chief Superintendent's mind, this tongue was definitely emerging from the animal's eyes. "Unless it's emerging from my own eyes . . ." A stretched-out tongue, which he thought must be hard as stone. But also incandescent. When mankind makes an effort, even stones can catch fire.

Indeed.

So Chief Superintendent Coudrier meditated.

In the rising dawn of his Napoleonic office.

The photos of a dismembered young girl on his blotter.

A nun converted to policing sitting in front of him. Silently.

Gervaise was not saying a word.

The Chief Superintendent was meditating.

His ears were following the passing swish of a street cleaner along the damp pavement.

In fact, when you looked at it closely, there was something dog-like in that horse. An epileptic dog, in fact. An epileptic dog was sticking out its stone tongue in Chief Superintendent Coudrier's mind's eye.

While, on the blotter, lay a butchered girl.

The Chief Superintendent looked up at Gervaise. He picked up the thread of the conversation where his reverie had left it. Ah yes . . . the suicide of old Beaujeu, Gervaise Van Thian's Belleville nark.

"Tattooed all over, Silistri tells me . . . from the base of his neck to the soles of his feet."

"That's right, Sir."

"And who tattooed him?"

But Coudrier already knew the answer.

"I did, Sir," Gervaise replied.

Before explaining:

"In the days when my father was investigating the murders of old women in Belleville, I asked Cissou to protect him. Cissou had quite an influence over the youths of Belleville. So long as Cissou was watching out for my father, no-one would touch him. More recently, he used to give me news of the Malaussènes . . ."

She went on:

"In exchange, he wanted to keep his memories of Belleville on his skin. It's the only pay he ever took. He used to bring me photos of buildings that had been pulled down."

The air-cushioned door opened to reveal Elisabeth, Chief Superintendent Coudrier's lifelong secretary, carrying a coffee tray. She would retire silently in three days' time. Just as he would.

"Thank you, Elisabeth."

The street cleaner was turning round the corner of the quay. A morning wash and brush-up.

"Gervaise, I know coffee is not your cup of tea, but when you sit up all night with a dead man, then you drink two cups without sugar the next morning. It's one of my rules."

"Very well, Sir."

(She calls me "Sir", the Chief Superintendent thought for a moment. With the same capital S Pastor used.)

In three days' time, retirement would knock down this capital for good.

"I have never asked you this, Gervaise, but where did you learn the art of tattooing?"

"In Italy, Sir, at the Santa Casa in Loreto, during the Marian festivities. The pilgrims there have tattoos done."

Chief Superintendent Coudrier knew the rest. As a nun in Nanterre in a home for repentant hookers (another of her father Inspector Van Thian's expressions), Gervaise converted both the ladies and their tattoos. She alone was capable of transforming a bright red erection into a radiant Sacred Heart, the arms of a pimp into the dove of the covenant, or the orgy on a young girl's flesh into the ceiling of the Sistine Chapel. Of course, Sister Gervaise's elders had protested in horror.

Such practices were just not on . . . Gervaise countered this revulsion by mentioning the tattoos worn by early Christians, such as Saint Joan of Chantal, the founder of the Visitation, who was tattooed with Jesus's name, or all the Crusaders of the True Faith who had fallen in the Holy Land with a cross tattooed over their hearts.

Once they had been defeated by History, Sister Gervaise's superiors then complained about the company she kept, her praetorian guard of repentant pimps, and the fact that she lived on Rue des Abbesses, in Pigalle, a God-forsaken red-light district. Gervaise replied that you cannot watch over hell from heaven, and that if angels can fall, fallen angels can also be saved. Sister Gervaise was not one for words, but her answers were always to the point.

For the moment, both Gervaise and the Chief Superintendent had fallen silent. Coffee.

Little cups, rimmed with gold, stamped with an imperial N.

The Chief Superintendent and his Inspector scalded their lips.

The first time Gervaise had sat down in this office was two days after her father's death, when old Inspector Van Thian had been gunned down in hospital, one year previously. As a nun divorced from her Mother Superior, Sister Gervaise had come to Chief Superintendent Coudrier, her deceased father's immediate boss, to join the force. With that in mind, she produced a rather dog-eared, but fully valid law degree. Chief Superintendent Coudrier, whose initial reaction was that this was some sort of father-daughter complex (an orphan's obsession, following in your father's footsteps . . .), had started by testing out the applicant's vocation. Zero vocation. Just determination. Sister Gervaise was determined. Someone was abducting her whores. Her repentant souls were vanishing one after another. Why hers? She had to find them again. She had a few leads, all of which led to the worst possible conclusion. She said she was ready to follow them through to the end. Sister Gervaise was not asking for police protection, she was asking to *become* the police.

Chief Superintendent Coudrier had made the applicant take an oral exam. Sister Gervaise at once brushed aside the theoretical questions and instead made clear what she *knew* about inner-city delinquency. The Chief Superintendent heard her out. And he heard this nun provide him with the solutions to a good half-dozen unsolved crimes, whose files he himself had laid to rest: the disappearance of a Securicor van in Rungis in October 1989, the triple murder on Rue Froidevaux in June of the same year, the kidnapping and death of the Frémieux boy in February 1990, the murder of Champfort the lawyer in May 1993, and so on. The nature of the crimes, the names of the guilty parties, their motives and subsequent careers were all there. Gervaise knew hell like it was the back of her hand. So why had she not mentioned all this to the police before? That was a misdemeanour! Because the culprits had either vanished in other bloodbaths, or else had repented, that was why. And Sister Gervaise named a couple of monasteries which were sheltering these saved souls in the perpetual silence of their secrets. Once he had thought the matter over, Chief Superintendent Coudrier could see no reason to complain if murderers sentenced themselves to life. Of course . . . but Sister Gervaise knew the difference between the impenetrable walls of a life sentence and the horizons of eternity. The openest of prisons is as air-tight as a snuff box, while the most air-tight of monasteries is open to the skies. The conversation took a crypto-theological turn and, little by little, Chief Superintendent Coudrier had started to feel less lonely. He missed Inspector Pastor. And, even more so, he missed Gervaise's father, old Inspector Van Thian.

And so, Chief Superintendent Coudrier had pulled strings so that, just one week later, Gervaise Van Thian could become a Trainee Inspector, attached to his team. Chief Superintendent Coudrier had become Sister Gervaise's Mother Superior.

Or *sis*, as old Beaujeu used to call her.

Old Beaujeu.

Cissou the Snow.

Victim of an optical illusion . . . a sacrifice to the "ultimate paradox of plastic expression", as it said in the papers.

Chief Superintendent Coudrier apologised to Cissou the Snow, but he had to admit that the suicide was taking his mind off the butchered girl on his blotter.

"Terrible business, this suicide . . . An awful misunderstanding . . . An art victim . . ."

Gervaise nodded.

"Suicide is imprudent."

So spoken without a smile, straight from the heart.

"And it's never an argument," the Chief Superintendent added.

Then let the silence settle once more.

Before asking:

"Have you had time to tell the Malaussènes?"

"Yes, Sir. I went to see them with Inspector Titus, while Silistri was waiting for the ambulance."

COUDRIER: How is Titus's head?

GERVAISE: He's got quite a lump. He's staying at home today. To have it X-rayed, I think.

COUDRIER : . . .

GERVAISE: Are you planning to discipline him, Sir?

COUDRIER: I'm planning to give him a dressing down. If Caregga hadn't knocked him out in time, he'd have gunned down two or three of those loonies and be in prison charged with murder.

GERVAISE: . . .

COUDRIER: I hate the idea of my men risking being sent down.

GERVAISE: . . .

COUDRIER: I need them too much.

GERVAISE: . . .

COUDRIER: I took Titus and Silistri off the special branch for your own personal protection Gervaise . . . And you must try to keep them under control . . .

GERVAISE: . . .

COUDRIER: . . .

GERVAISE: . . .

COUDRIER: Your second cup.

This was her punishment. Elisabeth's coffee was a rite of passage. A token of allegiance with Chief Superintendent Coudrier. He who drank it expiated his sins and could face any danger.

The sun had risen. Chief Superintendent Coudrier, whose windows always remained open on Paris's nights, went to close the heavy green velvet curtains with their swarm of imperial bees, and turned on his rheostat. The gold of the bees on the rims of the cups glittered in the half-light. The bronze emperor started to gleam softly. The limbs of the butchered girl suddenly burst out under the Chief Superintendent's eyes. How white they were!

The subject just had to be broached.

Coudrier allowed himself a final distraction by watching Gervaise drink her coffee. He thought about those rosaries. Recently, his men had taken to telling their beads during briefings. One officer after another. And yet Inspector Gervaise Van Thian, who thoroughly respected the secularity of the French republic, completely refrained from any evangelism. Just as she had sworn to do when being sworn into the force. On the cross. It was thus a sort of epidemic. Leather jackets, leather boots, identity bracelets, holsters, handcuffs . . . and rosaries. Such things happen. "Gervaise's Templars". That was what they were called in other departments. Coudrier just couldn't understand it . . . Unless it was . . . Perhaps . . . Yes . . . That itchy feeling at the tips of his own fingers . . .

Stop it.

Time for action.

He took a good look at the photo of the dead girl. How white she was . . . Blanched! Postel-Wagner, the forensic surgeon, had been adamant in his report. Her skin had been blanched. She'd been boiled alive.

COUDRIER: Between you and me, Gervaise, I would have preferred it if Titus had wiped them all out.

GERVAISE: . . .

COUDRIER : Among the "witnesses" we arrested, there are a few personalities . . .

GERVAISE: . . .

COUDRIER : . . . who are *dead famous*, as my grandsons would put it.

GERVAISE: . . .

COUDRIER : And if they had been *dead*, they would also be easier to swallow for the powers that be.

GERVAISE: And Inspector Titus would have been sentenced instead of them.

COUDRIER : . . .

GERVAISE: . . .

COUDRIER: They won't be put on trial, Gervaise.

GERVAISE: . . .

COUDRIER: The procurers will be tried, as will the cameraman, the technicians who copied the films, the distributors, the entire network which your operation has allowed us to break apart . . . but, among the voyeurs . . .

GERVAISE: . . .

COUDRIER: Only the less high-profile ones will be tried. Psychiatry will deal with the others.

GERVAISE: What about the surgeon?

COUDRIER: Not a trace.

GERVAISE: . . .

COUDRIER: Neither in the building, nor in the neighbourhood, which had been thoroughly cordoned off, believe me.

GERVAISE: . . .

COUDRIER: We have obtained some confessions, Gervaise . . .

GERVAISE: . . .

COUDRIER: . . .

GERVAISE: Confessions, Sir?

COUDRIER: The procurers and the cameraman have talked. Six of your girls are dead.

GERVAISE: . . .

COUDRIER: The surgeon killed six of them. In one year.

GERVAISE: . . .

COUDRIER : . . .

GERVAISE: . . .

COUDRIER: We have found their bodies.

GERVAISE: . . .

COUDRIER: I'm sorry.

GERVAISE: Do you have their names?

COUDRIER: Marie-Ange Courrier, Séverine Albani, Thérèse Barbezien, Melissa Kopt, Annie Belledone and Solange Coutard, the youngest of them.

GERVAISE: . . .

COUDRIER: . . .

GERVAISE: Could I have some more coffee?

By inflicting a third cup on herself, she was granting him some respite. She was allowing him to take the time he needed to find the right words to explain the rest. She sipped at her coffee silently. So, they had found the bodies. All of Gervaise's protégées had been flayed alive before the eye of the camera. That much she could work out for herself. She had no need of any explanations. The snuff-movie business . . . in the world of crime, nothing is unimaginable. Imagination keeps on surpassing itself. Just three days before retiring, it seemed to Chief Superintendent Coudrier that the French republic had been paying him all those years just so that he could learn this lesson: *no limit*. Every day had a surprise in store. Never a dull moment . . . "Objectively, I've never been bored, in fact . . ." Chief Superintendent Coudrier would have loved to see himself objectively. But things always happened subjectively. And right now he was beating about a subjective bush. Fumbling after the words . . . the right words . . . What was it all about after all? Nothing much really . . . Just how to tell Gervaise Van Thian that by trying to save those girls from their dissolute lives, she had packed them off to their deaths.

COUDRIER: And we also know why the "surgeon" was particularly drawn to your girls.

GERVAISE: Why?

COUDRIER: . . .

GERVAISE: Why, Sir?

COUDRIER: . . .

GERVAISE: . . .

COUDRIER: . . .

GERVAISE: . . .

COUDRIER: Because of your tattoos, Gervaise. He cuts off the tattoos and sells them to a collector.

GERVAISE: . . .

COUDRIER: . . .

GERVAISE: . . .

COUDRIER: . . .

There we are, then . . . It was as easy as that . . . The immediate consequences of bad news always come as a surprise. In this case, the slight tremble of a coffee cup against a saucer. Nothing but a faint chinking. *One always has sufficient strength to bear the ills of other people.* La Rochefoucauld had now slipped in and sat down on a corner of the desk. It was hardly the right moment for that! Chief Superintendent Coudrier sent La Rochefoucauld packing: "My dear duke, what with your aphorisms, you are nothing but a head shrinker."

Gervaise put down her cup and saucer as quietly as she could.

"Go on, Sir."

COUDRIER: How many girls have you tattooed, Gervaise?

GERVAISE: All the ones who wanted me to. I also offered to remove their tattoos, but most of them preferred modifications rather than having an ugly scar.

COUDRIER: How many?

GERVAISE: A hundred and fifty, maybe more.

COUDRIER: Are you still in touch with them all?

GERVAISE: No, Sir. Many of them go back into the world. With a new identity and a new address.

COUDRIER: Only one thing will stop the collector, Gervaise. That's when his collection is complete.

GERVAISE: . . .

COUDRIER: Your girls will continue to be in danger until we arrest our art lover.

GERVAISE: We're on to the surgeon. Things will quieten down for a time.

COUDRIER: True.

GERVAISE: . . .

COUDRIER: On the other hand, the risk will enable him to put up his prices. That's the market economy for you.

GERVAISE: In that case, he'll become even more dangerous.

COUDRIER: I'm afraid so. Like all good speculators.

GERVAISE: . . .

COUDRIER: . . .

GERVAISE: On the stock market, like everywhere else, speculation is always on other people's deaths. My father often used to say that.

COUDRIER: . . .

GERVAISE: . . .

COUDRIER: Your father and I did not vote the same way, but he did help me to think.

GERVAISE: . . .

COUDRIER: Then there is another mystery.

GERVAISE: Yes, Sir?

COUDRIER: The identity of the latest victim. The young lady in the photo. She wasn't one of your girls, was she?

GERVAISE: No, Sir. Maybe Mondine knew her. I'll ask her.

COUDRIER: Watch out for yourself, Gervaise. They've got you in their sights now. Whatever you do, stay close to Titus and Silistri. And your pimps, too.

GERVAISE: Very good, Sir. Is that all?

COUDRIER: That's all. And if you want my opinion, it's quite enough.

But it was not enough. As soon as Gervaise Van Thian had closed the double air-cushioned doors, the epileptic dog reappeared in the Chief Superintendent's mind's eye. Right in focus. He barely had time to be amazed before the phone rang.

And forced him to roll back the frontiers of the worst possible scenario.

"Oh no!"

The voice confirmed that it was yes.

He fell silent for a moment, took a deep breath then said:

"Bring me the letters, then call in Benjamin Malaussène and Julie Corrençon . . . Malaussène," he repeated. "And Corrençon. Send Inspector Caregga to fetch them. He knows them. And quick about it."

Chapter 23

Silistri drove Gervaise to Saint-Louis Hospital, where Mondine had awoken to find herself under the protection of the Knights Templars.

"She was still out when I saw her. The surgeon who sewed her shoulder back on was going to visit her later. She's going to be OK . . ."

Gervaise did not react. Silistri asked:

"How did things go with the Malaussènes?"

He was driving calmly. As if he had not slept for two days. He let the car glide along.

"How did they take the news? I mean, about old Beaujeu's death . . ."

The Malaussènes. Cissou the Snow.

Gervaise was grateful for this diversion.

"Better than expected."

"Tell me about it."

*

In the belly of The Zebra, Titus and Gervaise had been overwhelmed by the tribe before they could even open their mouths. Apparently, it was dinner time, and everything was boiling over in the wings of the old cinema: Clément's passion for Clara, Thérèse's anger against Jeremy, Suzanne's affection for the tribe, the saucepans on the cooker and Verdun's fury because she would not abide the slightest delay when it came to feeding times. Jeremy, the self-proclaimed conductor of this orchestra, was adding greatly to the confusion.

"Stop looking at me like that, Thérèse! All right, I admit the epilepsy bit was a stupid idea! OK, I'm a fucking idiot! Anyway, with Julius out of it, the whole show's off now. Pleased?"

"*Pleased* isn't quite the word . . ."

"As if this was a time to be picky about words . . . Jesus Christ, Clément, give us a hand won't you? Can't you see it's boiling over?"

"I've got a present for Clara."

"And this is no time for presents, either! Clara, stop gawping at Clément like a fish head on a slab and try to calm down Verdun!"

For little Verdun was screaming fit to burst.

(One hell of a day, all round, thought Inspector Titus.)

But Clara was already ripping into Clément's present with a crackling of paper, which finally revealed a state-of-the-art camera, a piece of Nippon electronics, a swarm of sparkling cells gathered around a frog-like stare.

"Oh, Clément, you shouldn't have!"

"It was a bargain, my dear!"

"But it must have cost you an arm and a leg!"

"It's just what you need to take the stills!"

Meanwhile, Jeremy was trying to offload Verdun, who was seething with rage.

"For fuck's sake, Suzanne, there's no room to put anything down in this shit-heap! And we've absolutely got to feed What An Angel if we want Verdun to put a sock in it. Where's What An Angel? Where the fuck's What An Angel?"

"Here!"

Inspector Adrien Titus felt as if his bump was swelling when he saw an Ogre's mask, with mad staring eyes and bloodstained lips, advance towards them.

"Here he is!" the Ogre's cavernous voice boomed in reply. "What An Angel's in here! I've gobbled him up!"

"Half Pint!" Jeremy yelled. "How many times have I told you *not to play* with the Xmas ogre! He's part of the *set*! And the *set* is not a *toy*!"

The Xmas ogre had tumbled over on to its side to reveal a curly-haired boy with rose-tinted glasses which were steamed up with tears.

"I drew him! He's *my* ogre! So get stuffed, Jeremy, and stop bossing people about all the time. That's all you are, a bossy-boots who doesn't even know how babies are made!"

While yelling almost as loudly as Verdun herself, the rosy-bespectacled Half Pint was clutching to his chest a platinum-blond baby who, quite unexpectedly, was grinning.

"Give me What An Angel! Can't you see he's hungry?"

But Verdun, who had screamed herself paralytic in Jeremy's arms, made any exchange of babies impossible.

So, Gervaise stepped forwards, tapped Jeremy on the shoulder, stretched out her arms and said:

"Let me."

Jeremy, who had not seen the two police officers come in behind Suzanne, threw Verdun into the stranger's arms, no questions asked.

And there was silence.

A Verdun silence.

The most unexpected silence of all.

The sort that stops planets in their tracks.

So much so, that Inspector Titus staggered, suddenly deafened by the beating of his blood in the lump on his head.

Complete immobility.

One by one, heads turned towards the newcomer.

Who was smiling at Verdun.

And at whom Verdun was smiling back.

(Yep, Inspector Titus said to himself, one of those silences where everyone in the cinema is awaiting *the* line which changes the course of the film.)

And it was Jeremy who came out with it, carefully articulating each word and staring into Gervaise's eyes:

"There was only one man alive capable of pulling off a stunt like that."

To which Gervaise replied:

"He was my father."

Clara's camera caught the sentence as it emerged.

Jeremy waited for the blinding light to fade.

"You're Thian's daughter? Uncle Thian's daughter?"

The utter pleasure of hearing the confirmation.

"And you're Jeremy."

(And so, thought Inspector Titus, our day in hell is now going to end up as a neo-biblical romance.)

"Gervaise?" Jeremy asked again.

Gervaise nodded.

"And the one who just photographed Verdun and me is Clara," she added.

(No doubt about it, Inspector Titus reckoned. This reeks of the promised land.)

"Gervaise . . ." Jeremy murmured.

Then, stretching out the name to test its elasticity:

"Geeeeervaaaaaaaisssssssse . . ."

But, at the same time, Inspector Titus spotted an idea germinating in the lad's mind.

(Not the sort who ever lets up for a moment, he thought.)

"If you really are Gervaise, Uncle Thian's daughter," he went on, "then you're the only person alive who can tell us why Verdun cries when What An Angel's hungry. It never fails. When What An Angel gets hungry, Verdun starts crying at once! Why? And don't forget that they're not even brother and sister, but aunt and nephew! It's stumped every paediatrician in town. Even Matthias! And Matthias Fraenkhel's no slouch!"

"It's because Verdun's an angel, too," Gervaise replied.

Silence.

She had plucked that one out of the air. It was the sort of answer Thian used to give her when she was little and used to pester him with questions. But Thian never simply replied. He always developed his line of thinking.

"Angels get bored sometimes," Gervaise developed. "And they're then attracted towards us by the warmth and force of our feelings. And your tribe lacks neither warmth nor feelings. Verdun chose you."

"If she chose us, why does she make such a racket?" Half Pint asked.

"She was just the same when she was up there," Gervaise answered. "And it isn't you she makes a racket about, it's about the ills of the world. Some angels are like that . . . and some people, too."

"What about What An Angel?"

"He was her friend up there. He came down to be with her a year after she was born so as to cheer her up. Ever since, Verdun reckons that she owes him, so she cries when What An Angel's hungry. She cries when What An Angel dirties his nappy. She'll also cry when What An Angel gets upset. It's called compassion. And compassion doesn't always put us into a good mood."

"Solidarity among angels," Jeremy murmured in the newly returned silence. "That's all we needed!"

It was a gawky girl with a bony voice who brought everyone back down to earth again by asking Inspector Titus, whom apparently no-one had noticed:

"You're police officers, aren't you? What do you want?"

*

"And so?" Silistri asked.

So, Titus and Gervaise informed them that Cissou the Snow was dead. So, the children started to cry, of course, and everyone lost their appetites, so the gas was turned off under the dinner saucepans, and so Gervaise witnessed the Malaussènes' "mourning sickness", their "ability to digest death and come up with life", as Thian put it, when trying to describe the tribe to Gervaise, and this time they proceeded as follows: Clément, who was telling them the story of a film every evening at bedtime, and who, this particular evening, had chosen *The Ghost and*

Mrs Muir, now decided to change targets and tell them the story of Cissou the Snow's life, who was, according to him, quite similar to the main character in the film, meanwhile, Titus complained of a double-sized headache and discreetly withdrew, while Gervaise, who had been asked to stay, took a place in the circle of bunk-beds, where the pyjama-clad kids dangled their attentive, slippered feet (the very scene Thian had so often described to her) and Clément, sitting on the storyteller's stool, began: "He was called Cissou as a distant memory of his native Auvergne, where cinq sous never equal six sous . . ." and Verdun dozed off on Gervaise's ample bosom, just as she had done so many times before on Thian's sharp ribcage, and Gervaise trembled with fear, almost with terror, when, absorbed by Clément's tale, she felt Thérèse's bony fingers take her hand, unfold it carefully, smooth out the palm, as though she was flattening a sheet of paper, then Gervaise could no longer withdraw her hand, because this gawky girl was so caught up in her reading that she was sagely nodding her head, and no matter how much of a nun you are, or how much you say that superstition is the last resource of the unbeliever on a godless planet, you still want to know, really want to know – do we ever really know? – what this nodding head, the smile on this harsh face and this sudden twinkle in her eye are going to reveal ("You know me," Thian used to tell Gervaise, "and you know that I have too much respect for your God-bothering to try to make you accept that Thérèse is the passport to the future. But one thing I do know is that she's never been wrong!"), and if Gervaise did not withdraw her hand, it was also to draw out this memory of Thian, and their old debate ("Come on, Thianie, everyone gets it wrong sometimes. We might even be one of God's mistakes!"), that's right, if Gervaise let her hand be, it was also to have the pleasure of proving Thian wrong, to hear this gawky girl come out with something improbable, completely impossible, which is precisely what the gawky girl did, after carefully folding back Gervaise's fingers, as if she had just placed a gold coin in her palm: "*You're a lucky woman, Gervaise. You're going to be a mother.*"

Silistri went through a red light.

"What? She told you you were going to have a baby?"

"That I was going to be a mother."

"Through the intervention of the Holy Ghost?"

"That's exactly what I wondered."

And Sister Gervaise apologised to the Trinity for even thinking of its third person in such an absurd situation, but the gawky girl, who was following her train of thought, pressed her point:

"I'm not joking, Gervaise. Within a year, you'll have a baby. Just as surely as Cissou left us this morning."

"OK," Silistri concluded, while parking in the hospital courtyard. "I'll have to keep an eye on Titus."

"And Titus on you," Gervaise replied.

Before opening the door, and adding:

"Meanwhile, I'll keep an eye on the Holy Ghost."

She put one foot out of the car.

"Wait."

Silistri grabbed her wrist.

"Wait a moment, Gervaise."

They had allowed themselves the right to smile, a little Malaussènian quarter of an hour, a slice of heaven in this torment. Silistri's grip clearly indicated to her that this was now over. Hell was back.

"Look at this."

He showed her a photo.

She took it like a punch. It was Cissou's naked body. Cissou and his tattoos. From his torso to the base of his neck. A map of Belleville on the cold skin of a fax. Someone had photographed Cissou the Snow's body. A body without a head. The body up to the frontier of the rope.

"The forensic surgeon?" Gervaise asked.

Silistri shook his head.

"When you replaced me at the morgue last night, I listened to the news on my car radio. They were talking about the spiriting away of The Zebra. We had been so preoccupied that we were the only people who hadn't heard about it. So, before going home, I dropped in to see my friend Coppet – she's a journalist – and she filled me in on Barnabooth's show. Then she added with a laugh: 'Some people wipe things out, while others remember them,' and she showed me this photo, which they'd just faxed her. Belleville on Cissou's body. Her editor wanted her to cobble together a piece about living memory versus the aesthetics of oblivion, or some other crap like that . . ."

"Who sold them the photo?"

"No-one. It's an agency snap. It must be in every editorial office by now."

"You're right."

She folded up the fax and Cissou's torso into four. Absent-mindedly, her nails ironed sharp the creases.

"I want to know who took it."

"So do I. I'll be back in two hours to pick you up."

Chapter 24

I N THE ECHOING hospital corridor, the two on-duty Templars looked rather relieved when they greeted Gervaise. The first cop indicated the door with his thumb.

"There's some quack in there who's been preening himself in front of Mondine for the past hour."

He shook his head.

"Normally speaking, I would have booted him out. But you're right, Gervaise, this thing really does calm your nerves."

He showed her the rosary which was dangling from his thumb. His team mate agreed:

"Plus it stops you from smoking. It's saving me a fortune!"

They held Gervaise back when she put her hand out to open the door.

"His name's Berthold. Watch out for yourself, Gervaise. He insists on being called 'Professor'."

"Professor Berthold, don't forget now . . ."

Once she had closed the door, Gervaise found herself facing an extremely white back, which was sounding off for the benefit of a circle of equally white coats.

"When you want to do the job properly, no operation is simple stuff, you bunch of morons! A successful appendicectomy, I mean a *really successful* one, requires seamstress's fingers of the sort that have been extinct since the seamstress who delivered your grandmother!"

The "morons" were taking down notes about seamstresses and grandmothers.

Berthold pointed at Mondine:

"The bastard who sliced up this lass here is the finest scalpel I've come across since meeting myself! He went for the tattoo on her shoulder with incredible dexterity. His initial plan was to bone her – I mean to remove her entire shoulder blade – to make an ashtray, perhaps – so he sliced through from the inside. But he was then disturbed and so went straight for the skin. A lightning incision!

Perfect! Not a trace of a shake! One second more, and he would have made off with this masterpiece. And what a masterpiece it is, my morons! Pontormo's *Deposition*! The most vivacious work to come out of sixteenth-century Florence. Life itself! As you'll be able to see when I take the wraps off the lass's shoulder! You'll see! The Virgin's lips, swollen with tears, the weight of her stare above her dead son, the density of her sorrow in that chill light! But, of course, you don't know of Pontormo, or Jacopo Carrucci! Jacopo was just like me! He didn't delegate his genius to second fiddles! He did everything himself, and never twice in the same way! Inventiveness! Inventiveness and life! You'll just have to see his *Deposition* in the altarpiece in Capella Capponi at Santa Felicità, if you want to believe in life! The truth of flesh in those dissolving shades of blue . . . And you've no idea of the added value that it has once it has been tattooed on to her baby-like skin! The lass's shoulder is the reincarnation of Pontormo!"

Professor Berthold was firing on all cylinders.

"Painting is the one form of culture open to surgeons, you bunch of morons! Not for the love of art, of course, but through a feeling for anatomy! Do like I did when I was your age! Skip your lectures and head straight for the Louvre, there's far more to be learnt there!"

Suddenly, he leant down over Mondine.

"But not you!"

He pinned her down on her bed with his finger.

"Never go to the Louvre, my little one! Never set foot there! I'll put that in my prescription! With a masterpiece like that on your shoulder, you'll end up in a frame! Who did it? I want one, too! Only bigger! The entire *Deposition*! So, tell me, who was it?"

With a flutter of her eyelashes, Mondine made eye contact with Gervaise, who had just stepped out from behind Berthold. She replied:

"I dreamt it, doctor. I dreamt of having it when I fell asleep, and when I woke up, there it was!"

"Not a bit of it, little one. It's cancer that works like that!"

A couple of white coats started.

Gervaise intervened, holding out her police card.

"Professor Berthold? I'm Inspector Van Thian. I'm in charge of this investigation. So you were saying that Mondine's shoulder was operated on by a specialist who . . ."

"A specialist? A virtuoso, Madame! A layer of gold leaf! Skilled in the counterfeiter's art! Let me put it this way: it could have been me! The only thing is, I don't kill people, I resurrect them. A simple career decision."

157

Gervaise was about to smile, when a nurse came up and on her tiptoes whispered something in Professor Berthold's ear.

"An abortion? What abortion?" Berthold roared.

The nurse hung on to the surgeon's shoulder and repeated what she had said.

"Tell Marty to go and fuck himself! The little twat is not about to start telling me how to do my job!"

The nurse pushed her head even further into the surgeon's ear.

"All right," he finally conceded. "I'm on my way. That Malaussène family is a right pain in the arse!"

Gervaise registered the Malaussène reference, but Berthold had already grabbed her hand to place a chivalrous kiss on it.

"Sorry, my lady inspector, even though I was just talking about resurrections, I'm off to do an abortion!"

Then, to the white coats:

"As for you lot, back to work! Cutting pregnancies short is private business, and strictly between the lady in question and me!"

Mondine's room emptied, as though sucked clear by Professor Berthold's departure.

In the freshly fallen silence, Gervaise clearly heard Mondine murmur:

"Sweet, isn't he?"

Gervaise sensed that this wasn't just a strange choice of adjective.

"I'm going to get my hooks into him."

Gervaise sat on the edge of the bed. Mondine was still staring at the door.

"You'll see, Gervaise, I'll be Madame Professor by the time I'm up and on my crutches."

Gervaise listened. Mondine had taken her hand.

"There are blokes like him in every walk of life. They start like that young and then never change. They're too full of sap, that's all. But when they've drained themselves, they're absolute lambs. They're big mouths, but they never say more than they really think. They have no ulterior motives. No souls, but no malice either. And a picture can make them cry. I like that. During my career, I had loads of blokes like that. They liked me, but it was only my career. With this one, my career comes to an end. You'll see."

Gervaise listened.

"We'll get married before God, then have a devil of a honeymoon. I'm not like you, Gervaise, I've always mixed the two of them up. That's what made me leave school young. They can't stand my sort of mix. I'm telling you all this, Gervaise, because you're you. I'm going to grab that dog with his vicious bark, and I'm going to hold on to him. If you'd like your pal up there to bless our union, then bless it He shall. And you'll be there to witness the blessing."

She was talking to the door which was still open, and crushing Gervaise's hand.

"I'm coming to a stop here, Gervaise. In the whitest of whites, like a true beginning. I'm going to hook up with Berthold and never touch another bloke again. Even free, gratis and for nothing."

Her eyes glanced round suddenly at Gervaise.

"I'm not dead, Gervaise."

Gervaise took her stare at face value.

"And I'm not mad either. It's a miracle!"

It was exactly the stare she'd expected Mondine to have on waking up.

"You can't imagine what you saved me from . . ."

The stare of a grown-up Verdun.

"I was in good company, Gervaise, with highly respectable individuals. They didn't bark. They made phrases, using proper grammar and loads of words. They were no Bertholds, they were refined. All of their motives were ulterior. Extremely ulterior. So ulterior no light can reach them. And, up front, all they have are words. Sugary words. Words to wrap you up like candyfloss. All very polite."

She fell silent for some time.

"I'm not dead, Gervaise, but I should be. They suspected something was up. They changed their timetable. If everything had gone to plan, you and your guardian angels would have shown up two hours too late. You'd have found a clean slab, an empty room and Mondine in bin liners. But something went wrong. They brought in this little red-head. She was an American, who'd apparently come over to France via Japan to be an au pair. A Yakusa product via Madame Mère's network, you know what I mean, no need for a diagram. A money earner placed in the household, who doesn't cause a family scandal. Clean and proper, plays the piano, speaks several languages, highly cultivated. Even wifey agrees. She can be left to look after the kids when they're off school. She's very well behaved. Just there to nurse the lord and master's glandular fever, that's all."

She suddenly looked down.

"If God exists, Gervaise, he isn't there for everyone. Or else, he's a gambler and we're his chips. He's a cheat. King of the three-card trick. Because instead of starting with me, as planned, they started with the red-head. They just couldn't wait. She had something which was driving them crazy. One of those tattoos you can't see, Gervaise, an *irozuma* made of rice powder, which was invisible on her extremely white skin and covered her entire body! They wanted it straight away.

Do you know how it works? You heat it up and the image appears as pale colours against the reddened skin. So they filled up an aquarium. The poor kid dived in laughing. She thought this was just one more exhibition. Because she hadn't been kidnapped. She'd come along of her own free will with the bigwig who'd taken her on. First off, I thought she was another voyeur like them. She let them undress her and put her in the warm water without the slightest resistance, then they put straps round her wrists and closed the top. As the heat rose, the *irozuma* slowly appeared and, while it did, the bigwig told us the girl's life story, really sweetly, like it was his own daughter . . . that's why I know where she was from . . . meanwhile, the camera went on filming. They wanted me to watch, too . . . just to terrify me."

She had now taken her hand away.

"Because, while they went on chatting about her so nicely, they kept on heating the water, Gervaise . . ."

She shook her head.

"They kept on heating it . . ."

She fell silent. Or rather, she continued her tale beyond the frontier of words, endlessly shaking her head. A long, silent tale which Gervaise followed motionlessly.

At last, her stare reappeared.

She said:

"Do you know what the worst part is?"

She'd taken her hand once more. She was gazing deep into her eyes.

"The worst part is that I'll forget. I'll forget, Gervaise. I'm going to lay siege to Berthold. And, when I'm on the other side of his defences, I'll get him to lead me to the altar. In a cathedral, maybe. Why not Notre Dame? And then your mother-fucker of a God will have to bless us. If He made us this way, then it's only fair for Him to bless us just as we are."

Then Mondine told Gervaise to leave.

"How many nights' sleep have you missed with all this?"

She packed her off to her home.

"One? Two? Your answering machine must be overflowing."

Mondine knew Gervaise's answering machine. She'd often confided in it.

"I'm not the only one in your life, Gervaise, there are all those other God-forsaken souls . . ."

Mondine knew about Gervaise's wake-up calls. Cissou the Snow was just the first on the list. More were to follow. Help, Gervaise! Her morning helping of distress. Then there were the evening calls. All those nights to smooth over . . .

sleep in peace, I'm here . . . I'm watching out for you . . . There are no monsters under your pillow . . . Gervaise is here . . .

"By coddling your whores, you're neglecting your old dad."

"And would my old dad prefer me to neglect my whores?"

But her old dad had been gunned down in this very hospital, far from Cissou's protection, and Gervaise had tattooed death on to the skin of her whores. "*It's not your fault, Gervaise . . .*"

She left the room.

"Where are you going?"

She brushed her Templars aside with a lie.

"I'll be right back."

She hurried out of Saint-Louis Hospital. "If You want to test me, Lord, why do it in another's flesh?" She wanted to be alone. "If You want to punish me, Lord, why do it with another's pain?" As far back as she could remember, it seemed as if He got at those around her, that He made her faith a fortress of simplicity around which people suffered, died, tortured one another and lost their ways . . . that in exchange for sparing her the torments of human contradictions, He'd placed her high up in the watchtower in the midst of a charnel house to keep vigil over this universal agony. And when she helped anyone, He turned her into the innocent instrument of that person's doom. "Why?" Her fury was unabated. "Why always *the others*? And why is it always *my fault*? To make me love You in spite of Yourself?"

It had all started when Thian, the little Tonkinese cop, had hitched up with Gervaise and her mother, Big Janine, and they'd all had to flee Toulon, pursued by an army of pimps who disapproved of this Asian love affair. The pimps wanted the mother and child back. Thian carried Gervaise on his scrawny chest in a sort of harness. Bullets whistled past their ears. But Thian was a fast and deadly shot. The pimps were gunned down, one after the other. They were Janine's Corsican cousins. Their family happiness was rooted in a heap of corpses. Why? Then Big Janine died. Why? Then Thian died as well. Why? Then Gervaise's whores starting dropping dead. Why? "Why *the others*? Always the others! Why?"

The roar of the car told Gervaise that, this time, He might be answering her prayer. Two wheels in the gutter, the other two on the pavement, a Mercedes radiator and a smoked-glass windscreen . . . A dustbin flew up in a shower of peelings, and the monster was on her. She dodged it by swivelling around two or three times on her heels, like a matador ballerina. But she ended up in the middle of the street, face to face with a second radiator coming from the opposite direction. "Two cars," she said to herself. "Jump Gervaise," the

Thian in her memory yelled. "If it hits you on the ground, it'll run you straight over!"

Gervaise jumped, her knees bent, feet drawn up below her buttocks. It was the top of the windscreen that sent her flying.

VIII

SOD'S LAW

COUDRIER: *I can see a terrifying case in the offing, and you will be its epicentre. Don't argue. It's practically inevitable.*

Chapter 25

THE SUGAR LOOKED like a white tornado in an extremely dark sky. It fell noiselessly into my coffee. Chief Superintendent Coudrier launched into his sermon.

"There are countless reasons why you were called in, Monsieur Malaussène."

Splashes. A pool in my saucer. Imminent drips.

"To sum up: obstructing La Herse the bailiff in the course of his duty, breaking and entering, wilful damage of property, incitement to civil disobedience, handling stolen furniture, assault and battery on the person of Monsieur Sainclair, the chief editor of *Affection* magazine . . ."

Chief Superintendent Coudrier's office hadn't changed since my last visit: the same bees embroidered on the closed curtains, the same rheostat, the same Elisabeth with her coffee, the same bust of Napoleon.

"Six charges in just the past three weeks!"

On the mantelpiece, the emperor was sulking. You couldn't blame him. Being made to turn his back on the mirror of *ad vitam aeternam* was one hell of a punishment for our little Narcissus with a hat. People should think of that before getting turned into busts.

"In terms of crimes and misdemeanours, the Malaussènes are a thriving family business!"

On the other hand, what can be more reassuring in this crazy world than a bronze bust on a marble mantelpiece? Even if it does depict a serial killer.

"Not to mention your knack for attracting everyone's suspicions whenever a particularly ghastly crime has been committed . . ."

Chief Superintendent Coudrier was seething with hidden rage. He was thundering, and the light intensified under the pressure from his foot. He repeated "ghastly", but only to himself. Then, quite abruptly, the light faded and his anger plunged into gloom.

"How is your dog?"

Like a petrified nightmare above a bridal bed, Chief Superintendent. And how are things with your own good self? It's not like you to ask after Julius as if your life depended on it.

But he didn't wait for me to answer.

"Let's get this straight, Monsieur Malaussène. I honestly cannot blame you for leading La Herse a merry dance . . . he himself has an unfortunate tendency to overstep the legal mark. As for Monsieur Sainclair . . ."

He pouted. He searched for the correct way to express his scorn.

"I have never liked the cut of Sainclair's jib. Even in the days of the Store . . . and *Affection* has done nothing to raise him in my esteem. Have you ever read his rag? No? You should. Just once. It's extremely edifying! And it's supposed to be about the medical world! So why exactly did you give him a hiding?"

Because I'm a grave, Chief Superintendent. Because I house the organs and memories of a certain Krämer, and because Sainclair wanted to resurrect Krämer in his columns. But what Krämer really needs is a good long rest, I don't want him to be woken up. I'm his grave and his keeper, the little stucco cherub and the slab of black marble . . . We all need to rest . . . The dead just a bit more than us . . . Krämer, Thian, Cissou, Stojil . . . It was a tiny death which whispered in my ear that evening, the tiniest of all deaths . . . dead at the very thought of being born.

"In the end, what does it matter? That is not the reason why you are here, to be quite honest with you."

To be quite honest, you seem to be fumbling for your words, Chief Superintendent. So what have you got to tell me? The abomination of all abominations? Cissou hanged himself, you know that? My child has given up the ghost, you know that? My dog has bitten the dust and Mother is dying of a broken heart for Inspector Pastor, you know that? So if you've got anything worse to tell me, don't hesitate. Hit me where it hurts, it'll take my mind off Half Pint's nightmares. Because Half Pint's started having nightmares again, you know that? His nocturnal screams are making the zebra's mane stand on end!

"I'm about to retire, Monsieur Malaussène."

"Where?"

It was the first question that occurred to me. I was so shattered by this bombshell that I didn't have a clue what to say. Retirement . . . Are you supposed to offer your condolences? Or else your congratulations?

He allowed himself a slight smile.

"To a small village outside Nice which, would you believe it, has the same name as you."

"Malaussène?"

"That's right. With a double 's'. I was born there. Do you know it?"

"I've hardly ever left Paris."

"A vow?"

"A necessity."

With Mum on the run and Julie on her adventures, someone had to mind the shop. No fox without an earth, and no earth without a concierge.

"My wife and I are retiring to Malaussène, to be with our friends the Sanchezes, who own the local café."

His smile was covering his thoughts, but his mind was already focused. I was sure that he'd willingly sacrifice his last three days at work if he could avoid having to tell me what was on his mind.

"I've always loved bees, and my wife has always loved honey."

Did he have me dragged in here to discuss his hives?

"My successor will not be overly fond of you, Monsieur Malaussène."

Right. So it wasn't about hives.

"He would have you locked up for just a third of the reasons I have just mentioned."

In other words, I had only three days of freedom left.

"Not that he's a bad chap. Don't get me wrong. It's just that he's . . . how can I put it? . . . an out-and-out public servant. And lacking in imagination to quite an incredible degree."

His eyes glided for a moment over the green meadow of his blotter.

"Imagination, Monsieur Malaussène . . . the route to all possible worlds. The ability not to judge a case by its appearances, not to mistake presumptions for proof, to consider that it is better for ten guilty men to go free, than for one innocent man to be condemned . . ."

He stared at me with an end-of-the-road look in his eyes.

"Imagination is a controversial subject in the force."

Then he added:

"And I know my successor well."

To judge by his ponderous eyelids and the brightening light, this knowledge clearly weighed heavily on him.

"He's my son-in-law."

Oh really? So that's how the force works, does it? A series of heirs to the throne. Nepotism. The little corporal handing out his duchies.

"Don't think for a moment that this is down to me. It is a pure career coincidence. At least, I suppose it is . . . Perhaps it comes from some deep-seated need to follow in your father-in-law's footsteps . . . Who knows? . . . Since Herr

Freud aired that sort of possibility . . . Then, of course, there is the desire for advancement. The prefecture . . . the minister's cabinet . . . the glorious abstractions at high altitudes! My son-in-law went to the *Polytechnique*, the School of Schools . . ."

The light intensified again under the pressure of his foot.

"But, to achieve this sort of ambition, you need spectacular results which are splashed across the papers."

A knowing look.

"And you and yours, Monsieur Malaussène, are an inexhaustible source of telegenic results!"

OK. I get it. He's retiring, he's abandoning me, and he's fretting about my family because he knows his own family only too well. Any moment now, he'll be inviting us along to the village that bears our name to gather nectar with him and his wife. I mean, the two of us have grown pretty close over the last few years. All that shit he's dug me out of . . . all those chats under the rheostat . . . and it's true that I've wound up getting rather attached to him. Yes, I'm rather attached to you, too, Chief Superintendent . . . It's not because you've got nothing to tell him that you can necessarily do without your confessor. I've grown attached to his questions, his office, his waistcoat, his figure, his flattened hair, his over-white forehead. I'm already sure that his departure will leave a gap in my scenery.

A slight drop in intensity. A friendly half-light.

"Coffee?"

OK for another drop. A stirrup-cup. I've grown attached to Elisabeth's coffee as well. To the turning of the little spoon in its melodious porcelain. To the silence of this room. To the curtains drawn on this man's goodness. That's it. To be quite honest, I've enjoyed being around a Chief Superintendent. Shame on me for the warmth in the cockles of my heart! I've loved a policeman! Which proves that nature accepts all sorts of love. And his sadness pained me.

"My son-in-law . . ." he repeated, as though still in doubt about his daughter.

He put his cup down. He increased the light. He looked straight at me.

"And his name's *Nepos*, Monsieur Malaussène, even though I've never pulled strings for him! Just imagine how little chance you will have if you fall into his clutches!"

For some reason this tautology sent shivers down my spine. So much so that I improvised a panicked defence.

"But it isn't the likes of La Herse or Sainclair who will help him further his career! After all, I didn't kill them! They're just trifles . . ."

His voice and hand cut me off.

"Have no illusions, my lad. Everything will be put into the balance. Absolutely *everything*!"

Silence, then a pained tone:

"But, in fact, you're right. That is not why you are here."

A pause.

"Now, listen to me carefully."

I listened.

"I can see a terrifying case in the offing, which will be in all the papers and you will be its epicentre. As usual, you will be perfectly innocent, but up to your neck in it. Only this time, I shan't be there to prove your innocence. Don't argue. I know you only too well. It's practically inevitable."

He broke off.

"I would have preferred you to come with Mademoiselle Corrençon."

"So would I."

So would I, I would far have preferred to come with Julie . . . but who ever takes our preferences into account?

He breathed deeply. He could no longer hold it back.

"Benjamin . . ."

That's right! "Benjamin." First-name terms! Then suddenly he was begging with me, as though on the brink of eternity:

"I am going to tell you something which will devastate you. But you must promise me not to do anything about it, and let the police take care of the matter. Otherwise . . ."

He broke off again. An explosion of light. An *a giorno* office. Half of him thrown towards me.

"Promise me, for heaven's sake!"

I stammered something which must have sounded promising enough, because he sat back down in the blinding light.

HIM: I know that Julie has gone to hospital.

ME: . . .

HIM: And I know why.

ME: . . .

HIM: I also know something else.

ME: . . .

HIM: . . .

ME: . . .

HIM: Did you receive this letter?

He stuck a letter under my nose. Its horribly familiar loops and curls were trembling.

I thought it wiser to keep my suspicions to myself . . . but unfortunately they now have been confirmed . . .

Yes we had indeed received this letter.

. . .this is such a rare condition . . .

Matthias's letter to Julie.

. . . we shall terminate the pregnancy next week.

Down to the last comma.

I know how empty words of comfort are . . .

"Why have you got a copy of this letter?"

"It isn't a copy, Monsieur Malaussène."

He fumbled for his words.

"Matthias Fraenkhel sent out *eleven* identical letters, one to each of his last eleven patients. All of them posted from Vienna. On the same date."

Perhaps I should not have given you so much hope . . .

"Benjamin, this was no therapeutic abortion. Fraenkhel decided to wipe out his recent patients' children. All of them. By using falsified tests and tampering with scan results. The foetuses were quite normal. I received proof of that this morning."

". . ."

"And these women trusted him so much . . . Not one of them had a moment's doubt. The surgeons all operated in good faith. Seven abortions have already taken place."

"Including Julie's?"

"I'm afraid so. I called the hospital when Caregga told me you were coming on your own. Professor Berthold had already operated."

*

The rest was yelled down the corridor. I didn't catch it all. He was telling me to come back, not to get involved. "You promised! You promised!" Yes, but the future is made of broken promises, Chief Superintendent. The latest members of parliament as well as your oldest friends will confirm the fact!

I legged it down the corridor and bombed down the stairs, several cops flattened themselves against the walls as their files were sent flying, heads stuck out of doors, which hadn't even had time to be closed again by the time I was leaping across the Seine. Take a Malaussène, hurt him, and he runs. He could grab a cab, dive down into the Underground, or grip on to the tail of an aeroplane, but instead, he runs! He makes the pavements tremble, laps up the tarmac, while balconies parade above his head. When passers-by turn round, he's already out of sight, in the twinkling of an eye . . . Malaussène runs, he runs in the straightest possible line and jumps as high as he can, dogs smell him passing above their snouts and traffic cops fail to notice him as he crosses intersections, he works up steam among the yells and hoots of protest, the screeching of rubber and squealing of whistles, the flights of pigeons and the fleeing of cats with arched backs . . . Malaussène runs, and it's hard to imagine who could run faster, making the world spin like this beneath his feet, unless it was a second Malaussène, perhaps, another swift piece of misery, and in fact there must be quite a lot of such afflicted sprinters if you judge by the way the world spins, because there's no two ways about it, the earth rotates beneath the feet of running men . . . and such circular ideas are the sole ones likely to occur to a man running across the surface of a globe, for he's running on a spinning ball, and so is condemned to marking time, to reasoning in circles, being sent back to square one by each step which brings him closer to his goal, it's true, take Malaussène for instance, he's just reached Boulevard de Sébastopol and is gobbling it up in one stride on his way to Saint-Louis Hospital, that's it, take Malaussène, take me! Then aren't I in fact running towards the beginning of this story? The moment when I leant over Fraenkhel's desk and, my eyes aflame, I asked him to clarify his position regarding that Saint Thomas quote: *It is better to be born unhealthy and deformed than never to be born at all.* "That's what you said at that lecture, wasn't it? I did hear you pronounce this quotation from Saint Thomas?" "Yes, and unfortunately that is precisely what I believe . . ." So . . . so . . . so how come Saint Thomas has suddenly morphed into Herod, the slayer of the innocents? What's the explanation? And why has the man who brought Julie into the world now murdered Julie's child? And why has this life innocently been snatched away from us by Berthold, to whom I owe my resurrection! Berthold, whom I can still hear saying: "You owe me a bit of procreation, for Christ's sake!" Run, Malaussène, the earth is round, and there's no answer, there are only people, the only answer is Julie, there's only Julie, Julie in hospital, Julie with an empty womb, Julie to be taken home, and since when have you needed answers when you're running towards Julie? The man running towards the woman he loves also makes the world go round!

Chapter 26

"**Y**OU LET HER leave on her own?"

Silistri's heels were echoing down the corridor.

"But, Joseph, she said she'd be right back!"

Silistri was heading for the operating theatre. The Templars were attempting to keep up with him, while doing their best to defend themselves.

"You know Gervaise! You'd never imagine she'd tell a lie!"

"You lost sight of her."

"We thought she was going to buy Mondine something."

"She said: 'I'll be right back.'"

"Yes, and now she's been brought back on a stretcher."

When Silistri spoke in such a thunderous basso profundo, fear raised all of the voices around him.

"Christ, Joseph, we didn't think she'd leave the hospital!"

"We thought she'd just gone downstairs to the shop."

"You thought . . ."

Silistri stopped dead and flattened the two men against the wall, which reverberated up to the roof.

"If she dies . . ."

An index finger tapped on Silistri's shoulder.

"If she dies, then turn this pair of dickheads over to me, Inspector. I'll kill them personally."

Silistri didn't turn round. He knew that the finger belonged to a good two metres of checked suit topped with a choirboy's voice. Toussaint Pescatore. The most picturesque of Gervaise's gang of pimps. Another variety of guardian angel. A tad outdated, perhaps: pinstripes, borsalino and signet ring. A kid with a taste for lasting values.

"And if she snuffs it, then you're probably going the same way, Silistri."

This final threat was backed up by the prodding of a short barrel, which

Silistri's experienced ribs identified as a Smith and Wesson. His grip relaxed around the Templars' necks. Silistri spoke in the same basso profundo, and still without turning round:

"Put your little dick away, Pescatore."

The barrel went a tad limp.

"Or else I'll confiscate it."

Smith and Wesson returned to the warmth of their nest, under the pimp's armpit.

"Now piss off."

But this wasn't so easy.

"And who's going to guard Mondine's room if me and the boys piss off?"

The cops looked round in the same direction. Three other eagle-eyed youths were now telling their beads outside Mondine's door, which had just been left unguarded by the Templars. Fabio Pasquetti, Emilio Zamone and Tristan Longemain, Pescatore's three gunmen. Gervaise's dark angels.

Silistri sketched a conciliatory smile.

"You're right, Pescatore, we've been crap today."

Without changing his grin, he shot his left hand up and grabbed the pimp where it hurt.

"Pull a gun on me again, my little Toussaint . . ."

The walls of the corridor were the same pale green as little Toussaint's face.

"Just draw one more time, you motherfucker, and I'll rip your balls off."

"If you do, don't count on me to sew them back on!" Berthold bawled into their ears.

Despite the surprise, Silistri kept up the pressure.

"Come on now," the surgeon went on. "Drop his bollocks, for Christ's sake. Can't you see you're strangling him?"

The pimp's lips were turning a ghastly blue. Tears were streaming down his cheeks.

"And can't you see we've got company?"

Berthold pointed to the operating theatre's double swing doors, which had just opened to reveal a pneumatic bed being pushed by a black and white nurse. A pink and white Gervaise was lying on it. She seemed to be enjoying a sort of distant sleep, far from her features, with a sceptical, slightly amused pout on her lips, a mixture of surprise and acceptance.

Silistri opened his fingers.

Pescatore's tears dried up.

"What's wrong with her?" the two men asked.

"She's asleep, that's what's wrong with her. Now, scram. My hospital isn't some sparring ground for cops and baddies."

Silistri raised his voice.

"Don't piss me about, doctor. Just tell me *exactly* what's the matter with her."

Berthold stared at him calmly.

"Or what? You going to put my balls in a vice as well?"

Before Silistri had had time to reply, Berthold raised one of his eyelids and examined the white of his eye.

"She's got *exactly* the same problem as you. She's knackered. That's all."

"Nothing broken?"

"Just a big bruise on her bum. She fell asleep in mid-air, and that's what saved her. She flopped down in a dream, first on to a florist's awning, then on to the bonnet of a parked car. When she hit the ground, she was already fast asleep. That's all there is it to it."

He pushed them aside and gestured for the bed to follow him.

Then he strode off in front.

"What are you going to do to her?"

"Three days of sleep and observation. In cases like this, you must never let the patients' guts out of your sight. There might be an internal haemorrhage."

"Which is her room?"

"The one next to Mondine. You're really going to have to get your rosaries going, lads. A double dose of the paters and the aves!"

In the room, where Pescatore and Silistri had followed Berthold, the nurse pulled down the blanket and sheet. Then, in a single movement from Berthold, Gervaise rose up to land gracefully on the bed. The whole thing looked practically choreographed, and Silistri could feel on his own skin the freshness of the sheet which fluttered down on to Gervaise's body.

"I advise you to do likewise," Berthold told him. "You're so exhausted that you'll probably end up gunning down some bystander. Are you married?"

Without grasping the logic of the transition, Silistri replied that he was.

"Then a good blow-job under a nice warm quilt is worth all the sleeping pills in the world."

No sooner said than Berthold was off. Pescatore and Silistri heard him booming in Mondine's room:

"How's life treating you, my dear?"

"All the stitches are pulling, professor . . ."

"Good sign! It means the meat's coming to!"

Mondine's door slammed.

Pescatore and Silistri slumped into the same silence. The sheet slid back. A sunbeam caressed Gervaise's bare arm. On it, all the colours of the spectrum formed an extraordinarily luminous rainbow. Silistri's first thought was that this was a mirage. But Pescatore knew better.

"It's her palette," he explained.

Pescatore opened Gervaise's hand.

"And she's had a summary made on her little finger. Look."

Sure enough, Gervaise had tattooed a sky on the fleshy part of the little finger of her left hand. A tiny patch Silistri had never noticed before.

"That's where she chooses her shades. Want to see?"

The young pimp had already opened his shirt. His entire chest was covered by Saint Michael slaying a dragon.

"It's a Domenico Beccafumi," Pescatore remarked casually. "In Santa Maria del Carmine in Siena. He was a mannerist godfather . . . in about the 1530s."

Silistri pulled up Gervaise's sheet and went to close her curtains.

"And I'm from Siena, too," Pescatore went on in the half-light. "My mother used to take me to see Saint Michael whenever I was a naughty boy."

Silistri let him natter on. He didn't believe in the piety of pimps. And yet, sometimes a pimp encountered a Gervaise and turned into a masterpiece.

"Sorry about just now, Inspector. I was beside myself."

Apologies . . . Such was the aim of this biographical detour. Silistri accepted them.

"You're a bit of a wop, too, aren't you?"

"In a way. A wop from the West Indies, with a mother from Alsace."

Pescatore nodded his head sagely.

"It's mongrels like us who make mankind, when you think about it. Cross-breeding is the future of humanity . . ."

Pescatore was apparently thinking.

Silistri crouched down beside Gervaise's bed. He told her what he'd come to say:

"As for the photo of Cissou, Gervaise, I know who took it and I know when. I don't know why yet, but I soon will. There may be a link with our collector. I'm going to discuss the matter with the photographer this very evening."

Was Gervaise receiving her mail? Her face showed no sign of emotion. It looked as though she was in doubt about everything, and had accepted this doubt with a sort of bemused indifference. This expression was unknown to Silistri.

"You'd do better to get an hour or two's kip before grilling anyone," Pescatore ventured. "The doc was right. You're living so much on your nerves that it will all end in tears."

Silistri looked up towards the pimp.

"Take my bollocks' word for it."

Silistri was about to thank him, perhaps even apologise in turn, when the din of a cavalcade in the corridor, a yelled-out name and the sound of someone falling made them rush towards the door.

Silistri's Templars and Pescatore's dark angels were pinning a man down on the floor, his arms and legs splayed, their four revolvers aimed at a head which was screaming out:

"Juuuuuulieeeee!"

Then it was Professor Berthold's turn to emerge from Mondine's room, push aside the pimps and cops, pick the prisoner up by his lapels and put him back on his feet, before saying:

"What the fuck are you doing here, Malaussène? And what's all this howling like a lamb to the slaughter? Don't you think you've already pissed me around enough as it is? Every time you set foot in a hospital, all hell's let loose!"

"Where's Julie? I've opened every door in the place, and I can't find her anywhere! What have you done with Julie?"

"Your Julie is as nuts as you are. She pissed off straight after the operation, while I had my back turned."

"And you let her go? You let her go? Berthold, you're even more of a dickhead than everyone says you are! I can't believe I'm hearing this! Where did she go?"

"Home! She went home! Where do you expect her to go?"

"Alone? In the state you left her in!"

"No, not alone. That wanker Marty rushed out after her, after I'd told him that she'd done a runner! He must be playing the good Samaritan even as we speak. If I were you, Malaussène, I'd run off home before he knobs her."

"All you're fit for is emptying out oysters, Berthold. The tool of your trade isn't the lancet, it's an oyster fork! One of these fine days, all your bullshit will come raining back down on your head, and you'll end up outside a restaurant scooping out sea urchins. That's your true vocation!"

Berthold hesitated for a second then, suddenly deciding to give up, he sighed deeply and threw Malaussène back into the arms he'd just saved him from.

"You were right, lads. Whack him. Then you can blow one another away. When the shooting's over, I'll send round some mops."

Chapter 27

JULIE HAD INDEED gone home, but the tribe had then whisked her away. Jeremy and his gang were sheltering her in their lair. Julie was playing Sleeping Beauty in the belly of The Zebra. They'd set her up a four-poster bed right in the middle of the stage. A large square one, with white sheets, just like in the song. Plus four bunches of periwinkles. Honestly. I'm not making any of this up. An avalanche of tulle tumbled down from the darkness of the flies, forming a seething cascade around her. The whole immaculate scene glittered in the half-light. All around the stage, photos of this bed fallen from heaven had been hung up and were drying – the choirs of angels captured by Clara's lens. Julie was asleep. In the wings, watchmen were guarding her. Julius the Dog, whose hammock had been shifted as well, was biting lumps out of the shadows every three minutes.

"We reckoned you'd feel better with us, Ben, while Julie conducts her grief management."

Her "grief management"? I stared at Jeremy. Jesus, this kid catches jargon like others catch colds.

"Doctor Marty agrees. Suzanne has decided to close The Zebra for as long as it takes. You do agree, don't you doctor?"

Marty confirmed:

"I also agree to speak to your brother alone. Go about your business, Jeremy."

Marty . . . the only person in the world Jeremy obeys, without first testing out the solidity of his authority.

Which didn't stop him from saying, on his way out:

"I don't want to take advantage of your presence, doctor, but before you go, would you be so good as to pop in and see Mum?"

Marty looked questioningly.

"She's stopped eating," Jeremy explained. "It was my turn to be the shoulder to cry on today, but I couldn't get a word out of her."

"What do you think the matter is?" Marty asked.

"Her heart, doctor. I mean the real one, not the pump. None of us dares ask her anything. It's too personal. But with you it's different. You don't mean anything to her, so maybe she'll speak to you . . ."

Marty promised, and Jeremy left.

Then we sat down together on the edge of the stage. We let our feet dangle into the darkness of the cinema. We remained for a time in a profound silence. Then Marty said:

"Julie will be up and about tomorrow. With Berthold, there's no risk of infection."

(I thought: There were no risks with Fraenkhel either, but kept it to myself.)

We listened to Julie's peaceful breathing and Julius's ivory snappings. The photos were dripping in a slight scent of developing fluid.

"And don't start telling yourself stories, Malaussène. This isn't your fault. You didn't lose the child through a lack of paternal fibre."

I looked at Marty.

He looked at me.

"I'm sure you're churning something like that over."

It was hard to deny it. We turned our eyes back to the cinema seats.

"As for Fraenkhel . . ."

I didn't really feel like discussing Matthias Fraenkhel.

"He can't have done this."

But nor did I want Marty to go. So I listened to him telling me how much he admired good old Doctor Fraenkhel. Who'd been his teacher on Rue des Saints-Pères, one of the few real human beings he'd met on his Hippocratic cursus, a good reason to become a doctor.

"Compared to Fraenkhel, we're all just social mechanics. And when I say 'we', I mean the entire world of healthcare. It's doctors like him who inspire us to use what little humanity we have to help our patients."

Matthias Fraenkhel's humanity . . . I did allow myself a slight objection:

"But he did write those eleven letters . . ."

Marty shook his head.

"I know. I spoke about it with Coudrier on the phone. Then with Postel-Wagner, the forensic surgeon. He's a friend of mine. Postel-Wagner was one of Fraenkhel's students, too. He just doesn't get it."

In the succeeding silence, I asked:

"Don't doctors go mad sometimes? Because of their jobs . . ."

He thought it over.

"In our profession, we're all a bit touched. We're either attracted or revolted by pain. In either case, we end up preferring illnesses to the ill, that's our form of madness . . . With Berthold as its finest example. In the constant struggle between clinical investigation and human emotions, the latter can never be allowed to win. They'd sweep away both doctor and patient. Some give up their careers because of an excess of compassion . . . I've seen that happen. Postel-Wagner transferred to forensics. He claims it's the best way to watch over the living. I know of others who speculate intentionally on suffering – they become the big stars. But most of us do what we can, we crack, we drag ourselves back up, we crack once more, then we get old. We're not very nice to know. We lose the fake jollity we had as medical students. But not through compassion. Through exhaustion . . . Illness is like Sisyphus's stone. Except that you can't imagine Sisyphus getting excited about a case of multiple sclerosis."

We were improvising away, like two actors grappling after the right words, in front of a theatre which was about to fill up.

"That's maybe what happened to Fraenkhel," I said.

"What do you mean?"

"A brainstorm . . . One strong emotion too many . . ."

"Maybe . . ."

Yes, in the throes of some violent emotion, maybe Fraenkhel had adopted the role I'd been pretending to play since Julie got pregnant. What's the point of being born, given the state of mankind and how things are with the world? A rekindling of the adolescent flame, which was all the more deadly for having been kept down for so long . . . then lo and behold he starts serially aborting tomorrow's children.

Marty remained sceptical.

"I really can't see what could have so utterly transformed a man like that. He hates death."

A moment's silence, then Marty muttered what sounded like an epitaph:

"His life was *life itself*."

God knows I had no desire to listen to stuff like this, so near Julie who had just been robbed of her reason to go on living by Matthias . . . Then suddenly I remembered how Clara had burst into our bedroom that morning, just after Julie had left and before Inspector Caregga arrived. "Benjamin, Benjamin! Half Pint's had a horrible dream!" "Sit down, my Clarinette, and calm down. What was the dream about?" "About Matthias!" Clara's heart was still fluttering. Half Pint had *seen* Matthias coming towards him down the central aisle of The Zebra, covered in blood, eyes staring madly, horribly pallid, the picture of martyred innocence

. . . not an image of suffering, but *Pain Personified*. I knew well that expression on Matthias Fraenkhel's face; it was just the same as the one I had seen during that conference, when a big pregnant girl had flung a lump of veal lights at him, hitting him plumb in the chest. Half Pint's dream was a genuine vision. I could still hear the spongy sound of those veal lights flying over my head. It had happened just after Matthias had quoted Saint Thomas: *It is better to be born unhealthy and deformed than never to be born at all.* I could still hear her yelling: "Here, cop that for something unhealthy and deformed, you fucking bastard!" I could see Matthias's bloodied expression. Matthias who had, that night, walked over towards Half Pint with exactly the same look on his face. As he advanced, he called my name. "He was calling to you, Benjamin. Half Pint says that Matthias was calling your name." Matthias walking through Half Pint's mind, covered in blood, crippled by rheumatism . . . an unfinished-off victim . . . apologetic pain . . . and calling out to me . . . to me . . . to me . . .

It took Julie's voice to bring me back to the land of the living.

"Is that you, Benjamin. Who are you talking to?"

Marty and I turned round.

*

On getting back to The Zebra, she hadn't said anything. Without a word of protest, she let them undress her, lie her down on the huge square bed and tuck her in just like when she was a little girl. While everyone was tiptoeing off the stage, she'd held back Suzanne, who sat down on the edge of the bed with the burdensome patience of someone waiting for confidences. But Julie simply told her about her encounter with Barnaby, and his refusal to let The Only Begotten Film be shown. She'd then asked Suzanne to summon a meeting of the college of film buffs that very evening. "Barnaby will be there. We'll probably have to make a decision." Then she fell asleep.

After Marty had gone, she didn't speak to me either. Not about the child, nor about Matthias, nor about Berthold. Not a word. Julie's silences are a basic healing process. The soul is at rest. The heart emptying out. The brain patching itself up. "When my father died, I didn't say a word for six months." A spot of advice to professional mourners: do not offer your condolences. Just be there, that's all. Lie down and wait. Which is what I did. I lay down next to her. She leant her head on my shoulder. We fell asleep.

Only to wake up again a few hours later amid a circle of attentive stares. We were surrounded by the Malaussène tribe and the film buffs. From big Avernon (the Judge Dredd of the static shot) to Lekaëdec (the Robespierre of dollying) not a single one missed the appointment. Sitting around us, bolt upright on their chairs, with those photos of the white bed hung up behind them, they were staring at us silently. It was like waking up in an incubator! Our bed was high up on a shadowy dais, while the stage lights wrapped the watchers in a glassy gleam. Discreetly, I nudged Julie. As though I'd given a signal, the tulle started rising up jerkily with a screech of pulleys, thus exposing the bed. A cone of glittering, sparkling light descended from the heavens to encase us.

Jeremy's idea of a good bit of staging . . .

Julie sat up, as white as a ghost in Suzanne's nightdress. Her Venetian mane decked by the shower of spangles, and her weighty breasts sticking to the linen under a veil of perspiration changed the nature of the silence.

She smiled.

"You really are the king of kitsch, Jeremy. Beside you, Walt Disney is a non-starter."

Some people laughed, including Jeremy whose ears had suddenly gone phosphorescent, then Julie got down to business. She thanked the seraphim of cinema for coming at such short notice, then gave them a brief summary of her conversation with Barnabooth the illusionist, Old Job's and Liesl's grandson, who was absolutely set against them showing Job's Only Begotten Film even once.

"And what's the reason for this censorship?" Lekaëdec asked.

"You ask him that when he arrives," Julie replied.

But things were not going to be as simple as that.

"I don't see any point in discussing the matter with him," Lekaëdec objected. "I mean, this is Old Job's business, isn't it? It's *his* film, after all!"

"For once, Lekaëdec's right," Avernon grumbled. "We're certainly not going to let some heir put a spanner in the works."

"The fact is," Suzanne added, "there's no less genealogical art than the cinema."

"Really great directors have never started dynasties like Bach or Strauss . . ."

"Or Bruegel . . ."

"Or Dumas . . ."

"Or Debré . . ."

"Or Leclerc . . ."

"Except for Tourneur, maybe, and then there's Ophüls!"

"The exception that proves the rule."

"Only actors reproduce!"

They were off. Julius the Dog marked time, seeing that each had the same opportunity to speak. Three minutes per person.

"An only begotten film! A man burns his life away under the lights to make *only* one film, and we're supposed to let his heir make off with the reels?"

"Talk about an heir! The negator of a century of pictures!"

"If this Barnabooth has got something against the movies, it's not up to Old Job to pick up the tab!"

"And if he's got something against Old Job, it isn't the movies which should suffer either."

At each turn of the table, the tension went up a notch.

"The cinema is *life itself*! Is the grandson out to murder the grandfather?"

"Can you imagine Mizoguchi with an heir?"

"Welles with descendants?"

"Or Capra?"

"Or Fellini?"

"Or Godard? Can you imagine an heir confiscating Godard's films?"

"Don't blaspheme, Avernon!"

Suddenly, I pictured myself in the shoes of the heir in question, this Barnabooth, who was due there any minute to enter the arena and face this mob of buffs. It did me good. It was one of those moments when, despite our inner torments, deep down we're pleased not to be someone else. That's how grief is managed. Little by little. Fleeting instants of joy amid bouts of despair, a stitch here, another there, until you're happy once more to be yourself . . . Yes, I guess happiness must be just that, the satisfaction of not being the Other.

I'd reached this point in my generous meditation when the "Other" finally showed up. By knocking on the door of The Zebra, just as Mum had done a few weeks back. But this time, we knew who we were expecting, and we were all eyes! The knocking didn't rise above the din of conversation. Only Suzanne heard it.

She raised her hand.

"Here he is."

The news gave rise to the silence of an ambush.

Another knock.

Jeremy clicked his fingers.

The stage was at once plunged into darkness. Only the emergency lights were still on in the stalls.

"Go on, Clément!" Jeremy whispered.

Clément ran silently to the door.

Julie's eyes were glistening slightly in the darkness. What was this childhood memory going to look like? What had the Barnaby from boarding school turned into, the first lover in the caves of the Vercors, the would-be see-through salamander, the negator of a century of pictures? Of course it wasn't Julie who was wondering all this, it was me. All I knew about Barnaby was that he'd been fifteen when he'd been in my place.

Clément had arrived at the door. He looked round at Jeremy, who was standing on the lip of the stage, one arm raised.

Jeremy lowered his arm.

The emergency lights went out and the converging fire of two spotlights hit the door just as Clément opened it, before flinging himself back against the wall. ("We're going to make our vanishing magician put in an *appearance*," Jeremy had decided.)

Not a bit of it. The door opened to reveal a figure with one hand on its face, the other on its heart.

Two shots rang out.

The spotlights exploded.

A shower of the sparks fell in the darkness of the cinema.

A second later, when Suzanne had put back on the house and stage lights, a tall man with mad staring eyes and dark hair was standing at the far end of the central aisle. In one hand he was holding a gun, which was aimed at us. With the other, he was pressing Clément against his chest to act as a shield.

Chapter 28

SILISTRI FELT THE lad's heart leaping in the palm of his hand. He could see a stage, a bed, a ring of pale faces around the bed, a terrified kid on the lip of the stage, and among the rumpled sheets a Desdemona with a fiery mane, about to pounce, giving him an Othello stare. Malaussène was standing beside her, slightly upstage. Silistri immediately thought: A play. A rehearsal. I've butted in on one of their rehearsals. Then he said to himself: Berthold and Pescatore were right. I'm going to end up fucking whacking someone.

The young lad's heart was racing so fast that it was drumming away inside Silistri's own chest. The Inspector freed his prisoner and put his gun back into his holster. The lad remained standing in front of him.

"You OK?" Silistri asked.

The lad didn't answer.

"Hey! Are you OK?"

Silistri took his head in his hands. He gently slapped his face.

"Sorry . . . it was the spotlights . . . they dazzled me . . ."

(What a reassuring excuse, he thought as he spoke. If I gun down everything that dazzles me.)

"I'm Inspector Silistri . . . I'm a policeman . . . Feeling better?"

"A cop? How many black kids have heart attacks in your station?" the boy by the lip of the stage yelled.

"Jeremy, shut it!"

The order flew out like a slap from Desdemona's mouth. And shut it he did. Silistri reckoned that kid looked just like the sort of wind-up merchant that he'd been at the same age. (Jeremy Malaussène, he thought.)

"Go on to the stage," he said to the lad. "I'll follow you."

The crossing of the tiny cinema seemed interminable. When he'd clambered up on to the stage, he apologised again. When Suzanne had introduced herself, he stammered:

"Tell me what I owe you . . . for the spots, I mean . . ."

A dry voice cut him off.

"The police is it? What do you want now?"

It wasn't Desdemona. This time it was a tall gawky girl. From the descriptions Gervaise had given him, Silistri supposed that the voice of officialdom must belong to Thérèse Malaussène.

"I'd like to ask Monsieur Clément a few questions."

Silence.

"Monsieur Clément Clément," Silistri specified.

From the converging stares, Silistri deduced that the Clément Clément in question was none other than his shield with the racing heart.

"Oh, it's you, is it?"

He hesitated for a second. Suddenly, he realised that there was nothing to be learnt here, that this was the land of innocence. A hundred miles away from those dead girls. But his automatic pilot had taken over.

"Just a couple of questions, sir. And sorry again about what just happened."

He decided not to take Clément aside, but to quiz him in public. He was going to regret that, too.

"Do you know this young lady?" he asked, showing round a photo of Mondine.

Jeremy glanced over Clément's shoulder, before shrinking back at once.

"You can have a look too."

Silistri handed Jeremy the photo.

"Pass it round."

Then, to Clément:

"You don't know her?"

Clément shook his head. The photo was now circulating. No-one knew Mondine. Which came as no surprise to Silistri. Julius the Dog snapped his teeth. Silistri glanced round at him incredulously, then asked Clément:

"What about this one?"

It was a photo of the little red-head. But not as a boiled corpse. It was a blow-up of the passport photo they'd found at her employer's address.

"No," Clément said. "Not at all. Never seen her before . . ."

Silistri gave it to Jeremy.

"Pass it round."

The little red-head circled about to no purpose. Her theatrical performances had been of a totally different sort.

"How about this one, then? Recognise that?"

The little colour that had flowed back into Clément's cheeks faded at once.

Silistri felt sorry at once. This wouldn't take his inquiries anywhere, and he knew it.

"Think before you speak."

Clément couldn't take his eyes off the maze of streets which covered the image of Cissou the Snow's headless body which he was holding in his hands. When Jeremy tried to have his turn, Clément instinctively clung on to it. Silistri ordered:

"Pass it round."

(While still wondering: What the hell am I doing here?)

"It doesn't ring any bells?"

(I don't need this confession, he repeated to himself.)

"They're tattoos!" Jeremy exclaimed. "It's Belleville!"

"Recognise it?" he pressed on, still staring at Clément.

(At their age, I wasn't putting on plays, he thought in a fit of anger. At their age, I was nicking cars. I was nicking cars, but I wasn't photographing stiffs.)

"It's the body of Monsieur Beaujeu," Silistri explained. "Or Cissou the Snow, if you prefer."

After his third car theft, old Beaujeu had given little Silistri the hiding of a lifetime.

"Why did you take this photo?"

Silistri owed his career in the force to that timely hiding.

Suddenly exhausted, he let his automatic pilot take over once more.

"*Article 225 of the penal code*," he recited. "*Paragraph 17: any denigration of the dignity of a corpse, by any means whatsoever, is punishable by one year's imprisonment and a fine of 100,000 francs.*"

The photo was being passed round.

"Why did you take this photo? And why did you sell it?"

This was more than mere silence. And more that just immobility. This was a stage full of statues.

"I think I'm right in saying", he said, peering round at the entire Malaussène tribe, "that you were all the family Cissou the Snow had left . . ."

Then, amid all that shared grief, Silistri suddenly just *knew* what he was going to do with this photo of old Beaujeu. A staggering revelation! He felt like heading off straight away, rushing round to Titus's place to tell him his idea. But he stayed there. Something inside him was stubbornly picking away at this young lad, who was now turning into another decomposing corpse under his stare.

"You went into his room just after he'd committed suicide. You then left again, without informing anybody so as to fetch a camera. You returned and photographed the body from every conceivable angle. An hour later, at three thirty p.m., you sold the photos to a friend who works in a press agency."

The photo was being passed round. Julius the Dog was snapping his teeth in vain. A timepiece has never brought time to a stop. Suddenly, the tone of Silistri's voice changed:

"You won't be charged," he said softly. "But, before I go, I just want to know *why* you did such a thing."

Not a movement. Silence. Time passing . . . and passing, with stares closing in on Clément the Budding Bayleaf. Then, when the photo reached her, the warm voice of an oval-faced girl could be heard, yes, a round voice from an oval face, which said:

"I know why."

(Clara Malaussène, thought Silistri.)

Clara broke the silence and the immobility. She walked over to Clément. She was holding her new camera. She just said:

"O Clément . . ."

Without raising her voice, but having to rummage for his name in the depths of an astounded sorrow, and then drag it slowly back up to the surface.

"O Clément . . ."

She opened the back of her camera and pulled out the film. With a faint, apologetic smile, she said to the Inspector:

"He did it so he could buy me a new camera."

She let the film fall to the floor, until it coiled around her feet. When the camera was empty, she handed it to Clément.

"Go away."

Without raising her voice.

"Just go away."

Then she took down all the photos of the white bed and left the stage.

*

Outside, the camera exploded against the wall of The Zebra. Then Clément kicked what was left of it across the boulevard. A convoy of fruit and veg on its way from the market in Rungis ready for the street stalls the next day attempted to flatten it into the asphalt. Then a passing green car sent the metal cap into the gutter. Its final burial took place in a sewer hole at the corner of Rue Ramponeau, beneath the bristles of a phosphorescent broom.

Clément ran. He didn't give a damn where to. He ran through the night, doubled up in sorrow, anger and shame. An expressionist refugee, casting on the walls the shadow of a sycophant. Fritz Lang's M, John Ford's informer, Clément was running through a blinding array of accusing images, he pushed open the doors of the night, while being pursued by Raymond Bussières's broken hands: *Look at me hands, laddie, you're nothing but a bastard* . . . Then he heard Sénéchal's groan, with the voice of Reggiani: "*But I don't want to be a bastard*. But Clément had betrayed a dead man, and so was far more of a bastard than Sénéchal or Gypo, who had, after all, merely betrayed the living, which is only human . . . Clément was running like a grave robber pursued by the mummy's curse. In the vengeful fury, the Pharaohs were beaming him the worst images he had in his celluloid memory: a sandstorm in which the shadow of the wind machine could be seen, Christopher Lee's grotesque gait, the rapid echoes in a studio supposedly enclosing the desert, and Clément himself rushing along in ghastly shorts and a papier mâché helmet . . . He was a complete monster, the object of eternal, universal scorn. Belleville's last shutters closed as he approached. He fled as though wiping himself out. Never again would he return to the scenes of his happiness. "It was for love!" he yelled in the silence of his skull. "For love!" He sobbed as he fled, still repeating: "For love!" and the quality of the images picked up: Grémillon's camera and Charles Vanel's voice in *The Sky Is Yours!* Clément ran on, screaming out his love for Madeleine Renaud and that the sky was theirs, his and Clara's, but it wasn't! There was a difference! Too great a difference! Clara had thrown him out because of a fundamental difference! He was the boy with green hair! The Elephant Man with his broken heart! He had nothing left to hope for! How far would she have gone to prove her love for him? As for him, he would have been capable of anything. For Clara! For her love! That was the real difference, and all of them, hidden behind their eyes, were all part of that single gaze! The single gaze of the pimps of reality, the priests of the image, aimed at his irreconcilable difference! They were judging him! Their lack of feelings left them with the moral high ground! They had held him in the fire of their stares because they were bodiless and heartless! They had cursed him!

"Excuse me!"

He'd got back to Fritz Lang and reached Place de la République by the time the kid caught him up.

"Excuse me . . ."

It wasn't one of the Malaussène kids. It was a little Vietnamese boy he'd never seen before, and who was now out of breath.

"Excuse me! But this bloke asked me to give you this!"

A tiny tape recorder. Panting, Clément stared up Rue du Faubourg du Temple. The kid had vanished. While getting his breath back, he examined the machine. Smooth metal, which fitted into the palm of your hand . . . Clément retreated into the shadows of a doorway, turned the tape on and placed it against his ear.

The voice was soft, persuasive, a little nasal.

"You have run far enough. It's time to stop and think. They've accused you of despoiling an image, but they intend to do far worse. Don't blame yourself. Come and see me in an hour's time. We'll have a nice little chat."

Clément listened to the message again. And again. As though dousing his sorrows. It was the voice of consolation. And it was making an appointment with him somewhere on the Champs Élysées. It said it belonged to Barnabooth, the illusionist. *"You know, the Barnabooth who made The Zebra vanish!"*

At that very moment, Silistri burst into Titus's and Tanita's bedroom.

"I've got a present for you, Titus."

Adrien Titus's bruised head rose up from its conjugal duties.

"Haven't we got time to finish?"

"The time it'll take for me to fix a punch."

"A professional present?" Tanita asked.

Silistri apologised.

Tanita brushed aside his apologies.

"Go into the other room and wait your turn. My present to you is on the stove."

Half an hour later, when Titus appeared in the living-room, he found Silistri fast asleep.

"Shall I wake you up or get Hélène?"

Silistri opened one eye.

"OK. So what about this present?" Titus asked.

"The surgeon. I'm giving you the surgeon on a plate."

Titus gazed round the room, as though looking for the whore killer.

"Is he here?"

"Could just as well be. This time, we're going to nail him, Titus."

"No kidding? You've got a plan?"

"That's right."

Silistri's gaze darkened.

"And it cost me dear."

IX
THE INTERVAL

Benjamin, tell me the truth.

Chapter 29

MUCH LATER THAT night, Julie said:

"Benjamin, tell me truth."

It was the first time she'd asked me such a thing. I finally murmured in reply:

"Yes, my love?"

She hesitated for a few seconds, then asked:

"Really speaking, you couldn't care less about the cinema, could you?"

I didn't wonder what lay behind her question. With Julie, I'd got out of that habit. I simply thought it over. The cinema . . . let me see now . . .

"In fact, you couldn't give a tuppenny fuck."

"Not really. Not completely. Let's say, I couldn't give much of a tuppenny fuck . . ."

"To a buff, that's the worst possible answer. Just imagine Avernon's face if he heard you say something like that. It would be like telling him you prefer the interval."

We were whispering in the darkness, lying on our backs, arm against arm, beneath the canopy of the four-poster bed in the empty theatre. Without transition, Julie asked her next question:

"And what about wine?"

"What about wine?"

"Apart from your Sidi-Brahim, are you interested in wine?"

"You mean . . . do I know anything about it?"

It was as if we'd just met.

"Yes. Do you know anything about wine?"

"Zilch."

Then, still without budging an inch, she said:

"I've got a suggestion to make."

It was a simple idea, which she expressed in simple terms:

193

"We're going to deal with our woes by doing things we couldn't give a fuck about."

She would hire a truck and take me to her native Vercors, where we'd fetch Old Job's film collection. At the same time, we'd take delivery of his Only Begotten Film, no matter what Barnaby had to say.

"Old Job faxed me. He's expecting us. On the way, we'll take the opportunity to do *my own personal* wine tour."

We'd then bring back all that celluloid to Suzanne and the film buffs. We'd treat them to the time of their lives, while we were going through hell. Long live the cinema!

I asked:

"What about Clara?"

"Clara's decided to be miserable for a week with your mother."

That's all right, then.

"When are we leaving?"

"Tomorrow."

*

"Well?"

I spun the wine round in my glass, gave it a good sniff, drank a drop, gargled with it and chewed away, just as I'd seen it done. Then I looked up towards the heavens, nodded, knitted my brows . . . I regretted not being able to wiggle my ears. Finally, I said:

"'Tsallright."

Outside, the white truck was patiently waiting for the tasting to be over.

Julie mimicked me:

"'Tsallright . . ."

Her imitation echoed with loving pity . . . a twist of scorn . . . and the massive iceberg of her knowledge bobbing up and down in the resulting cocktail.

"Irancy wine, Benjamin, is far finer than 'all right'. It's a prestigious red which ages well. The particular example languishing in your glass comes from a variety of grape which is practically extinct, as rare as a whale in Japanese territorial waters: the *tressot*, my dear chap, a 1961 tressot, which is also an extremely good year! A vigorous, ruby wine! Look at it at least, if your tastebuds are that useless!"

"How come you know all this, Julie?"

In the truck which was conveying us to our next stopover, she smiled.

"From my father, the Governor."

The Governor had decided to educate her palate.

"When I was six, he plunged me into wine like other parents stick you in front of a piano. I resisted, like kids always do with their musical instruments, but there was no making him budge. Even today, I'm not that keen on wine, but I do know about it. As you will see!"

She was taking her revenge on me for her oenological childhood.

"Is that all you can tell me about this Chablis, Benjamin? Nothing about its body, its delicacy, its colour, its limpidity? OK, let's get things straight. What does it *taste* of? I'm waiting . . . What have you got in your mouth?"

"A taste of grass, maybe . . . something green?"

"Not bad. Stone and cut straw, in fact. Chardonnay grapes. A 1976 *Montée du Tonnerre*. A *premier cru*. Remember that! *Nineteen seventy-six*! Make a note. On the way back, I'll test you."

The truck headed off again. Julie drove unflinchingly past an ambush of gendarmes, despite the fact that, what with the little Burgundy sparkling wine, the Vézelay *côteaux rares*, plus the Sauvignons of Saint-Bris and the Chablis with its green glints, our bloodstreams were becoming encyclopedic. If one of those boys in blue had asked us to blow in the bag, we'd have finished our journey in a hot-air balloon. So far as I was concerned, this haze of tipsiness suited me fine. It was practically the first time I'd left Paris, and I'd started to get homesick as soon as the key was in the ignition. I had to ward it off. So I settled down into the warmth of wine, vapours and Julie's voice. It was an internal journey.

Once we'd passed Dijon, Julie avoided the Côtes-de-Beaune and all the Côtes-de-Nuits. The truck crossed the Saône and headed for the Jura. If the map was accurate, this was not the most direct route.

"My father the Governor always went this way. Which means I've never drunk any Beaujolais and not a drop of Bordeaux."

She laughed.

"But you'll see, Jura wines are something else!"

*

She spoke about her father. She spoke about her childhood. She spoke about Old Job. She spoke on and on as she drove. She spoke just a decibel louder than the engine. She kept on speaking. About Old Job, about the Vercors and the Loscence valley, the caves, Barnaby, Liesl and Job again, about plonk and the movies, as the truck purred onwards . . .

You never know how grief is going to unravel. Normally, when she was down, she shrank into silence, and now here she was doing the talking for both of us. As if she was telling stories. With a title for each one. Often taken from one of my questions. Take this one for example:

"How did Job first get into the cinema?"

Job and the Cinematograph

"Because of his father. When he was five, his dad took him along to a special showing. In the Hofburg Palace in Vienna, in the presence of the Emperor Franz Josef in person. Almost a century later, Job can still remember it all perfectly. As you'll see, if you ask him to tell the tale. He loves that."

And she loved the story, too.

She told it.

"Emperor Franz Josef didn't believe in the movies. He was also against electricity, typewriters, telephones, cars and railways. Like his grandfather, Franz, he suspected the railways of propagating revolutionary ideas more rapidly. He was still going to the toilet with a candle in his hand when the entirety of Vienna was producing light and dark by pressing on a switch! Emperor Franz Josef was a stubborn, yet conscientious monarch. He always weighed up the pros and cons of any progress. When the scales tipped to the pros side, he sat down firmly on the side of the cons. So he summoned all the industrious industrialists Vienna had to offer so they might opine (as Job puts it) about the Lumière brothers' invention – the cinematograph. Old Job's parents had been invited. And they took along their little boy. There were three films on the programme: *Employees Leaving the Lumière Factory*, *Queen Victoria's Jubilee* and *Arrival of the Train at La Ciotat*."

Julie was telling me what Old Job had told her.

As for me, I was listening to Julie and I was at the movies. I could clearly see the magic ray of light across the ageless darkness of the Hofburg as it passed above those aristocratic heads and slapped reality on to the wall in front of them: *Employees Leaving the Lumière Factory*. An invasion of proles! Women in bell-skirts and men in shirt sleeves and straw hats. Just as though they were walking through the wall.

"As an added dramatic effect," Julie said, "the projector jammed just before the janitor closes the factory gates."

And all of the Lumières' employees were suddenly frozen there, like motionless spectators! How scandalous! Not only had all this scum turned up with their hats on and wheeling their bikes to gatecrash this party, they were now behaving as if the showing had been organised for them, and the subject of the Lumière brothers' film had been: *The Habsburg Royal Family, with Their Relatives and Hangers-on, Caught Staring into Space*. Did what happened next start because of the spectators' anger? First, there was a little glow in the middle of the screen, then a scattering of iridescent swellings, gobbling up the workmen and women, and they finally found themselves back in their own company, in a ghastly stench reminiscent of burnt flesh. The projectionist stammered out his apologies. A second projector then showed *Queen Victoria's Jubilee*. This time the nobility was astonished to find itself on and off the screen at the same time. They all had fun trying to spot one another in the crowd paying homage to their gouty cousin. And when they discovered themselves, they pinched themselves and checked their pulses to make sure that it was only their images bowing and curtsying in the depths of the screen. After that, a locomotive smashed through the wall of the Hofburg, knocking over several members of the audience. It was Louis Lumière's *Arrival of the Train at La Ciotat*. (That evening little Job discovered he had eyes to see.) Once it had stopped, the train's wooden side opened to receive a couple of country bumpkins – peasants to top it all! – with the young girl clearly looking extremely intimidated about having attracted so much aristocratic attention. So much so, that she hesitated for a moment on the step of her carriage, as though wondering whether she'd picked the wrong class.

"It's hard to explain, Juliette," Old Job would say. "But it never occurred to a single one of the spectators at the Hofburg that the girl was in fact intimidated by *the presence of the camera.*"

"You mean . . . they thought *she could see them*?"

"No, of course not, no more than they really thought they were being invaded by the Lumières' workforce, or gifted with ubiquity at the Queen's jubilee. But . . . how can I put it? They had an *aristocratic eye*, see what I mean? They were used to seeing the world as a picture book and now they were being shown *the real world*. Can you understand that, Juliette? Make my day and tell me you can understand."

She nodded. Old Job's voice sounded like a movie projector. She liked the way it crackled.

"Their eyes were now powerless to change what they saw. I was only young, but I was watching them closely, you know. It was all going on in front of them, with nothing they could do about it, just like many things to come of which they were still unaware. And yet they maintained their aristocratic stares. It was highly entertaining . . . highly entertaining . . ."

"And what did the industrialists think?" Julie asked.

"About the cinematograph? They all thought it was a dead loss. 'You can't industrialise magic lanterns.' A real chorus of cretins. When they finally woke up in 1908, it was too late. Since then, my father's factories had reeled out so many miles of celluloid that the earth looked like a bug's eye spinning in the cosmos."

The inn was every inch an inn, the bedroom panelled with undressed timber and the bed covered with a granny's eiderdown, the open window looking out over the purple flank of a mountain, with the white truck in the stable with its ration of oats, and Julie and I leaning over some amber wine.

"Savagnin, Benjamin, is the name of the grape. Remember?"

"Savagnin."

"Exactly. A wine of legend, called *vin de voile*. It's the crown prince of the Jura wines. The grapes are harvested late, then the wine's put in seasoned oak casks where it stays for at least six years, until a veil of yeast forms on the surface. Hence its name. And its amber colour. It's also called *vin jaune*."

"*Vin jaune* . . ."

The names of wines, towns and grapes buzzed around my head. Tastings in Salin-les-Bains, in Poligny, in Château-Chalon, in L'Étoile, in Lons-le-Saunier, in Saint-Amour, the sharp purple juice of the *trousseau*, the delicate pink of the *poulsard* and now the savagnin with its marvellous *vin jaune*, "the crown prince of the Jura wines".

"A marriage of green walnuts, grilled almonds, hazelnuts . . ."

(Green walnuts, grilled almonds, hazelnuts . . .)

"Not to be confused with *vin de paille*, Benjamin, a famous and extremely rare wine . . . but we'll see about that tomorrow . . ."

(That's right . . . tomorrow . . . tomorrow . . .)

There was a little black box on the bedside table. When we got into bed, Julie picked it up and pointed it like a gun in front of us. Immediately, a plastic cube facing the bed lit up. It was called a television. A window on to the world, apparently . . . Fat chance. When this window opened, it looked straight out at ourselves. Or, to be more precise, at a map of Belleville. A map tattooed on to a man's skin. The commentator's voice was saying:

"*The Christos of this world wrap things up, while the Barnabooths make them disappear. Both possess an aesthetic of oblivion in this now valueless society, but there are also anonymous people out there struggling to remember, so much so that they have their memories engraved on to their flesh . . . Monsieur Beaujeu, the Belleville locksmith, was one such . . . in his neighbourhood, he was known as Cissou . . .*"

The commentator's voice guided the camera along the Rue du Transvaal on Cissou's chest towards the intersection of Rue Piat and Rue des Envierges, and those heights which give such a breathtaking view of the destruction of Belleville. And I suddenly felt the chill of the photo which had been torn from Clément's hands, the chill of a corpse, the chill of Cissou's absence and, in the warmth of our shared bed, I realised that by losing Cissou, we'd lost yet another reason to keep going; that, after Uncle Stojil and Old Thian, Cissou had struck camp too, Cissou, for whom I had not wept at the time, had torn out another one of my ties to the world, because it wasn't a friend I'd lost, it was the best part of myself, as is always the case when a friend departs, an anchor had been ripped out of the midst of my being, with a bloody lump of my heart stuck on the raised anchor, and now it wasn't just the wine which was spilling out from my eyes, but the tears of my tears, that bottomless vat of suffering, the eternally fertile vine of pain, so thoroughly rooted in the earth of our grief.

I sobbed my eyes out in Julie's arms, then Julie started as well, we emptied ourselves out until we passed out into what is called sleep, a respite from what you wake up again to find, a lost child, one friend fewer, another war, and the distance left to be covered despite it all, because apparently we too are reasons to keep going, so you mustn't add another departure to a departure, suicide is fatal to the survivors, you have to hang on, hang on whatever happens, hang on by your nails, hang on by your teeth.

Chapter 30

"MONSIEUR BEAUJEU'S FAMILY *is invited to come forward. The body will be kept at their disposal for one week.*"

Then there followed the address of the morgue and the phone number.

Chief Superintendent Coudrier turned off the television.

Inspector Titus said:

"There we are. We've made a press announcement and it will be on the news on all the TV channels till tomorrow evening. It's Silistri's plan."

Postel-Wagner, the forensic surgeon, looked up with genuine astonishment.

"A plan?"

"Old Beaujeu didn't have any family," Inspector Silistri explained. "We checked, right down to his roots in the Auvergne. Not a soul left. There's only one person in the world who would want his body now. Someone who loves tattoos, if you see what I mean. A sort of surgeon . . ."

The three men were bathed in a stench of formalin and cold pipe tobacco. Their voices echoed off the white tiled walls of the morgue. The forensic surgeon spoke cautiously. Almost the way you might talk to kids about to light the fuse on a stick of dynamite.

"And you *really* think it will work?"

Titus and Silistri gazed at each other wearily.

"It's a working hypothesis, doctor," Chief Superintendent Coudrier intervened. "A diagnosis."

Postel-Wagner's eyes twinkled.

"If diagnoses were infallible, Chief Superintendent, our morgues wouldn't be so full."

"And forensic surgeons would come to their conclusions more quickly," Titus remarked.

Postel-Wagner paused to fill the massive head of his meerschaum pipe. A match set it blazing. The three men vanished from sight. All that remained was the doctor's voice:

"The dead deserve our patience, Inspector. Their bodies contain all sorts of interesting things. There is more to life than police inquiries. There are also organic inquiries."

When he'd flapped his arms to chase away the smoke, Doctor Postel-Wagner grimly discovered that the others were still there.

"So," he said, "if I understand you correctly, Beaujeu's body is to be the carrot, with me dangling it in the air. Is that it?"

Chief Superintendent Coudrier cleared his throat.

"That's one way of putting it."

"Then I refuse."

Silence. Smoke.

"Listen, Wagner . . ." Titus began.

"Call me 'doctor'. It's not because I'm a stickler for titles, just that I'm not sure we'll ever be friends."

This was said with such candour that it shut Titus up. The doctor's tone was merry and slightly nasal.

"I'm refusing for several reasons," he explained. "Firstly because, thanks to all this media hype, tomorrow we'll have a crowd of curious people, who have nothing to do with the killer, queuing up to see Cissou the Snow's tattoos."

The argument hung in the air for several seconds.

"We'll do the sorting," Inspector Titus said. "And then kick the nutters out on their arses."

"A morgue isn't a sorting office," the forensic surgeon remarked. Then added softly: "And then I don't see why you should call tattoo lovers nutters. There's nothing wrong with them, so far as I know."

(I see, got a tattooed butt, Titus thought.)

"And I have no tattoos," the doctor murmured, drawing on his pipe.

Chief Superintendent Coudrier got the discussion moving again.

"What are your other reasons for refusing?"

"The danger, for one thing. I don't work alone. And if I can believe the case report, this character will stop at nothing. One of the girls was kidnapped in broad daylight, right in front of her family and her husband was gunned down. I can't allow my staff to be put at risk like that."

"There'll be so many coppers in this morgue that he won't be able to pull off any of his stunts," Inspector Silistri objected.

"He's already given you the slip once, even though you had all of your men on the case. He cut up that girl practically before your very eyes."

True.

True.

True.

Silistri tried wheedling.

"Doctor, we've got to get this character. We want him as a present for Gervaise when she wakes up."

The forensic surgeon smiled sweetly.

"All of us would like to do something for Gervaise, Inspector. You don't have a monopoly on devotion. I've known her far longer than you have. She studied law with my wife. Sister Gervaise is an old friend. I'm the oldest of her Templars."

(He's starting to get on my tits, Inspector Titus thought.)

"And I'm not sure if Gervaise would approve of your methods," the doctor added.

"Oh really? Why not?"

Titus and Silistri were startled.

"The repose of the dead, for example. The dead really need a good long rest."

(Exactly what Malaussène said about Krämer, Chief Superintendent Coudrier thought.)

Coudrier sometimes wondered why he liked Doctor Postel-Wagner and had such exasperating esteem for him. And he had just found the answer. Postel-Wagner was a touch Malaussènian. In fact, his job as a corpse opener, about which he spoke with such tenderness, was no less incongruous than the goat horns on Malaussène's head.

(I must ask him one day why he chose forensic science, the Chief Superintendent said to himself.)

But then the imminence of his retirement flashed into his mind.

(I won't have time, he thought. Tomorrow afternoon, it's all over.)

The Chief Superintendent's tone hardened:

"Sorry, doctor, but you have no choice."

He raised a hand to sweep away any objections and pointed at the television.

"As of now, even if we left with Monsieur Beaujeu's body, chummy will think it's here and come looking for it. If I were you, I wouldn't risk him paying you a visit without police protection."

"Or without Cissou's body," Titus added.

"Blokes like that tend to get stroppy when they don't find what they're looking for," Silistri explained.

"You wouldn't want that to happen . . ." said Titus.

Postel-Wagner lit another match. The three officers vanished once more.

"Spare me your nice-and-nasty routine, gentlemen . . ."

Then, to Chief Superintendent Coudrier:

"I repeat, I will not have any member of my staff being put in danger."

The Chief Superintendent frowned:

"Very well. Then tell them all to stay home until the operation is over."

"That's easier said than done. We're up to our eyeballs in work."

The emperor suddenly felt weary.

"Don't set me any insoluble problems, doctor."

"Forensic surgery solves insoluble problems, Chief Superintendent. Problems which are dead and gone."

(Malaussène, the Chief Superintendent thought. That exasperating habit of going proverbial.)

"Well, doctor?"

Postel-Wagner stretched out his tall, slightly stooping frame, knocked his pipe against the palm of his hand over the zinc jar he used as an ashtray, then proposed a solution:

"I usually work with a male nurse and two student doctors. I think it's important not to change staffing levels. Our visitor might be put on his guard if there's a crowd. So all I need are three men in white coats to replace my normal team. One in the role of the nurse, who will stay at the door to keep out the curious, and another two as my students, who will work alongside me as usual in the operating theatre."

"OK, doctor. Then the rest of our men will be hiding outside."

Doctor Postel-Wagner smiled pleasantly at Inspectors Titus and Silistri.

"You'll see, it isn't very difficult. You'll just have to help me cut up the corpses."

Something froze in the two officers' blood.

"And then you'll have to put the innards back where they came from after analysis. We'll start this very evening. I'm running late as it is."

Titus and Silistri tried in vain to make eye contact with their superior.

"Very well," Chief Superintendent Coudrier said. "Now that we've reached an agreement . . ."

Then he slipped his heavy coat over his shoulders, which gave him that lonely look of an emperor out campaigning. He held out his chubby hand to the doctor.

"You'll see. It will work perfectly."

"One chance in ten," the forensic surgeon estimated.

"I think you are being pessimistic."

Postel-Wagner's smile was appeasing.

"Let's just say that I'm a well-informed optimist."

He pointed round at the metal drawers in the walls of his lab, containing the waiting bodies.

"I live in the midst of my informers."

(Malaussèneries, Chief Superintendent Coudrier thought, on his way out.)

Postel-Wagner held him back.

"No, go out the back way. If 'chummy's' already heard the news, then he'll probably be watching the place. Follow me."

For the second time in their lives, Inspectors Titus and Silistri had lost their mother.

When he got back, Doctor Postel-Wagner gave them a smile of condolence.

"You were right," he said. "We owe this to Gervaise."

Chapter 31

"MMMM!" JULIE SAID as she stretched. "Didn't we have a good cry last night!"

She smiled at me. A beam of postcard mountain sunshine was licking the counterpane on our bed like a stroke of watercolour.

"I hadn't done that for ages," she added.

She tried to remember.

"Not since . . . No, I'd rather not remember the last time."

She ran her finger over the scarred border of my skull.

"We cried like pissheads for Cissou's health," I said.

"We cried for everything which deserves our tears."

"And cried ourselves dry. That's *vin jaune* for you!"

"No, that's the TV for you," she corrected me.

*

Thirty kilometres farther on, it was my turn to say:

"Tell me the truth, Julie."

Yup, we'd now been dwelling on the essentials for the past two days.

"You're taking us up into the mountains so we can nab Matthias, aren't you?"

She answered at once:

"Matthias can't possibly have done that."

It rang out like a certitude. But she nevertheless added:

"Of course, if we find him at Old Job's place, we'll ask him what happened."

"If Matthias was at Old Job's place," I said, "the cops would already have nicked him. The Fraenkhels must be as famous as wolves in the Vercors."

"They're completely unknown under that name," she replied. "Old Job is a Bernardin. That's their name. The Loscence Bernardins."

"They're not called Fraenkhel?"

"Bernardin."

The engine purred on for some time in our silence.

"Only Matthias is called Fraenkhel."

She concluded:

"And it's for that reason he can't possibly have done what he's been accused of doing."

Matthias Fraenkhel or Everyman's Honour

The story was simple, and had taken place over fifty years back. The story of a basic choice.

"In 1939, Matthias married Sarah Fraenkhel, who'd recently emigrated from Cracow, and who was to be Barnaby's mother. When the first anti-Jewish laws were passed in 1940, he hid her in his house in Loscence. After that, he went back to Paris, called in at the town hall of the seventh *arrondissement*, where his birth had been registered, and changed his name."

"Changed his name?"

"Instead of Bernardin, he became Fraenkhel. He quite simply did what the other forty-five million citizens ought to have done."

O Matthias . . . Matthias or everyman's honour.

"What about Sarah? What was she like?"

"Come back to earth, Benjamin. Don't think for a minute that Matthias did that out of love. Not entirely, in any case. If he hadn't met Sarah, if he'd been single or married to a gentile, then he'd have called himself Cohen or Israel or something like that . . . Pacific resistance is Matthias's style. Pacific and silent. You know what he's like. Certainly no evangelist."

"And they let him?"

"He had to bribe the clerk in the registry office, who must have been delighted to get a bit of baksheesh from what was obviously a suicidal idealist . . ."

"And Matthias was able to continue practising?"

"His waiting room was already packed with upper-class ladies. He was France's youngest obstetrician. They adored giving birth in the hands of an angel. High-society people mistake principles for whims. And so they forgave him. He was so fashionable that women went on bearing children in Doctor Fraenkhel's surgery, even though there was *Fraenkhel* engraved on the brass plate on the door. Pretty Aryans with round bellies pushed and pushed, while carefully avoiding having to pronounce his name."

Julie kept to her route and her story.

"Then things got worse in spring 1944, when they all went crazy. They gave him a choice: him or Sarah. When he came back from Auschwitz, he'd lost half his weight. And had a number, tattooed on his forearm."

"What about Sarah?"

"I never met her. Apart from all this history, they were just a normal couple, you know. They got divorced at the end of the 1950s, just after Barnaby was born."

*

The next wine was rare and famous. We drank it over the valley of Arbois which was redolent with calm. It was the prestigious *vin de paille*.

"Well, Malaussène?"

She'd told me the whole business before filling my glass. About the carefully selected grapes being laid to dry on beds of straw for two or three months. The fruit then mummifies and the sugar becomes concentrated. You let the must ferment for one or two years, then the wine ages in its cask for another four years.

"So?"

So, it wasn't bad.

But I was supposed to say more about its not-badness.

"It's a white wine, sweet of course, very fine . . ."

Julie smiled.

"Very fine indeed, Benjamin . . . As they say in these parts: *The more you drink, the straighter you go!*"

*

The white truck drove straight on to the next vintage.

Julie was speaking less.

This made me suppose that she was thinking more.

And that isn't good for troop morale.

I let our conversations of yesterday kindle today's spark.

"So what were the Bernardins doing in Austria at the turn of the century?"

"They are the descendants of Octave Bernardin, who deserted from our imperial army. A sub Bernadotte, who betrayed Bonaparte. He settled in Vienna and made his fortune under the Restoration."

Silence.

Don't let certain silences take root.

"So, what effect did that film show in the Hofburg have on little Job?"

The Oracle of the Central Café

After the evening at the Hofburg, some public showings were allowed in Vienna, but little Job refused to attend. This was the start of his principle of never seeing a film twice.

"An event cannot be repeated. Any film worth its salt should be seen only once, Juliette. What gives it life is the memory it leaves you with."

Instead of going to the showings in Vienna, little Job preferred to go and drink hot chocolate at the Central Café. His German nanny dropped him off there every day at four o'clock then picked him up again at six. (A secret agreement between them, which Job's father discovered one day and, in exchange, demanded two hours of German nannying.) The Central Café buzzed with intelligence, and little Job was one of its attractions. He moved around the tables, pontificating like an adult. Every time his head popped up from the cigar and pipe smoke, someone would ask him a question of topical import.

"So, Jobchen, what's your opinion of the cinematograph?"

"What opinion do you expect me to have of an invention? We shall have to wait and see."

The idea the Viennese youth had got into its head was that if nature had provided mankind with eyes, the cinematograph had given us *our vision*.

"We'll have to see how this vision is used."

"As a celebration of movement, Jobchen! The cinematograph is a celebration of movement! Of life itself!"

"Movement? Stuff and nonsense!" little Job exclaimed. (Stuff and nonsense was his father's favourite expression, and he adored it.) "Triple stuff and triple nonsense! In this case, movement is merely an expression of duration. Movement is simply the means to an end, a simple tool! With their cinematograph, the Lumière brothers have given us far more than just movement. They have allowed us to *seize the passage of time*."

"Really? How's that, Jobchen?"

They picked him up. He was whisked up into the air and placed on the bar. This was usually how his German nanny found him, standing on the counter.

"So, Jobchen, what's all this about time?"

Like a true tribune, little Job raised his hands for silence.

"You've all seen the employees coming out of the Lumières' factory, you've seen them coming towards you and you've clapped your hands and yelled: 'They're moving! They're moving!' So employees move, do they? What a discovery! Did we have to wait for the invention of the cinematograph to find out that employees move? That bicycle wheels rotate? That gates open and close? That trains arrive in stations? That aristocrats bow? That ageing queens move more slowly than young ones? Is that really all you saw?"

The discussion was now so passionate that nobody in the Central Café budged an inch. Then a female voice was heard:

"What about you, then, Jobchen? What did you see?"

Job looked round for the woman. She was smoking a long pipe and had a little girl on her lap. Beneath her mother's amused smile, she was directing a sky-blue stare at Job, in which could be read a promise of eternity.

"Between the instant the gates opened", he replied, staring back at the little girl, "and the moment the projector jammed, thirty-seven seconds went by . . . thirty-seven seconds," he repeated, pretending to count them on his fingers so that she could understand.

A sudden wave of emotion made him stop. His eyes clouded over. He concluded, almost in a murmur:

"The cinematograph gave me thirty-seven seconds of the lives of those men and women. Of each of those men . . . and of each of those women . . . thirty-seven seconds of their existences. I'll never forget that."

Then, his eyes now fixed on the little girl.

"We'll never forget that."

*

"And the little girl was Liesl?"

"However did you guess, Benjamin? You're really quick off the mark!"

Once she'd stopped taking the piss, she opened a bottle of roussette. Down in the distance, the white sunlight was making the lake of Annecy gleam like zinc. Quite a bar counter! With a great collection of glasses awaiting us.

"After this Savoy roussette, I'll get you to taste some Abymes, a slightly sparkling wine, which is quite splendid. Then we'll hit some red mondeuse. Great name, isn't it? You'll see, it's a grape which gives a strong, highly coloured red wine . . ."

Chapter 32

"TRY NOT TO breathe too much, it will only take me a second. Hold the dish straight, Monsieur Silistri. And I can do without your comments, Monsieur Titus. Show some respect. After all, this was a senator."

The senator in question had let himself be sliced open from the lower jaw to the pubis without making the slightest objection. Silistri had then inherited a huge, granular liver, which was as hard as wood and pinkish with white spots. This masterpiece of cirrhosis emerged from the senator with a ghastly noise of suction. Then the statesman had given up his spleen, his kidneys and his pancreas. Silistri passed them on to Titus, who neatly arranged them in little zinc dishes for later examination. The senator let them get on with it. He was giving off a faint odour, with the suggestion of some other fragrance.

"Can you smell anything?" Postel-Wagner asked.

Titus and Silistri forced themselves to sample the air.

"An old cask, maybe," Inspector Titus hazarded. "Made of oak, I'd say. The sort of cask which produces livers like this."

"You have a good nose. But there's something else. A scent which accompanies the visceral rosé wine."

The senator was duly sniffed.

"Green almonds, wouldn't you say? Remember the apricot jams of your childhood?"

Silistri's mother never made jam.

"Cyanide," Postel-Wagner concluded with a nod. "I've got some bad news for you, senator. Someone cut your djinn."

The forensic surgeon was lecturing the corpse.

"Someone was after your money. Or a seat as President of the Council. The family and politics are two common causes of death, just like cirrhosis . . ."

Between two sheets of glass, under the microscope, the senator concurred. A dialogue had at last begun.

"I quite agree, senator. A botched job. A rudimentary poisoning. Either you were in somebody's way, or you had been a burden for your kith and kin for too long. Hence the rush. They were counting on your cirrhosis to get permission to bury you. What's more natural than dying in public, over dinner, with a glass in your hand, when you've got a liver like yours?"

Postel-Wagner glanced at the file.

"Yes . . . yes I see . . . but that was counting without the fact that another guest at the party was Doctor . . ."

He turned the page.

"Doctor . . . Fustec! An excellent diagnosis, my dear chap! Bravo!"

Without turning round, he called out:

"Inspector Titus? Would you mind taking down a letter of congratulations for my colleague, Doctor Fustec?"

He looked back down his microscope.

"Meanwhile, Monsieur Silistri can give the senator his organs back. He's told us what we wanted to know."

As nothing seemed to be moving behind him, the doctor turned round.

"Anything wrong?"

The two Inspectors, standing beside the gaping senator, had seen better days. Titus tried courageously to brighten up the situation.

"In our future, I can't see roses . . ."

Silistri was in no shape to chip in.

"We'll get back at you for this, Postel. At the next opportunity, I'm going to strap you down in a chair and show you some videos which will make you wish you'd never been born. You may autopsy bodies, but we autopsy souls. And let me tell you, cirrhosis of the soul is something else . . ."

The forensic surgeon cut short this diatribe by removing his white coat and handing the Inspector a leather-clad flask which had been plumping up his right buttock.

"Have a drink and calm down. It's over."

The smell of the whiskey mixed with the stench of the irrevocable.

Silistri didn't budge. He was keeping his breakfast balanced in his throat.

"No? You're wrong. This is a lovely drop. My wife's Irish, you know."

The forensic surgeon emptied half the flask, handed the rest to Titus and opened the door of the operating theatre, which led into the main corridor.

A child was waiting there, sitting on a wooden bench.

"Who on earth are you?" Postel-Wagner asked in sudden delight.

"Thomas. Me finger 'urts," the child added without transition.

"Thomas Mefingerurts?"

On guard duty by the main entrance, Inspector Caregga glanced up from his rosary, then nodded towards the kid.

"He says his grandmother knows you."

"His grandmother?"

"Madame Bougenot."

"Oh, Madame Bougenot! Of course! How's her hip?"

"All right, doctor. She told me to come here. Me finger 'urts."

Two seconds later, the forensic surgeon's merry face appeared through the door.

"Tidy the senator away, gentlemen. We're now going to deal with the quick. An exceptional whitlow!"

Without a word of protest, the senator returned to his chill limbo. Titus and Silistri were getting the hang of it. This was the third time that morning they had switched between the dead and the living.

*

"Say what you like," Titus observed, "but a morgue with a waiting room is distinctly off-putting."

The three men were laying the table for lunch in the doctor's office.

"There's more to life than the dead."

Postel-Wagner laid the places in the French fashion – forks to the left, prongs downwards.

"True, but that doesn't make our life any easier," Silistri moaned.

The knives now took up the opposite positions, cutting edges inwards.

"The agreement was that we'd follow my usual routine to the letter," Postel-Wagner reminded them. "And the entire neighbourhood knows that I give free consultations and have lunch in my office."

He handed a bottle and corkscrew to Silistri.

"Mind you, my patients do not abuse my generosity. All I get are emergencies."

"That kid's whitlow was an emergency?'

"There's a boy the same age in drawer B6. Septicaemia. A whitlow when treated badly can be fatal. We even suspect the mother of letting the pus build up."

Then, without transition:

"Don't shake that bottle up, Monsieur Silistri. It's a Baron Pichon Longueville '75. That may not mean much to you, but our senator's liver had been marinating in it for years."

Before Silistri could respond, the door opened to reveal Inspector Caregga, who was carrying the tray which had been ordered from the next-door restaurant just the same as every day.

*

Following the forensic surgeon's routine, they then had a forty-five-minute rest break, which they used to analyse the present situation. There had been far fewer nosy parkers than Postel-Wagner had feared – just half a dozen of them. And Inspector Caregga's build had dissuaded them from playing at mourning families. Cissou the Snow slept in peace. So the question now was: who was going to come, and when?

"If anyone does."

Postel-Wagner was peacefully smoking his pipe and opening his mail.

"The surgeon will come," Titus insisted.

"He needs time to get himself a fake ID card," Silistri added.

"All the same, it's a big risk," Postel-Wagner objected.

"And pots of money in perspective," Titus explained.

"Just put yourself in the collector's shoes," Silistri suggested. "You know, the one who pays the surgeon. For the last two days, he's been drooling over old Beaujeu's Belleville as seen on TV. It's an absolute masterpiece in the world of tattoos. Something like a live version of an ancient city map."

"Live?"

"Manner of speaking . . . Our collector has had girls cut up for much less than this . . . And the surgeon's taken incredible risks . . . And here we are offering them the corpse . . . A fresh corpse to be picked clean in the morgue."

"A piece of cake, compared to what they've done so far."

"If the collector doesn't get the idea, the surgeon will. He'll offer to procure it."

The two Inspectors carried on with their ping-pong. At each exchange, they became more convincing.

"What if they smell a rat?" Postel-Wagner asked. "After all, you've already tried baiting the hook with Mondine."

"They'll start by asking round Belleville, where they'll discover that old Beaujeu is really dead. And at the address in the report. And with no family. They'll check out all of the information given by the TV and the press. And find that it's all true. They've no reason to suspect anything."

"Unless it's their suspicious natures . . ."

For the first time, Silistri smiled at Postel-Wagner.

"All the more reason, Postel."

(Intimacy, the forensic surgeon thought. Whether I want it or not, intimacy is creeping in.)

Silistri leant over him.

"With people like our surgeon, suspicion is a driving force. In cases where we would give up, it gets them going. A taste for risk and an obsession with precautions is a cocktail this sort of bastard can never resist."

"So why are we taking so many precautions, then?" Postel-Wagner said snidely.

"Because if the surgeon saw an entire squad of coppers in front of the morgue, then he would give up despite everything. He isn't crazy."

"He isn't?"

"He's weird, doctor. But he isn't crazy."

Silistri's gaze grew more distant. As for Titus, he sat down by the window, where he started telling his beads. Postel-Wagner withdrew into his post. Thus do conversations die.

A magazine slipped out of a slit envelope. Postel-Wagner picked it up. It was *Affection*, the pseudo-scientific weekly.

There was a huge headline – THE MAN-EATING BACTERIUM – followed by an article about necrotising fasciitis, an unpleasant streptococcus which occasionally devours an entire body in a few hours, but which is extremely rare and has been more or less under control since the nineteenth century. However, the article, written by the editor Sainclair in person, presented it as the latest example of divine wrath, predicting a worldwide epidemic, with gory details, shock-horror adjectives and juicy examples – the nocturnal decomposition of a man in bed with his wife, of a baby in its cot, and so on. Utter terror.

Postel-Wagner turned the page: CELEBS' OBSTETRICIAN GOES MAD. A photo of Fraenkhel. An article written in a spirit of hysterical revenge for the loss of medical honour. Postel-Wagner shook his head. Matthias Fraenkhel had been one of his teachers.

"This *Affection* is a pure infection."

Binned.

And yet, there was no room for doubt. Postel-Wagner had personally carried out post-mortems in two out of the eleven cases of unnecessary abortions. And the conclusions he'd sent to Coudrier were adamant: the foetuses had been perfectly viable.

The pipe the forensic surgeon rekindled was a thoughtful one.

From far off, Titus asked:

"What sort of killer weed do you put in your pipe?"

Postel-Wagner cleared away the cloud.

"And what sort of prayers are inspired by your rosary?"

A revolver leapt into the Inspector's hand.

"For the forgiveness of sins."

At that moment, the phone rang.

Postel-Wagner answered, listened, nodded twice then hung up.

"It was Chief Superintendent Coudrier. Someone's been going round Belleville asking questions about Cissou the Snow. He says he's his nephew. It sounds like you'll soon have a few sins to forgive, Titus."

Chapter 33

"So," I said, "if my calculations are correct, Liesl and Old Job were together for over eighty years, is that right?"

"Eighty-seven, to be precise. After their encounter at the Central Café, they were never apart."

We'd emptied the lake of Annecy in our wine glasses. The white truck was now swaying towards Grenoble.

"Quite a love story!" I said.

The white truck twitched nervously.

"Love, love and more love! You're starting to get seriously on my tits with all your crap about love, Benjamin."

(Oh dear . . . we're in a mood.)

Her hands clenched round the wheel, her eyes fixed on the horizon, Julie was now driving like a thing possessed.

"You almost make me want to go out and start shagging around again."

Foot down. The white beast leapt forwards. I clutched on to the door handle and to the subject of our conversation.

"So, eighty-seven years of loveless life together, is that it?"

Screaming round bends.

"The world according to Malaussène: with love, or without! No choice! Love's an obligation! You just must be happy! Guaranteed bliss! The soul mate! A universe of people staring into each other's starry eyes and muttering: I love you, you love me, what are we going to do with all this love? It's enough to make you puke. To make you want to become a widow-maker!"

"A widow-maker?"

"That's right! A maker of widows! People who liberate us from all this love! Who give us the chance to live life as it is: unlovable!"

I looked at the sky. Not a single cloud. A blue fury.

"Where did you catch this religion of love, Benjamin? Where did this lovey-dovey claptrap come from? Hearts stinking of bouquets of flowers? You call that love? At best, it's just an appetite . . . and at worse, it's a habit! Whichever way, it's just play-acting! From the come-on of seduction to the lies in a break-up, passing by unspoken regrets and unutterable remorse, it's all just an act! Cowardice, confidence tricks and deceit, that's love for you! A way to cook our own books! To lay the daily table! So go and fuck yourself with your love, Malaussène! Open your eyes! Look out the window! Buy a TV! Read the papers! Learn statistics! Go into politics! Get a job! Then you can come back and tell us about love!"

I listened. I listened. The sky was blue. The engine had bolted. I was miles from Paris. On a trip. Imprisoned by the outside world. No ejector seat.

Then she started muttering in Spanish:

"*No se puede vivir sin amar . . .*"

She sneered. She slapped the steering wheel with her open palms. Foot right down, she yelled:

"*No se puede vivir sin amar! Ah! Ah!*"

A war cry.

The truck swerved to the right, and bounded up on to a hump of brown earth. Dust. Handbrake. Windscreen. Stillness. One wheel's turn from the brink. Gasping for breath. She opened the door. She jumped out. She stood out against the rocky valley. She kicked a stone. Silence fell, fell.

Fell.

She crouched over the void.

Eternity.

She stood up.

The sky on her shoulders. Arms down her sides. Eyes staring at her feet.

She got her breath back.

She turned round.

She got back on to her seat.

She said:

"Sorry."

She added:

"It's nothing."

She didn't look at me, didn't touch me.

Ignition.

"It's over."

She repeated:

"I'm sorry."

Reverse.

The white truck set off again.

She told me the story of Liesl and Job.

Liesl first. Liesl's childhood.

Liesl in a World of Sounds

1) *Notes*: When Herma, Liesl's mother, used to play the piano, the child's tiny fingers would flutter around as though hovering to gather nectar. When asked what on earth she was doing, Liesl replied:

"I'm catching the notes."

2) *Words*: For her, words were like notes: butterflies pinned on the spreading board of her memory: firstly "Herma" and "Stefan", her parents' names. Liesl didn't go in for "mummy" and "daddy", she *named* them straight away, with her brows creased, as though checking out a memory.

Herma found this funny.

"Look, she's trying to remember where she met us."

Her first words had nothing to do with childhood: *Österreich, Zollverein, Neue Freie Presse, Die Fackel, Darstellung, Gesamtkunstwerk* . . . they fluttered out of adult conversations to nestle among the names of those who had uttered them: Schnitzler, Loos, Kokoschka, Schönberg, Karl Kraus.

"Ethics and aesthetics are one and the same!" Uncle Kraus exclaimed, while damning Reinhardt's theatrical productions.

"*Ethics and aesthetics are one and the same,*" Liesl repeated, pushing away her untouched plate.

"You're not going to tell me that she understands what she's just said!"

"Aren't I?" Karl Kraus replied ironically. "Just look at her plate! My niece knows exactly what she is saying."

3) *Sounds*: The first noise Liesl absorbed was the clock above her crib. With its ticks and tocks . . . A Junghans clock which she hung on to for the rest of her life.

"Listen to the clock," she said to Julie. "Listen to it with all of your being. Each 'tick' is different, and each 'tock'. I can clearly remember each and every one of them."

*

"Do you reckon that's possible?"

The white truck had returned to its rhythm of long-distance narrative.

"What?"

"Those ticks and tocks. Do you reckon she could really remember them all?"

Julie looked round at me. She just couldn't believe I was asking that.

"You're a child, Benjamin. Remind me to give you a mythology lesson."

For some time, there was the silence of the road. Then Julie asked:

"Do you know what her last words were?"

"Her last words?"

"Liesl's last words. On the tape recorder."

"The last words to be recorded before she died?"

"*Lasset mich in meinem Gedächtnis begraben.*"

"Which means?"

"*May I be buried in my memory.*"

Liesl's Memory

After meeting little Job at the Central Café, Liesl phoned him up several times a day. Liesl adored the telephone. It was modern magic: you were both here and there at the same time. Liesl's ubiquity.

"You're not here and yet we're together," she said into the ebonite receiver.

"We're together, and yet you aren't here," little Job's voice answered politely.

But the real shock, the wonder of wonders, took place a fortnight after they first met. That evening, Herma and Stefan took Liesl and Job to the theatre, where they saw a performance of Feydeau's *La Main Passe* in the original French. When the curtain came up, they discovered a man (Chanal) alone in his living-room (but soon to be caught unawares by his wife, Francine) talking into a machine. And the machine *repeated every word the man had said*! The machine had a memory which was even more reliable than Liesl's! A memory which was *non-selective*.

"What's that?" Liesl asked her father.

"A tape recorder," Stefan replied.

"Who invented it?" Liesl asked.

"Valdemar Poulsen," Stefan replied. "He's Danish."

"A long time ago?" Liesl asked.

"In 1898," Stefan replied.

"How does it work?" Liesl asked.

"By non-volatile magnetisation of a steel wire," Stefan replied.

"I want one," Liesl declared.

"Listen to the play," Stefan replied.

". . . *que ma voix traverse les mers . . .*" the machine recited, in the actor's voice.

"I want one," Liesl repeated.

As soon as she was given her first tape recorder, Liesl set about preserving the world's memories.

First came the voice of Uncle Kraus.

"Uncle Karl, would you repeat for the tape recorder what you've just said?"

He bent down over the horn and repeated what he'd just said:

"Vienna is a testing ground for the destruction of the world."

"Now listen."

The machine repeated, in his nasal tones:

"*Vienna is a testing ground for the destruction of the world.*"

Then followed the annexation of Bosnia-Herzegovina, the assassination of Archduke Franz Ferdinand in Sarajevo, a world war lasting four years, millions dead, the crumbling of the Austro-Hungarian Empire, the October Revolution, the return of the Bernardins to France, the marriage of Liesl and Job, the birth of Matthias and the creation of The Only Begotten Film.

*

"The birth of Matthias *and* the creation of The Only Begotten Film? So the film came after Matthias?"

The white truck had finally found a motorway. It was now gliding alongside a river.

"Matthias helped them out a lot in the making of the film. Whenever I saw them, Matthias always devoted his free time to Liesl and Job. When Liesl came back from her travels, and Job took some time off from work, Matthias locked himself up for hours with them. That's the whole problem, in fact."

"What problem?"

"Various problems. Matthias and Sarah getting divorced, Barnaby's feeling of being left out . . . What united Job and Liesl didn't have much to do with your vision of love, Malaussène."

"I see."

"What do you see?"

"A shared project. Profitable love. *Love isn't looking at each other, it's looking together in the same direction.* That kind of reasonable bullshit. Creative, efficient love. The manufacturing of love as *Associated Destinies Ltd.* Setting off into the wide blue yonder with a shared project, and watch out if you get in the way! Puke-making. Obviously, Barnaby couldn't ever find happiness. There's no happiness to be found in a five-year plan, and even less in a hundred-year one! As for me, Julie, I have no project to offer you, not the slightest idea, and if one ever occurs to you, tell me at once so I can jump off the gravy train."

A brief response to her monologue earlier. But I didn't develop my point. I just said:

"Stop in the car park over there."

"Can't it wait?"

"I want to make a phone call. Stop."

She stopped. The truck door swished open in front of the phone box. I slid all my change into the comfort machine.

"Hello, Mum?"

"Yes, number-one son, it's me."

"All right?"

"Fine, my little one, having a nice trip?"

"Perfect. Are you eating?"

"I'm seeing that your sister eats."

"Is she eating?"

"I'll hand her over to you."

"Benjamin?"

"Clara? How are things, my Clarinette? Are you eating?"

"I have some good news and some bad news for you, Ben. Which do you want first?"

"Are you eating?"

"Julius is better, Benjamin."

"What do you mean, he's better?"

"Better. All fresh and rosy. He got down from the hammock in fine fettle. Now he's out prowling round Belleville. The fit didn't last very long this time."

"Any after effects?"

"A slight one."

"What sort?"

"The snapping of his jaws. He's still snapping them every three minutes."

"Jeremy must be pleased. He can have his role back now."

"No he can't. That's the bad news."

"What, Jeremy? Whatever next? What's he done this time?"

"Nothing. It's The Zebra."

"What's The Zebra?"

"Suzanne has received an expulsion order from La Herse the bailiff. She's got to be out in a fortnight's time. We'll have to shift all the sets and the furniture. We're thinking of using the Koutoubia's cellar . . ."

"But Suzanne's as safe as houses. She's under the protection of the King."

"What king?"

"The King of the Living Dead."

"Oh yes . . . Well, in fact she isn't. Suzanne called him up. No-one knows where he is. We can't find him anywhere."

"Look, Clara . . ."

"This is important for Suzanne."

"Look . . ."

"She's very courageous, you know. She's got the entire neighbourhood up in arms. There's going to be quite a protest."

"Clara . . ."

"They can't demolish The Zebra, Benjamin! It's a historic monument! There's already a petition going round . . ."

I gave up trying to butt in. I'd never heard Clara talk so much before, I let her substitute one sorrow for another, which is the beginning of a cure, I let her explain how minor historic monuments are the finest monuments of all, that as far as she was concerned she'd sacrifice ten Arc de Triomphes if they could save The Zebra, and how the death of Cissou was not going to enable that bastard La Herse to have a free hand (she didn't say "that bastard", it isn't in her lexicon, not even in her lexicon of sadness). Concerning Cissou, she added:

"And have you heard? The police got it wrong. He did still have some family."

"Really?"

"A young man dropped into Amar's. He's his nephew. He wants to claim the body. He wants to have it buried in the village where Cissou was born, beside his father, Cissou's brother."

Clara thought it wonderful that Cissou was now going to get a family funeral. She thought that being reunited with your loved ones underground after a life on the surface spent in exile was a good way to approach eternity, in fact that was what Amar wanted, too, he wanted to be buried in Algeria, Amar had had a long chat on the subject with Cissou's nephew.

"Having a family tomb in a village is almost a privilege these days, don't you think, Benjamin?"

I let her go on. I said to myself that stuffing herself with words was already some sort of nourishment, and while she was feeding her soul, I watched the machine gobble up my coins, I enjoyed a feast of love, snug in the receiver, as though in one of those seashells where the heart of the sea is beating.

*

Silence.

Lying in our hotel bedroom, window wide open over the Vercors, Julie and I drank in silence.

Just a quick word about the essential, the woes of The Zebra.

"We'll see about that with Job," Julie replied.

Curtain.

The bubbles of the clairette were occupying our silence.

Clairette de Die, to be drunk chilled, with the Vercors over your head.

The last rays of the sun set the rock faces ablaze. We drank. *Clairette Tradition*. A little wine from the plains at the foot of a cliff. A merry grape for a black mood.

Twin beds.

Each to his and her own.

A bedside table between them.

And the Vercors standing there, an awesome mass in the dusk.

I thought of the poor sods who'd thought they'd be safe there during the war. Standing, alone, on a sheer island, with a view over the world. They'd forgotten that disasters always come from the skies.

We let the blaze burn up the rock faces. The mountains fell asleep with all their weight.

Trying to find something to say, I said:

"The coppers got it wrong. Cissou did have some family. Or a nephew, at least."

"Long live the family," Julie murmured.

X
THE INTERVAL'S OVER

The interval's over, my lass. It's time to go back to your place in the big shit-heap.

Chapter 34

"**S**o what's our nephew waiting for, Christmas?"

Their Belleville colleagues had given them a description of the "nephew". Titus and Silistri knew that he was about to call by. They'd been on the lookout all night, alternating two hour vigils over Cissou, while Doctor Postel-Wagner slept with one eye open. And now they'd spent another entire day waiting but also opening, emptying, analysing and sewing back up stiffs as though they'd been born to it.

"What the fuck's keeping him?"

"Maybe it isn't the surgeon. Maybe it's a genuine nephew . . ."

"If he was a genuine nephew, he'd already have been round. Old Beaujeu didn't have any family."

"So what now?"

"So, we keep them peeled and we nab him."

"What if he sends someone else?"

What was tiring Titus and Silistri even more than the wait was having to play at being male nurses, while casing visitors with policemen's eyes. Seventeen had been in that day. All claiming to be members of Cissou's family. Titus and Silistri got rid of them the gentle way. They reckoned that the nephew would send someone round to have a look-see. They now had to spot the mole without alerting him or her and without being identified as coppers. Batches of police records paraded through their medical minds. These mental gymnastics were draining them. Even fresh corpses looked suspect to them.

"Telling the difference between the fake and the genuine is one thing . . . But the fake fake and the genuine fake is something else . . ."

"Such a dilemma is symptomatic of our times," Postel-Wagner remarked.

Titus and Silistri had ended up taking a liking to this doctor of the dead. When Postel-Wagner left them to do his rounds – he also treated the needy and bedridden – the two Inspectors felt rather lost. They greeted him with relief on his return. Apparently his life was a constant toing and froing between the quick and the dead, as though he were in a hurry to provide the former with what the latter had just taught him.

"There's some truth in that," the surgeon admitted. "When you open up a corpse, you're seeing the future of a newborn baby."

The day went by.

No nephew.

Cissou the Snow was resting in peace.

"We've failed," Silistri sighed.

"He must have sussed us out," Titus agreed.

"Whiskey anyone?" the doctor suggested.

The flask was passed round.

"What's for dinner?" Titus asked.

A barrack-room routine.

They were just choosing from the menu of the nearby restaurant when there was a knock at the door. It was Inspector Caregga. He pointed down the corridor with his thumb.

"It's the kid you saw yesterday, doctor. He's in a terrible state."

Caregga disappeared.

Despite the fact that the little boy was at the far end of the corridor, Postel-Wagner could read all the terror in the world in his dilated pupils.

"Thomas Mefingerurts? What's up?"

"Come quickly, doctor! Please!"

The child was sobbing in spasms. Postel-Wagner strode over to him.

"What's the matter?"

"It's Grandma, doctor. She's fallen over!"

Postel-Wagner froze.

"Fallen over? Has she hurt herself?"

"She's not moving."

The child was trembling all over.

"I'm coming."

When he took his bag from the hatstand, the two Inspectors were still staring at the menu.

"Pick something cold for me. I might be some time."

"And to drink?" Titus asked.

"A Château-Bonbourg '87."

"I thought that was a bad year."

"Château-Bonbourg never has bad years."

They just had to cross the boulevard. The boy's hand was icy cold in Postel-Wagner's grip. He was walking in short, stiff strides, his knees frozen with terror.

"How's the whitlow?"

The boy didn't answer.

"Did you bathe your finger like I told you to do?"

The boy didn't answer.

"Don't be frightened," Postel-Wagner said, while pressing the lift button.

But the boy was frightened.

"Your grandma's made of solid stuff. I was the one who fixed her."

The lift stopped on the third floor. When Postel-Wagner stepped out on to the landing, the boy's hand was no longer in his. Absolutely terrified, the lad had shrunk back into the corner of the lift. Postel-Wagner crouched down. He spoke as gently as he could.

"OK, Thomas. Go back to the hospital and stay there with the nurses. I'll come and fetch you later on. Just give me the keys to the flat."

The boy shook his head jerkily.

"Have you forgotten the keys?"

No. He shook his head. No, no, no. As though his neck was out of control.

Postel-Wagner smiled and reached out.

"Come on, Thomas. Give them to me."

Behind him, the door opened. Then a quavering voice said in his ear:

"Doctor?"

Without standing up, Postel-Wagner turned around. Thomas's grandma was leaning over him. Very old, very grey, very frail and very pallid, her eyes expressing the same terror as her grandson. Postel-Wagner leapt to his feet.

A tall woman in a pink suit was standing behind the old lady. She called to the boy in a tone of grinning menace:

"Thomaaaas!"

The boy rushed into his grandma's arms.

"There, there," the tall woman said.

Brutally, she pulled the boy and old lady towards her, before backing into the flat. Standing in her Diana-pink suit, and with her jangling bracelets, she looked like a real piece of Chanel posh elegance.

"Do come in, doctor," she said amicably. "And close the door behind you."

Postel-Wagner did so.

It was only when the door was shut that he saw the gun in the woman's hand.

"Oh yes!" she said. "You were expecting a nephew, but now you have a niece.

I couldn't be both here and in Belleville. The police are getting better at the art of making descriptions."

The niece was an extremely big girl, with a carefree expression on a face dotted with freckles and lit by two strangely bright eyes. Blonde, permed, broad shoulders, long powerful muscles, a wrestler's wrists and muscular legs. (Is she a drag queen? Postel-Wagner wondered. From the hips and lack of Adam's apple, no, he decided. Just an iron lady.)

The niece pulled the grandma and boy into a small living-room and motioned to them to sit down on the old settee.

Then she slumped into an armchair, crossed her legs and, with the tip of her gun, pointed to a chair for Postel-Wagner.

When he'd sat down, the niece took a long look at the boy, then, sounding sincerely sorry, she finally said:

"You've been a naughty boy, Thomas."

She had a tomboy's raucous tones.

"It was wrong to lure the doctor into an ambush."

She shook her teacherly head.

"What made you do that?"

The grandmother was hugging the boy, his head hidden in her armpit.

"Look at me when I'm talking to you. Why did you do it?"

The boy lifted up his head and Postel-Wagner was amazed to see an expression of surprise mixed with terror on it.

The niece smiled at him.

"Because I told you to?"

The boy nodded.

"Really?" the niece sounded amazed, and was now looking at the doctor for confirmation. "Really? And if I'd told you to go and throw yourself in the river, would you have done that, too? Do you always do as you are told, Thomas?"

"You said . . ." the boy stammered. "You said that Grandma . . ."

"I told you I'd kill your grandma if you didn't come back with the doctor, is that it?"

The boy sniffed and nodded.

"And you're right. I would have killed her," the niece admitted gravely.

Then, leaning towards the boy:

"But that's still no reason to betray the doctor. A hero, a real hero, would have sacrificed his grandma rather than betray a friend. Heroes in the Resistance used to do that. Because the doctor's your friend! He cured your whitlow! He's a real friend, isn't he? Well, isn't he?"

"Yes," the boy admitted.

"And you betrayed him! I'm very disappointed with you, Thomas. And I'm sure your grandma disapproves. Isn't that right, madam?"

(I'll jump her, Postel-Wagner thought. Then chuck the lot out the window, her, her gun and her chair! He suddenly felt quite capable of doing so.)

But the niece winked at him.

"One move, doctor, and I'll stick a bullet in grandma's hip. After all, that's why you're here isn't it?"

She sniggered. A charming release.

"And it would soothe Thomas's bad conscience."

She fell silent for a moment, then sighed:

"I mean, what are the young people of today coming to? And to think, they're supposed to be the future of mankind . . ."

"Good point," Postel-Wagner butted in. "Let's talk about the future . . ."

The niece stared at him with apparent incomprehension. She thought for some time then, without taking her eyes off Postel-Wagner, said to the boy:

"You know what, Thomas? The doc's not such a nice friend as all that."

The boy glanced at Postel-Wagner.

"He locked my uncle in a fridge," the niece said.

The boy didn't react.

"Can you imagine it? Locked in a fridge!"

"Maybe he's dead," the boy said with a start.

"Dead?" the niece repeated. "Dead? My uncle? Never. Of course he isn't dead. What makes you think that?"

Then she added:

"People never die when you really love them."

Then, leaning over the boy again, and clearly articulating each word:

"If your grandma ever dies, my little Thomas, then it will be because you didn't love her enough."

Postel-Wagner's hands gripped the arms of his chair.

"Isn't that right?" the niece asked him, with a hint of candour. "Don't we always die of unrequited love?"

"Your 'uncle' has been expecting you for the past two days."

"He's expecting me?"

The niece's face lit up with childlike joy.

"Can we go and see him?"

She was jumping up and down and clapping her hands.

"Can we go now?"

For a moment, Postel-Wagner was speechless. Then he slowly stood up.

"OK, come on."

"Great!"

Then, when they were going out of the living-room and into the hall, she called out merrily:

"And you two stay sitting on the settee, OK? Not a move, or I'll kill the doctor. Got that?"

The grandma and grandson stared at her silently.

"I swear it on both of your heads!"

She pointed at their heads with the barrel of her gun. Neither the grandma nor the grandson was capable of making the slightest movement.

"Right, let's go."

Postel-Wagner heard the parquet creaking beneath her feet all the way down the corridor. Then, when he reached out for the door handle, he felt the barrel of the gun in his ribs.

"Not another move, doctor."

Postel-Wagner froze, then started to turn around.

"And don't turn around either. I've seen quite enough of you," the niece added sharply.

Postel-Wagner stayed put.

"Putting old Beaujeu on the box in search of his family was a nice try," she admitted. "You had me fooled for a while. Otherwise I wouldn't have bothered sending someone round Belleville to check. But where you really took me for an idiot was using undercover cops. Don't you know that pigs stink? Even from inside a car? I'd even recognise the stench of a pig from inside a coffin! So how many of them have you got playing doctors and nurses in the morgue? Two? Three? More?"

Postel-Wagner didn't respond.

"So," the niece said. "At least one."

(Shit, Postel-Wagner thought.)

"It's lucky I met little Thomas and his whitlow yesterday . . ."

"Yesterday?"

Postel-Wagner had jumped.

The niece's lips were pressed up against his ear.

"That's right! Yesterday at noon! A little boy coming out of a morgue isn't a common sight. So I asked him a few questions . . ."

Silence.

"I spent all last night working on him and the old dear. I psyched them up a bit . . ."

(Oh no, the doctor groaned inwardly.)

"Now, listen to my instructions. I want you back here at two a.m. in an ambulance with old Beaujeu inside. Two o'clock. That way, we'll avoid the traffic. I don't want to get caught in a jam and I don't want to be followed. As I'm far from home, I'll also need some gear to skin the body. You know what's required. After all, we're in the same line of business."

"You wouldn't rather I did it in the morgue?" Postel-Wagner asked.

A giggle rippled over the nape of his neck.

"No, doctor," the niece murmured into his ear. "I wouldn't. First off, you'd make a balls of it. Secondly, you'd be depriving me of a considerable pleasure. And thirdly, I want to take all three of you for a drive with my uncle."

Change of tone.

"Two a.m. on the dot. You'll park in front of the entrance to the building. You'll open the passenger door without getting out of the ambulance. I'll come down with the old dear and the whitlow. If there's the slightest hitch, I'll whack both of them."

She paused, then went on:

"Don't think. Don't try and find another solution. Talk your friends out of laying siege. Fort Alamos take time, and grandma and grandson would die . . . of fear."

Postel-Wagner didn't react.

"OK?"

"OK."

The niece sighed with relief. Then, in a carefree tone:

"And no pig on the stretcher pretending to be my uncle, clear? Don't try anything smart. Just you and my uncle. Let's keep this in the family."

Silence.

"You'll drive and we'll go the way I direct you. If anyone follows us, all three of you are dead. If we make it, I'll dump you all in the middle of nowhere when it's over. OK?"

Postel-Wagner didn't answer.

"One more thing. Don't forget that from now till two a.m. I'm going to keep talking to them. Did you hear what I can do *with words*? So, be here on time, and don't draw out their agony. I mean, be humane. Otherwise, all you'll find will be two basketcases who'll never listen to a single word again. And from what I can guess about you, you'd never forgive yourself for that."

Chapter 35

A T TWO ON the dot, an ambulance parked in front of the building. Postel-Wagner leant over and opened the passenger door towards the darkness of the hallway.

Then his heart started to count the seconds.

Somewhere upstairs, the lift door slammed. The cables shook. The lift creaked as it came down. Its arrival was announced by a halo of light, spread out like a puddle across the floor tiles of the hall. Then it came to a juddering halt. The first thing that Postel-Wagner saw emerge on to the iridescent tiling was the child's small, rigid frame. Then out came the grandmother, her head shrinking into her shoulders. Postel-Wagner started. Behind the old lady, people were talking.

"Not at all," the niece's raucous voice proclaimed. "It's nothing serious . . . A few days' rest after the operation and that will be an end to it."

The few words spoken by the second voice were lost in the dimensions of the hallway.

"Absolutely!" the niece trilled. "If we wait any longer, it could be the death of her."

The niece's voice rang with competency.

"That's often the way it goes with minor operations. There's nothing much wrong, but you let it drag . . . then suddenly you've had it!"

The child had reached the first of the hall's doors. He stopped like a remote-controlled toy, his eyes blank, his limbs stiff. The old woman came to a halt behind him. Her hands seized his shoulders. Postel-Wagner wondered if this was instinctive protection or the reflex of the drowning.

"If she'd been better advised . . ." the niece's voice went on.

Then Postel at last saw her.

She was wearing a white coat and a professional smile. She was talking and gesticulating at an elderly man, who was nodding timidly.

"I'm so pleased you agree!" the niece affirmed as she, too, stopped in the wide doorway.

"At our age, what we really need is rest," the old man muttered.

"And discreet neighbours, too," the niece chipped in.

She looked him straight in the face. Her green eyes sparkled.

"When she gets back," she said, pointing at Thomas's grandmother, "be a good chap and stop being so intrusive . . . as a neighbour, I mean . . . stop disturbing her all the time."

The old man jumped.

"I'm not telling you to stop dropping by completely," the niece corrected herself, in a sympathetic tone. "I'm just asking you to stop tiring her out."

"Yes, yes of course, doctor . . ." the old man stammered.

"You're mistaken," the niece protested with a peal of laughter. "I'm only a nurse. The doctor's over there in the ambulance. Look . . ."

The old man bent over. Postel-Wagner's gaze met a pair of eyes full of surprise, timidity and gratitude.

"Now, if you'll just let us get in."

The niece stood the man up and pushed him to one side, but without releasing his shoulder.

"Get in, Thomas."

With her other hand, she gave the boy a brisk slap on the head. He then crept in beside Postel-Wagner.

"Not so close," the niece ordered. "The doctor needs to be able to change gear. Where are your brains?"

Thomas pulled back, as though he'd just had an electric shock.

"That's right," the niece said. "Your turn now."

Two fingers in the ribs, hitting her just over her liver. The old woman doubled over and was thrown on to the seat next to her grandson. In the same motion, the niece shifted behind the old man and pressed him against the rear door.

"Where on earth were you going at such a time?"

The man tried to reply, but the pressure and pain from the half nelson she was holding him in took his breath away.

"At your age! You should be ashamed of yourself!"

The old man was sobbing with fear. The niece relaxed her grip slightly.

"Open the door."

The old man felt for the handle, found it, and managed to open it. He was then torn from the vehicle, shoved aside violently and, as he collapsed on to the tiled floor, the rear door of the ambulance slammed shut and the gun's grip hammered down on to Cissou's head, which was hidden beneath a white sheet.

"Good," said the niece. "It isn't a pig. And it's dead."

She pulled back the sheet, revealing the tattooed body in the gleam of the street lights.

"And it's my uncle, sure enough . . ." she murmured.

Then, all joyful:

"Look, Thomas, how lovely uncles are when they have a legacy."

The boy didn't turn around. Postel-Wagner felt the waves of his fear in the backrest of the seat they were sharing.

"Giddy up, cabby!" the niece exclaimed, tapping the doctor on the shoulder.

The forensic surgeon started up the ambulance, then slowly drove down the deserted avenue.

The niece was still ecstatic.

"Did you notice, doctor? I didn't expose myself once during the entire operation. I was always covered by someone else. That's the real art of body armour!"

She leant over the front seat.

"Remember that, my little Thomas. A man should always shield a woman."

Postel-Wagner changed into second.

Once again, the revolver's grip whistled through the air. In three sharp blows, the ambulance's radio was demolished.

"No radio for children. It's full of wars, murders, tribal music, scandalous stories . . . it's very bad, very bad indeed."

The first intersection was now about fifty yards away. Postel-Wagner asked:

"Right, left, or straight on?"

The niece chuckled.

"You've really got nerves of steel, doctor. Left. Into Avenue Ledru-Rollin."

Then:

"Did you like the radio, Thomas? Or did you prefer the TV?"

Postel-Wagner noted the past tense. Something froze in his mind. The boy didn't reply.

Postel-Wagner drove on in second gear, without the slightest jolt.

"Don't you ever do more than twenty miles an hour, doctor?"

The niece glanced over her shoulder. She gave her tomboyish laugh.

"Is it so we can be followed more easily?"

But Avenue Ledru-Rollin was empty in the rear-view mirror.

"Come on, this isn't a funeral, get a move on!"

Postel-Wagner slowly put his foot down.

"The white coat was a nice touch, wasn't it? Funnily enough, Thomas's grandad was a barber. Then he died."

Postel-Wagner slowed down again, as though paying careful attention to what was being said.

"Another one Thomas can't have loved that much," the niece went on.

"Don't you ever shut up?" Postel-Wagner asked adopting the tone of the conversation.

The niece quietly thought the question over. She placed an ostentatiously thoughtful finger on her lips.

"No," she said at last, "I don't. And do you know why not?"

"No, why?" Postel-Wagner asked.

"Because the day I shut up, I'll never speak again."

The ambulance was now crawling along.

"And when a woman shuts up that much, it's the end of the world."

She put her mouth to Postel-Wagner's ear.

"Talking of ends, doctor, if you keep playing silly buggers, it'll be your end. Turn right into Rue de Charenton and, for the last time, get a move on!"

Postel-Wagner took the bend at exactly the same speed.

"Foot down!" the niece suddenly bellowed, pushing the barrel of her gun under the doctor's jaw.

Postel-Wagner's foot rammed down the accelerator and the ambulance lurched forwards. Hanging on to the back of the seat, the niece made no reaction. But then came a crash. The stretcher had broken itself free from its moorings, banged into the tailgate and forced it open.

Cissou the Snow's body was thrown out into the darkness.

"Shit!"

The ambulance came to a screeching halt.

Staring wide-eyed at the open door, the niece and the doctor watched the stretcher slide away in a shower of sparks.

"Jesus Christ!"

The niece turned round, her pupils dilated.

"Did you do that on purpose?"

"You were the one who told me to speed up," the doctor objected, still staring fixedly at the stretcher.

"True," said the niece. "OK, back up. And quick about it."

The doctor did so. The gaping rear door neared the stretcher like a sperm whale's maw.

"Stop!"

They were now just a few yards away from the body.

"Get out. Go round and put the stretcher back."

"It weighs over two hundred pounds," Postel-Wagner remarked.

The niece peered down the empty street. She seemed to hesitate, then made her mind up.

"No, doctor, I'm not getting out of this ambulance. Get out, pull the stretcher to the door. I'll stay inside and help you put my uncle back in his rightful place. That's all I can do for you, apart from killing you."

The forensic surgeon opened the ambulance door, went to the back and grabbed the handles of the stretcher. While Postel-Wagner was approaching, his shoulders bending under the strain, the niece turned around to Thomas and his grandmother.

"You see," she said smiling sweetly, "he tried to get you left here all on your own, but I stayed!"

When she turned around again, the doctor's back was occupying the open tailgate.

"Well done!" the niece said. "You're no Mister Universe, but you made it! Now, listen carefully."

A pause.

"Are you listening to me?"

Postel-Wagner nodded.

"You're going to crouch down then push the stretcher up as far as you can. I'll grab the handles, then you go round and lift it up from the other end. Right?"

Another nod.

"And I'll put my gun in my pocket, doctor. The slightest false move, and I'll drop uncle and whack you. How does that sound?"

"Perfect," the doctor replied.

"Good? Ready then? At the count of three, knees bend, arms stretch. One . . . two . . . three!"

Knees bent, arms extended. The stretcher handles passed from Postel-Wagner's grip to the niece.

"Fine. Now pick it up from the other end. Quick!"

As soon as the forensic surgeon had grabbed the other pair of handles, the niece started to pull back. She moved slowly, bent double with the effort and because of the ambulance's low roof.

"The wheels have had it! They're not rolling any more!"

With one pushing and the other pulling, the stretcher finally returned to its place.

"Made it," the niece said.

"Made it," Postel-Wagner said.

When the niece looked up, she was surprised to see a smile of shared effort on the doctor's lips. A genuinely satisfied grin!

Whose true meaning came home to her when she stood up to feel the cold mouth of a gun pressed against the nape of her neck.

"Made it," a third voice echoed.

At the same time, a hand slipped into her coat and relieved her of her gun.

"OK, you can turn around now."

What the niece saw when she did so looked scarcely human. A sort of living mattress, which was dark, supple and dangerous. An image she knew only too well. A dreaded vision, which had slipped into the ambulance through the still-open side door, as noiselessly as if it had hatched out inside her own skull. A face with no eyes, but which was nevertheless staring at her from behind a visor which reflected the glimmers of the night.

The state.

As though to confirm this revelation, sirens started up and the darkness sparkled with blinding lights. Alone in the middle of the street, the ambulance became a sort of star beneath their projectors. The left-side door opened. A shape identical to the one pinning down the niece seized Thomas's grandmother in its padded arms.

"Come on, madam, it's all over."

More forms were appearing from practically all of the neighbouring doorways, and the parked cars. The niece didn't turn around. She knew that more automatics were already aimed at her through the whale's gaping maw.

"Stopped speaking, have you?" a child's voice suddenly asked.

Kneeling on the front seat, Thomas was staring at the niece.

"Not another word?" he pressed the point.

Sure enough, the niece didn't have another word.

"Look at me when I'm talking to you."

The niece glanced round at Thomas. She could almost see her own smile on the boy's lips. This impression was confirmed when the lad raised an eyebrow in resignation and declared in a voice which was sweet, reasoned and just a tad viperish:

"Well you see, you've stopped speaking, but it isn't the end of the world."

Chapter 36

G ERVAISE WAS TO remember her awakening for a long time.
It was – she was later to say – as if I was being pulled up to the surface by a lifebuoy or a balloon, then sucked up into the light. A dream was lingering in the depths, and I was ascending! I was in no hurry to arrive, but the balloon had ideas of its own. The water was rushing over my skin at an incredible speed.

She popped up like a cork amid applause and streams of champagne.

"We got her, Gervaise!"

She opened her eyes in a hospital room, surrounded by her guard of pimps and Templars. Everyone was talking at the same time and they were all congratulating her friend, Postel-Wagner, who didn't know where to put himself and so was hiding behind the smoke of his monstrous pipe.

"We got the surgeon, Gervaise!"

"We nabbed the nephew!"

She seemed to understand that Postel-Wagner had helped in the arrest of "the surgeon" (who was also called "the nephew", or "the niece", which was even more confusing).

Titus and Silistri had unfolded a map of Paris on the bedroom floor. They were explaining to Pescatore's pimps how they'd screwed the niece by setting ambushes at every single junction in a radius of 800 yards. At the same time, they spoke to Gervaise, praising Postel-Wagner's guts, the brilliant way he'd rammed his foot down just at the vital moment at the corner of Rue Charenton and Avenue Ledru-Rollin, one of the seventeen mousetraps they'd set up for two a.m.

"Real balls, I can tell you!"

How the sabotaged moorings of the stretcher had snapped, just as planned, when the vehicle lurched forwards and how the tailgate had swung open because it was only being held shut by a piece of string.

They told her that she, Gervaise, had slept like an angel under the protection of Pescatore's pimps during all of the forty-eight hours that the operation had lasted. A staff shortage. But perfect service. A fly couldn't have got into Gervaise's bedroom. These ponces deserve to be made cops. No kidding. What an excellent example of social rehabilitation that would be!

The fallen angels and the archangels would be reconciled! The sacred alliance of times before Time itself! Gervaise woke up in paradise regained. Her first instinct was to thank the One whom Mondine called her "pal up there", but for once Gervaise held back her prayers. Instead, she praised Humanity.

What she was now beginning to grasp was that the boys in blue and the ponces had saved her whores. By arresting the surgeon (who had turned out to be a surgeoness) they had nicked both the brains and the bistoury. Now all they had to do was nab the collector. But, without the surgeon, the collector was no longer a threat to her girls. They could sleep peacefully beneath their tattoos.

She also understood that the strategist behind this entire operation was the fat man with an oily lock of hair, who was bending over her in his waistcoat embroidered with imperial bees.

"I would not have liked to retire in the knowledge that our young lady was still unapprehended."

Gervaise looked at him blankly.

"That's right. I've retired. As of eight o'clock this morning."

Chief Superintendent Coudrier pointed at his men.

"They've given me a set of fishing rods. This is going to be a rural retirement, Gervaise."

All of which made for rather a large amount of information. But, while Gervaise did gradually take on board the arrest of the niece, Postel-Wagner's heroics, Coudrier's retirement and their hunt for the collector, what she still couldn't fathom was why this male-dominated champagne-swilling nineteenth hole was taking place in a hospital bedroom, and what she was doing in this bed with its green sheets which smelt of her own sweat.

The answer came from a whirlwind dressed in a white coat.

"When are you lot going to shut up and bugger off?"

She recognised Professor Berthold from the sound of his voice and the quality of his prose.

"Who's running this piss-up? You is it?" he asked Coudrier.

"Not since a quarter of an hour ago," the former Chief Superintendent replied.

"I'll give you another five minutes," the surgeon decreed. "Get these rugger-buggers out of here, or the kid will go under again."

Then he spotted Postel-Wagner behind his cloud of pipe smoke.

"And what the fuck are you doing here? Are your fridges hungry? Come round to whip up a bit of custom?"

"I missed you, Berthold. I wanted to give you a big kiss."

Berthold, Marty and Postel-Wagner: university buddies . . .

When they'd finally all gone, Gervaise obtained her final piece of wake-up information.

"You were sent into orbit by a car out for your skin," Professor Berthold explained. "But you're a solid lass, and all it did was give you three days' kip. Believe you me, when you have a job like ours, it's good to take three days off. Turn around," he ordered, lifting up her nightdress.

The surgeon's hands examined her. Ankles, knees, hips, spine, shoulders, vertebrae, torsion, flexion, rotation. He frowned.

"Fine. Solid stuff we've got here . . . A lovely bod. No structural damage from the impact."

He slapped her bum.

"On to your back now."

He fingered her belly.

"Does it hurt here? Or here? No? What about here? Nothing?"

It didn't hurt anywhere.

"Perfect. Your guts are all where they should be. You haven't even had the slightest haemorrhage."

He pulled down her nightdress and stood up.

"Fine."

He suddenly looked embarrassed. He glanced round at the closed door, pulled a chair over to the bed, sat down and stared at Gervaise intently.

"Tell me something . . . The lass next door, there . . . Mondine . . ."

(Already? Gervaise thought.)

"Mondine worships you, she's told me everything about you, about your God Almighty, your answering machine, your redeemed whores, repentant pimps, your ecstatic cops . . . the lot."

He leant further over.

"So could you . . . I mean, could you in turn tell me a bit about her?"

"Like what, for instance?"

"She's been around, hasn't she?"

"Yes, for the past thirty-one years," Gervaise replied.

Berthold stared at her, while nibbling his lips.

"I see," he said at last.

He repeated himself.

"I see."

He stood up.

"I see what's going on."

He shook his head.

"The guardian-angel bit! Saint Joan watching over her flock."

He just couldn't make up his mind to leave.

"Not the slightest scrap of gen about Mondine, then? Very well . . . very well . . ."

(Grew up too fast, Gervaise thought, like most boys – she didn't say "men", but "boys", an inheritance from her mother Jeanine.)

Berthold was almost squirming.

(Mondine didn't have to ask anything about you, Professor, Gervaise thought. She gave you a full scan in three minutes flat.)

He finally made up his mind to leave. His hand flopped on to the door handle.

"You can go home today, after one final X-ray. The interval's over, my lass. It's time to go back to your place in the big shit-heap."

Gervaise called after him as he left.

"Professor Berthold?"

He turned around.

"Yeah, what?"

And then Gervaise at last told him what he was dying to hear.

"All I know about Mondine is that, if I was one of the boys, I'd like to wake up next to her."

Chapter 37

"TWINS ARE MADE in beds of the same name."

At the foot of the Vercors, I too had a memorable wake-up that morning.

Julie had slipped into bed with me. And to make things up, she'd whispered:

"Twins are made in beds of the same name."

It rang like a coded message from London, Free French Radio, a message of liberation on my crackly wireless.

"I repeat: 'Twins are made in beds of the same name.'"

Our hands were already kneading the future into shape when a thunderous knocking at the door put paid to the event.

"Madame! Monsieur! Downstairs quick! The police are here! They're asking for you!"

Julie would willingly have made the forces of law and order twiddle their thumbs for a bit, but something inside me stopped me from fathering under police observation. I rushed downstairs, tucking in my shirt and polishing my conscience.

In reception, a guest was bellowing. The chambermaid-cum-night-porter was trying to calm him down.

"Not so loud, sir! It isn't even seven o'clock! You'll wake up all the guests! I'm on my own here, I don't want any trouble!"

Obligingly, the moaner kept bellowing, but in whispers.

A blue-clad officer was noting down these roars on his catch-all notepad.

"Are you Monsieur Malaussène?" the inevitable second officer asked when he saw me arrive.

I said that I was indeed me.

The second officer produced another notepad.

"Room twenty-five?"

The right number.

"You had a white truck?"

"Yes."

"Well you don't any more. It's been stolen."

"Along with this gentleman's vehicle," the first cop added, indicating the bellower who was now improvising around themes of insecurity, immigration, lost values, the corrupt left, the corruptible right, whatever are we in for next, sleeping nightwatchmen, a sluggish police force and a firm hand is what we need.

"It took you half an hour to get here! I timed you! A full half an hour!"

"You're not the only person we have to deal with, sir," the first officer remarked.

"Unfortunately," the second officer added.

"That's no way to reply to a taxpayer!" the citizen exploded.

"Not so loud, sir," the chambermaid pleaded.

Upon which, Julie put in an appearance. The two Biros froze in mid-air and the shouter's mouth remained agape. I must say I've never got used to it myself. Every time Julie appears, all I can see is Julie.

"Our truck's been nicked," I said, to break the spell.

"Do you have the necessary papers to identify the vehicle?" our cop asked us, as though just coming to.

"They were inside it," Julie answered.

Then added:

"It was a hired truck."

The pen froze again.

"You left the papers inside?"

He was now staring at us with increased appetite.

"Very foolish of you. In this sort of case, it's often an indication of complicity."

(And God knows, we should watch out for any indications of complicity!)

"Where were you going?"

Julie took over the answers.

"To the Vercors."

"You moving house?"

"We were going to pick up a collection of films."

"Where?"

"From Monsieur Bernardin, in the Loscence valley."

"Which can easily be checked," I said.

The ballpoint rolled over destiny's notepad. Then it stopped abruptly. The cop looked up. I noticed he was now grinning. (A grinning green-eyed officer.)

"Bernardin from Loscence? Old Job?"

He bent his inquisitive sparrow's head to one side and asked:

"You from the plateau?"

"I was born there."

His grin broadened.

"I'm from Saint-Martin. Where were you born exactly?"

"At La Chapelle. In Les Rochas."

"The farmhouse behind Les Revoux? The one that belonged to the Colonial Governor?"

"To Governor Corrençon, yes. He was my father."

"Oh, then you must be Juliette!"

"The very same."

*

That's the way it goes with indications of complicity . . . All you need is a cop with a Biro who just happens to have been born in the same village as you and the most suspect of indications becomes a reason for a good natter. It was Saturday morning. Just after dawn. Our cop was getting ready for his weekend off at home in the Vercors, when news of this theft had emerged from his radio.

"Seven minutes before I was due to be off duty!"

All in a tizzy at having discovered a neighbour, he got the formalities out of the way in no time, asked his team mate to hand in his report for him at the station in Valence and then offered to give us a lift up to the heights in his own car.

"Anyway, there's nothing we can do at this stage. Your motor will be over the border in Italy by now . . ."

So there we were, the three of us, ascending the rock faces of the Vercors along a track called Les Goulets, which pierces the massif like a tunnel through your dreams. God knows why, but these dripping intestines, where beech trees spring up from the rock and creepers tumble down over clumps of moss, conjured up a clear vision of Clément the Budding Bayleaf. It would have reminded our Clément of *Beauty and the Beast* – the Cocteau version. He would have pictured muscular arms emerging from the rocks to point out the way, candlestick in hand. He would have started to tell the kids the story, and their eyes would have sparkled. So what lies behind this weeping wall? To what destiny are these candlesticks emerging from the rocks pointing us? What miraculous road is scattered by so many saints, whose villages we crossed: Saint-Nazaire, Saint-Thomas, Saint-Laurent, Saint-Jean, Sainte-Eulalie? O guardian saints of the Vercors, where are you leading us? Into the innards of the devil? And, as ever when Clément narrated his favourite films, what I would have heard was silence, the silence of ecstatic kids, the silence of Clara in love, yes, right at the start, before all the intellectual bullshit started, what marked the beauty of a tale was silence . . . O Clément! . . . Silly you . . . Why did you do that? . . . Why flirt with death in the heat of love? . . . But that's the way it goes . . . Love can't even save us from ourselves . . . That's why we're mortal . . . And you, my Clarinette . . . the most candid of women in love . . . setting off passions so passionately devoid of scruples! . . . your mother's daughter . . . so threatened in her naive love affairs . . . an innocent devastator . . .

"A penny for them, Benjamin?"

Julie's question cut me off right in the darkest reaches of the Grands-Goulets. A mountain stream could be heard raging just beneath our wheels. A pathway marked "Extremely Dangerous" went down into the abyss.

"Two years ago, a girl was killed going down there," our green-eyed copper explained. "And a few tourists before her."

"Your Vercors is a maw," I said.

The cop laughed defensively.

"This is the easiest way up, you know."

My sweetie upped the ante:

"The Vercors has to be earned, Benjamin!"

The eternal pride for one's roots.

"And, right at the bottom, there's the devil's piss pot . . ." I mumbled. "I've got vertigo and I hate travelling. Belleville, where are you?"

Leaning half out the window, I yelled into the depths of the abyss:

"Where are you, Belleviiiiiiiiiiiille?"

The young officer burst out laughing, then put his foot down and hooted his horn. The car bounded forwards and suddenly we burst out into heavenly light.

"Jesus Christ!"

A phosphorescent explosion! The devil's guts leading out into heavenly pastures! The saints hadn't lied to us: these really were the green fields of Eden. The roof of the world!

It left me speechless.

Them, too.

"It does that to you every time," Julie confirmed.

*

The first thing I saw in the shadows of Les Rochas was the kitchen table. The sun laid a golden cloth on it as soon as Julie opened the first shutter.

Julie's table.

"So, that's where you were born?"

"Yes, thanks to Matthias and his trusty penknife. It was a Caesarean. My father the Governor boiled the water on this stove."

An antique Godin model, with holly leaves running across its white enamel. Serial number 603. Praise be to thee, old range.

"The water came from the spring and the wood from the garden. You can trust me, Benjamin. I'm a completely natural product."

"Does it still work?"

"Well enough to feed and heat you. This old Godin is a commune's dream. It'll heat generations to come!"

The green-eyed copper had dropped us off at the junction of the main road and the dirt track. Julie had insisted on walking the rest of the way. She liked arriving alone in this solitude, with no-one aware of her coming except the hollyhocks which were besieging the farmhouse. She was now speaking from a distance, opening the shutters in another room, then another, little by little revealing the scenes of her childhood. The light of the Vercors didn't play hard to get. Les Rochas was a nest of shadows woven by light. Wood fire, linen sheets and cooking apples: the fragrances of a generation.

"Who came from the Vercors, your father or your mother?"

"My father. There's even a village with the same name! My mother was Italian. Emilia Mellini, from Bologna. There are a lot of them round here. They come here to work as lumberjacks."

Her voice crossed the silence of the centuries and the rooms.

"Didn't the Germans burn down the farmhouse?"

"Even with the worst will in the world, you can't burn everything . . . They blew up the school further down the hill, there in Tourtre. People found exercise books in the trees as far up as here."

I was following her at a distance. I went into each room just after she'd left it. I was discovering the scent of her aged twelve. In the bedroom, I was caught between the two creators of her face. She, the stunningly beautiful Italian, photographed while still young, in her frame, staring at him on the opposite wall, standing amid the hollyhocks on the eve of his death, a skeleton floating in his white Colonial Governor's uniform, with love in his eyes, directed straight at the facing wall. Standing between them, I took a pace back. How he was looking at her! How he was looking at her across all those years!

"Your idea of love, Benjamin . . . He never remarried."

Julie's voice in my ear, which added:

"Which made me furious."

"What did she die of?"

"Cancer."

We were whispering.

"Did he talk about her much?"

"Now and then . . . in odd turns of phrase . . . 'the patron saint of the hollyhock' . . . 'as sweet as your lumberjack mother' . . . Or when I got angry: 'Yes, Julie! Again! More Italian fury!'"

"No other women, then?"

"The occasional whore."

In his frame, the Governor listened to us in powerless amusement, his hands open, as flat as hollyhock leaves.

"When he missed her too much, he used to chop down the hollyhocks."

Julie had already told me about these fits of hollyhockicide. A struggle against grief. Lost from the start. There's nothing so vivacious as hollyhocks.

"He was a bit like you, Benjamin – a woman, or a cause. Once his wife was dead, he chose a cause: decolonisation. He put it quite plainly: 'I'm working to disempire France.' He was in Saigon when he first met Liesl, in fact. Liesl dragged her microphone round all the battles of Indo-China."

While little Julie was in a boarding school in Grenoble.

"Do you know what I used to dream of?"

"Tell me."

"Of a stepmother, whom I'd drive to suicide. Or else who'd be my friend. I lacked a female presence in my girlhood."

"What about the Fraenkhels?"

"Matthias was already divorced by the time I went to stay with him. And Liesl wasn't a woman. She was just ears."

Chapter 38

O LD JOB HAD his routine. We respected it.

"Never disturb him in the morning," Julie said. "He's a night bird."

"Let's go round after lunch then."

"You're forgetting about his nap. You'll see the notice on his study door: *Nap time from 16.00 to 17.05. Do not disturb on pain of death!* It's been there ever since I was a little girl."

"After his nap, then."

"That'll be fine. Just after five. That was the time I used to leave Barnaby in his caves and go and watch Job's latest acquisitions."

"Wasn't Barnaby jealous?"

"Barnaby is jealousy made flesh."

"Was he your only boyfriend?"

"I was friends with all the boys on the plateau, the Chapays, the Mazets, the Bourguignons, the Malsangs . . ."

"What did you play at?"

"None of your business."

All this spoken while she was filling a rucksack with provisions purchased at Sainte-Eulalie, because Julie had decided to spend the day on the jagged crests of the cliffs.

"It'll rebuild your lungs and legs, Benjamin."

The conversation continued along the windswept heights.

"You are silly! What do you imagine we played at? Potholing, skiing, family get-togethers, hunting, rock-climbing, poaching, lumberjack contests . . ."

"And Old Job's film collection . . ."

"No. Liesl and Job enjoyed their solitude. As did my mates, too, in fact. They were two different worlds."

Then, suddenly:

"Look!"

A finger pointing across the void.

I thought she was showing me the landscape, the world way down there, flattened into a road map, with no limit except for the cutting-off point of the horizon.

"No, there!"

It was an eagle. About thirty feet *below us*, a massive, devilishly serious-looking eagle was making it a point of honour to remain motionless in the gusts of wind. The master of the breezes! The entire world between its wings.

"It's on the lookout."

I immediately thought of the rabbit it was after, two or three hundred feet below, rummaging about in the low grass, highly active, in love maybe, about to start a family, with career prospects, agate eyes and silky fur, transparent ears and twitching nose, another one of nature's masterpieces . . .

"Let's have lunch."

*

Five or six hours further on, the wind had calmed, the sun was torrid, my lungs were in my shoes, and we at last arrived in the Loscence valley. Julie pointed once more.

A large farmhouse was awaiting us beneath its tiles, all alone in a valley from which the fulsome fragrance of cut grass was rising up to us.

"Is that Job's house?"

One of the five chimneys was sending up a ribbon of smoke straight into the heavens. Julie smiled.

"Job will be expecting us in his study, by the fire."

"In this heat?"

"Summers are short round here. Job doesn't have enough time to warm up between one winter and the next."

We went down in stages, as though coming up from the bottom of the sea. Whenever we paused, Julie added to her commentary.

"The right wing, with its windowless walls, houses the film collection. Three hundred square yards of barn, where Barnaby used to sabotage miles of film in secret."

"What do you mean by sabotage?"

"New editing. Cut and paste. Barnaby had a theory called cine-syncretism. Count Dracula meets King Kong in the salons of Marienbad . . . that kind of thing. Suzanne is in for a few surprises."

"And Old Job never noticed?"

"How many times do I have to tell you that Job never watches the same film twice? Come on, let's go."

*

I recognised that door. It was huge and studded and framed in a stone arch. Its knocker was a grimacing bronze centaur, its chest pierced by an arrow, who was holding in its arms an unconscious woman with dangling limbs.

"I recognise that door!"

"Yes, it's Count Zaroff's. Schoedsack gave it to Matthias after his niece had had a baby, and Matthias of course gave it to Job."

"Why of course?"

"Because Matthias would have paid his salary over to his parents if he thought they'd appreciate it. As for presents from actors, directors and producers, he and Job had so many they didn't know what to do with them. They were real heads of state. They got showered with them after every roll of film sold and every birth. You'll see. This house is a museum of illusions."

I was no longer listening to Julie. I didn't like the way the centaur was looking at me. It was as if the vapours of all that plonk had faded away for the first time since we'd set off. I could clearly remember where we'd come from, where we were, the real reason for this excursion and who we'd presumably run into on the other side of the door. I grabbed Julie's wrist just as her fingers gripped the door knocker.

"Wait a second. Are you sure you want to see Matthias?"

A glance.

"I don't expect he's here. But if he is, then we do have a couple of questions to ask him, don't you think?"

Two rapid knocks, a pause, then a third, echoing into the heart of the house.

"It's my code. This way, Job won't have to come down."

Sure enough, Count Zaroff's door wasn't locked. It creaked open – naturally – to reveal a vast hall of gleaming floor tiles, which glittered as far as the robust rails of an oak staircase which made no sacrifices to sobriety.

"What about the staircase? Recognise that, too?"

No, I didn't. We weren't from the same planet.

"Renoir! It's the staircase from *The Rules of the Game*. The tiles, too. Plus the hunting trophy over there."

"What about the fairground horse?"

A merry-go-round horse, with wild staring eyes and ghastly teeth was bridling up in the shadows to the left of the door, as though it was about to pounce on the visitors.

"A gift from Buñuel's *Los Olvidados*."

For the second time that day I thought about Clément the Budding Bayleaf. I could even picture the face he'd have if he ever crossed this threshold. Clément in paradise! He'd have no problems identifying Trnka's dolls from *The Good Soldier Schweik* laid out on a Victor Louis console-table – presented to Old Job by Sacha Guitry – or Rashomon's accursed sword suspended above Lon Chaney's harmonium, and he'd have recognised the gallery of portraits which punctuated the flight of stairs below Topkapi's extraordinary chandelier.

"Is this the family?" I asked Julie, pointing at the series of portraits. "Generations of Bernardins?"

Julie was going up in front of me.

"Shhhh!" she whispered. "No, they're from Bergman. The complete set of paintings and medallions from *Smiles of a Summer Night*."

"You ought to keep the film collection here. Take down The Zebra brick by brick then rebuild it in the barn."

"Be quiet!"

She smiled. She was in front of me. She was getting younger each step she took. A gesture. "Stay put!" Finger on her lips. "Silence!" A childhood ritual. Pretend to surprise Old Job who was obviously expecting her by now. She'd go in without knocking. "How are things with the oldie?" Girlish cheek, which would at once earn her an equally ritualistic reply: "I hate youth. It's disgusting the way the young love the old!" And it would be the beginning of a long evening.

When Julie reached the door, she showed me the sign. Sure enough, it read: *Nap time from 16.00 to 17.05. Do not disturb on pain of death!* in neat, violet loops and curls. She put it back without making a sound, gave me a final girlish grin, turned the door handle, opened it and went in.

And Old Job's study exploded.

Exploded.

Almost noiselessly.

Just like a gust of wind.

Julie was thrown back against the wall of the corridor in slow motion. Propelled out of the study by the dragon's breath which tinged her with its flames.

Only then did I hear the explosion.

And saw Julie's hair catch fire. I screamed. I leapt towards her. I wrapped my torn shirt round her head and pushed her downstairs. The three doors we'd passed on the way up exploded one after another. The house had been booby-trapped. We got our breath back a bit on Renoir's floor tiles then fled this hell-hole, doubled up, stumbling, rolling in the grass, as far away as possible under a shower of broken glass, my shirt still round Julie's head, my arm protecting her. At that moment, the front door too spewed out its mouthful of hellfire.

"Watch out!"

We rolled over and the bronze centaur buried itself in the earth at the very place where we'd just been lying breathlessly.

"Further away! Quick!"

Julie's hand in mine, I headed off.

"Run!"

"I can't see anything!"

"Faster! Run! I'm here! I've got you!"

Explosion after explosion. Blowing out windows and raining down roof tiles. Each one followed by an eruption of rapacious flames, abruptly folding back into themselves in crackling hunger.

A dive behind a lime tree.

"Let me see!"

I unwound the shirt. Julie screamed.

"Gently!"

Her eyebrows came away with it.

"Oh! Jesus Christ!"

She hid her eyes. Hands blackened by the fire. Wrists swollen.

"Take your hands away, Julie. Let me see!"

She doggedly pulled her hands away. Along with her hair and lashes!

"Try and open your eyes."

She tried. God knows she tried. Eyelids puffy. Her entire face was twitching, looking up to the sky, blotched with burns. I stood between her and the sun. The shadow of my face on her scorched skin.

"I can't!"

Another explosion. A downpour of roof tiles in the leaves of the lime. The collapse of the roof frame.

"Who did that?"

Sudden tears. Tears of fury between swollen eyelids. Her eyes opened. She pushed me away. She leapt to her feet and faced the house. Eyes wide open!

"Who did that?"

"Hide, Julie!"

It was raining roof tiles. I pinned her against the tree trunk. But she couldn't take her eyes off the house.

"It's systematic! One room after another! A chain reaction!"

Chapter 39

WHICH WAS PRECISELY what we told the sergeant in charge of the local gendarmerie.

"It was systematic. One room after another."

The she added:

"I must have set off a system of fuses when I went into the study."

The kepi's peak was being maintained dead straight above the catastrophe.

"Did you see anyone in the study?"

"No, I don't think so. But it all happened so quickly! The first explosion set off a chain reaction!"

"Where had you come from?"

"Les Rochas, just behind Les Revoux."

"On foot?"

"That's right. Our truck's been stolen."

"What truck?"

"A truck we'd hired. We were supposed to be moving some films."

"With the owner's agreement?"

"Yes. Monsieur Bernardin had made me his heiress, at least when it comes to his film archives."

"Was this officially recorded?"

"Yes, it was. I had a fax in the truck. Monsieur Bernardin was going to give me the official notification along with the reels."

"What about sir here?"

"He's my partner. He was with me. He got me out of the house."

"Can you confirm that?"

"Every word of it."

Clear-cut questions. A toneless inquiry. A voice that went with the uniform. Polite. The barest hint of a personality. The other gendarmes taking photos and searching the surrounding countryside. The firemen hosing down the eruptive crater.

"Here's the doctor."

A fair-haired medic who leant over Julie's face and declared that there was nothing serious.

"It looks far worse than it is."

Ointment, lint, bandages. My Julie was mummified.

"I'm not hurting you?"

"No, it's OK."

"You must have been worried about your eyes."

"A bit. Benjamin wrapped my head up in his shirt."

"Good move. Now, hold out your hands. The worst burns are here, on your wrists . . . You must have been protecting your face by clenching your hands and crossing your arms."

The entire region was converging into the Loscence valley. Plus Julie's pals, at first drawn by the fire, then finding her there, by the black maria. But they knew La Juliette too well to show any signs of emotional effusion.

CHAPAYS (*re* the bandages): They really suit you, know that?"

MAZET: La Juliette looks good in anything.

JULIE (taking care of the introductions): Robert, Aimé, Benjamin.

Paws. Solid paws. Friendly fists, rather weather-beaten by the winters.

CHAPAYS (looking at the fire): Jesus. Quite a fireworks display. Was there anyone inside?

JULIE: I don't think so. I didn't see anybody.

MAZET: Look on the bright side. Every time Parisians put in an appearance down here, they give us something to talk about for the next thirty years.

Despite the circumstances, what shook Julie beneath her cottonwool and bandages was apparently a brief burst of laughter.

THE DOCTOR: Don't move.

THE GENDARME: Do you know each other?

CHAPAYS: Since we were kids. This is La Juliette. You're not going to cause her any problems, I hope?

THE GENDARME: Normally speaking, no.

Chapays and Mazet glanced at each other in a clear condemnation of any way of speaking apart from the normal one. There was a clear feeling that La Juliette was sacred territory, and that the constabulary would do well to kneel down and worship like everyone else.

CHAPAYS: If you need anything, Juliette . . .

MAZET: We'll be there.

And off they went to lend a hand to the firemen who were still busying themselves around the volcano.

"There we go," said the doctor, tying the last knot in the dressings. "When it starts to hurt, take two of these every three hours. And these, too."

Exit the doctor. The north wind started blowing, stirring columns of sparks. The sergeant shivered slightly in his blue shirt.

"Are you from these parts?" Julie asked.

The officer smiled.

"No, nor are any of my men. It's a rule in the gendarmerie. Otherwise, our work would be impossible. I'm actually from Alsace."

It was the barn's turn to collapse. A row of seats was cast up into orbit.

"That was their private cinema," Julie explained.

"Do you have any idea?" the officer asked. "I mean, who could have had this much of a grudge against them?"

Julie hesitated for a moment.

"No . . . No really, I don't."

This almost dreamlike conversation was interrupted by the arrival of a second kepi.

"Come and see, sir! We've found something!"

Then, to us:

"You come along, too. You might be able to help us."

He went on ahead.

"It's up there, on the Maupas road."

He clambered up through the undergrowth. We followed. He crossed a stone track, then plunged into a wood of spruces, whose lower branches were crumbling into dust.

"Look!"

And look we certainly did.

I think I've never looked so hard in my entire existence.

Or seen so much.

There, in front of us, in the middle of a clearing, half camouflaged by cut branches, was our truck.

The white truck we'd hired.

No doubt about it.

"That's our truck," Julie said.

"The one which was stolen?"

"That's right."

A third gendarme opened the double rear doors. The truck was full of rolls of film.

The sergeant made no reaction. He just climbed inside and motioned to Julie to do likewise. He read out aloud the film titles on the metal cases.

"Is this Monsieur Bernardin's film collection?"

"Yes," said Julie.

"And this is definitely the truck which was stolen?"

"Yes," one of his men replied. "We found the rental agreement in one of the glove compartments. Corrençon, isn't that right? Mademoiselle Julie Corrençon?"

"Yes, that's right," Julie said.

Question from the sergeant to his underling:

"And did you find a fax from Monsieur Bernardin?"

Answer:

"There were no faxes, sir."

Sergeant to Julie:

"Where did you put it?"

Starting to catch on, Julie shook her head.

"In the glove compartment, with the other papers."

"There are no faxes in the glove compartment, sir," the officer repeated.

I chipped in at once:

"The theft was reported to two police officers, who lodged the complaint at the main station in Valence."

What a strange feeling it is when you yourself don't believe what you're saying, and yet you know it's true. The earth opening beneath your feet . . . a free fall through solid ground . . .

*

"I'm sorry," the sergeant said as he hung up.

And I knew that, right then, between the four walls of this high-altitude gendarmerie station, he was going to announce that Valence said no. With his hand still on the receiver, the sergeant shook his head. He looked genuinely sorry. He was not one of those cops who justifies his coppery existence by preferring lies to the truth. He liked innocent citizens. He would have preferred it if the station at Valence had confirmed our tale. But it hadn't.

"There were no reports this morning of a stolen truck."

Julie remained silent.

Julie had caught on.

Julie was measuring the perfidious extent of the frame-up.

The depth of the pit.

I went on battling. But I knew I had as much hope as a herring in a Baltic fishing net.

"There was another guest at the hotel whose car had been stolen! And the girl in reception can confirm what happened. She was there when we arrived yesterday evening. Then she woke us up this morning when the two Inspectors turned up."

"We'll check that too, of course," the sergeant replied. "Which hotel was that?"

I repeated the name.

While typing it into his Minitel, he asked:

"Had you reserved? Is there any written trace?"

"No, we were just passing through. But we did pay by cheque."

"Which you gave to the receptionist?"

"That's right."

"OK, I'll ring them. I'll also call back the station in Valence about the theft of the car. Do you know what make it was?"

Memory, o memory . . . I rummaged through the fat bellower's diatribes. A real firework display which had been set off by the theft of a car. And no . . . no . . . not the slightest trace of any make. Even though it had meant so much to the dickhead!

"I reckon it must be big," I guessed. "And new."

"Never mind. If the theft has been reported, we'll have the make and the owner's name."

*

Well. No point dealing with the rest in detail. I too gave up the fight. Not only did the station in Valence say that no cars had been reported stolen between seven and eight o'clock that morning, but it had even received notification that a person had gone missing from that very hotel at ten o'clock. The student who had been taken on to do the night shift until the end of the month had mysteriously vanished, and the guests had woken up to find the hotel empty. The manager was in a panic, she was a steady girl, his very own niece who had been entrusted to him so that she could earn some holiday money. She was planning to visit Iceland with some fellow students. There was no sign of my cheque, and of course not the slightest trace of our stay, given that we'd arrived late, had been checked in by the girl in question, then gone at once to our room. The other nine guests had found their nine cars in the morning. There had been no tenth guest. As for the green-eyed cop who was supposed to be from Saint-Martin-en-Vercors, there was no police officer his age in the micro-population of Saint-Martin, nor for that matter the slightest young man with green eyes.

It was no longer a pit.

It was a sump.

Julie and I were spinning round inside, like a pair of flies, waiting to be ejected any moment now at the Antipodes, through the planet's arsehole.

Which now suddenly gaped even wider.

"Boss! We've found some bodies!"

"Bodies?" the sergeant asked, turning round towards the officer who had just burst into his office.

"Yes, in the house. Charred bodies. Three of them."

XI
THE RETURN OF THE GOAT

And you're sticking to your story?

Chapter 40

"**A**ND YOU'RE STICKING to your story?"

Chief Superintendent Nepos decided to repeat the said version so that I could gauge the full depth of its absurdity and then change it in accordance.

"If you are to be believed, Monsieur Malaussène, you and Mademoiselle Corrençon are supposed to have rented a truck in order to take possession of a collection of films she is supposed to have inherited (though she has no documentary evidence), and this truck is supposed to have been stolen (and the theft reported to a non-existent policeman) on the forecourt of a hotel (where no-one saw you), then hidden near the very place you were going so as to implicate you in the murder of Monsieur Bernardin and of his son, Doctor Matthias Fraenkhel. Is that it?"

Alas! Old Job . . . and Matthias . . . had been found dead in the ruins . . . along with a third as yet unidentified body.

"Quite an elaborate scheme, requiring a full supporting cast, don't you agree?"

Indeed.

But he still insisted on summing up:

"A truck thief, a false guest to shout about the theft of his own car, two other men to impersonate police officers, at least two others to booby-trap the house . . . who can possibly hate you so much that he's raised an entire army against you, Monsieur Malaussène?"

This really was the big question. Who hated me? And why that much? What had I done to you?

Chief Superintendent Nepos just couldn't believe in so much hatred.

"On the other hand, you certainly knew Doctor Fraenkhel."

On the other hand, we did.

"He was Mademoiselle Corrençon's gynaecologist."

True.

"And a close family friend."

True.

"You trusted him completely."

True.

"After what he did to you, you could easily have wanted to kill him."

False.

"Which is what is called a motive, Monsieur Malaussène."

And will soon be called a judicial error.

But what could I say? What can you say when you're the unfortunate depositary of the true truth? Man doesn't live on truth, he lives on answers! And Nepos was a man. O young men of generations yet to come, mark my words: know nothing, just have answers to everything. God was created from such a preference. God and Statistics! God and Statistics are answers which are going from strength to strength.

"No, Monsieur Malaussène, your story is unbelievable."

If the only problem we had in life was believability . . . Take this office, for instance, Chief Superintendent Coudrier's former office . . . How can a room's decor be so totally changed in such a short time? How, in just a few days, can that redolence of the First Empire – gold and green shadows jealously obscuring their host's meditations – turn into a room which is so *transparent*: broad bay window open over the city, white carpet and halogen lamps, double glass doors behind which flows the glittering stream of the corridor, translucent chairs which seem to hold the suspect suspended in mid-air, a bright glass desk . . . What had become of the dark ebony and matt-green velvet? Of the leather-padded door and the creaking floorboards? The rheostat lamp and the Récamier sofa? The imperial killer and his mantelpiece? Elisabeth, where are you? Coffee, Elisabeth! A nice cup of coffee . . .

"If my opinion is of any interest to you, Monsieur Malaussène, here it is."

Chief Superintendent Nepos knew nothing about hatred. His voice was calm. Staring at impeccable nails, he relentlessly stacked up the blocks of his thinking. Chief Superintendent Nepos worked hard at being a straightforward chap.

"I do believe that you hired the truck in order to take delivery of the film collection and of this 'Only Begotten Film' (which we're still looking for among the reels). You had said as much, as your cinematic friends have testified, so this point does seem incontestable. It is also quite possible that the films are a sort of legacy intended for Mademoiselle Corrençon. We shall have to check, but it is quite possible."

Eyes on his squeaky-clean hands. Apparently Chief Superintendent Nepos didn't look at much else. The bald mirror of his pate reflected the suspect's guilt.

We were supposed to see ourselves in the thinker's skull. A mirror which must have made many a villain confess!

"But there's something else, Monsieur Malaussène. I think that neither you nor Mademoiselle Corrençon has been able to bear the murder – and murder it certainly was – of the child you were to have."

The Chief Superintendent was a man of delicacy. He placed his silences perfectly. And didn't make them last longer than they should.

"It is at this moment that our two versions of the story begin to diverge."

With the sort of negligible divergence that fills up prisons.

"One question first. You and Mademoiselle Corrençon were the only people who knew that Doctor Fraenkhel had taken refuge in the Vercors with his aged father. Why didn't you inform my department?"

A question of culture, sir . . . And, at the time, "your" department was still your father-in-law's.

"Here's the rub, Monsieur Malaussène. Instead of tipping off the police, you decided to go there yourselves and ask Doctor Fraenkhel to explain himself, which I can quite understand."

Matthias was actually the last person I wanted to see on the plateau of the Vercors. But just try to introduce such a *human* piece of data into a *logical* sequence. Just try, and see what happens . . .

"Publicly, you were going to take delivery of the collection plus The Only Begotten Film. But in reality you were out to interrogate Doctor Fraenkhel. Then there was a murder. Two murders. Three, with the unidentified body."

Who are you, you other corpse? What surprises do you have in store for me?

NEPOS: Who is the third victim, Monsieur Malaussène?

ME: . . .

NEPOS: We'll find out sooner or later. The forensic surgeon . . .

ME: Julie and I thought the house was empty.

NEPOS: That's absolutely impossible. A sign found on the door of Monsieur Bernardin's study indicated that he was having an afternoon nap, and that he didn't want to be disturbed. And yet, according to what you said, it was when you opened this very door that you set off the first explosion.

ME: The sign dates back over twenty years.

NEPOS: Perhaps, but Monsieur Bernardin had hung it on his door that fateful day.

ME: He put it there every day.

NEPOS: In a house where he'd been living alone since the death of his wife? That hardly sounds likely.

ME: It was a souvenir of the days when there were children in the house.

NEPOS: Monsieur Malaussène . . . We found Job Bernardin's charred body in the study, sitting in its desk chair, with its skull smashed in, facing the hearth and that sign on the section of the door which hadn't burned.

ME: If Julie didn't see Old Job, then the chair must have been facing away from the door.

NEPOS: Unfortunately, Mademoiselle Corrençon's escape means we cannot ask her that.

Julie's Escape

A roll of clouds and drums. The blue sky suddenly turned the colour of asphalt. A Vercors fury. Instantaneous. One of those summer furies which are played behind closed curtains. Perpendicular lightning and horizontal hailstones. A bombardment. The heavens explode. The earth takes the blows. The murder squad's R-25, which had come from Valence to pick up Julie and me, was caught in the torrent. The two cops cracked jokes: it's like Beirut! It's like Sarajevo! That's the Vercors for you. It was the same last time. We go out for a nice family stroll, you know, to go berrying, and it ends up like a military operation. The fucking Vercors for you! The windscreen's going to smash if it keeps up like this! The left wiper's already had it. Can you see the crossroads? Watch out there in front! In front! It's coming straight at us! Braaaake! Till the impact. A soft impact. Soft and heavy. Shit! What the hell is it? Hay! A downpour of round hayricks rolling down from the heights. Jesus fucking Christ! Peasant semaphores towards the car window. Not my fault! Lightning! The rear of the truck gave in on the way up. That's right. A bolt hit the lock. The farmer didn't seem that put out. Standing under the storm. His fine face being pummelled by hailstones. He looked familiar. But I won't say who it was. I'd have willingly kissed him, but . . . handcuffs. Handcuffs hooked on to the door handle. Malaussène, the dangerous criminal! No handcuffs for Julie. Because of her burnt wrists. Just a muscleman beside her. One move darling, and I'll . . . Poor bastard. Didn't know Julie. His guts were still digesting the darling's elbow when the nape of his neck cracked under a rabbit chop. Door open, and Julie's leap into the thicket. Julie's race towards freedom. Lightning. Thunder. Wonderful! Shit! The other cop next to me drawing his gun. Shit! Shit! Don't fire! My foot in his ribs. A bullet in the trees. Run, Julie! A pistol whip to my head. Curtain.

An Irrefutable Summing up in a Transparent Office

CHIEF SUPERINTENDENT NEPOS: This is what really happened, Monsieur Malaussène. You and Mademoiselle Corrençon claimed that you were going to the Vercors in order to take delivery of a collection of films as well as this Only Begotten Film. But your real objective was to find Doctor Fraenkhel and question him. You did so. The conversation became heated. There was a murder. Two cumbersome witnesses – or else people you considered to be Doctor Fraenkhel's accomplices – his father as well as a third unidentified person suffered the same fate. You then panicked and attempted to cover up the murders by blowing up the house. You hid your truck in the forest of the Loscence. And you tried to pass yourselves off as victims of a booby-trapped house.

BENJAMIN MALAUSSÈNE: Who'd believe such a thing, for Christ's sake?

NEPOS: That's precisely my point, Monsieur Malaussène. For your story to be credible, it had to appear incredible. You even went so far as to leave incriminating evidence in your truck – a stick of dynamite and a bomb fuse. Mademoiselle Corrençon knows how to use this sort of explosive. All the local potholers use it for widening openings in caves.

ME: But why would we have done that?

HIM: As I've already told you, Monsieur Malaussène, you accumulated clues to your guilt in order to create the impression that *other people* had placed them. Your reasoning went as follows: the police will never believe that a pair of murderers could be quite so inept at concealing their crimes. On the contrary, if someone had tried to frame you, then this is just what they would have done . . .

ME: . . .

HIM: In other words, it was well thought out.

ME: . . .

HIM: And, to a degree, such staging pleads in your defence.

ME: . . . ?

HIM: Of course! Because it rules out premeditation. Only someone in the throes of panic could have dreamt up such a scheme. Thus, you did not go there *in order* to kill Doctor Fraenkhel. But you arranged all of this stage-managing *because* you had killed him.

ME: . . .

HIM: . . .

ME: But . . . what about the girl at the hotel? The student? She knows we spent the night there and that our truck was stolen!

HIM: Yes, the missing student . . . that is a good question.

ME: . . .

HIM: . . .

ME: . . .

HIM:: You didn't go back and kill her, did you? To eliminate a witness?

ME: . . .!

HIM: Because if you did, that would change the nature of the situation.

ME: . . .!!

HIM: Of course it would! Because for that murder, there would be no doubt about premeditation. But you wouldn't have done that, would you? Surely you didn't go that far?

*

You can escape from any situation. Imprudent swimmers have extricated themselves from the larder where they've been dragged by ravenous crocodiles. Yes, that's right! In Cameroon! In Florida! Absent-minded parachutists have jumped without their backpacks and have still died in their beds. Every day, convicts escape from prison and real-estate agents manage to remain at large. People with insurance policies have even received their repayments. But no-one, ever, has escaped from the clutches of a son-in-law bent on liberating himself from his father-in-law. This is what I suddenly realised when Chief Super-intendent Nepos at last raised his clear eyes to stare at me.

"Times have changed, Monsieur Malaussène."

I didn't catch on at once. But he soon filled me in.

"My predecessor would have seized on to this network of presumptions and used it to prove your innocence. He claimed you were a textbook case, the living proof of how appearances can be deceptive. A scapegoat. An expiatory victim. You rammed that idea into his head. Thanks to you, he trained – or rather derailed – generations of police officers. He made them so wary of the obvious that now not one of them is capable of detecting a crime that is being committed in broad daylight. The subtlety virus . . . *If the guilty party looks that guilty, then he must in fact be innocent.* It flatters a lowly copper's. intelligence. As for me, Monsieur Malaussène, I reject his thesis. It's no more than a novelistic conceit. In real life, deeds are deeds, misdeeds are misdeeds, and most of them clearly point to their perpetrators."

I stopped listening to Nepos. I had also just realised why the office had morphed. The *successor* syndrome. The New Man has arrived and, with him, mankind is renewed! This, of course, can lead to problems for those men who are being renewed, involving sackings, premature retirements, sidelinings, exile, melancholy, resignations and solitude. Solitude. A successor! You wipe out, uproot, obliterate the past with your gaze fixed on the future. I reckon Coudrier's old team must have been thrown on the junk heap with the furniture. But that's the way it goes: new man, new ways. The cretinous chant of the successor. You think you're being modern. But you fail to understand that modernity is as old as the hills. That it must be the most hackneyed of all traditions. I'll eat my hat if they haven't also changed the make of the staples which are pinning together the papers in my file. And Chief Superintendent Nepos sincerely thinks he's being original. He's here now! And we're really going to see something! The graphs on the wall are a clear sign, the classification of crimes, geographical distribution, criminality curves, percentages, social-insecurity forms. No more guestimation. From now on, everything's scientific. "Now, the only form of science, Monsieur Malaussène, is the one that is based on facts!" Nepos thinks he's talking calmly, his highly educated lips slowly frame their words, but behind this blue-eyed civil servant there's a palm tree being shaken. Furiously. Stop it, you silly bastard. Just stop it, you daft cunt! It isn't Coudrier who's hanging on for his life up there, it's me! Coudrier's gone fishing! Coudrier couldn't give a toss! He's fishing! With his mate Sanchez! In Malaussène! My namesake village! Coudrier isn't in the slightest bit obsessed with his son-in-law! He's putting a worm on his hook! With a bottle of rosé chilling in the stream . . .

And, as if to confirm my worst suspicions, Chief Superintendent Nepos's voice concluded:

"There is, of course, nothing personal about all this, Monsieur Malaussène. So far as I am concerned, you're just another suspect. You have the same rights as everyone else. No more, no less. Your case will be examined thoroughly and dispassionately. If there is any room for doubt, you can count on me that the doubts also will be methodical ones."

Where are you, Elisabeth? Didn't you hear me just now? Coffee, Elisabeth! I beg you. A little cup of coffee. It's the least you can do when the doors of a life sentence have just been opened in front of me.

But it wasn't Elisabeth's voice that came through the intercom, and it wasn't Elisabeth's outline in the glass door. Another one of New Man's miracles – the transformation of a good old vicar's housekeeper into a spanking new secretary, who had nothing more to offer than a nervous smile on a competent face above a miniskirt.

And it wasn't a cup of coffee she was holding.

It was a fax.

She minced over and placed it on the desk.

"Thank you, Mademoiselle."

Chief Superintendent Nepos's office was so transparent that it looked as though Mademoiselle walked straight through the wall.

A fax.

A moment to read it.

"This will be of interest to you, Monsieur Malaussène."

Time to finish.

"The identity of the third victim."

Time to look up at me blandly.

"Marie-Hélène Desgranges, Monsieur Malaussène. Does that name mean anything to you?"

No. Luckily enough, it meant nothing at all.

"Are you sure?"

Sorry, not a thing. I've never heard of any Marie-Hélène Desgranges.

"Nineteen years of age, Monsieur Malaussène . . . a student . . . with a holiday job working nights in the hotel where you claim to have spent the night . . . Must I remind you of its name?"

" . . ."

It was in my own silence that I heard the final blast of typewriter fire which had been nailing our words to the walls since the start of the interrogation.

Chapter 41

A GROUP OF JAPANESE tourists, sitting in mid-air, their legs dangling in space . . . That was what Julie could see in the mirror.

"Out of there, Barnaby!"

Alone in Old Job's Paris flat, Julie was talking to a wardrobe.

"Come on out or I'll come in and get you."

The wardrobe replied:

"Hush now, Julie. And do like me. Watch the show."

The mirror in the wardrobe was not reflecting Julie. Instead, it contained the inverted image of a television set. And the TV set contained a group of Japanese on Place du Palais-Royal, sitting in space, crossing and uncrossing their legs, standing up and skipping above the ground, going up and down invisible stairs, without ever succeeding in touching the ground, to the great delight of the surrounding crowd.

Julie was in no mood for this.

"For the last time, come out of the cupboard, Barnaby, or I'll smash it into firewood."

"Just listen to the commentator crapping on, Julie, and relax. After all, he is talking about my art."

The levitating Japanese above Place du Palais-Royal once again caught Julie's eye. No matter how hard they tried, they really were incapable of touching down. They looked forlorn, as if they were the only ones gravity refused to nail on to the common plot. All around, the equally Japanese Place du Palais-Royal was laughing.

The commentator's voice:

"*If the Columns of Buren caused a scandal in the days of the Architect-President, then Barnabooth's sarcastic vision will surely sow the seeds of further controversy. Were Buren's striped pyjamas art? Is Buren's disappearance under Barnabooth's stare art? Are Barnabooth's vanishing tricks a tourist attraction, or the aesthetic verdict of a masked avenger? Is Barnabooth a passing fad, or the highest form of criticism? Who will now dare to create under his eliminating stare?"*

"Who indeed?" a voice ironically echoed from the depths of the wardrobe.

(For fuck's sake, Julie thought, this character massacres his family, burns his childhood memories, frames up Benjamin and me, forces me to assault a police officer, drops me into an underground existence, and here I am like a silly cunt watching him make the Columns of Buren disappear, while listening to his sarky comments about reactions to his art!)

She tore the TV set away from its socket and threw it into the mirror. Implosion, explosion, assorted noises, bright flashes, showers of sparks. Smoke. Silence, at last.

And Julie's face.

The wardrobe was empty.

But the voice was still there.

"What have you done, Juliette? Wrecked the wardrobe? Did you really imagine I was waiting for you in a wardrobe?"

Mouth agape. Arms dangling.

"I'll kill you," she said at last.

"Wasn't all that death and destruction in Loscence enough for you? Are you set on destroying Old Job's furniture in Paris as well?"

"I'll kill you."

"That's another reason why I wasn't in the wardrobe."

"Where are you?"

"Where do you imagine? On Place du Palais-Royal of course! This programme's being broadcast live. Making the Columns of Buren vanish requires my presence and skill. With a huge contract in perspective with the Japanese. These dancers are just great, don't you think?"

"I've just been to the Palais-Royal!"

"I know, and you didn't find me. Juliette, if you want to talk to me, then you'll need a transceiver. But as for seeing me, no way. So just forget it. No-one can see me. And I'm not making an exception for you, Miss Journalist!"

Then he yelled:

"I really did it, Julie! I've succeeded!"

That voice! Julie was recognising Barnaby more and more in his voice. The less she saw him, the more familiar he got. That voice . . . a barely deformed echo of a child's shrill, distant voice: "I'll do it, Juliette! I'll succeed!"

*

Centuries before, one afternoon in their early teens, Barnaby had asked her to come to his room.

"My room, at three o'clock on the dot, Juliette. If you're just one minute late, you'll ruin everything."

This was the same time as when Liesl, Matthias and Job used to lock themselves up in what they pompously called their "laboratory". Whenever the other three disappeared, Barnaby would suggest some activity to Julie, and Julie would always accept.

"At the stroke of three, in your room? OK."

Julie and Barnaby had synchronised their watches.

"You're really going to see something, Juliette."

When she opened the bedroom door, she screamed. It led out to nothing. To a void. The door was open and there was nothing behind it. No more bed, no more chest of drawers, no more walls, no more ceiling, no more beams, no more floor, no more corners, no more volume, no more surfaces. Nothing. Just white opacity. She'd put out her arms, then leant back on the closed door, which had in turn vanished. She felt giddy and sick, like in the absolute blackness of the potholes they explored. She slid down on to her heels. Everything inside her had gone woolly, as though by opening this door, she had opened a void inside herself, a void crammed full of cottonwool, an unbreathable emptiness. She struggled for breath, her heart beating in her mouth.

Finally, when she had got over the surprise, she saw him. Somewhere in that space without space, in what she supposed must be the upper left-hand corner of his bedroom, she saw Barnaby's face. And only his face. As though sliced off by a razor and glued down on to white paper. A face with closed eyes and no body. She tried to look away, but the quantity of surrounding whiteness forced her eyes back to this floating mask. Her first thought was how frail Barnaby seemed. How small faces are, with nothing to surround them! And how oval! Unreal! And yet how perishable!

Then, as if by magic, an open book appeared before his face. A book with no fingers to hold it. A book which Julie recognised as being the one they were both into at the time: Valery Larbaud's *Barnabooth*. Then she heard Barnaby's voice – so shrill without its body – reading out some lines they both knew by heart. The face was reading, with its eyes still closed. But, behind the lids, Julie could clearly see Barnaby's eyes moving in the path of Barnabooth's verses:

Go and tell Shame that I'm dying for her love;
I want to plunge into infamy

As though on to a soft bed;
I want to do everything that's justly forbidden;
I want to be covered with mockery and disdain;
I want to be the basest of men.

Then there was the crackling of a short circuit, and a whole stretch of the room reappeared in a stench of burnt wires and melted copper – the window, bed and chest of drawers, which had been masked by white sheets. The face high up to the left was now staring wildly and saying: "Fuck! Fuck! Fuck! Fuck!" During the subsequent spluttering, Barnaby's body had reappeared gradually: feet, legs, hands, elbows and shoulders mounted up to his face in a Mexican carnival atmosphere. A thousand tiny projectors exploded one after the other, following a complex itinerary. And Barnaby at last reappeared in his entirety, as Pierrot Lunaire, hanging a few inches from the ceiling, white in his white room, in a long nightie filched from Liesl, feet and hands enclosed in socks, which turned them into rabbit's paws, and a bed cap pulled over his ears – a white bat caught in the web of climbing ropes, Valery Larbaud's *Barnabooth* dangling in front of its eyes on nylon threads which had been pinned on to the ceiling. "Fuck! Fuck! Fuck! Fuck! . . . Fuck! Fuck! Fuck! Fuck! It didn't hold up even for one minute!" And Julie's burst of hysterical giggles, as she slapped the floor, while Barnaby raged and threw the Larbaud at her.

"You little idiot," he said. "You'll never be more than a cardboard cut-out!"

His fury and resolution as Valery Larbaud bounced off the wall:

"One day, I'll really do it! One day, I'll succeed!"

*

And succeed he had. He was now nothing more than a voice. Julie was listening to the wreck of a wardrobe.

"No, Juliette, I didn't kill my father, nor my grandfather! I didn't burn down the house in Loscence! And I didn't stuff your truck with incriminating evidence."

"It was you, Barnaby! You blew up every single one of those rooms! God knows, we've widened enough potholes together! You used the same amount of explosives at the same intervals."

"A good clue, Juliette. This proves there must be an experienced potholer in the gang."

For a moment, she was tempted to believe him.

"Just dare to tell me you weren't there!"

"Why would I have done such a thing?"

274

"You were there, weren't you?"

"For revenge? Is that the only thing you can come up with, Juliette? Vengeance! Barnaby murders Old Job, because Old Job had robbed him of his father, is that it? And just to round the story off nicely, Barnaby then slaughters his father and destroys the house?"

"Were you there, or weren't you?"

"Vengeance! That's all you people can think of! But I'm not out for revenge! Barnabooth is no avenger! Did you hear about my production of *Hamlet* in New York?"

"Don't start pissing me off with *Hamlet*, Barnaby!"

"It sparked off one hell of a scandal. Because instead of going out for revenge, all my Hamlet wanted was to erase this world of murderers and cheats. To make all the liars vanish! Lying and dissimulation turn us into ghosts. The King, the Queen, Polonius, even Ophelia, are dissolved in social deceit, are no more real for Hamlet than his father's ghost. Why should Hamlet avenge a father who was as rotten as his uncle? Why should Hamlet kill an uncle who is as ghostly as his father?"

All Julie could do was wait. Another thing Barnaby had always had in common with Hamlet was a tendency to soliloquise.

"To *erase*, Juliette. Not to eliminate, but to *erase*. To wipe out deceptive images. Do you still understand what such words mean? I'm an eraser, not a murderer! During the play, I erased the entire state of Denmark. My Hamlet's stare wiped out the other characters. As soon as he looked at the other actors, they vanished, one by one. All those dialogues spoken in absolute emptiness. Just imagine the crap the critics came out with!"

"Barnaby . . ."

"I'm no avenger. I don't measure myself up against others. I've broken the chain! Do you hear me? *Erase! Erase!* That's the point! And no memories. Absolutely no commemorations! I didn't go to Liesl's funeral, nor to those of Job and Matthias. I refuse to commemorate! I'll believe in commemorations when the Germans come to mourn *our* dead and we go to kneel down before the graves in Algeria, when Arabs grieve for the Jews whose throats they've cut, and Jews for the Palestinians they've shot down, when the Yanks gather solemnly on the ruins of Japan and the Nips weep over the bodies of Chinese and Korean women . . . Then, and only then, will I mourn for my dead ones . . ."

He suddenly fell silent.

"OK, so you want to know if I was in Loscence?"

She didn't even have enough strength left to be surprised.

"Well, yes I was. I had told you that I wasn't going to allow The Only Begotten Film to be shown. So I went there to get the reel."

"Alone?"

"No. With your Clément. You lot had made the poor kid feel so guilty about Cissou the Snow that he was dying to make amends. He agreed to help me."

"Since when have you needed help, Barnaby?"

"I didn't want to go inside the house. Too many memories. And the kid wanted to cleanse his conscience. When I told him that showing the film would be as big a crime as displaying Cissou's tattoos, he agreed at once."

"And then?"

"He was a nice kid, Juliette. He lived for the cinema. But you lot handed him an Ophelia."

"For Christ's sake, Barnaby! Don't start on *Hamlet* again!"

"He asked me: 'Where are you taking me, Barnabooth, to the Beauty or to the Beast?'"

"Did he see you? Did you show yourself to him?"

"I repeat: I don't show myself to anyone. No. We had two cars. Him in front, me behind. I'd equipped him and told him which way to go."

"And then?"

"And then? . . . And then? . . . And then? . . . You should hear yourself asking your questions, Juliette."

"Don't start again, Barnaby . . ."

"It isn't even to save your Malaussène that you're questioning me now . . . I'm an expert in the tones of people's voices . . . 'And then?' 'And then?' . . . The obscene lure of the scoop! You hacks are all out of the same mould! It's *how* that interests you, not *why*, isn't it? How many copies sold? How many listeners? How many colleagues are already on to it? How many times has the same topic already been dealt with?"

"So, Barnaby, did you kill them before or after Clément arrived?"

A stab to stop the tirade against journalism. But she'd apparently hit him too hard. The succeeding silence lasted almost as long as the outburst. She was now sitting in front of a stubbornly mute wardrobe. She knew that he was waiting for her next question, and that this question would only lengthen his silence. He knew she wouldn't in fact ask it, and so finally said:

"When Clément went to the house, there were at least two people inside. A man and a woman."

(Here we go . . . Julie thought.)

"Did they jump him?"

"Not at once. They didn't see him at first. He went straight to Old Job's study. I'd drawn up a plan of the house so that he wouldn't waste too much time in ecstasy before all those knick-knacks. They only spotted him when he was going into the study."

Another silence.

"You really managed to make that poor kid feel rotten."

And then:

"Because he felt he had to act like a hero."

And:

"He fooled them for a while, but they finally sussed."

Silence.

"And they killed him?"

"Clément must have rushed to the door. The woman yelled: 'Stop him!' And there was a thud. It was the last thing I heard."

"And where were you?"

"Round the back, on the forest road. See where I mean?"

"What did you do?"

"I hesitated. I started to come down towards the house, then I saw them come out. A tall woman and a bulky man. The bloke was carrying Clément over his shoulder. The girl got into a red Fiat, and the big guy took Clément's car, which was parked on the Maupas road. Five minutes later, they drove past me. I ran to my car. Once they'd left the woods, they turned right on to the Col de Carri road. I followed them from a safe distance. Too safe, in fact. Because by the time I reached Col de la Machine, all I could see was the red Fiat, which was setting off at full speed. They'd pushed Clément's car off the top of the cliff. It's probably still there, in the woods of Combe Laval."

"What make is it?"

"A small white Renault. We'd hired it."

"What did you do next?"

"I climbed down the Laval rock face. I had my climbing ropes in the boot."

"And?"

"He was dead, Juliette."

Silence.

"Barnaby?"

"Yes?"

"I believe you."

BARNABY: . . .

JULIE: There's just one thing . . .

277

BARNABY: Yes?

JULIE: . . .

BARNABY: Yes, Juliette?

JULIE: Why didn't you then go back to Loscence? You knew we were on our way, didn't you?

BARNABY: I didn't know when you were coming.

JULIE: And you couldn't be bothered to wait? To warn us? Or tell the police about Clément?

BARNABY: So they could pin the murder on me? No thanks.

JULIE: No, you preferred them to arrest us instead.

BARNABY: Of course not! I didn't know the house was booby-trapped!

JULIE: Do you want me to tell you the real reason you went back to Paris?

BARNABY: . . .

JULIE: To prepare your show.

BARNABY: . . .

JULIE: Barnabooth's idea of purity . . . The morality of Barnabooth, the universal giver of lessons . . . Murderers have occupied Old Job's house, a young man is killed practically before his very eyes, his childhood sister is in danger of getting involved, and what does Barnabooth the non-avenger do? He who erases and doesn't commemorate, the one and only Barnabooth, Barnabooth the pure, this Noah of the human species, what does our new Hamlet do in such circumstances? Will he watch out for his kith and kin? Will he tend young Clément's grave? Not a bit of it! He dots a full stop. He erases it all . . . then off he goes to Paris to make the Columns of Buren vanish.

BARNABY: . . .

JULIE: A contract is a contract.

BARNABY: . . .

JULIE: A career is a career . . .

BARNABY: . . .

JULIE: And a show like this requires careful preparation.

BARNABY: . . .

JULIE: So there's no way he's going to jeopardise it by getting caught up in some tabloid story . . .

BARNABY: . . .

JULIE: Barnaby, are you listening to me?

BARNABY: . . .

JULIE: When you went down to see if Clément was dead, you had something else in mind as well.

BARNABY: . . .

JULIE: You went to get back the transceiver. Leave no traces.

BARNABY: . . .

JULIE: . . .

BARNABY: . . .

JULIE: There's no point making yourself invisible, Barnabooth. You can be spotted from miles away. You're the foulest piece of shit the world has ever dropped!

(Right, so what do I do now? Julie had installed the silence of a vanishing trick in the ruins of the wardrobe. What do I do now?)

She glanced around. Apart from these two visits to Barnaby, she'd never set foot in Job's Paris office. She recognised nothing about her old mentor in it. Nor anything about Liesl. It was one of those Champs Élyséean offices whose sole purpose is to display the "surface" of a company. Apart from the unreflecting mirror, Barnaby hadn't added a single personal touch, and the wardrobe had now seen better days. (Well I'll go then, Julie thought while remaining seated.)

"I'm going."

She finally stood up.

"Where?"

The wardrobe had recovered its voice.

Without replying, Julie headed towards the corridor.

"Don't be silly, Juliette. Come back and open the false bottom in the wardrobe."

She stopped. She stared round incredulously at the wardrobe. A false bottom?

"You open it by sliding your hand underneath. There's a catch there. It's a sliding panel. If you haven't completely demolished everything, it should still slide out."

She retraced her steps and did as the wardrobe directed. It slid open.

"Take the envelope."

A small brown paper envelope.

"It's the conversation between Clément and his aggressors. I taped it."

The envelope contained a tiny tape recorder with a cassette inside.

"Sit down comfortably and listen. Then you'll understand why I came back to Paris."

Julie sat back down in front of the wardrobe. When she took the recorder out of the envelope, Barnaby concluded:

"They stole Job's and Liesl's film, Juliette."

Chapter 42

T HE TAPE STARTED WITH a muffled exclamation:
  "Jesus, it's Count Zaroff's door!"
Which was at once reprimanded by Barnaby's voice:
"Don't waste any time getting ecstatic, Clément."
But, when he went into the hall, Clément had been incapable of holding back a second cry of amazement.
"Trnka's dolls! Is this what you call knick-knacks, Barnabooth?"
Then Barnaby's furious whispers:
"Are you trying to wake everyone up? Go upstairs quickly, and spare me your comments on Bergman's medallions."
Clément was teasing Barnaby.
"I'm more interested in Renoir than Bergman."
"Go on!"
Julie could hear Clément's weight on the stairs. She pictured him going up towards Old Job's study, Clément following the beam from his torch, completely overexcited by the cinematographic nature of the experience. Clément climbing towards his destiny on the staircase from *The Rules of the Game*. What must have been going through his mind? She heard him mumble:
"OK, I'm there. I've reached the study, with the notice about the nap."
And Barnaby's irritated reaction:
"Well, if you're there, go inside!"
Julie could clearly hear the handle turning.
Barnaby's and Clément's whispering grew barely audible: directions through the chaos in the study, identifying the three possible hiding places.
"No," Clément whispered. "It isn't here."
"OK, well try the top of the mantelpiece."
Until a woman's voice burst in:
"What are you doing here?"

280

And Clément's extraordinary reflex response:

"Christ, you're beautiful! He told me you were beautiful, but I never expected you to be as beautiful as this. Put your gun away, you'll only end up hurting yourself."

Pause. Rewind. Listen again:

"*Christ, you're beautiful! He told me you were beautiful, but I never expected you to be as beautiful as this. Put your gun away, you'll only end up hurting yourself.*"

(Amazing, Julie thought. Clément pretended that he *knew who she was*. An instantaneous reaction. Without the slightest hesitation.)

Intrigued by the "he", the girl hesitated.

"Who are you?"

Clément went on with his act.

"I don't know if I should tell you this, but what he likes most about you are your freckles."

The girl sniggered.

"I know better than you what he likes . . . Anyway, what the hell are you doing here?"

Another instant reply:

"I've come to get the film of course!"

A few minutes before his death, Clément was play-acting. Clément was playing at playing. Clément was shooting his own film. Clément the Budding Bayleaf was taking the chance to play the role of a lifetime. His every sense sharpened by the danger, he was coming out with a series of likely answers in a scenario he knew nothing about.

Meanwhile, he was relaying as much information as possible to Barnaby. He was describing the girl in front of him!

"And you're limping? Have you hurt your knee? He didn't tell me you limped."

"The film left the day before yesterday."

"It left, but it hasn't arrived. That's why I'm here."

"What do you mean it hasn't arrived? Cazo went back with it the day before yesterday."

Pause. Rewind.

"*What do you mean it hasn't arrived? Cazo went back with it the day before yesterday.*"

Continuation. Clément's tone hardened.

"So what are you still doing here? If the film's gone, you should have gone too. They're expecting you! You're not trying to pull a fast one on us, are you?"

Incredible!

"This is our business. It's got nothing to do with the King."

Back!

"*It's got nothing to do with the King.*"

"*. . . nothing to do with the King . . .*"

Then, suddenly a man's voice:

"Who are you talking to?"

And Clément's voice, suddenly wavered:

"Hey, given up the theatre, have you?"

The man's voice:

"Are you part of the set-up?"

The woman's voice:

"Apparently Cazo hasn't shown up yet."

Clément's immediate follow through:

"The King sent me to fetch the film."

Pause! Pause! Rewind! Again! Again!

"*Hey, given up the theatre, have you?*"

"*Are you part of the set-up?*"

Again!

"*Hey, given up the theatre, have you?*"

He knew him. Clément knew the man!

"*Are you part of the set-up?*"

And the man recognised Clément.

"*Hey, given up the theatre, have you?*"

Clément knew him, but not well enough to remember his name.

Girl's voice:

"*Apparently Cazo hasn't shown up yet.*"

And Clément's immediate gambit:

"*The King sent me to fetch the film.*"

But there was an audible shake in his voice. He hadn't been expecting to find this man there. But, if they had sent him to fetch the film, then he would have been told that the man would be there, all of which he immediately realised.

The man's voice:

"Oh yes? With an electric torch? And without giving us warning?"

Clément's panicked voice:

"We thought you'd gone. That's what was planned, wasn't it?"

The man's voice:

"Planned by who?"

Clément's exclamation:

"You so much as touch me and I'll spill the beans to the Viet's daughter!"

The girl's yell:

"Stop him!"

Then a series of dull thuds.

Then silence.

Then Julie alone, leaning over the machine. A final replay:

"Who are you talking to?"

"Hey, given up the theatre, have you?"

"Are you part of the set-up?"

"Apparently Cazo hasn't shown up yet."

"The King sent me to fetch the film."

"Oh yes? With an electric torch? And without giving us warning?"

"We thought you'd gone. That's what was planned, wasn't it?"

"Planned by who?"

"You so much as touch me and I'll spill the beans to the Viet's daughter!"

"Stop him!"

(The Viet's daughter? Julie thought. Gervaise? Gervaise . . . What the hell's Gervaise got to do with all this?)

*

"Juliette? Do you know who he meant by the Viet's daughter?"

Julie got to her feet.

"This time, I really do have to go, Barnaby."

"Take the transceiver. We have to keep in contact outside. I've prepared one for you. It's in the left-hand cushion on the sofa."

Then, while Julie was plugging herself in:

"And the King, Juliette? Who's the King?"

Chapter 43

THERE WEREN'T THAT many kings around who were quite so interested in Old Job's work. There was only one, in fact, and Julie could picture His Majesty perfectly: a smug laugh across porcelain choppers, an open shirt revealing a luxuriant peroxide fleece, matching neck chain, bracelet and signet ring, a frank hug and direct address. Forty years of betrayed ideals dissolved into a puddle of repentance at Suzanne's feet: "I admit that I've become the King of the Living Dead, that I've wasted my footage and never sent you reeling . . ." Then this cry: "I want to see it, Suzanne. Kneel me down on a ruler with a dictionary on my head if you want, but I've *got* to see that film!" Neither Suzanne nor Julie had gauged the true extent of that need. The King of the Living Dead wanted to see Old Job's Only Begotten Film. And at any price. The ghost of a film buff still wandered around the caverns of his brain, looking for the truth. Suzanne had sent the King of the Living Dead packing, so the King had decided to serve himself. And the means at his disposal for self-service were considerable . . .

Barnaby had pressed the point:

"And the King, Juliette? Who's the King?"

Julie had exchanged the King's identity for his Paris address, which Barnaby had unearthed in the twinkling of an eye.

In the taxi which was taking her to the King of the Living Dead, Barnaby kept on bargaining.

"What about the Viet's daughter?"

Julie was being driven round with Barnabooth in her brain. The bandages which were covering her burns, and which gave her the sharp face of a snake-woman, concealed the receivers she had placed in her ears. Massive convex sunglasses added bluebottle eyes to her snaky looks.

"The Viet's daughter? No idea."

Barnaby was spluttering with rage.

"Julie, I did give you the King's address."

"After I told you who he is."

"Juliette, who's the Viet's daughter?"

"Tell me what this film's about, Barnaby."

"I don't want anyone to see it, and I don't want to tell anyone about it either."

"Even me?"

"Especially you."

"I don't know who the Viet's daughter is, Barnaby."

"Are you talking to yourself?"

This question came from the outside. In his rear-view mirror, the driver was looking worried.

This bluebottle-eyed woman was rather scaring him.

"I'm mad," Julie answered.

"How do you mean, mad?" the cabby asked.

"Completely off my trolley. I'm talking to someone inside my head," Julie explained.

"Who are you talking to?" Barnaby asked.

"Someone who's out of my head," Julie replied. "He wants to know who I'm talking to. What's your name?"

"My name's Raymond."

"I'm talking to Raymond," Julie told Barnaby, while staring at the nape of the cabby's neck through her sunglasses.

"I mean . . . we aren't really talking," the driver corrected her, keeping his eyes fixed on the road. "You can't really call this talking."

"And what do you really call talking?" Julie asked with a hint of irritation.

"Are you asking me that?" Barnaby asked.

"Listen, Hamlet, who paged you?" Julie said. "Now shut up or I'll erase you."

The driver, who had been hoping to take this turban-clad visitor via the tourist route, changed direction and took a short cut.

*

When she arrived at his address – a modest little mansion on Avenue Henri-Martin – Julie realised at once that she'd never again have the chance to speak to the King of the Living Dead. She immediately spotted the journalists scattered around the crowd and understood why they were there, with their massed cameras and mikes. And why the crowd was there, being kept back by the police. And why there were all these discreet tears. It all stank of the death of a star, of lucrative mourning. From what she could hear, the actor-cum-producer's obituary must have been ready for some time.

"It was bound to happen the way he drank."

"It's a wonder he lasted as long as he did."

"It's a bit of a record."

"Apparently he hadn't washed for the past seven years."

"Really?"

"Honestly. He wore talc and aftershave and was tanned to hide the dirt."

"A real king, in fact."

"A nabob's trappings concealing a tramp's body."

"Yes, that was in the last interview he ever gave . . . The temptation of bumming."

"So, is he really dead or isn't he?"

"He's gone, barring complications."

"*He's gone, barring complications*: that's a Flers and Caillavet line, from *The Green Jacket.*"

"Well spotted, Jeannot!"

Julie had erased Barnaby and was now listening and looking around. The King was dying in the American Hospital in Neuilly. What of? No-one knew. An emergency admission. A big secret which had lasted all of one night. He might already be dead. They were expecting his body to arrive at any moment.

"*Whatever his final illness was, a star has been taken away from us, yes, a star has gone out . . . and the assembled crowds . . .*"

The character who was whispering this into his mike with the finest tones of compassion was holding a *pain au chocolat* in his other hand.

Julie turned Barnaby back on.

"Barnabooth?"

"Who's the Viet's daughter?" Barnaby asked.

"That's not what matters right now. The King's dying."

She described the crowd around the King's house and repeated what she'd heard.

"Like Pandora's box," Barnaby observed. "He saw the film and it was the death of him."

(No, Barnaby, Julie thought. I'm not going to ask you twice what's on this reel everyone's dying to get hold of.)

"I'm going in," she said. "I'm going to take a closer look. I'll plug you back in later."

"No point. I'm here."

She jumped.

"What?"

"I'm here. Just by you."

She couldn't resist staring round at the crowd.

"You look very nice in that raincoat, Juliette."

"Here's your toy back, Barnabooth."

She tore out the receivers and threw the tiny headset into the bin. Then she took a deep breath, tightened the belt of her beige raincoat, folded up the collar, moistened a finger, stained her cheeks with eyeliner, plumped up her lips with grief, moored her sunglasses beneath her turban and, thus disguised as an image of inconsolable mourning, she set off through the crowd. Her colleagues' cameras went for her at once. Flashes surrounded her as she advanced. She walked on, shrinking her head into her shoulders, but keeping her hips expressive. People drew to one side. So did the police.

In the hall, the butler offered to take Madame's coat. She replied with a brusque refusal and continued straight on. With a silent shimmy, the butler got to the massive door before her, and opened it.

The jet set turned round. But, as there was no shortage of inconsolable widows, they soon looked away from Julie and started chatting again, each peering over each other's shoulder in search of a more profitable person to talk to. Between these swift glances, icy stares, peeks and leers, Julie slid in between the movie world's eyes. She was looking, and she found. Firstly, Suzanne, standing alone by a window, done up like the ace of spades, staring out into the garden in genuine sorrow, but quite capable of breaking into her crystalline laughter if anyone were indecent enough to set her off. Right, so Suzanne was there. Julie was grateful for a hint of warmth in this icy summer. She went on looking. Then, there in front of her, at the end of a diagonal patch of gleaming parquet, her eyes happened upon Ronald de Florentis. Just as he'd been in Saint-Louis Hospital at Liesl's deathbed: the mane of hair, godlike build, but now sitting on a wing chair. An old man. How old could he be? The same generation as Job? But he was still in business. OK. Go for it. When Julie had reached the old promoter's side, she went round behind him, then leant over his ear:

"Ronald?"

He seemed to awake with a start.

"Who is it?"

Yes, an old man. He really had been asleep.

"It's me, Ronald. It's Juliette."

He turned round in amazement.

"Juliette? Job's god-daughter?"

"The very same."

"What on earth are you doing here, my little Juliette? The police have been looking for you for weeks!"

"I know, Ronald, I know. But I didn't kill Job. Can I talk to you for a minute?"

"Why, of course!"

"In private?"

A gesture of impatience.

"I've never spoken or slept with more than one person at a time."

His career secret.

"Ronald . . . what did the King of the Living Dead die of?"

"It's impossible to say."

"What do you mean it's impossible?"

"His wife discovered him last night in a critical condition. So she phoned the American Hospital."

"In a critical condition?"

"She was horrified. Struck dumb with terror. She had to be sedated. And not a word from the hospital since."

"Was he murdered?"

"No, the doctor's signed the death certificate. He died two hours ago. We're now waiting for his body."

"Suicide?"

"Not that either."

"Had you seen him recently?"

"Every day of the week until last Tuesday night."

"Were you preparing something?"

"Just a purchase and distribution which was hard to set up. A bit complicated. It was wearing me out. An international deal. Everyone was in on it. The Americans, Japanese, Europeans . . . a global event. An exceptional cultural occasion for one and all. The film of films."

"Can you tell me more about it?"

A tall waiter loomed up presenting a champagne glass full of dancing medicinal bubbles. Ronald stopped him in his tracks.

"I'm in conversation."

The tall waiter vanished, like a foldaway flunkey.

"You know that Job had been making a film since the year dot?"

(Jesus Christ . . . thought Julie.) Then replied:

"Of course!"

Ronald flared up.

"Of course? What do you mean, of course? I didn't know about it!"

288

"Only the family were in on it, I think . . ."

"The family, is it? And isn't seventy-five years' friendship worth all the families in the world?"

A few heads turned round. His lion's stare made them swivel back again.

"What's all this got to do with the King?" Julie asked.

"It was Job's film he was selling us."

(Bull's-eye, Julie thought.) But still asked:

"With Job's agreement?"

Ronald de Florentis looked at her as if she'd just grown a second head.

"Obviously! We had a 200-page contract, signed and sealed airtight. You knew Job!"

(But that's precisely the point, Julie thought. I did know Job.)

"What's the film about?" she asked off-handedly.

"No-one's allowed to know until it's released," Ronald replied. "No-one. It's stipulated in the contract. Secrecy is the crux of the entire operation. If we want everyone to see it, no-one must know what it's about."

"Why did you pay a fortune for a film which no-one, or practically no-one, knows anything about?"

"Before coming to see me, the King did the rounds. Three or four decision makers saw it. They're the best men in their field."

"Were you one of them?"

"No, I'm just a middle man. I'm setting up the financing by using the facts which are at my disposal, that's all. But, believe me, I'm dying to see it! We'd been friends for seventy-five years! A unique piece of work! And not a word to me! Never the slightest glimpse! And then he sells it to that . . . that . . ."

But then he suddenly remembered he was in "that's" house, waiting for "that's" body.

Julie felt sorry for him.

"So, you bought something you haven't seen?"

"That's right, on behalf of a partnership, and quite a partnership at that! All the sluice-gates of legal financing suddenly opened at once. They want to turn this into the event of the century."

*

Then the King made his entrance. In a coffin. Lid screwed down. His final mansion house. People formed a circle. Except for Suzanne.

Julie followed her towards the door.

Once outside, she dogged her at a distance.

Then overtook her on her way down into Métro Pompe.

Julie then twisted her ankle right in front of Suzanne and yelled out in Roman pain.

Suzanne rushed over.

"How are the children?" Julie asked between two outbursts of oaths imported from Rome.

"Julie?" Suzanne murmured, leaning over her ankle.

"How are the children?" Julie repeated in her ear.

"Fine," Suzanne whispered. "No problem. Someone left a cassette at the mother's place. It states that you're both innocent and that they can prove it. So they're not too worried. You know what they're like . . ."

"A cassette?"

Another passenger bent down, claiming to be a doctor. Hardly had he touched her ankle, than he leapt back up again.

Julie yelled:

"*Ma che vvole 'sto stronzo? Guarda che me la rompe davvero la caviglia! Aòh! . . . A'ncefalitico! Ma vvedi d'anna affanculo! Le mani addosso le metti a quella pompinara de tu' sorella!*"

The quack fled from this Roman fury.

"I need to see Gervaise," Julie went on at once.

"That's simple. She comes to see us from time to time. I reckon she's grown attached to Verdun."

"You're all being followed, Suzanne."

"Yes, all of us. They're after you."

"That so-called doctor just now . . ."

"He was a copper?"

"Or a suitor. He'd been following you for the past ten minutes."

"So it's your fault if I'm missing out again."

"Suzanne. I just have to see Gervaise. And fast."

Chapter 44

FLANKED BY INSPECTORS Titus and Silistri, Gervaise was busy following a bunch of keys down the echoing corridor of a women's prison. The bunch was bouncing up and down against the shot-putter's hip.

The shot-putter said:

"She never speaks to anybody. Not a single word since she arrived."

The shot-putter's hands looked capable of hanging oxen on to coat hooks.

"And vicious with it."

The shot-putter nodded her buffalo-like head.

"The only solution was solitary confinement."

Gervaise sensed the fear in the shot-putter's voice.

*

The niece had assaulted her three cellmates. One eye put out, a cheek cut to the bone, a broken arm. Suddenly, just like that, for no apparent reason and in a Sphinx-like silence. Buckets of blood in the cell. But not a single drop on her pink suit.

Solitary.

"Nepos's men haven't got a peep out of her. After all these weeks, they still don't even know who she is."

Inspectors Titus and Silistri were now enjoying what Titus called "a good lay-off". Since Chief Superintendent Nepos had forbidden them to take part in questioning suspects, they had abandoned their role to their new boss's logical methods. "Methodical Interrogation." But Nepos had got nowhere. His men came back looking haggard. Apparently this particular jailbird never slept. What they saw in her inquisitorial stare was the vanity of their inquiries and the ambiguity of the truth. The prisoner's gaze pushed you back into your own lies. The Inspectors came back with bags under their eyes and a desire to confess. They had doubts – methodical ones, of course – about the method. In despair, Chief

Superintendent Nepos had finally had to fall back on his father-in-law's threesome. Once more, Gervaise had extricated Titus from Tanita's arms, Silistri from Hélène's sheets, and now the three of them were following the shot-putter across the flagstones of a prison which echoed with that enclosed sound of all prisons.

"Can you hear that?" Silistri asked.

"What?" Titus asked.

"Can you hear the echo of our footsteps on the concrete?"

"Of course."

"This is the sound which made me go straight."

True enough. The last time little Silistri stole a car, old Beaujeu had given him a good hiding, then taken him to prison. He had a friend who was a turnkey and who had left them in the corridor all day. Cissou had simply said: "Listen."

*

"Here we are."

The warden pointed to a cell door.

Titus at once looked through the peephole.

The niece was sitting there, the same as ever, bolt upright on the edge of her bed, eyes fixed on the door, still impeccable in her pink suit. Titus's first impressions were confirmed. She really did look like one of those starchy bitches from fashionable boutiques who came round to inspect the work of Tanita, his little dressmaker. Tanned and blonde, squeezed into their classy suits, with tinkling bracelets, steel legs and abrupt delivery, they pontificated about Tanita's delightfully futile calicos, and laboured to turn life's lightness to lead. They wanted fashion to be like their perms. Standing behind them, Titus mimed sodomising them, while Tanita was showing them her designs and staring candidly back into their marble eyes.

What Silistri saw in this woman sitting up in the armour of her suit was quite different: a headhunter, a personnel manager, a human-resources director, a calculating supplier for the dole queue, who will trim down a company as coolly as a butcher prepares a leg of lamb. One of those starchy killers who made Hélène remark, when weary and philosophical after a long day: "You know, sometimes I prefer softies to iron ladies."

In the end, Titus and Silistri both found the niece absolutely ordinary. Each era has the norms it deserves. And this norm was becoming increasingly murderous.

Silistri moved aside to let Gervaise take a look.

"No."

292

Gervaise refused the peephole.

"Open up," she said to the warden.

The shot-putter did so. Not without some hesitation. But open she did.

"You stay outside."

The two Inspectors did as they were told.

"Then lock the door behind me," she said to the shot-putter, before adding: "And close the peephole too."

*

Apart from the bed bolted to the wall, the cell boasted a stool, which was bolted to the floor, and a small table, which was bolted to another wall. (The chaining of objects is the imprisonment of man, Gervaise thought.) A writing pad and a ballpoint pen had been left there for the niece by Chief Superintendent Nepos's methodical Inspectors, "in case you'd rather write it all down".

The pages were still blank.

Gervaise sat down on the stool.

Her knees brushed against the niece's knees.

Gervaise remained silent.

Two eternities.

When Gervaise finally spoke, it wasn't to break the silence. It was more to lift the veil which was obscuring language. Language could now either fly free, or else remain in its pit.

"Hello, Marie-Ange," Gervaise said.

The niece made no reaction. This revelation of her true identity smashed open her silence, but she bravely took the blow.

"I didn't want to believe it was you," Gervaise said again. "But when they showed me the anthropometric photos . . ."

In fact, Gervaise hadn't recognised her at once in these photos. At first, there had been an impression of complete ordinariness. A face far too much like all other faces. "But no-one can be this normal," Gervaise said to herself. And she decided to take a batch of photos home with her. She'd sat up all night looking at them, without seeing any more than the mask of a businesswoman. But the mask didn't really fit the face. Gervaise decided to have the photographs photographed. She did what her father Thian would have done. She went to see Clara Malaussène. Clara and Gervaise had then locked themselves up under the red lamp. In Gervaise's arms, Verdun stared at the two women with her projector eyes. They started by making blow-ups of the niece, enlarging her eyes, lips, ears, jaws. Nothing came of it. She'd had a nose job, her eyebrows had been plucked, her mouth had gobbled up her lips. If this face had ever been known to someone, the niece had since worked hard at making it unrecognisable. "What if we made it a bit hazy?" Clara suggested. Gervaise glanced round in surprise at Clara, as she bent over the tray. "As hazy as the truth," as Chief Superintendent Coudrier sometimes put it. "We are specialists in haziness." Clara had then watered down the woman's features. Then, as it appeared in the light of the projector, a face started to take form in Gervaise's memory. Yes, it was then, in front of that far-off out-of-focus image, that the penny dropped. It was Marie-Ange's broad, beautiful features! "Could you ruffle her hair?" Gervaise asked. With a couple of strokes of gouache, Clara gave the hair back its natural freedom. "And sharpen the nose . . . Now thicken the eyebrows," Gervaise suggested. "Plump up the lips . . . Make them fleshier . . ." And, under Clara's brush, her memories crystallised. "Yes . . . Marie-Ange . . ."

When she left Clara Malaussène, Gervaise just said: "Make my day and eat something." Then, to Verdun: "I'll be back soon."

Outside, Gervaise ran through and through the list of murdered girls which Chief Superintendent Coudrier had recited: *Marie-Ange Courrier, Séverine Albani, Thérèse Barbezien, Melissa Kopt, Annie Belledone* and *Solange Coutard.* How had they been identified?

To answer this question, Gervaise went to see her friend, Postel-Wagner. The doctor of the dead gave her half a litre of coffee. "By the usual means of identification. Dental records, for the most part . . ." "What about Marie-Ange's body?" she asked. "Oh her! She wasn't so much killed as utterly annihilated. But we found her ID papers in her clothes." "Didn't you find that odd?" Gervaise asked. "Why make a body unidentifiable, then leave ID papers lying around?" No, this hadn't raised any suspicions. "Coudrier must have put it down to sadistic excess. Don't forget, those loonies made no particular effort to conceal the identities of their other victims . . ." Then Postel-Wagner asked: "And you? Are you OK? You're looking a bit run down to me . . . Drop by and see me when you've got a moment, and I'll give you a quick check-up."

*

And now here was Gervaise, alone in a cell, face to face with a sort of Judas – the oldest of her repentant whores. Her first disciple. The one she'd loved. And who had now slaughtered the others, having faked her own death.

"It must have been easy to set up, once you'd pulled the wool over our eyes. You knew all the girls. And you knew their tattoos."

Then Gervaise fell silent. She didn't feel like asking any questions. She knew

Marie-Ange, and she could already hear her answers. She could read them in her stare. Another thing Postel-Wagner had said about the niece came back to her: "She reasons and moralises like a paranoiac, in a very *constructed* way, follow me?" Yes, Marie-Ange had an answer, explanation and justification for everything. In a few words, she had been able to frame an ethics of prostitution. She amused Gervaise. "Morality is just a question of syntax, Gervaise. Politicians learn that in their cradles. They should make me Minister of Morality." But today, Gervaise was not amused. In Marie-Ange's eyes, Gervaise was reading the silent answers to the questions she wasn't asking:

I made it, Gervaise! I've become what you wanted me to become. I've "reinserted" myself. You wanted me to go back and finish my medical degree, didn't you? To follow in my father's footsteps and become a surgeon? A real chip off the old block! "Treat people, and you take away one reason to be bad," that's what you used to say. Well, I did exactly that, Gervaise! I treated them all right. I operated! I removed *every single* reason to be bad. And it's all thanks to you, Gervaise! Why did I do it? Because of my love of art, of course! For my love of *your* art!

And so on.

The rhetoric of evil. "They always try to involve us," Thian used to say about hardline criminals. "They slip *their* crimes into *our* way of thinking," Chief Superintendent Coudrier explained. "They have no choice," Thian agreed. "It's that or admit they're nuts." "It's incredible how similar real killers are in their desire to appear unique," Chief Superintendent Coudrier went on pensively. "That's why prisons are so fucking boring," Thian concluded.

"You've been really nasty to me," Marie-Ange suddenly said.

Gervaise didn't catch on at once.

Marie-Ange still had her sharp tomboy's voice.

"Not nice at all, Gervaise . . ."

The tomboy was upset.

"Putting me in prison like this . . ."

Gervaise didn't reply.

"What's going to become of me in prison?"

Marie-Ange gave her a distraught stare.

"Do you think prison's the answer?"

She leant over towards her.

"I mean, do you . . . really?"

She sketched a timid smile.

"And in solitary confinement as well!"

She shook her head.

"Just when I'd finally found my vocation . . ."

She frowned.

"Who am I going to be able to kill now?"

She stared at her earnestly.

"Killing was my life, Gervaise! I live to kill! Jesus, can't you understand that? Have you no humanity? Who am I supposed to kill in here?"

Gervaise's expression must have changed, despite herself, because Marie-Ange suddenly burst out laughing.

"You really are a daft cow sometimes, do you know that?"

Her laughter was genuine. A real fit of the giggles, shaking her from head to toe, even dishevelling her hair a little.

"Poor old Gervaise! What must be going through your mind as you look at me! You thought you had my number, didn't you? Filed away with all the others! Our little neighbourhood paranoiac who justifies her crimes. Who blames her mum and dad, society, the system and all that crap. Well no, Gervaise. That's not what murder's about. It's a job, like any other. And as profitable as charity!"

Gervaise asked:

"Who was buying the tattoos, Marie-Ange?"

The laughter stopped as quickly as it had started. Marie-Ange replied in the earnest tones of a close collaborator.

"Do you want the name of the organiser, or of the collector?"

"Who was buying the tattoos?"

Marie-Ange looked relieved.

"OK, the name of the organiser. Just as well, because I don't know who the collector is."

She hesitated for a second.

"Are you sure you really want to know, Gervaise? You're not going to like the answer, you know."

Gervaise listened.

"It must already have been a bad enough shock for you to find out that I was the one doing the work . . . I'm sorry, I really am. You didn't deserve that. Not you. I sometimes felt sorry for you when I was at work. I used to say to myself . . ."

She broke off.

"You really want to know who was buying the tattoos?"

Gervaise didn't repeat her question.

"Sure sure?"

Gervaise waited.

"His name's Malaussène," Marie-Ange said at last.

Gervaise went tense.

"Benjamin Malaussène, Gervaise. You know, the saint with his lovely family, Louna, Thérèse, Clara, Jeremy, Half Pint, Verdun, What An Angel, and that disgusting fat dog and a mother who gets laid as much as I did, but for some obscure reason no-one seems to hold it against her."

Gervaise remained silent. Marie-Ange looked at her compassionately.

"I know how you feel, Gervaise. It always makes a nasty noise when a Jesus falls off his cross."

Gervaise didn't at once understand her body's reaction. It was like a wave. It rose up from inside her like an unstoppable geyser, it burst out of her mouth and the pink suit was covered in it.

Surprisingly, Marie-Ange made no attempt to protect herself. Not her body, nor her face or her hair or her legs. When Gervaise finally stood up, with an acidic taste in her mouth and tears in her eyes, Marie-Ange had shifted back along the bed and, leaning her back against the wall, was giving her a distant stare. A stare of total understanding. At last she said, in a voice full of satisfaction while licking her lips:

"And to top it all, you're pregnant. I couldn't have asked for more."

Chapter 45

"MALAUSSÈNE?" SILISTRI SAID. "The Malaussène we know?"
"The Belleville Malaussène?" Titus asked. "With all those kids? The Zebra Malaussène?"

"Malaussène," Gervaise repeated while getting into the squad car.

"Do you reckon that's likely?"

"Likely or not, that's what she said, and it's what Nepos will immediately believe and go and tell the magistrates."

"Malaussène . . ." Titus murmured.

Then he added:

"What with that Clément Clément photographing hanged men's tattoos, this isn't going to make old Malaussène's life any easier . . ."

". . ."

Gervaise fell silent.

Silistri glanced round at her.

"This has really been a shock for you, hasn't it?"

With her acid throat and burning nostrils, all Gervaise wanted to do was go home.

"Is that why you puked up over her lovely suit?" Titus asked. "Because of the shock?"

"No."

"No? Why then? Are you ill, Gervaise?"

The two men were looking at her anxiously. They couldn't bear the thought of Gervaise being ill.

"No," she said. "I'm pregnant."

*

Titus and Silistri literally blew the bar's door off its hinges. The shock sent the bouncer reeling beneath the tables. They weren't used to police raids at the Ace of

Spades, and this was definitely the first time they'd ever seen anything like this team of a Creole and a Tartar, brandishing their cards and yelling Pescatore's name.

"Pescatore? Is there anyone by the name of Pescatore here?"

And the seven-foot frame of Pescatore slowly rose to its full length, in its checked suit, cards still in his hand and, like any good grass, pretended not to recognise his contacts.

"Who's asking?"

"One of his lover boys," the Tartar whispered, baring his teeth.

"You're Pescatore?" the West Indian asked.

"Sometimes. To my friends."

"We'll be waiting outside."

"What if I stay inside?"

"If you stay inside, no-one else leaves, that's what," the blue-eyed Tartar replied. "We've got a nice big padlock."

*

"What's got into you, coming to see me here?" Pescatore asked as he joined Titus and Silistri in the street.

"Are you carrying?"

"Of course. Why? You need a hand?"

"Give," said Silistri, clicking his fingers.

"What?"

"Give."

"Trust us," Titus added. "You'll get it back."

"What have I done now?"

Pescatore gave a boyish sigh then laid his Smith and Wesson in Silistri's palm.

"Keep it nice and warm," said Silistri, handing the Smith and Wesson to Titus.

Then, pushing Pescatore into a doorway:

"Remember your three men who guarded Gervaise when she was out of it in hospital, can they be trusted?"

"With your life! No-one could have got into that room. Nor into Mondine's room either."

Pescatore's seven-foot frame shrivelled to a tiny ball under Silistri's fist. Something about the liver. Then a splitting migraine. When Pescatore's head had finished ringing, he heard Silistri say:

"Gervaise is pregnant."

And Titus conclude:

299

"You'll get your piece back when you bring us the one who did it."

*

"Fabio! Emilio! Tristan!"

Leaning over the same billiard table, the three pimps were wondering if it was a better bet to go for the red off the cushion, or else hit it full on with a bit of left spin, when the boss's voice erupted behind them. There was something urgent in his delivery. All three of them turned around at once. Pescatore's fist hit each chin in sequence.

"Gervaise is pregnant!"

They'd have loved to get up, but Pescatore's feet had taken over.

"Who did it?"

They thought they were secure under the table, but it suddenly rose up above their heads and looked as if it was about to drop.

"Who?"

*

From the cell where she'd spewed, via the warden shot-putter, the guards on the gate and the drivers of black marias, the news spread from the prison to HQ.

"Gervaise is pregnant."

"You're kidding . . ."

"No, honestly."

The Templars' halos suddenly went rusty.

"The Templars diddled their saint."

"Really?"

"Absolutely!"

Laughter.

"Maybe it was the saint who laid the Templars."

And blows.

"Say that again dickhead. Just one more time, motherfucker!"

"I was only joking."

*

So it goes with news that kills.

When Professor Berthold went into Mondine's room that evening (a Mondine who'd healed up ages ago but who'd become an indispensable part of the hospital staff), he noticed she was looking a little off-colour.

"Whatever's the matter, my little Pontormo?"

300

"Gervaise is pregnant."

Three words. But pronounced with a woman's searching, ultraviolet stare, which casts its beams on the darkest lies hidden in the depths of deception.

"Was it you, professor?"

"To a sleeping patient?" Berthold erupted. "I'm supposed to have . . . Me? . . . With a sleeping patient? For fuck's sake, Mondine, if it was anyone else but you who'd asked me that, I'd . . ."

"But it is me," Mondine butted in. "So don't throw a wobbly."

But Berthold's explosive reaction had convinced her.

"There's no morality in love, professor. Only questions."

She pushed her hand into Berthold's mane of hair and ruffled that head which was all bark.

"And I'm satisfied with your answer."

End of chapter. Return to her own anger.

"Never mind," she said darkly. "I'll slice the bloke who did that into tiny pieces."

She said again:

"He did it to Gervaise . . . to Gervaise."

*

When she got home, Gervaise's first instinct was to check her answering machine.

"You have five messages," a female voice said behind her.

Gervaise turned around. A woman was standing framed in the bedroom door.

"I heard you come in and I hid. I wasn't sure it was you."

"Are you Julie?" Gervaise asked.

Julie nodded.

"I was afraid Suzanne wouldn't manage to get the keys to you," Gervaise said. "They're all under such close surveillance."

"She sent them via Nourdine, the youngest of the Ben Tayeb boys."

"Fine," said Gervaise. "How about some tea?"

They silently went to work in the kitchen, each intimidated by all the things they'd been told about the other one.

"It was a good idea to come," Gervaise said. "No-one will think of looking for you here."

"True, but I'm not staying. It would be too compromising for you."

Gervaise suppressed a laugh. In terms of being compromised, the little squatter in her belly was already doing a good enough job.

"Don't worry about my honour, Julie. You can stay here."

Sitting over tea, they summed up their two cases. Julie played Clément's tape to Gervaise. She explained how when Clément yelled "I'll spill the beans to the Viet's daughter". it sounded like a sort of last will and testament. Clément wanted Gervaise to hear the tape, and Gervaise agreed that it did mean that Benjamin was off the hook. Gervaise then showed some photos of Marie-Ange to Julie.

"No, I don't think either Benjamin or I have ever seen her before," Julie said as she handed back the photos. "Why?"

"Because she says it was Benjamin who was buying the tattoos."

"Good God," Julie mumbled.

"You may not know her, but she certainly knows you," Gervaise concluded. "And she'd do anything to put Benjamin in the frame."

"Good God!" Julie repeated. "But why?"

"That's what we're going to have to find out," said Gervaise, then added: "And stop calling God good, you'll give Him a big head."

Upon which, Gervaise turned to her answering machine.

"And what do you have to say for yourself?"

What the machine had to say was the same as everyone else was saying.

"People are saying you're pregnant, Gervaise. What the hell's going on? Come and see me at once and I'll examine you."

*

Half an hour later, Gervaise was lying on a freshly scrubbed corpse slab, while her friend Postel-Wagner was concluding that, yes, she was indeed in the family way.

"And you hadn't realised?"

"My periods were late when I came out of hospital," Gervaise explained. "But I put that down to the shock . . . I thought things would get back to normal later."

She smiled.

"The funniest thing is that Thérèse Malaussène predicted it."

"When?" Postel-Wagner asked, while filling his pipe. "Before or after you were in hospital?"

"Before. The very day before my accident. When I went to tell them that Cissou had died."

Two or three thoughtful puffs, then Postel asked:

"And do you believe in soothsaying?"

"No, I don't. But in this case, you have to admit . . ."

"Not a bit of it, Gervaise. When Thérèse told you that, you were *already* pregnant."

"Oh no! I'm quite sure I wasn't."

"And for a good two months," the forensic surgeon confirmed while puffing away.

"But I was as regular and periodic as a nun could be!" Gervaise protested.

"You must have had bleeding, which you mistook for your periods. This inquiry has been extremely telling for you, don't forget. Too many sleepless nights, too much emotion . . . Who did you meet two or three months back?"

"What do you mean, who did I meet?"

"What new acquaintances did you make? To put it another way, any new faces? Men other than your incorruptible bodyguard of pimps."

Gervaise frowned.

"The two Inspectors who helped you catch Marie-Ange," she said at last.

"Titus and Silistri?"

"Yes. Chief Superintendent Coudrier transferred them from the special branch for my protection."

Postel-Wagner shook his head sadly.

"Well, no matter how unlikely it might seem, I'm afraid you will have to look in that direction, Gervaise . . ."

*

During the night of Saturday to Sunday, the door of the Ace of Spades opened once more. This time, the big Creole cop was alone.

"Pescatore!"

The pimp followed the cop outside again.

"Here's your piece back, Pescatore. Your men had nothing to do with it."

*

The next day, at about one p.m., Hélène and Tanita had finished their shopping and had sat down in the Envierges bar.

They let a long awkward silence pass by after Nadine had served them their glasses of Sunday port.

"So," Hélène asked at last. "Do you reckon it was yours, mine, or both together?"

"It was her," Tanita answered gravely.

*

It was Chief Superintendent Nepos who had the final word.

"You know me, Gervaise. Your private life is none of my business. But your . . . condition . . . is fomenting such frenzy in the squad . . . such a network of mutual

303

suspicions . . . that their work is suffering . . . you do see what I mean . . . unity is indispensable . . . utterly indispensable . . . of course, I'm not talking about disciplinary measures . . . you're a good officer . . . whose work is . . . remarkable . . . excellent, even, in many respects . . . but . . . what I mean is . . . the well-being of the station . . . or . . . put it this way . . . if you offered your resignation, I wouldn't refuse."

Chapter 46

"STOP HIM!" THE girl yelled. Then a series of thuds. A brief struggle. Clément had been outclassed. Silence. The mike must have become unplugged during the fight. What struck me about that woman's cry was the hatred in her voice: "Stop him!" Clément! Clément! Just to think that I thought you'd be in heaven in that house! O Clément . . . heaven's no place to die!

"And there we are."

Chief Superintendent Nepos's voice brought me back to the transparent reality of his office. He'd been observing me since the tape came to an end. He could see tears in my eyes. He rewound the cassette to give me time to dry them. A click. The cassette was ejected. Chief Superintendent Nepos picked it up between two fingers and showed it to me.

"This confirms what I was telling you last time, Monsieur Malaussène."

What was it exactly that the dickhead had been telling me last time?

"The credulity of officers trained by my predecessor is boundless, and your credit with them limitless."

He stared at me. He looked bewildered. He stared at the cassette.

"According to them, this tape should get you off the hook."

And doesn't it? Doesn't Clément's death prove I'm innocent? After all the effort he made to relay clues to the killers' identities? Did he die for nothing?

Chief Superintendent Nepos carefully placed the cassette in a drawer, crossed his hands and once again aimed the perfect mirror of his skull at me.

"Let's try to think methodically, shall we? What exactly does this audio tape tell us?"

He changed tack at once.

"Or rather, no. Let's take things one at a time. Firstly, where does this audio tape *come from*?"

From Barnaby! At the beginning, you can clearly hear Clément talking to Barnaby.

"From a certain Barnabooth. Do you know this man, Monsieur Malaussène?"

"Only by name."

"Evidently. After all he does pass himself off as being invisible. Our department interviewed him, since he is the son and grandson of two of the victims, but we were not permitted to see him. In this art-besotted republic, officially recognised artists apparently have certain privileges . . ."

He let his annoyance vanish along a thin smile.

"Now, this Barnabooth is the conjurer of our élite artistic community. The in thing . . . You make the *Mona Lisa* vanish and the jet set is in ecstasy. So it would seem that proof of your innocence has been provided by a master illusionist, Monsieur Malaussène."

Then, in a pedagogical tone:

"Leaving aside the fact that tape recordings, like photographs, cannot be used as evidence in court, this cassette could of course have been recorded by just about anybody, just about anywhere. That Barnabooth was present on the scene of the crime just prior to your arrival, and that he was recording what was going on in the house, is not only unlikely, it is also impossible to prove. Especially as we have not found a transceiver on Monsieur Clément's body, in the wreck of his car, or in the ruins of the house. So much for point number one. Secondly, what does the tape actually tell us?"

That Clément was murdered, Chief Superintendent, and that you couldn't give a toss – or to put it another way, that the lad's heroic self-sacrifice doesn't enter into the logical construction of your investigations.

"It tells us that someone has apparently *stolen* Monsieur Job Bernardin's Only Begotten Film. But other, far more reliable sources indicate that this full-length feature film of a duration of three hours is currently being sold under the terms of a legally drawn-up contract, through which we have been with a fine-tooth comb, Monsieur Malaussène, and in which Monsieur Bernardin's wishes are expressed in terms which are crystal clear. Given that the beneficiary of this contract has recently passed away, we have not had the opportunity to question him. We paid a call on his lady wife, who has been deeply affected by her spouse's sad demise . . ."

Chief Superintendent Nepos rumbled on. He spoke the language of those frozen terrains where there's no death but *sad demise*, where wives are *lady wives*, where husbands are *spouses*, and where sorrow *affects* rather than devastates. Chief Superintendent Nepos spoke the glossy tongue of those registers in which forenames pile up behind patronymics – which turn into titles when times get rough.

"Are you listening to me, Monsieur Malaussène?"

I feel like I've been listening to you ever since I got my birth certificate.

"Is it correct that Monsieur Bernardin promised to give you The Only Begotten Film, as all those film enthusiasts are claiming?"

"It is."

"Just as I feared."

He opened his mouth to explain the cause of his fears, but the phone butted in.

He picked up the receiver.

"Yes? Good, very good. No, no. I'll only be another minute or two. That's right. I'll call you back."

He hung up.

"Now, where were we . . .? Oh yes. Unfortunately, Monsieur Bernardin broke his promise."

He fell silent.

"Which is extremely unfortunate."

He looked up at me.

"You claim that you had gone to Monsieur Bernardin's house to take delivery of his film collection *and* The Only Begotten Film?"

"That's right."

"Even though he had in fact sold the film to someone else."

"We didn't know that."

"But you found out when you arrived."

"When we arrived, we didn't see a soul. The study blew up as soon as Julie opened the door."

"Please, Monsieur Malaussène, let us not return to your yarn . . . it is as unlikely as this cassette."

I fell silent.

He fell silent.

We fell silent.

And I left him the pleasure of a logical conclusion.

"I must admit that old Bernardin's death had puzzled me," he admitted. "I could see no reason for it. Your motive for killing Doctor Fraenkhel was clear. Just as it was for that student. And if you had also come across Clément, then . . ."

Silence.

"But today I have a better understanding of Monsieur Bernardin's death. He had betrayed you and you took your revenge. This is a perfectly credible motive. Especially when you consider how much the film is worth. The sum on the

307

contract. Which has now been transferred to Monsieur Bernardin's account . . .
That's right, we have checked that, too . . ."

Silence.

"A tidy little sum, as a matter of fact . . . What you were after, Monsieur
Malaussène, was not so much a film as a gold mine!"

He fell silent.

Then he went on in his pensive tone:

"Just imagine it . . . Some police inspectors give me evidence which is supposed
to prove your innocence, but which in point of fact provides me with the real
motive for the killings! They really have been abysmally trained . . ."

*

He slapped down in front of me what the machine had been typing out behind
me.

I didn't sign it.

I stood up and put out my wrists to the gendarme who was acting as my
guardian angel.

Nepos gestured to me to wait.

He pressed a button on his intercom.

"Show her in," he said into the machine.

Then, to me:

"There's someone here who is dying to see you."

A tall woman in a pink suit came in, wearing handcuffs, but with an impeccable
perm. The suit wasn't exactly brand new, but it suited her like one of those
qualifications which never go out of fashion. When the woman saw me, she
flashed me an urbane smile.

"Benjamin! How are things since last we met?"

She had a boyish voice.

"And the family? Do you get any visits?"

I didn't know her from Adam or Eve.

"Does Verdun still cry when What An Angel's hungry? Has Julius recovered
from his fit yet?"

And, in a tone of true compassion:

"Has your mother got her appetite back?"

XII
IN PRISON (AT PRESENT)

There's nothing more coherent than a judicial error.

Chapter 47

My Jailer

PRISON IS THE present. The present is what people in prison are trying to escape from. There is no other punishment.

Faucigny, the governor of my particular prison, knew that only too well. He made his present as continuous as possible. His ideas were simple. He was a born pedagogue.

"Pleased to be back in Champrond, Monsieur Malaussène?"

For, either thanks to Nepos's spite, or to an administrative coincidence, it was indeed in Champrond where I'd been imprisoned. Here where Uncle Stojil had ended his days with Virgil.

"I've been told that you like explosives, Monsieur Malaussène."

Faucigny was broad in the beam, with grey eyes and bushy eyebrows. He said horrible things, which his country accent softened up marvellously.

"Those bombs in the Store, a few years back, and the ones in the Vercors just recently . . . home-made bombs, bombs with timers, fire bombs . . . you just like bombs, and I suppose this has been the case since you were a boy."

Faucigny smiled amicably beneath the steel grip of his stare.

"I can quite understand this taste for bombs, in fact . . . the thrill of the ignition, the surprise of the flash, the din of the explosion, the propulsion into space, the downpour of debris when the puff of smoke begins to rise, the crackling of the flames . . . it's all rather beautiful really."

Faucigny was a weatherman announcing the end of the world with a smile.

"I'll cure you, Malaussène . . ."

I could no longer remember when Faucigny had given me this bracing speech. Yesterday? A month ago? Ten years back? To the various indicative tenses, Faucigny had added a new one: *the present unprogressive*. It's the tense which prison guards dream of, the present of perpetual regret, the eternity of the tooth under the drill of remorse, an unlimited instant of agony, a stretch of time stretching endlessly on, in which all hope is dead, even the hope of dying . . . the present unprogressive, Faucigny style, the torture tense.

I no longer knew when Faucigny had spoken to me.

All I knew was my cell.

My cell in Champrond was enough to make honest citizens jealous. I could just hear them. It's all right for some! Just imagine it! We're now lodging dangerous criminals in stately homes! With stone arches and vaults! Not even any bars on the windows! Unbreakable glass! A cell with a view over cornfields, if you don't mind. Rolling meadows to soothe a murderer's eyes . . . With cretonne curtains to dim the sunlight. And, to cap it all, a television!

"I inherited a cultural prison, Malaussène, and I've turned it into an educative one. A culture which doesn't educate is a dangerously fertile terrain for crime. Just look at Julien Sorel, or Raskolnikov . . . My predecessor, Monsieur de Saint-Hiver, whom you knew so well, did rather neglect this side of the question . . . He was an idealist . . ."

Faucigny wasn't like Saint-Hiver – the deceased former governor of Champrond Prison and Clara's first love – he was down to earth and good at eye contact.

"Nowadays, whether we like it or not, we get most of our culture by the television. Beyond these walls, television is the primary incitement to crime. Inside, I've transformed it into a pedagogical tool. Do you like watching television, Malaussène?"

One prisoner per cell and one TV set per prisoner. On the taxpayer's money! *Your* money! That's right, ladies and gentlemen, it was your money that bolted this television set to the wall in my cell. It was your money that sealed it inside a plastic coating thus making it indestructible. It was your money that connected all of these sets to Faucigny's central control panel. And it was Faucigny, paid with your money, who switched on the programmes at any time of the day or night, when we were waking or sleeping, for a few seconds, or several hours, with no way to turn the sound down, change channels or switch the thing off.

The first time, the shock pinned me to the wall. I thought Champrond Prison was exploding. That it had been built over a volcano, eruption time had come and the walls were collapsing over our wicked heads. Wrong. It was just my telly coming on. A mighty explosion, up there in the cube of my set, setting an infinite succession of echoes off the four walls of my cell. Ever since, each time had been like the first time. Faucigny's version of the present. My cell could explode at any moment. Such was Faucigny's grand theory. You like explosions, do you Malaussène? Well, you're going to get some. My cell was the epicentre of carpet bombing. Then please fill up the moments of respite by panicking about when hostilities will start again. Of course, I could look away from the screen, but I couldn't escape the noise, even by keeping the mattress over my head. Every explosion that had been shot since the cinema discovered sound was now being set off in my cell. Ammunition dumps, houses, oil refineries, safes, booby-trapped cars, the bridge over the River Kwai, Captain Nemo's island, Pierrot Goes Wild, my cell was exploding twenty-four hours a day. Faucigny's simple idea. Cure evil with evil. Therapy by overdose. I supposed that rapists got treated to the screams of beaten women, cut-throats to the bubbling of cut-throat blood, serial killers to serial killings . . .

The result was the same for all the inmates: telephobia, stony stares and mechanical gaits during daily exercise, a constant trembling of the entire body, occasional epileptic fits, refectory plates which stayed full.

There were even scenes of panic during the return to the cells, muscular refusals, but Faucigny's turnkeys were always sufficiently convincing to make their boss's educational project go through.

Door bangs.

Bolt in the lock.

Peephole.

Silence.

Me.

And the set, up there.

Chapter 48

The Scent of the Sentryman

I SHOULD HAVE BEEN mad by then, or have hanged myself from my bedstead, the window latch or central-heating pipe, as others had done. But Faucigny had decided to gild the lily.

"I reserved a special cell for you, Malaussène. It belonged to your friend, Stojilkovitch. You do remember Stojilkovitch, don't you? He armed the old ladies of Belleville and wanted to translate Virgil into Serbo-Croat. He died here last year."

The table, chairs, dictionaries and waste-paper bin had been removed, but I recognised the cell at once. And Uncle Stojil took up residence inside me as soon as I took up residence in his cell. I wasn't invaded by memories of Stojil, but by Stojil in person. It wasn't his appearance or the sound of his voice (Faucigny had stolen my eyes and my ears), no, it was Stojil's very being which insinuated itself inside me, that subtle and powerful aura of his very being, his *odour*, that aroma which followed him like a shadow and which stood to attention behind him whenever he came to a stop. If the truth were known, I recognised Stojil's old cell as soon as I set my nostrils on it. Stojil was lending me his sentry-box. I shut myself up inside it after the surprise of the initial explosions. And it was then that his voice came back, an inner voice which even the most volcanic eruptions couldn't drown out.

"There's a smell of feet in here, don't you think so?"

He liked asking that. And, when your ears had flushed nicely, he'd explain:

"Don't apologise. It's me."

Then, more gravely:

"The scent of the sentryman."

My old uncle Stojil had started his sentry duty young, against the hydra of Nazism, then against the ogre of Stalinism, so close to us, behind the gates of the Balkans, in days before me.

"Any sentryman worthy of his name never looks at his feet."

Oh, Stojil's voice, so warm, so powerful, and so low it seemed to be coming back up from your own innards.

"Fancy shoving wood around?"

In his lingo, this meant playing chess. And, while that TV set kept on exploding, I recalled each and every one of the games we'd played.

"D5, lad!! If your bishop takes d5, my queen takes c3!! And if you reckon you can hit back by taking my queen, my bishop mates you from a3. It's the mate from Boden versus Schulder, in 1860, a textbook checkmate. And I did tell you to watch the diagonals! You're not on form today."

How many times did nightwatchman Stojilkovitch beat me in the shadows of the Store?

Bombs went off during the day. At night, it was my defences that exploded.

And the bombs in the Store made me deaf.

Faucigny didn't know that.

The explosions in the Store used to make me go deaf.

Faucigny, bombs deafen me! Turn up the volume, I can't hear your telly any more!

Exactly the same phenomenon as at the time of the Store: a piercing noise in the geodesic centre of my brain, then a terrible pain spinning around its own axis before suddenly bursting out my ears. For a few seconds, I was hanging in my cell on a white-hot wire which was running through my head.

Then the pain died down.

And I was deaf.

Sorry, Faucigny, knives make me shit myself, guns make me puke and bombs make me deaf. No matter how much you want to live without convictions, when your body says no, it's no.

Interestingly enough, these bouts of deafness used to turn me into an ultra-lucid chess player.

"Check from the bishop on d5, Stojil, and if you take it with your knight, my queen checks you from f8. Of course, your king could nab my queen, but then my rook moves down to c8 to finish you off. Checkmate! I did tell you to watch the perpendiculars."

"I wouldn't go so far as to say that you play well, lad. But you're making progress, you're making progress . . ."

Chapter 49

My Visits

SELF-DEFENCE? CONTRARINESS? Whenever I left my cell, the silence of the corridor gave me my hearing back. I still had the migraine, but my ears opened on the tinkling of handcuffs, the clicking of locks and the rhythm of the footfalls in the deep stone silence.

"Mum's eating, Ben! She's got her appetite back."

This was one of the pieces of good news which Jeremy brought to the cellar now used as Champrond Prison's visiting room. Each of them visited me in turn: Jeremy, Clara, Thérèse, Louna, Half Pint . . . But, most often, Jeremy came instead of Louna, who was too busy at the hospital, or of Thérèse, too busy with the stars, of Clara, who was too upset, or of Half Pint who was too much of a half pint.

In the end, all I saw was Jeremy.

"Mum's got her appetite back. She's not exactly stuffing herself, but at least she's eating normally. And talking, as well."

"What's she saying?"

"It's hard to say. She talks to herself. Like she was speaking into her blouse. Like she was cradling someone on her chest, see what I mean? Between her . . . you know. She shuts up as soon as we arrive."

"Have you told Marty?"

"No point. I mean, she isn't really ill, is she? Apart from that, she's quite normal. She's Mum. She gets up at eleven, stays in the bathroom till twelve, emerges as beautiful as ever, she helps Clara cook, she burns things, she's Mum down to the ground. As happy as though she was in love. Now she's started eating again, she sometimes gets Clara eating, too. It's hunky-dory, Ben. Life is starting all over. And Julius is better. But you knew that already . . . He's still snapping his jaws every three minutes, but otherwise, he's better. Then there's Gervaise. Gervaise has replaced Thian in Verdun's affections. Some things change, others don't, as they say . . ."

A pause.

"And what about you, Ben? How are things?"

Champrond's visiting room used to be the confessional in a lepers' house. Two crossed vaults divided a huge lofty cellar of chalk into four. You went to one of the corners, the turnkey locked an iron grille behind you, then you talked facing the wall, with your back to your visitor. Since the seventeenth century, everyone's secrets had run along the crest of the vault diagonally to the person opposite, just as clearly as if they had been whispered into his ear. Yes, just a murmur sufficed. It was relaxing. Like a promise of absolution.

"Clément would have loved it here!" Jeremy exclaimed during his first visit. "There's a scene like this in Fellini's *La Dolce Vita*. You know, when Marcello confesses his love for Anouk Aimée, while she's getting snogged by that fair-haired bloke."

Jeremy never ran out of conversation. He was not one of the visitors who dried up after one too many visits. Words started when he arrived, and he was always the one the screw interrupted when visiting time was over.

"I've had practice, Ben. It's a bit like when I used to visit you in hospital and you couldn't answer. I had to fill in . . ."

He entered the visiting room, sat down in his corner, and got going:

"Hi, it's me. But you can always pretend it's Clara, your favourite sister."

Then he served me up the family news, from Clara's benevolent viewpoint.

Or else:

"Good afternoon, Benjamin. It's Thérèse."

And Thérèse it was.

"Gervaise is rounding out nicely, Benjamin. I do know that dowsing leaves you cold, but my pendulum is adamant that it's a boy."

"Still no news of any father?"

"She's taking it easy. She isn't even trying to find out who it was. A good horoscope is better than a bad father."

But generally Jeremy came in his own name. He read to me. Since Clément's death, the repossession of The Zebra and its occupation by support groups, Jeremy had dropped the theatre completely. He had now transformed his play into a novel. His idea was to give a blow-by-blow account of the doings of his goat of a brother. He'd got it into his head that this would be the best plea in my defence. As words cropped up under his pen, he used them to knit me an apologia which would keep me warm during my life sentence.

"There'll be four books in all. One about the bombs in the Store, one about the junkie granddads in Belleville, a third one about your brain death, then another one about what's happening now. But I'm not writing them one after the other. I'm writing them all at the same time, as things occur to me. It's a bit like the way a film is made, see what I mean? You shoot such and such a sequence depending on the weather, or the mood your diva's in, then you stitch the whole thing together at the end. What do you reckon, Ben?"

I reckoned Queen Zabo would be hot on his heels.

"Good thinking, Jeremy."

"Shall I read you a bit?"

No-one has ever worked up the courage to say no to this sort of question.

"Of course, I'd be delighted."

"After all the stories you told us when we were kids, Ben, it's the least I could do . . ."

Keep stitching, Jeremy . . . invent a novelistic hero, an irreproachable brother besmirched by others' guilt . . . keep stitching . . . and give yourself a good role while you're at it. When life's like this, then novels should be however they want to be. And if you need any stuff on the human condition, then ask me. I've got plenty on my hands right now.

Chapter 50

Madame, My Investigating Magistrate

TAKE THIS SPECIMEN of humanity, for instance. Madame, my investigating magistrate. Madame was a little, curly-headed creature with limpid eyes and a girlish complexion. When she packed me off to the assizes, there were tears in her eyes.

"You must have suffered so, to do such a thing!"

I quote.

"Losing a child . . ."

I'm not kidding. I had a *mother* examining my case.

"I'm a mother, Monsieur Malaussène."

Which allowed her *to understand* what I'd done. (And thus have no doubt that it was me!)

As for me, it took me a while to suss out how her head functioned. When I realised that her brains beat like her heart, I knew I'd had it.

A mother's heart.

Which seemed to find it quite normal (and clearly legitimate) for someone to blow up an entire family, plus a few passing friends thrown in, because he's been deprived of his darling little baby.

"I could well have done the same . . ."

Quote! On my mother's life! Quote!

And so, the assizes.

*

While awaiting this apotheosis, return to the present unprogressive of Faucigny . . . Stojil's sentry-box . . . and our games of chess.

"You reckon it's mate in one, lad, but look: I move my rook to c8, you block with your knight, my queen checks you from h7, your king takes it, my bishop then checks you again, your king moves down and you're in perpetual check.

Stalemate, Benjamin! That's how our mountain bears defend themselves when they're wounded."

O Stojil, how I loved you!

But then Madame my examining magistrate called for me once more.

*

"Monsieur Malaussène . . ."

Her huge innocent eyes (straight out of Walt Disney) glittered with a welling tear while my handcuffs were being taken off, then she pointed me towards a seat. I didn't know what I was in for yet, but she did, and things didn't augur well.

"Monsieur Malaussène . . ."

She looked for the courage to begin by staring into the eyes of my taciturn brief.

"I have been obliged, by letters rogatory, to ask Chief Superintendent Nepos to open an inquiry into matters prior to those of which you have been accused today."

A trembling of fingers as they fiddled with my dossier.

"And things aren't looking good, Monsieur Malaussène."

Saliva.

"Not good at all."

She finally got round to reading me Nepos's report. After just three lines, I saw what was up. After having shaken Coudrier's palm tree so hard that I had fallen down at his feet, Nepos was now trying to rip it up by its roots. Methodically. One root at a time. He had been to see Madame about my previous. One by one, he mentioned all of the crimes that had blossomed around me over the past few years. Firstly, the Store: five bombs, six dead and me. Then the case of the Belleville druggies: an inspector gunned down in broad daylight, the iffy suicide of a Chief Superintendent, a bookseller injected with caustic soda, and me there at the very same time and place. Then the J.L.B. business: the attempted murder of Krämer in prison, the murder of the governor of Champrond, my sister's fiancé, and me, weighed down with motives until a .22 long-rifle high-penetration bullet packed me off to the brain death of a coma. To which could be added the six prostitutes murdered over the past few months, on my orders, according to the tall girl in the pink suit who was sticking by her guns. Which made six plus three equals nine, plus two equals eleven, plus six equals seventeen. If we then added the four murders in Loscence, we arrived at twenty-one murders, not forgetting those others which a more thorough investigation might still reveal.

"It's not looking good, Monsieur Malaussène, not good at all."

320

Especially not, considering that Madame *understood* my motives perfectly. This didn't mean that she approved of what I'd done ("I'm a mother, but I'm also a magistrate"), no, but she was quite happy to understand . . . at the Store I was avenging those murdered children, in Belleville I was attacking racism and flying to the succour of the elderly, by slaughtering Saint-Hiver I was preserving Clara's virginity and, when posing as J.L.B., I was fighting for literature; as for the six murdered prostitutes . . . Madame of course had no prejudice against prostitution, but all the same . . . she could quite understand why any person with religious feelings would have such a violent reaction against holy images being tattooed on to the flesh.

"Your weak point, Monsieur Malaussène, is your sense of the sacred. Your motives are so crystal clear . . ."

Chapter 51

Cell-Room Thoughts

M ORAL: DO WHAT you want, so long as you don't have any motives.

*

If ever I get out of here, I swear to remain utterly unmotivated.

*

My thoughts turned, of course, to Justice. To my country's Justice. I had always approved of those who declare publicly that they trust their country's judicial system. They emerge from the magistrate's office, they stand boldly on the steps outside, they smooth down the lapels of their jacket and declare to the extended microphones: "I place my trust in the Justice of my country." They're right. And Justice is extremely grateful to them. As for me, I could picture little Mahmoud, aged eighteen, one of the Ben Tayebs' cousins, who was collared in a car park where he and other kids were stealing cars. Five years, of which zero years suspended. Serves him right. Should have placed his trust in the Justice of his country.

Chapter 52

M'Learned Friends

"THEY'RE FALLING OVER each other to defend you, Malaussène. And not just any old barristers! The finest silks in the business! There were even fisticuffs outside the prison gates. Our learned friends are just dying to get at you."

Faucigny was amazed.

"In some respects, it's an honour to have you here."

But he didn't forget his democratic principles.

"I hope you remember what a privilege it is to live in a free country!"

Then, as I didn't seem to realise it:

"No, of course you don't. It seems normal to you that society defends your sort of vermin. Very well. Which one would you care to see first? Even though it is contrary to our usual rules, I'd prefer you to see them in your cell rather than in the visiting room. The less my inmates see of you, the better."

*

M'learned friend Ragaud was exultant:

"Guilty, Malaussène! We'll plead guilty! With our heads held high!"

"We" was him.

And he was me.

Or, what he imagined me to be.

"After all, what have we done? We've punished our child's murderers! We've defended our legitimate right to give life! We've fought for the unimpeachable right to be born! They took away a tiny little life, a defenceless innocent, and we interrupted the course of their criminal existences. We had no right so to do, of course! But the time has come at last to reconcile legality and legitimacy! At the end of this century, when our most basic values are the laughing stock of the sophisticates, I'm going to make you the champion of legitimate defence! Head held high, Malaussène! All I can see in you is someone to be immensely proud of!"

I looked at him.

I stood up.

I knocked at the door.

The turnkey opened it.

I said:

"Don't want this one."

Ragaud didn't argue. He put his papers away, then got to his feet.

"So you'd rather have me against you, would you Malaussène? How foolish of you. I know myself. I would not like to have me on the other side. Attacking you will be so much easier. If there is one thing that matters today, something of utmost urgency, it is to rid society of criminals with belief systems. They exist on the margins of society, they nail children to doors, they kill you if you get in their way, they do not know what their own father's name is, and they imagine they have the right to procreate! Not to mention your cosmopolitan acquaintances . . . Believe me, for a barrister such as me, attacking someone like you will be a piece of cake."

Before the screw closed the door again, Ragaud wrinkled his nose. His moustache bristled.

"There's a footy smell in here, don't you think?"

And m'learned friend Gervier came in.

*

"Kicked him out, did you Malaussène? Good on you. We'll now have him in the opposite camp. But it won't be the first time I give that fascist a hiding. He's rubbish when up against the real heavyweights."

Gervier had sharp eyes and an electric delivery. His perpetual motion abruptly ceased.

"Jesus, it doesn't half stink in here, can we open the window a bit?"

We couldn't.

So instead, he got the air circulating by dashing backwards and forwards in short strides.

"You blew up the World of Big Business, Malaussène. Well done! You snuffed a prison governor. Pure justice! And today you're sowing panic in the Republic of Images. You know how to hit where it matters. Excellent work. And ten years before getting caught! It's a record."

Gervier got so heated that his glasses steamed up. He leant his opaque lenses over me and murmured:

"I know the assizes like the back of my hand, Malaussène. And this is going to be fun. The trial won't be for some time yet. You can rely on me for that! If they insist on denying you bail, we'll draw your custodial spell out so long that it will become ridiculous! I'm going to give you a life in custody, my lad!"

I wasn't quite sure what he meant.

So, he explained:

"It's obvious! I'll go into court. I'll produce a stack of demands for getting the case thrown out. After that we'll appeal. I'll claim that the court is incompetent and the charges inadmissible. They won't give a damn, but it will give us more time. Time enough to work up public opinion against them. I know these judges only too well. They all obey orders while the long arm of the law has got them by the short and curlies. By the time one of them has found the balls to stand up and be counted, you'll have sown the seeds of revolution in the penitentiary!"

He was still striding up and down my cell when the screw peered round the door.

"Don't want him either," I said.

Gervier stopped in surprise.

"What? Really?"

Then, not at all put out:

"Fine, then."

And, on his way out:

"Too bad. In that case, I'll see what I can do against you."

*

M'learned friend Rabutin saw things differently. But, as soon as he entered, his nose came to the same conclusion.

"This cell reeks."

His admirable face remained unmoved. He didn't sit down. He stood up straight and handsome in his impeccable suit.

"I'll be quite straight with you, Monsieur Malaussène. You have no defence."

And, before I could reply:

"But that is no reason to allow you to undergo such conditions of detention."

He added:

"Even a habitual criminal has a right to dignity."

Then, as the habitual criminal made no reaction:

"We'll demand better prison conditions."

*

"Excuse me, dear colleague."

"Excuse me."

"After you, sir."

"No, please . . ."

"Thank you."

"Thank you."

"See you soon, dear colleague."

"In court?"

"Yes, next Thursday. I've booked a table at Félicien's at noon. Would you care to join us?"

"Of course."

"Till Thursday, then."

"In court."

"In court indeed."

M'learned friends Rabutin and Bronlard were chatting away at my cell door. The more I self-efface you, the more you advance me. At last, one went out and the other came in, the door closed and Bronlard and I were alone.

"You were right to pack off those three ideologists with their causes, Benjamin. Convictions are poor counsellors when it comes to convictions. They form a screen."

He sat down.

"You don't mind if I call you Benjamin?"

Not a hair out of place. A fraternal smile. He opened an attaché case which stank of fees.

"Talking of screens . . ."

He produced a wodge of paper which he placed on my bed.

"Talking of screens, I've decided to ask the court's permission to have the trial broadcast."

What?

"Yes, this will be a public trial. On television. And I am about to obtain permission. It will be a first in France. It's been absolutely forbidden until now. But you are no ordinary defendant, Benjamin. You can't be judged behind closed doors. I'll see to it. Have no fear. Believe, me, this is going to be the trial of the century. Several channels have expressed an interest. On prime time, naturally. The Americans are already making a screenplay of your adventures . . ."

The Americans are scripting me?

"So I've brought along the first batch of contracts . . ."

His nostrils suddenly flared.

"Shame that smells can't be filmed. Your cell would be of interest . . ."

*

In the end, I asked the screw:

"You don't know one who'd pay attention just to me?"

"One what?"

"A lawyer. One who'd believe I was innocent, even just a little bit . . ."

The screw thought it over. He wasn't a bad bloke. He really did stop and think.

"There's my brother-in-law's cousin . . . But he's really young. A beginner. Still learning."

"He'll do fine."

Chapter 53

My Trial

No, no, no. Not a word about my trial. Go and read about it in your daily paper. I mean, they're the ones who fired the first shot. The artillery of the press softening me up . . . A continual bombing from the papers to wear down my defences . . . Those shells cased with "is accused of having" so as not to blow up in the gunners' faces. Word has it that Malaussène (photo) and his diabolical partner (photo) are accused of having blown up a house and everyone in it. Word has it that their main motive was not revenge, but theft. Word has it that they murdered a young receptionist (photo, yes, that's her, the poor lass) and a student (photo of poor old Clément), because they were awkward witnesses. Word has it that Malaussène has been filled up with the bodily organs of a serial killer (photo of Krämer) and that this has apparently driven him completely barking.

Yes, it all started with Sainclair's article in his magazine *Affection*, entitled: "The Criminal Transplant". Circulation then shot up, and *Affection* became the one the others followed, pecking at its heels like a flock of sparrows. Malaussène to get the circulation going! The whole street of shame was on to him! With pictures! The transplanting of murder. Just perfect! Televised debates, round tables and trick cyclists doing their pieces. A case worth dwelling on. After all, they'd spent years transfusing death in blood, so why not now transplant murder along with the murderer's heart? Had Mary Shelley been right? Malaussène = Frankenstein's monster. One of those marvellous nineteenth-century intuitions. *Affection* led the dance. Sainclair defended his arguments on TV shows with the utmost aplomb. Berthold of course went ballistic: the transplantation of behaviour? Whatever next? Never heard such crap! The truth of the matter was that he, Berthold, had pulled off a genuine surgical exploit, while I, Malaussène, was buggering the whole thing up on purpose by blowing people up. I'm like that. That's just the sort of person I am. Quite capable of burning down an entire city to drop my saviour in it. Have the bad guys been doing it any differently over the past two millennia? Berthold joined the camp of the martyrs. Nailed up on his caduceus, he denied me.

This business about a transplanted killer appealed to my lawyer. (The screw had been right, he was young, still learning.)

"If we can't convince them of your innocence, then we could always fall back on diminished responsibility."

Fat chance. I can still hear Ragaud's voice from the bench opposite:

"They would have us believe", he yelled (Ragaud can yell without raising his voice, and such an ability has a name. It's called the power of conviction), "that the spirit of crime has been *transplanted* into this man's breast. He's not the killer. It's the *other* within!"

Silence. A long shake of the head.

"I find the way the defence belittles your intelligence, ladies and gentlemen of the jury, quite extraordinary."

Silence. Dismayed whiskers. Palpable rage from the belittled jury.

"That said . . ."

That said what? Ragaud raised an eyebrow of doubt, the one that comes up with the shoulders in tow.

"This could in fact be correct . . ."

Incredulous surprise from my lawyer.

"The defence may well be right," Ragaud went on in a pensive tone.

My lawyer turned half around and patted my hand, as though to say "see, it's working . . ." (He was a beginner. He must have seen this gesture in films.)

Ragaud's chin drooped into his hand.

"When you transplant a man, it may be like grafting a plant . . ."

Self-approval from his snowy head.

"It is even highly likely."

He sounded increasingly convinced.

"It may well be true that the accused, in the throes of mimesis, felt the need to take away other people's lives . . . There are some psychiatrists who would certainly go along with that . . ."

My lawyer smiled and leant back, arms out, victory in sight.

(His chance to be on TV for sure.)

"In other words, a plant-cum-man," Ragaud continued still in the same pensive tone.

Then, to the jury:

"Most of you, ladies and gentlemen of the jury, are like me, city dwellers and not botanists or gardeners . . ."

Sure enough, it was a real set of concrete faces staring from their box.

"And, like me, you know practically nothing about grafts, saplings, rejections, suckers, scions, and so forth . . . We have no idea how to make cuttings, to layer or to provine . . . But, ladies and gentlemen, if there is one thing we know about, it is this . . ."

Twelve pairs of ears eagerly pricked up to find out what they knew about.

"Figs do not grow on pear trees, and dogs do not have kittens. Even when grafted together!"

Ragaud was yelling (this time, really yelling).

"And that the secret behind this botanical miracle" – he pointed at me – "is that a killer's organs were transplanted on to a murderer's soul."

A sudden awakening of my lawyer.

"That's right, a murderer!" Ragaud repeated. "And one who was no longer a beginner in his trade when he burnt alive those unfortunate inhabitants of that quiet, Alpine dwelling."

My lawyer leapt to his feet.

"I . . . We . . . Mere suppositions . . . !"

"Seventeen," Ragaud roared. "Seventeen suppositions of seventeen murders! Bombs, knives, syringes, revolvers, culminating in four executions by arson in Loscence! Without mentioning those poor girls sliced up for the benefit of God knows who . . ."

"It isn't true!"

(I swear it, my lawyer yelled out: *It isn't true!* My defence complained that it was *not true*. The only defence he had for me was that it was *not true!*)

Even Ragaud himself looked sincerely dismayed.

*

No, no, no. You can't recount your own trial. Who can recount their own death throes? All you can do is record a few impressions. As the days go by, you grow numb. You feel your innocence draining away like a suicide's blood in the warm water of his tub. You vaguely agree to this loss . . . with a sort of world-weariness, a placid stupor at the sheer variety, quantity and originality of the tricks pulled by the enemy.

I can still hear Gervier's first question. A juicy one, right from the word go:

"What do you think of Irancy wine, Monsieur Malaussène?"

And I replied, as though being quizzed by Julie, amazed at being able to remember:

"Excellent. Sixty-one being a particularly good year!"

"I quite agree. And what about Chablis, Monsieur Malaussène? How would you describe its taste?"

"Stone and cut grass."

"The name of the grape?"

"Chardonnay."

"A good vintage?"

"A *Montée du Tonnerre* '76."

Gervier nodded approvingly. He was now questioning me as though I were an honoured guest.

"And what could you now tell me about the *vin de voile*?"

"The *vin de voile*?"

"Or *vin jaune*, if you prefer."

"Oh yes . . ."

I honestly tried to remember what Julie had told me about wines from the Jura.

"Firstly, the name of the grape."

"Savagnin, I think."

"Spot on. And could you tell us a few things about the secrets of how it is made?"

I could. For once I was being asked to speak the unclouded truth. So I could.

"A late harvest . . . kept in seasoned casks . . . for about five or six years . . . then a veil of yeast forms on its surface."

"Right, hence the name. And is it good?"

"A hint of green walnuts, grilled almonds, hazelnuts . . . yes, it's good."

Gervier grinned broadly.

"We like the same wines, Monsieur Malaussène."

Then, turning to the jury:

"Such is life, ladies and gentlemen of the jury. The prosecution and the accused can share the same tastes. If Monsieur Malaussène and I dug a little deeper, we would find others . . . Perhaps we like the same books, the same music . . . And that is why . . ."

He thought for a moment.

"That is why murderers are featureless."

A few seconds more.

"Or rather they have your features, or mine, or anyone else's."

Then, to me:

"One more question, Monsieur Malaussène. When did you acquire this connoisseur's knowledge of wine?"

I immediately saw where he was coming from. My hair should have stood up

331

in anticipatory horror, but instead I gave myself an inward fatalistic smile, and answered the question honestly.

My lawyer spun round at once.

"Are you completely mad?"

(Ah, he's beginning to catch on . . .)

Gervier stared at me long and hard, then said:

"Thank you, Monsieur Malaussène."

Upon which, he then addressed the jury. If he still sounded like a party guest, then it was one with a bad attack of spiritual indigestion.

"No, ladies and gentlemen, I am not representing the interests of some prestigious vintner. Not at all . . ."

Silence.

"I'm a dead university student."

The words came from the pit of his stomach and from behind the thick lenses of his glasses – *I'm a dead university student* – and everyone believed him.

"A student who worked in July in order to have a little fun in August."

He fell silent once more.

"A student who was not very well off and who, one evening last summer, took a bottle of *Clairette Tradition* up to the room of a couple who knew a great deal about famous and local wines."

Silence.

"Who'd visited twenty-five cellars along their pleasant journey into crime . . . it was a memorable pilgrimage, ladies and gentlemen of the jury . . . sixty-four vintages savoured slowly before turning a young student – who desired only to live on love and air – into a dead student."

Then, this final question:

"And how was the *Clairette Tradition*, Monsieur Malaussène?"

*

"It must be admitted that my young and learned friend's job is far from easy . . ."

Bronlard shook his splendid head of black hair with its silvery glints. Like Gervier, Bronlard was the incarnation of the memory of a student. This time of poor old Clément, who had been still practically a child, and whom I had flung from those rocky heights in his four-wheeled coffin.

"A violent death, just like that of Monsieur de Saint-Hiver, the former governor of Champrond Prison and Clara's first love . . ."

Dot dot dot . . .

"It is dangerous to be in love in Monsieur Malaussène's household."

Period.

Bronlard was genuinely compassionate about how young my brief was.

"My youthful and learned friend is struggling courageously to defend the indefensible. And in so doing, ladies and gentlemen of the jury, he is an honour to our profession."

That's right, Bronlard had decided to defend my defence.

He leant over my brief.

And spoke to him.

Alone.

He explained.

Calmly.

Without waggling his sleeves.

The right profile presented to the right camera.

Because Bronlard had indeed managed to get my trial televised!

Hence the measured play-acting.

He knew how cameras amplify gestures and accentuate words.

No unnecessary movements.

No thoughtless words.

"No, Malaussène did not go up to the Vercors to avenge his dead child. Alas, it is not a wounded father whom you are defending . . ."

My lawyer listened, his ears turning red, and the legal benches turned into school benches and Bronlard's voice into his master's voice.

"There is a simple fact you need to understand. Your client is no occasional murderer. He is neither impulsive nor, I should say, is he sentimental. What sort of father goes on a wine-tasting tour after losing his child? No, your client is a relaxed, meditative killer who took his first step in his murderous career many years ago – and the first step is by far the hardest one to take. Once this point has been crossed, all that matters is self-interest. At first, men kill gratuitously. Then they kill for profit. And in this case, the profit, the object of desire, was a film . . . the movie heralded as the film of the century! And which a student in love with the cinema was trying to conceal from covetous eyes!"

Silence.

"And it cost him his life."

Silence.

"He was just a little younger than you, my friend . . ."

What compassion in Bronlard's stare as he bent down over my beginner!

"Your client . . ." he murmured.

He stopped to think. He weighed his words. He whispered into the black mike which was invisible on his black robes.

"Your client is an effacer of life."

Close-up on the effacer of life, whose eyes were being hypnotised by the monitor. It was the first time that I'd seen myself on TV. There I was, right in front of myself. A gendarme at each side, staring straight out in front, then – zoom in – only me in the camera's eye – zoom again – still me, even closer up, lost in my contemplation of myself.

"An effacer of life who is not averse to his own image," Bronlard concluded.

That dig took some time to cross my stupor before exploding in my neurons. When I looked up, they were all looking at me intently. *Looking at me looking at myself.*

*

The relentless logic which honest citizens attribute to killers.

How nicely they fit together your early childhood, your personality, your motives, premeditation, modi operandi, the act of murder itself and the after-slaughter service . . . it all fits together! Like tenons and mortises! Everything "makes sense" . . . words and silences . . .

They don't want truth, what they want is coherence.

And there's nothing more coherent than a judicial error.

And you still want me to tell you about my trial?

*

The soberest one was Rabutin. He was preaching for Matthias's memory. But, initially, I was the one he spoke about. In a sort of summing-up, for the benefit of the jurors.

"Like you, ladies and gentlemen of the jury, I have paid the utmost attention to what my learned friends have said. And the conclusion I have reached will come as no surprise to you."

Rabutin . . . I'd never seen anyone so vertical. His face carried on exactly from where his body stopped. Two precise creases fell down like plumb lines in the impeccable folds of his robes. A man of conscience, in fact.

"This man . . ."

He gave me a perpendicular stare.

"This man is a man."

Such was his conclusion.

"Quite simply a man, like you or me."

334

He developed his point.

"In fine fettle one day, hospitalised the next, undergoing transplants, just as any of us might, traumatised just as some of us may be; a man of taste who selects the finest wines, but who also has a commonplace love of his own image; a man in love, who has not revealed his partner's hiding place to the police – would we have done as much in his place? – but, above all, a man who was about to become a father . . ."

Pause.

"Whose paternity was interrupted."

Panoramic stare round the jury.

"Perhaps one of you here, ladies and gentlemen of the jury, has experienced just that agony."

Two of them raised instinctive fingers then lowered them at once.

"Terrible, is it not?"

And what silence there was in the courtroom at the mention of such woes!

"Now imagine if that life had been taken away by force."

Everyone started. Ragaud had suddenly leapt up from his bench, Bronlard was staring keenly from his, and Gervier from behind his glasses ready to strike like a cobra, while my youthful brief was nodding his head vigorously in amazement at this unhoped-for succour.

For that was indeed what was happening.

A miracle.

A reversal of allegiances.

Blücher coming to save Grouchy.

Rabutin pleading for my sorrows.

And on he went in a pensive tone:

"We would avenge ourselves, too . . . All of us . . ."

This time Ragaud leapt into the arena. But Rabutin pinned him down.

"Especially you, sir, who have so often pleaded in defence of such actions. Why then be surprised if the accused has become one of your followers? After all, he is a man, a genuine human being! And this is quite simply self-defence! Which *legitimately* procures a revenge which *legality* outlaws! Those are your very words, my dear sir. All I am doing is following you into your own semantic field . . . which corresponds precisely to the domain of your principles!"

Ragaud was speechless.

Gervier highly amused.

And Bronlard was looking round to find the right camera for a knowing smile.

All of which allowed Rabutin to proceed.

"As far as we are concerned, the revenge hypothesis cannot be excluded. So let us just suppose that Doctor Matthias Fraenkhel was killed by the hand of an avenger."

A negligent wave.

"In this case, the murdered witnesses, the burnt house and the stolen film occur only *after* the initial cause. The sluice-gates of violence had been opened, and the killer punished himself by aggravating his crime . . ."

The change in the jury was instantaneous. I read in their eyes that I had become an acceptable killer. Not one they'd invite home, of course, but one who was almost pardonable, and certainly comprehensible.

"That is precisely what I have been saying!"

We'd forgotten about my lawyer. It was his childish voice which had just butted in.

"That is precisely what I have been saying!"

A titter ran round the court.

Which didn't disturb Rabutin's serious demeanour.

"And it was plausible, sir."

He didn't call my lawyer his "young and learned friend", he didn't look at him condescendingly. No, he called him "sir".

"Plausible, but also regrettable," he added at once.

A pause.

Then:

"Because Doctor Fraenkhel had *absolutely nothing to do* with this abortion."

What?

(This was one of the few moments when I got seriously interested in my trial.)

What? Matthias was innocent? Thank you, m'learned friend, Julie had been sure of it, and nothing would give me greater pleasure. But how do you know that? Where's the proof?

"The letter Mademoiselle Corrençon received was a fake."

Which is what's called a last-minute revelation.

Rabutin then explained. He explained how the inquiry had been so slapdash, that they had checked Matthias's handwriting on only one of these embryonicidal letters. And chance would have it that this very one had indeed been clinically justified and in the doctor's hand. All of the others were copies. Rabutin had insisted on them being examined. Ten fakes out of eleven! Including the one which had packed Julie off into Berthold's clutches.

Who did it? Who did that to Matthias? Who did that to us? Just bring him in! Just leave him to me for a couple of minutes! Who did it? Who?

Rabutin's question echoed my thoughts.

"The question now is: who wrote those letters?"

Yes, who? Tell me who!

My eyes in the monitor were screaming out that question.

A terrible tension in Benjamin Malaussène's features.

Then Rabutin asked:

"Monsieur Malaussène, did you *really* want that child?"

The whole courtroom was hanging on my lips.

"I ask this because all of the reports collected from your employers, doctors and friends seem to indicate the contrary. All of them!"

An iceberg.

A courtroom changed into an iceberg.

My silence.

My lawyer's silence.

Their silence.

Oh, the motionless din of silence!

"Ladies and gentlemen of the jury, this is a man. A man who knows his fellow men."

Here, then, was Rabutin's conclusion: I, Benjamin Malaussène, in fact faked those letters in order to get rid of an unwanted child. I then murdered Doctor Fraenkhel in the name of fatherly vengeance – which was certainly a mitigating factor – in order to conceal the true motive of the crime: the theft of The Only Begotten Film! In this way, I'd murdered Doctor Fraenkhel twice over – once by destroying his professional reputation, then by destroying his very person. This was merely an hypothesis, but eight of the ten graphological analyses he had commissioned confirmed it. The author of the letters was none other than Benjamin Malaussène, seated here in the box!

"Ladies and gentlemen of the jury . . ."

Rabutin wasn't a bad guy. He was just a little more coherent than the others, that's all. And probably better, too, if his conclusion was anything to go by.

"No-one should try to influence the decision you are to make . . . But if it should happen that, after your deliberations, this man returns to prison, then it is your duty, and my duty too, to see to it that he is treated as a human being."

*

And you really want me to tell you about my trial?

Chapter 54

The Verdict

IF THERE IS a record for deliberations, then I broke it.

Four minutes, thirty-one seconds precisely!

Two hundred and seventy-one seconds counted out in heartbeats.

Two hundred and seventy-one seconds of hope.

Hope!

Hope...

Tell me about it.

You go home and find that your love left ten years back. Gone with your heart, furniture, carpet and best friend. Ten years back. For the first four years, you bathed your feet every evening in your tears. Then time passed... ten years passed ... The foot bath went cold, your tears evaporated, the heart made a new nest... You go home that evening to a home renovated by another. Ten years later. Hello darling, hello my love. A quiet drink. A nice meal. Then the doorbell rings. Your heart leaps into your soup, you watch it bound off the table and on to the floor, you can't hold it back, it rushes off to open the door. What if it's her? What if it's her!

Hope...

You're on your hospital bed, it's been some time now that your body's been emptying itself into the surrounding bottles, your encephalograph is as flat as an official speech, all that's left is your nose lying on the pillow. The white coats examine it and can't believe what they discover. Your nostrils are palpitating! Your nose still has hope!

Hope...

It's time for the great political hold-up, the race for troughs to stick snouts in. You've got to choose between the eternal, the shameless, the ineradicable, the appallingly unmentionable, but you still go along, you pick one of the names, your voting slip hesitates for a moment above the slit, but you finally let it go and your vote tumbles silently into the utter darkness of the ballot box . . .

Hope . . .

As insane as hope . . .

You're in court, charged with twenty-one murders. A Judaean ass bearing all the sins of the world! Not the slightest mitigating circumstance! The press has pumped you up into the greatest monster of the century. Compared to you, Jack the Ripper is the man everyone would want their daughter to marry. You're every family's nightmare, the terror fermenting in the heart of mankind, absolute evil, older than time itself. The lawyers have gobbled you up raw for breakfast. After their summing up, the jurors would have willingly eaten the rest, if there had been anything left. They strode out as one man.

And still you hope!

After all, you are innocent.

There must be one Just Man to cry out your innocence!

You've always believed in the existence of the Just.

Or a last-minute witness.

The stirring of an uneasy conscience.

The upsurge of truth!

It wasn't him, it was me!

You hope . . .

Each and every second of the trial drove you deeper into the shit, every word undermined you, your own lawyer's silences hovered like a gravestone over the debate. And you know that gravestones don't hover for long. You know that.

And still you hope . . .

In the corridor where you wait, the gendarmes at either side of you are poker-faced. Are they waiting, too? Are they counting the seconds? You glance round at them. What does a military policeman hope for? The sergeants hope to become sergeant-majors, the warrant-officers chief warrant-officers. The wisdom of armies. Slices of hope in the vending machine of a career. And what does a marshal hope for, once the last slice has been consumed? Marshals hope for the Academy. For only immortals are exempt from the torment of hope.

How many cretinous thoughts can go through one mind in 271 seconds of insane hope? Cretinous and futile, if you think about what's going on in the jury room.

Quite simply, I was hoping that the jurors were going to make me a free man again. They were good people who had been unduly influenced by lawyers, that's all. But the judge would set them right. After all, he must have seen any number of genuine culprits! He must be able to tell the difference between a guilty man and a Malaussène! He must know that bigwigs only accuse or defend you for their own interests! He knows that, the judge knows what the barrister business is all about! He knows fine well that nobody can possibly be *that guilty*! The judge is a serious fellow, he may even be my Just Man.

Sitting on my wooden bench, I blindly paid over all my hope capital to the judge. I didn't even want any interest. All I wanted was freedom. That wasn't much to ask for, was it? Who could possibly envy my freedom? Is it too much to ask for the return of an epileptic dog lording it over a family of loonies? What's more, can you even imagine what my charges will get up to if I'm kept away from them for too long? That's what society (sorry, Society) really has to fear. This is a non-negligible side to the question, your honour! I must be sent home at once! This is the best turn you can do to Society. All you do is sentence, sentence, sentence; why not try a little prevention for a change? *What will a child like Verdun be capable of if she grows up without me?* Have you wondered about that, your honour? I have! Did you see Verdun when she was *born*? I did! That year, my mother didn't give birth to a baby so much as to a powder keg! An atomic bomb which will go off beneath your respectable arse if you let her simmer on without me . . . Get me out of here, for Christ's sake!

My inner being was pleading, pleading and threatening . . . threatening and sobbing . . . it wasn't me, it wasn't me . . . can't you see that *it can't possibly have been me*?

Two hundred and seventy-one seconds . . .

The red light started flashing above the door.

"A new record," said the gendarme to my right.

"Congratulations," said the gendarme to my left.

"Let's go," said the gendarme to my right.

"It's time to pay the bill," said the gendarme to my left.

*

It's amazing how much they were all looking forward to seeing me again in the courtroom! No-one tires of contemplating a murderer. From his initial anthropometric appearance to his appearance during the verdict, including his appearances during the trial, the murderer's appearance is in for constant quizzing. You examine it for *differences*, just as keenly as you examine a newborn baby for similarities.

It was just that expression that I saw on the jurors' faces when I returned to the box: nine faces peering down into the cradle of monstrosity. At something other than them. A thing born of a different species . . . And the countless eyes of the public confirmed my impression.

"Will the defendant rise."

The gendarme to my left nudged me.

The one to my right raised his eyebrows.

I was on my feet.

"After due deliberation, to the first question the court has answered 'yes' . . ."

It took me some time to grasp the meaning of the three questions which the court had asked the ladies and gentlemen of the jury during their secret deliberations, but it finally came home to me.

Had the jury declared me guilty of the crimes of which I had been accused?

"Yes."

Were they premeditated?

"Yes."

Were there any mitigating circumstances?

"No."

This is what they'd come up with during my 271 seconds of hope. There was a stir in the courtroom, which was immediately quashed by the judge's hammer.

Like the three blows struck before the final act.

Sentence!

"In consequence, the court sentences you to life imprisonment, with a minimum period of detention of thirty years."

Explosion of universal joy! I'd never made so many people so happy at the same time. I was Monsieur Quatorze Juillet in person! All we needed now were the fireworks. Neighbours embraced. All of them had been delivered from evil. Alleluia!

The last thing I remember about these festivities is the face of the judge on whom I'd pinned all my hopes. He was leaning towards me, while hammering on his desk like a thing possessed, and yelling out over the din:

"Just consider yourself fortunate to be French, Malaussène. In the States, you'd have got three millennia! Or a nice little jab!"

XIII
THE WHOLE GRAVEYARD'S TALKING ABOUT IT

"One hell of a film," Marty sighed. "The whole graveyard's talking about it."

Chapter 55

"**I** CAN'T!" HALF PINT yelled. "Cut that bit out at once!"

His tears had burst out so suddenly that he was soaked to the waist before it occurred to him to dry them.

"Wait!"

"No, I'm not waiting! I'm not! Not a bit of it! Cut it out!"

"But it isn't finished yet!"

"I don't care! Cut it! Dump it! Tear it up!"

"Things will sort themselves out, you'll see! There's going to be a dramatic twist!"

"Oh no there won't! Leave your dramatic twists out of it. He's been sent down!"

"We're going to help him escape. I've got a cunning plan!"

"Even if we pull it off, he's still been sent down!"

"Half Pint's right," Thérèse butted in. "If you want my opinion, it's decidedly off of you to put Benjamin in such a situation."

"And do you know where you can stick your opinion?"

"Hush, Jeremy," said Clara. "Don't talk to Thérèse like that."

"But she's a total pain in the arse! Thérèse the wind-up merchant! Like always! I mean, just look at her! Little Miss Divine Justice in fucking person!"

It's true that, way up there on her bed, sitting in the jutting angles of her nightdress, staring pointedly down at Jeremy, Thérèse did look like a stainless-steel allegory of Justice.

"Say what you like, but in symbolic terms, what you're doing to your elder brother is extremely suspect."

"But I'm not *doing* anything to him, for Christ's sake! I'm *telling a story*! Can't you tell the sodding difference?"

"What about Half Pint? Do you think he can tell the difference?"

And Half Pint's tears gushed out even faster. This wasn't just a sign of sorrow any more, it was a dam breaking.

"And Verdun? Do you think she'll be able to tell the difference when she's a bit bigger?"

As though she'd been waiting for Thérèse's green light before chipping in, Verdun promptly opened her blazing eyes and volcanic mouth. Her pit-like fury then woke up Julius the Dog, whose wailing was added to the concert. All we needed now was the bass rhythm provided free of charge by the neighbours' brooms – they duly arrived – followed by the beginning of curses from the courtyard – so did they.

"OK! OK! OK! I get the picture!"

With a vengeful kick, Jeremy sent the storyteller's stool flying to the far end of the bedroom and flung his writings into Thérèse's face. Then he left, slamming the door behind him. What An Angel's smile tried in vain to play down the gravity of the situation, and so it seemed to me that it was time to act.

"Clara," I said as I got to my feet, "try and save what can be saved, while I go and catch Jeremy before he throws himself under a train."

*

I found him in the kitchen, with his *poète maudit* head buried in his arms, amid the dirty dishes, potato peelings and other leftovers we hadn't had time to tidy away, given that the poor sod had been in such a hurry to read us his last fifty pages.

I went for the direct approach.

"Cut the crap, Rimbaud, and give me a hand with the washing-up."

Stacking the plates, I asked:

"So how does the last chapter end? What was your dramatic twist?"

Apply to the author and you assuage the pain. He explained the business to me while collecting the cutlery:

"After the judge's final words, you remember: 'Just consider yourself fortunate to be French, Malaussène . . .' "

"Yes . . . 'In the States, you'd have got three millennia! . . .' "

". . . 'Or a nice little jab!' Yeah, that's it. Well, at that very moment, I spring up behind the cunt, stick a gun to his head, while brandishing an armed grenade in the other hand, and tell the gendarmes to hand you their pieces, then lie down on the floor."

"Swipe me. And then?"

"Nothing. That's where I stopped. It's a striking end, you see?"

"I certainly do."

I placed the glasses in the foam beside the plates, then turned on the tap over the second basin. Jeremy liked doing the washing-up with me, especially since I'd got out of prison. He calls it our "double sink-tank". I make the bubbles, he rinses and wipes. It gives us time to talk critical.

"Answer me honestly, Ben."

"Of course."

"Do you like it?"

"Yes."

"Are you just saying that?"

"I'm saying what I think."

"Do you reckon it was a good idea to put you away in Champrond?"

"It was nice to have old Uncle Stojil's reek back again."

"I did that for the unity of place. And what did you make of the lawyers?"

"Truer than life."

"You don't think they're a bit over the top?"

"That's exactly what they're like. How come you know so much about the legal profession?"

"From Zabo. She's got some learned friends."

Zabo . . . since the disappearance of The Zebra, Zabo had decided to morph our dramatist into a novelist. She was pampering our Jeremy. Every two days, he gave her what he'd produced. The Queen and the apprentice then locked themselves up in her office and, word had it, got into serious negotiations. The apprentice defended his turf, he gave way readily when it came to spelling mistakes, or errors of grammar and composition, his childish tics and other signs of immaturity, but he was fighting tooth and nail to keep the life sentence. The Queen reckoned it was exaggerated. Her felt pen swished, her scissors snipped. The Vendetta Press reverberated. People crept along the walls. The Queen expanded the themes. Jeremy worked up the emotional side. The Queen wanted a more mannered style. Jeremy stuck to the Malaussène method: "That's how Benjamin speaks, that's how he tells us stories, that's even how he thinks! I mean, I do know him better than you do!" "Thinking, speaking and writing are three different things!" the Queen retorted, pen in hand, and proof aplenty. Style battles in the war of the novel. The Queen knew what she wanted. And she was going to get it, while carefully allowing Jeremy to think that he was still the author. France's youngest novelist!

"And what about the 'maternalistic' magistrate, who does you in because she understands you too well? What did you make of her?"

"An amusing idea. Yes, she was funny."

"That was Zabo's idea. Do you reckon it's possible?"

"What, a mother like that? Of course it's possible. Watch out, you're overflowing."

He turned off the tap. Then spent several seconds contemplating the basin.

"Tell me the truth, Ben. Are the trial and verdict *really* credible?"

"I almost believed it myself."

"And *you*? Did you find yourself to be a good likeness?"

"You never really recognise yourself, you know. But I reckon you've got me pretty well right . . ."

Silence had returned to the bedroom. The door opened slightly. Clara's head appeared. She looked at me questioningly and I reassured her with a quick nod. The door closed again silently.

"Can I ask you a question, Ben?"

Leaning over the basin, sleeves rolled up, Jeremy presented me with his ethical profile.

"About what Thérèse said . . . Do you think you can put *absolutely everything* in a novel?"

*

I know, I know, you can put anything and everything in, but you can't drag your readers through eight chapters only to inform them once it's over that all this tragic tension, this sense of injustice which grew with every word, and the terrible verdict at the end, were all just a joke and things in fact didn't turn out like that. Such a conceit would be an abuse of trust, and would deserve punishment. Defenestration of the book in question, at the very least! It's true, I know it, mea culpa, et maxima with it! But *who* has the guts to stand between Queen Zabo and her cash register? Who'd have the balls to get in the way of Jeremy in the throes of novelistic delirium? Who'd be heroic enough to stop him dishing us up our daily ration of words? Who's ready to be sacrificed at the altar? Any takers? If so, step forward and I'll give you the keys to the shop.

And, then, what's with all this disappointment?

What does it mean *deep down* (as Thérèse would put it)?

Does it mean you'd have preferred to see me sentenced for life *really really* (as Half Pint would put it)?

Thirty years minimum?

Thanks.

That's all I can say really: thanks a lot.

If those very people who are most intimately aware of my innocence also want me sent down, then something is rotten in the state of reality.

Need coherence, do you? Just like judges? You'd sacrifice an innocent man just to maintain coherence . . . Better a judicial error than a poor literary conceit, is that it?

Bravo.

Thanks again.

So much for humanity . . .

*

Which is also to forget that not everything in the Zabo/Jeremy version is completely wrong. It certainly contains a fair amount of inventiveness, but that goes without saying! However, there's also some truth in it. We can separate them, in fact, into two distinct parts: what's false, and what's true.

1) What's False

My imprisonment in Champrond? False. It was simply due to a Jeremyesque need to cast up the odoriferous shade of Stojil over our woes. And, sure enough, Uncle Stojil's shade has been sadly missing of late!

Would you have preferred a description of the penitentiary in which I was *really really* banged up for the last few months? No point. Penitentiaries are indescribable. They're just like you imagine them to be. Everything comes to a halt. The pen is one place where the pen isn't mightier than the sword.

So, no Champrond, and no Faucigny. No lawyers, either, or trial, or verdict. Who'd have swallowed all of that? Far too improbable! A prison governor obsessed with educational sadism? Steady on there! Reversible lawyers, as brilliant on one side as on the other? Pure defamation! Jurors doped by the press? Never! Jurors are free spirits! With minds of their own! As for judicial errors . . . What? Here in France? When? Where? You're kidding me . . . The only thing that makes people believe in judicial errors is the whingeing of the guilty!

2) What's True

On other hand, it's absolutely true that I've just spent several months in the can, far from my loved ones and my beloved one.

It's also absolutely true that Chief Superintendent Nepos tried his hardest to turn my past against me, and that he nearly succeeded.

Absolutely true, too, that an investigating magistrate was put in charge of the case. A certain Judge Képlin, who will remain nameless . . . A magistrate like an investigative machine, of no novelistic interest at all. And if he'd had his way, there really would have been a trial and I really would have been sent down for life.

Finally, it's also quite accurate that a lawyer did agree to take on my defence. He's a friend of a friend of a friend, young, a beginner and who – to his credit – wishes to remain anonymous. My thanks to him, while we're on the subject. He did what he could. You did what you could, dear and learned friend. And it wasn't easy.

During all that present time, I didn't count the weeks or the months. All I know is that it was long. In my cell, in the evening, it was comforting to know that Jeremy had taken the tribe in hand at the hour when nightmares beckon. A reading in the prison visiting room during the afternoon to work up his confidence, then back home with my blessing. "Brilliant, Jeremy, just great! Keep it up!" I was of course a tad pissed off with Queen Zabo about the way she maintained the illusion of his genius after she'd completely rewritten his text but, I said to myself, after all, that's life for you . . .

It was long, and could easily have been even longer . . .

But believing in the worst would mean admitting that my tribe could imagine, even for a second, that my innocence could be put up on trial. Believing in the worst would be to picture a world in which Coudriers didn't keep tabs on their sons-in-law. Believing in the worst would mean not to count on Gervaise, her dark angels and her Templars. Believing in the worst would be to forget that Julie never escapes to no purpose.

Believing in the worst would mean accepting that it's over.

I'm not like that.

Chapter 56

"*H*EY, GIVEN UP *the theatre, have you?*"
        "*Are you part of the set-up?*"
"*Apparently Cazo hasn't shown up yet.*"
"*The King sent me to fetch the film.*"
"*Oh yes? With an electric torch? And without giving us warning?*"
"*We thought you'd gone. That's what was planned, wasn't it?*"
"*Planned by who?*"
"*You so much as touch me and I'll spill the beans to the Viet's daughter!*"
"*Stop him!*"

Inspector Joseph Silistri stopped the cassette before the series of thuds.

"Do you recognise any of the voices?"

"The two men, but not the woman."

"So?"

"The young one's Clément."

"And the other one?"

"Well, I might be wrong, but . . ."

"You want to hear it again?"

"Yes please."

"It's Lehmann," Jeremy replied. "It's Lehmann's voice. I definitely recognise him."

Thus did Inspector Silistri identify Lehmann's voice, by playing the cassette to Jeremy Malaussène, who'd managed the "spatial relationship" of our family saga.

"Are you sure?"

"Ab-so-lutely."

Inspector Silistri then wanted to hear more about this Lehmann.

"He used to work in the Store, when Benjamin was acting the goat there. He was the one Ben used to do his weeping number in front of."

"And you'd asked Lehmann to play himself in your show?"

"Yes. That must be why Clément mentioned the theatre."

"And does the name 'Cazo' ring any bells?"

"Not at all."

"And the girl's voice? Nothing there either?"

"No."

"It doesn't matter. You've already done your brother a big favour."

"Will he be released now?"

"Not immediately. He's got more than just Clément's death on his slate."

"And will this tape convict Lehmann?"

"No, it isn't actual proof."

"So what are you going to do now?"

"Nothing much. I'm off the case. I'm just going to complicate Monsieur Lehmann's existence a bit. Got his phone number?"

*

During the following weeks, Monsieur Lehmann's existence became distinctly complicated. It all started with a late-night phone call, while he was in a deep sleep. Lehmann answered with a curse. A voice he recognised at once said:

"Hey, given up the theatre, have you?"

Lehmann was so taken aback that he didn't answer. He just hung up as though the receiver were red hot. A sleepless night. Inspector Silistri then let him get his beauty sleep for a few nights. The memory faded. Probably a bad dream. Yes, definitely a bad dream.

Then the phone rang again:

"Hey, given up the theatre, have you?"

"Who is it? Who's there?"

In the pit of his terror, Lehmann didn't know what to expect. What he heard next was even more terrifying. It was his own voice in reply:

"Are you part of the set-up?"

"What is all this? Who are you? Who are you?"

No answer. Just the syncopated silence of a phone that's been hung up.

And so on.

Until Monsieur Lehmann smashed his phone to pieces.

A week later, it was the intercom that woke him up. Six floors below, someone was ringing his doorbell. Someone in the entry hall was calling for him. What time was it? What the hell was the time? He barged into the furniture on his way to answer.

"Who's there?"

"*The King sent me to fetch the film,*" Clément's voice answered.

Monsieur Lehmann moved out.

He took refuge in a hotel on Rue des Martyrs. He paid in cash and didn't give them his name. He felt like death when, one evening, he walked past reception and he heard the night porter say:

"Monsieur Lehmann?"

He was too slow to reply that he wasn't Monsieur Lehmann.

"There's a letter for you."

The letter just said:

"*You so much as touch me and I'll spill the beans to the Viet's daughter!*"

*

"Why are you doing this, Joseph? Why don't you just question him in person?"

Gervaise was astonished. This was not the way the police worked. Old Thian would have disapproved.

Silistri defended his approach.

"It's healthy for someone like that to start believing in ghosts. Once he's marinated in fear long enough, he'll tell us everything we want to know."

Gervaise didn't agree.

"I don't believe you. If you just wanted him to talk, you'd question him. So why don't you?"

"He won't cough just like that. He's a hard nut."

"I still don't believe you. You're doing this to get your own back on him, Joseph."

Gervaise explained:

"You're angry. You're angry and you're taking it out in this Lehmann because you've got him in your clutches. What's made you this stroppy?"

But it wasn't that easy to make Silistri talk. You had to tell him what he had to say. Gervaise did so.

"Stop it, Silistri. Titus isn't the father of my child."

"How do you know?"

"I'm as sure as I am that it isn't you."

A convincing point.

"But it must have been someone!"

"Is that really necessary?"

"What?"

Silistri looked at Gervaise, then he looked at Malaussène's woman, who was watching the match as an impartial umpire.

353

"I mean, is it really necessary to know who it was?" Gervaise clarified her question.

Silistri looked to the umpire for assistance.

"Did you hear what I just heard?"

Malaussène's woman had heard.

"Gervaise does have a point. There are so many unknown factors about having a child. So what difference does one more make . . . ?"

The holy alliance between the veil and feminism, Inspector Joseph Silistri thought when back on the street. That was all they needed! He'd been protecting Gervaise for months . . . just to be told that the identity of her rapist was of no importance.

A pair of bollocks is a pair of bollocks, Gervaise. And I'm going to rip Titus's off.

The fury which was blinding Inspector Silistri was also keeping his eyes open. His nights had become as sleepless as Lehmann's. Yes, Lehmann. How about taking Lehmann in hand a bit . . . He set off like a sleepwalker towards Lehmann's new hide-out.

Chapter 57

"MARIE-ANGE, O MARIE-ANGE, you really screwed up when you shopped poor old Malaussène."

Twice a week, Inspector Adrien Titus spent a good half an hour in the cell of the pink-suited niece. And always at the same time in the afternoon.

"How past it can you get? Holding salons like this went out with the Great War."

He produced a thermos from the depths of his jacket, poured out some tea and offered her some *petits fours* in a wicker basket.

"They're from Dalloyau's, if you don't mind. I take care of my customers."

The first few times, she refused to touch the tea. She looked down her nose at his *petits fours*. She remained extremely attentive in her pink armour.

"Isn't your suit starting to pong a bit?"

One afternoon, he arrived with a fresh suit in the same Diana pink.

"Try it."

She didn't react.

"It's from my wife. She's in the rag trade."

The next time, Marie-Ange was wearing the clean suit.

"Give me the other one. I'll get it dry-cleaned."

*

He put his cards on the table with the very first words of his first visit.

"Marie-Ange, Marie-Ange, you were wrong to shop poor old Malaussène. You don't know him. You'd never set eyes on him before. This means you cannot be believed, and that's where it gets fascinating. Why shop some poor sucker who's a total stranger?"

She didn't reply.

"That's what I'm wondering about . . ." Inspector Titus murmured while serving tea across the doilies.

She followed every move he made.

"I mean, if he was famous, I could understand it. It's good fun pissing over a statue. Statues are never dry. There's always at least one droplet of suspicion left: '*Apparently he isn't what he seems . . .*' A real pleasure for arse-lickers and leg-lifters."

Little by little, she drew towards the tea. Then she drank a cup. Then she ate the *petits fours*. Without taking her eyes off him. Without uttering a word.

"But Malaussène is no celeb. He's unknown outside the circle of his friends, relatives and dog."

They gulped down the little chunks of dunked cake.

"And you don't know his family, but you've been talking away knowledgeably about them to Nepos's boys . . . the dog, the mother, the brothers and the sisters. You haven't missed a trick."

Generally, their little chat finished on a shared silence.

*

"So, it occurred to me that . . ."

Inspector Adrien Titus picked up the thread of the conversation where he'd left it.

"It occurred to me that, if you don't know Malaussène, you must know *someone else* who does. And this someone is not exactly a bosom pal, but he's told you everything about him."

He smiled.

"What a fibber you are . . ."

He had his wicker basket. From it, he produced two small white polystyrene containers.

"I've brought you some ice cream today."

Despite herself, she glanced at the name of the manufacturer on the label. She was never disappointed.

"And so, it wasn't Malaussène you were getting the tattoos for, but for someone else who talked a lot about him."

That afternoon, they enjoyed their ice cream without adding another word.

*

On the following occasion, he spoke more:

"So, you don't know Malaussène. But you shopped him instead of this other person who you were really supplying with tattoos and who does know him. That's the mistake you made, Marie-Ange. Because he does know Malaussène,

356

and knows him well – dog, mother, brothers and sisters – we'll find him soon enough."

She put down her cup without finishing.

Titus licked up the sugar from the bottom of his.

"That was your bright idea, wasn't it? Our friend didn't tell you to shop Malaussène if you got caught. And he was right. Because this isn't a lead you've given us, Marie-Ange. It's a direct route to the organiser."

Then, just before leaving:

"Here, they're from my wife."

He laid three rectangles of silk on her prison bed.

*

"O love! Love! Love and lies . . . You really must be besotted with him to slip up like that. I mean, you're so self-controlled. It wasn't enough just to cover him with your silence, you had to accuse someone in his place. And you wanted it to be a nice present for him. Malaussène . . . does he really hate him that much?"

She went on coolly drinking her tea.

"Then something else occurred to me. If you're capable of doing all this for our fortunate friend, then you could do even more."

All she could do was go on courageously drinking tea, eating her *petits fours* and licking her fingers.

"Like accuse yourself, for instance."

There, she put down her cup and saucer before they trembled in her hands.

"You're not the surgeon, Marie-Ange. It isn't you."

Her eyes were still expressionless, but she didn't know what to do with her hands. She dried them on a square of white batiste.

"The surgeon's our friend there. It's him. He was the one you were taking Cissou the Snow's body to on the night you were nicked. A map of Belleville on human skin – what a marvellous present for an art lover. Was it his birthday or something?"

Titus refilled the cup as soon as Marie-Ange put it down.

"You're just his procurer, Marie-Ange, that's all."

Then added, with a hint of sympathy:

"His favourite procurer."

Titus gave a long shake of his head.

"Even though that cunt's heart's full of shit!"

*

Inspector Adrien Titus observed the devastating effects of the truth in Marie-Ange's stare. Tiny shells were exploding in the blue of her eyes, sparks flying down to set her heart ablaze. She'd have gone for anybody else's throat, but him there, this cop, had suddenly started talking about the man she loved. One hell of a cop! An enemy fit for them! She hadn't said a word, not the slightest scrap of information but now via the logical steps of his deductions he was talking to her about her love! He was filling the cell with that passion! What a great seer he was, this Tartar-eyed pig!

Inspector Adrien Titus would have so liked to agree with her. But he knew he was just a down-to-earth officer, bred up on prosaic truth. Not a seer at all, Marie-Ange, definitely not . . . All his skills and deductive power derived from an anonymous letter which was hidden in the inside pocket of his jacket, next to his heart.

What did this letter say?

The letter said what Inspector Titus paraphrased to Marie-Ange.

Gentlemen of the police,

I am sorry to inform you that the person you are holding in custody, called Mademoiselle Marie-Ange Courrier, is the greatest liar of her sex and her era. Nothing she has told you is true. She is guiltless of all the crimes she claims to have committed. Her lies are designed quite simply to protect the real culprit.

If you do not give me back my little liar within the next fortnight (counting from this postmark), on the fifteenth day I shall kill again, this time among your officers. You cannot imagine how dull my life is without my little liar. The truth is so depressing, gentlemen . . . however, since you set such a price on it, you can have it in return for Mademoiselle Courrier, in the form of a full signed confession. So this is the deal: free falsity and you will garner truth. Keep her in irons and I shall kill your officers. As of the fifteenth day.

Please consider this letter as an ultimatum.

Inspector Adrien Titus knew the letter off by heart. He didn't like the way it was written. "Gentlemen of the police" . . . "Mademoiselle Courrier" . . . "free falsity and you will garner truth" . . . A smug git sounding off. Such was Inspector Titus's opinion. And he couldn't help sharing it, in a roundabout way, with Marie-Ange.

"Does he pick your clothes?"

Yes, the pink suit came from him, she wore it only for him.

"And the perm? Was that his idea, too?"

A helmet of respectability on the free head of a whore. What compassion . . .

"Revamped Cacharel . . . I'm sure the creep speaks the same way he dresses you."

That did make her nearly jump.

"OK. Let's say, we've now defined what we're looking for as a squeaky-clean arsehole who speaks the same way he dresses you."

- *

Titus made his weekly report to Gervaise, being careful not to choose the same day or time as Silistri.

"To start off with, she was wondering whether to drink tea with me or not. Then she thought, why not? She's a liar and a player, you were right about that, Gervaise. She likes duels. But it was a bad decision to eat the *petits fours*. It's harder to control your emotions with your mouth full. Stomachs spew up what brains can keep down."

Titus was shamelessly staring at Gervaise's belly as he spoke. No, it was definitely not the Holy Ghost blowing up that Montgolfier.

"Gervaise, remind me to interrogate Silistri when his mouth's full."

"Leave it out, Adrien. You know it wasn't Joseph."

"I don't know anything, Gervaise. And since it wasn't me . . ."

"You sound as if you wish it was."

This last observation came from Malaussène's woman. Ever since she'd holed up in Gervaise's place, Malaussène's woman had become her shadow. On her own, she'd replaced all of Gervaise's guardian angels. Titus asked her:

"You looking for a slap, or what?"

*

The next afternoon, when he went into Marie-Ange's cell, he set off on a different tack:

"Did you know that I've got no right to come here and piss you around?"

A point of law.

"I'm off the case, Marie-Ange. You belong to Nepos now. I'm here undercover."

She was now helping him to dress the table. Doilies, saucers, cups, teaspoons, lovely little embroidered batiste napkins . . . On those afternoons, they played at tea parties.

"And since when do Inspectors visit prisoners in their cells? It's unheard of."

He had brought along an entire collection of rare jams.

"Each visit costs me 500 francs. I have to bribe my way in. For that, I could treat myself to a whore or a psychiatrist."

He filled the cups.

"Truth has a price . . ."

He was delicate enough not to add on the cost of their little love feasts.

"That's just to tell you you can kick me out if you want."

Apparently, she didn't.

"Especially considering that 'Nepos's methodicals' don't believe me. Because they believe you."

But they discussed something else that afternoon.

"How did you guess Gervaise was pregnant, Marie-Ange? Just because she puked all over you? Or can women sniff out buns in their rivals' ovens?"

She had a fleeting smile of disgust.

"I have a problem," he confessed.

It was his turn to put down his cup for a long think.

"I can't help wondering who the father is."

She grabbed the teapot and served him. She had the right fingers for the job. She kept the top delicately in place.

"Thanks," he said.

Then he asked:

"You don't have your own theory about that?"

She looked at him.

"Because I do," he said at last.

She was extremely interested, and relieved that he was finally on to someone else.

"A terrible suspicion. I can't sleep at night."

True enough: his features were drawn, his skin ashen, his eyelids more slanted than usual, and his stare more feverish and mean. An insomniac fury.

"What's the explanation, Marie-Ange? For months, I've been investigating a snuffer who slices up whores, I've heard the screams, seen the bodies, viewed kilometres of horror, I've got a stock of nightmares to last me the rest of my life, and what's stopping me from sleeping is the fact that I can't catch the owner of a spermatozoid!"

He suddenly looked up.

"Shall I tell you the fucker's name?"

But instead he left without another word, choking on his fury. The cell door slammed behind him.

Chapter 58

O N T H E M O R N I N G of the fifteenth day, Chief Inspector Julien Perret, one of Chief Superintendent Nepos's methodicals, was leaving his home on Rue Labat on his way to headquarters on Quai des Orfèvres, when he turned his back on a cloudy sky to unlock the door of his Quinze Citroën (he liked collectable cars) and then felt the cold twinge of a blade slice into his spinal cord just above the fifth cervical vertebra. He was immediately robbed of the use of his arms and legs and of all other sensations. So he didn't feel what happened next. He was finished off, then his body was transported in the boot of his car, which was being driven rather recklessly by a total stranger he would never have lent it to.

*

Meanwhile, Chief Superintendent Coudrier had other cases on his mind, twiddling his thumbs outside the door of what had once been his office. He'd now been waiting a good thirty minutes for the pleasure of seeing his son-in-law. This was a long time for a father-in-law, but not that long for a recently retired, patient fisherman. It wasn't the disappearance of the imperial trappings or the modifications made by Xavier (his son-in-law's forename) which surprised him. So much had been foreseeable. Xavier would always be Xavier. Bay windows, glass doors, aluminium frames, light, light and more light, and not a single familiar face on the entire floor of headquarters . . . Chief Superintendent Coudrier had pictured all this on the way between his hotel and Quai des Orfèvres.

"You're not going to stay in a hotel, sir. I'll put you up," Inspector Caregga had suggested after picking him up at the airport.

"Are you no longer in love, Caregga?"

Inspector Caregga's neck had blushed in his Normandy pilot's jacket.

"Then don't spoil your chances. It was already good of you to come and fetch me."

And, before Inspector Caregga could repeat his invitation:

"What are you working on these days?"

"Red tape in admin, sir."

"Red tape . . ."

Chief Superintendent Coudrier had had personal experience of this sort of career upset on two or three occasions, and always in the same historical context – after a change of boss.

"Take my word for it, Caregga, that won't be the case for long."

*

"I'm sorry, Father, really I am, we're up to our ears . . . What with the elections, anti-terrorism, all those political shenanigans added to our routine work . . . but you know that better than I do, please, take a seat."

Chief Superintendent Nepos pointed his father-in-law towards a sort of transparent tub perched on a chrome tube.

(Is he offering me a bidet?)

Chief Superintendent Coudrier sat down on it gingerly. It was an unpleasant sensation, as though he was slipping down into the bottom of something. He clung on valiantly to his old leather briefcase.

"How are Martine and the children?"

"Fine, Father, couldn't be better. The twins are making good progress with their German. We finally opted for coaching. It is, of course, rather dear, but we had no choice. The situation was becoming alarming."

"And Malaussène?"

It sounded as if Chief Superintendent Coudrier were enquiring about his third grandson.

Silence from the other side of the glass desk.

"How many crimes has he been accused of this time?" Chief Superintendent Coudrier insisted.

But it wasn't enough to break the glass.

"The last time I had to deal with Malaussène," he went on, "he was suspected of having murdered his sister Clara's fiancé and of having sent out a hitman to cut the throat of a certain Krämer, one of Champrond's inmates. This was quite a low score for him. On previous occasions . . ."

"Father!"

"Yes?"

Chief Superintendent Nepos placed a vast amount of hope in the following sentence:

"I have no intention of discussing Malaussène with you."

"Why ever not?"

Hope wasn't enough.

"Listen, Father . . ."

"Yes, Xavier?"

"I don't have the time. I really don't."

As far back as Chief Superintendent Coudrier could remember, Xavier had never had any time for him. Nor for Martine. Nor for his children. It was as if time had swallowed up Xavier whole as soon as he emerged from his mother's womb. If you happened upon him alone in a room, he jumped out of his skin as though you'd caught him on the loo. No time . . . The obsessive dream of a career had gobbled up all his time. No time, just a healthy appetite.

"Even though I've come all this way to give you some information . . ."

"The Malaussène case is closed, Father. My men have no need of any further information."

"You have officers here who have no need of information? Well done, Xavier, that is a genuine innovation."

Chief Superintendent Nepos strove to hold back the drops of sweat which were glistening on his brows. Nothing doing. The sight of his father-in-law with his paunch and oily lock always made him break out into a sweat. He's the obese one, and I'm doing the sweating. Xavier's impeccable bald patch harboured this kind of thought. Never mind, he said to himself at last, if he will insist, let's get this over with.

NEPOS: Listen Father, the Malaussène case isn't just about what happened in the Vercors. Judge Képlin has decided to reopen all his previous files and make fresh inquiries.

COUDRIER: I see.

NEPOS: I'm sorry.

COUDRIER: Sorry? Why on earth are you sorry?

NEPOS: I mean . . . this wasn't my decision, and . . .

COUDRIER: I had no doubt about that, Xavier. And so, anything new?

NEPOS: Not really. But there are several grey areas . . .

COUDRIER: For instance?

NEPOS: The suicide of Chief Superintendent Cercaria a few years back. Malaussène was in the architect's house at the time. There are witnesses among his colleagues at work.

COUDRIER: Anything else?

NEPOS: Father, believe me . . .

COUDRIER: Anything else, Xavier?

NEPOS: . . .

COUDRIER: . . .

NEPOS: The bombing campaign in the Store. There's no trace of any guilty party in your conclusions. But Malaussène was on the scene of the crime on each occasion. Six deaths, Father!

COUDRIER: And?

NEPOS: I'm really sorry, Father, but the list is long and my time is short.

COUDRIER: . . .

NEPOS: . . .

COUDRIER: . . .

NEPOS: . . .

COUDRIER: . . .

NEPOS: Look, Father, I'll play along with you if I must, but you should understand that times have changed. These past years have seen too many scandals build up, with culprits who have either been covered up for, or else miraculously proved to be innocent. Such cases so thoroughly discredit our institutions that democracy itself is in danger . . . The requirements of transparency . . .

COUDRIER: What was that?

NEPOS: Sorry?

COUDRIER: The last word you said . . .

NEPOS: Transparency?

COUDRIER: Yes, transparency, what in God's name does it mean?

NEPOS: . . .

"Transparency is a cretinous concept, my lad. When applied to the quest for truth it is, at best, useless. Can you imagine a transparent world? What would your transparent truth then stand out against? Are you an admirer of that . . . Barnabooth, Xavier? Transparency is only good for illusionists!"

"Father . . ."

"Now shut up and hear me out, because I'm here to do you an extraordinary favour. It isn't your catchphrases that will change the way this country works. Human truth is opaque, Xavier, there's the real heart of the matter! You're making yourself look ridiculous with your *transparency*! If I let you get on with it, you'd soon be shedding a tear about *exclusion* after sidelining all of my men. It is not enough just being able to use the jargon, my boy! You need more than that if you want to avoid the really deep shit . . ."

Chief Superintendent Coudrier suddenly broke off.

"Is there any coffee in this place? Don't tell me you sidelined my coffee pot with the rest! Get me a cup of coffee! No, two! You'll have one with me! And without sugar!"

The order went into the intercom. Somewhere, a coin dropped into the slot of a machine.

The father-in-law's eyes were flashing.

"You think I'm different from you, don't you Xavier? Do you really imagine that the first time this Malaussène character landed in my office I didn't react in just the same way? A gift from the gods! A real serial killer! I'll soon be sitting at the minister's right hand! That's what's pushing you on, isn't it? The minister's right hand . . . just try and tell me I'm wrong!"

Chief Superintendent Nepos blinked.

"What's this lamp on your desk?"

"A halogen."

"A halogen . . . Isn't it bright enough as it is? *Mehr Licht, mehr Licht,* always more light, my poor German scholar. So, who are you going to vote for?"

"Sorry?"

"In the presidential elections. Who are you voting for?"

Chief Superintendent Nepos was now fighting for his second wind under this varied cross-examination by a multiplying horde of father-in-laws. The arrival of the coffee signalled the end of the round.

"Not a word during coffee."

And not a word was said. The coffee pot wasn't Elisabeth. The coffee pot's skirt was well above its knees.

Chief Superintendent Coudrier placed the empty cup on his son-in-law's desk.

"That was coffee?" he asked.

Then:

"So, who are you voting for?"

"Um, well, in fact I haven't really . . ."

"I see. Then stay inside your voting booth, Xavier, and avoid any risk of transparency . . ."

He carried straight on:

"You have identified some 'grey areas' in my files, is that correct? Well, you are perfectly right about that. Take the person behind the bombing campaign in the Store for example . . . the name of the culprit certainly does not appear in police records."

He undid the clasps of his ancient briefcase.

"And it wasn't Malaussène."

He produced an imperial-green cardboard folder.

"You really want to know who it was?"

Before Nepos had time to reply, the name flashed before his eyes, written in bright loops and curls, in the gleam of his halogen.

The succeeding silence ended with a barely audible whisper:

"No! You don't mean it was . . . our . . ."

"Your candidate? No, my lad, it was his uncle . . . on his father's side! Same family. Same name. You'll find all the relevant information in this file."

But Chief Superintendent Nepos's fingers remained at a respectful distance from it.

"Fancy a little transparency, Xavier? Pick up the phone and call the minister. This won't be news to him, he knows the story off by heart. But then you won't be on his right hand, nor on his left for that matter, nor even here, you'll be out on your ear. *Exclusion*. Like my men and my coffee pot. Go on, call him!"

Chief Superintendent Coudrier barked out the order.

"Call him, Xavier. After all, what we want is transparency!"

"Father . . ."

"Call him!"

But it was the phone that called Chief Superintendent Nepos. A ringing tone which pinned him to his chair.

"That might be him now! The Minister of the Interior in person! Go on, answer it!"

It rang on.

"Answer it, for heaven's sake! That noise is driving me mad!"

It wasn't the minister. But, to judge by Chief Superintendent Nepos's crumbling face, it was worse, or nearly.

"When? . . . Where? . . . Is forensics there?"

Then he hung up and leapt to his feet.

"One of my men has just been killed. Excuse me, Father, but I really must go."

"I'll come with you."

*

The weather didn't seem to want to clear up. Wisps of fog hung between the banks of the Seine. Postel-Wagner's head emerged from the boot of a black Citroën.

"You're here are you, Postel? Not been sidelined? You're more fortunate than my bust of Napoleon."

There was a corpse in the boot of the car, but a discreet smile, all the same, below the forensic surgeon's moustache.

"Good to see you again, Chief Superintendent."

Access to the river bank had been blocked. Flashing lights were turning in mourning. No sirens. Not a word. The shock of headquarters losing one of its own.

"Who was he?" Chief Superintendent Coudrier asked.

"Inspector Perret," Chief Superintendent Nepos replied.

"Perret?" Chief Superintendent Coudrier asked.

"He was new," Chief Superintendent Nepos admitted.

"His spinal cord has been severed just above the fifth cervical vertebra," the forensic surgeon explained. "Then he was finished off by being stabbed through his heart, just below his shoulder blade, here. A single blow. It happened about an hour ago."

"Then the murderer parked his car right in front of headquarters," Chief Superintendent Coudrier observed. "Quite a cold-blooded bastard."

"Who informed us?" Chief Superintendent Nepos asked.

"We were tipped off by phone, sir," a young inspector replied, incapable of taking his eyes off the corpse.

"And what was Perret working on?" Chief Superintendent Coudrier asked.

"On the Malaussène case," Chief Superintendent Nepos replied.

"Which one?" Chief Superintendent Coudrier asked.

"Father, please . . ."

"There's something else," the young inspector said. "A message pinned to his jacket."

"Let me see."

Coudrier put out his hand – a purely professional reflex – but Nepos intercepted it.

Gentlemen of the police, this is now the morning of the fifteenth day. Counting from my postmark. Consider this note as a renewed ultimatum. Of the same duration.

Chief Superintendent Nepos apparently couldn't believe his eyes.

"Ah yes," Chief Superintendent Coudrier whispered into his ear, "looks like you're going to have to make up your mind to give him back his little liar."

His father-in-law's words took some time to penetrate Chief Superintendent Nepos's stupor.

"What did you say?"

"We'll discuss the rest in your office, Xavier. Take my word for it, it's better for everyone."

Scraps of conversation broke through the glass door, echoing off the walls, until access to the floor had to be blocked off, just as it had been beside the Seine.

Chief Superintendent Coudrier was brandishing under the nose of his son-in-law the letter which had announced in no uncertain terms the murder of a policeman.

"All I can see is that you received this threatening letter but chose to ignore it," Chief Superintendent Coudrier thundered. "And now one of your men has paid the bill!"

"Father, for the last time, how do you know about this letter? Am I to think that . . ."

"What?" Chief Superintendent Coudrier suddenly muttered. "To think what? What must you think, son-in-law?"

Chief Superintendent Nepos was panting for breath, suffocated by the very nature of his suspicions.

"That I'm the one wielding the scalpel, for instance? That I've abandoned my fishing rods with the idea of finding you at the wheel of a Quinze Citroën . . . is that it?"

"No, Father, of course not . . ."

"Why of course not? Since when has a policeman had the truth written all over his face? And it could very well be true, after all! I like Malaussène! Malaussène would have made an ideal son-in-law! I would be quite capable of topping your entire squad to get him out of the can!"

"Father, that isn't what I meant . . ."

Chief Superintendent Coudrier's fist slammed down on to the glass desk.

"Oh yes it is. It's precisely what you meant! It's what you *would have liked to be the case!*"

He suddenly calmed down. He'd hurt himself when hitting that horrible desk. He added, *mezza voce*:

"But for that, you need will-power."

NEPOS: . . .

COUDRIER: . . .

NEPOS: . . .

COUDRIER: I don't like you, Nepos. And the reason has less to do with my daughter's misery and my grandsons' isolation than with the fact that you've forced me to adopt the grotesque role of a father-in-law.

NEPOS: . . .

COUDRIER: Someone in your office sent me a photocopy of the letter. It was a case of *transparency*, old chap.

NEPOS: . . .

COUDRIER: Has it even occurred to you to have the handwriting analysed?

NEPOS: . . .

COUDRIER: No, of course not. You have at least noticed that it is handwritten? And in an interesting hand at that . . .

NEPOS: . . .

COUDRIER: The same sort of camouflaged script as the one used to forge Doctor Fraenkhel's letters . . . a bad imitation of Malaussène's writing . . .

NEPOS: . . .

COUDRIER: . . .

NEPOS: . . .

COUDRIER: You'll just have to get used to it, old fellow. Malaussène is depressingly innocent. And if you want to arrest the real serial killer, then you'll have to shift up a gear. Otherwise, he'll knock down your entire squad like coconuts on a shy.

NEPOS: . . .

COUDRIER: . . . and your career will suffer.

NEPOS: . . .

COUDRIER: If you're still alive, that is.

NEPOS: . . .

COUDRIER: I have no advice to give you, Nepos, but if I were in your shoes, I would consider it suicidal to keep Inspectors Titus, Caregga and Silistri on the sidelines.

On his way out, he added:

"Oh yes! I was forgetting that business about Chief Superintendent Cercaria's suicide."

Once again he opened his old calfskin briefcase and removed an envelope.

"Here."

Without stepping forwards, he held it out. Chief Superintendent Nepos made a final effort to walk over to his father-in-law.

"What is it?"

"Inspector Pastor's confession."

"Inspector Pastor?"

"Yes . . . Inspector Pastor had a personality which was . . . somewhat different from yours, my poor chap."

Chapter 59

MONSIEUR LEHMANN'S LIFE was getting increasingly complicated and his ghosts more and more restive. They spoke to him at all times of the day and night, with a distinct preference for the least foreseeable locations. When Lehmann asked for the tab for the pastis he'd drunk in a bar, a hand had jotted down on it these apparently anodyne words:

"*Apparently Cazo hasn't shown up yet.*"

Brandishing the bill, Lehmann rushed over to the barman.

"Who wrote this?"

The barman pulled back.

"Calm down! It was your mate by the pinball machine over there."

"Where?"

No mate, of course.

"He's gone. He wanted to give you a surprise."

When Lehmann went to relieve his fear against the ceramic of the toilets, his gaze wandered among the graffiti, only to come to a halt on this trivial question:

"*Oh yes? With an electric torch?*"

In the street, monstrous children surged up in front of him.

"*Are you part of the set-up? Are you part of the set-up? Are you part of the set-up?*"

He soon gave up trying to catch them.

He stopped going to bars.

He stopped going to the toilet.

He pissed on the walls of the city.

He gave up everything.

He even thought of giving himself up.

An Italian pimp expressed his concern to a police inspector, who was half Italian himself.

"Stop the slaughter, Silistri. Your pal's going to wind up topping himself."

Inspector Silistri didn't agree.

"That would be bad news for you, Pescatore."

"It's out of my hands. He's going nuts. If he can't find a rope to hang himself then he'll just give up breathing."

Inspector Silistri very much wanted Monsieur Lehmann to stay alive.

"OK, we'll try one last trick."

The last trick came into contact with Lehmann's feet that very evening, when he slid them into the sleeping bag he was using instead of a bed in the stairwell of a disused building on Rue Tourtille. Lehmann grumbled, withdrew his legs and dived in with his head and arms. He re-emerged with a cold plastic box between his fingers. He then had to go outside in search of a lamppost to identify it. It was an audio cassette. The label could hardly have been more explicit:

"The kid's execution was recorded. Go and warn the others."

*

The effect was instantaneous. Suddenly freed of his ghosts, abandoning all of the precautions he'd been scrupulously taking thus far, perhaps thinking that his friends would be in great danger if he didn't warn them, or else imagining that this handwritten note came from one of the gang, Lehmann rushed off through Paris.

When in panic, you don't politely ring on doorbells. You ram home the intercom button till your arm's buried in a mess of plastic and concrete.

A strange voice answered Lehmann's call.

"Who's there?"

A rather offish voice, yet cooing with it. Feminine, too.

"It's me! It's Lehmann!"

"What the hell are you doing? Didn't we say . . ."

"Was it you who sent me the cassette?"

"What cassette? I've no . . ."

"Open up, this is serious! You must listen to it, you must . . ."

There was a click.

Lehmann vanished into the darkness of the lobby.

Beside the button Lehmann had leapt on, Inspector Silistri read a strangely inoffensive-sounding name, with a medieval ring to it, just the job for a troubadour: Pernette Dutilleul.

*

But Inspector Silistri was no troubadour. Once arrested, Pernette Dutilleul quickly gave them the name of a certain Cazeneuve (aka Cazo), who tried to get away from Inspectors Caregga and Silistri, which earned him a bullet in his right elbow – armed resistance – and another one in the back of his left knee – attempted escape. Whereas Lehmann had retired, Dutilleul and Cazeneuve both worked for *Affection*, a monthly medical magazine, run by a certain Sainclair. Now, Sainclair, Cazeneuve, Lehmann and Dutilleul had a point in common: they had all been employees of the Store in the days when Benjamin Malaussène worked there as a scapegoat. When Inspectors Caregga and Silistri visited Monsieur Sainclair's home, the flat was empty. When they obtained a warrant to search the magazine's offices, he was not to be found there, either. But his publication was not going to suffer from the absence of its editor. The next four issues had already been finalised, and there was no lack of material for the future. Among other projected features, Inspector Silistri noted the following:

"Illness in Cinema History", a special issue planned to mark the centenary of the movies.

"Tattoos and Their Motivations".

"Plastic Surgery Considered as One of the Fine Arts".

"Lying: A Pathology or a Way of Life?"

"The Criminal Transplant" (in which the psychological effects of organ transplants were scrutinised and, in particular, a recent case in which a certain Malaussène was the antisocial hero). Large parts of the article, which had been prepared in advance, anticipated a trial which had not yet taken place.

All of these subjects fascinated Inspector Silistri. Especially the last two. And even more so after a search of Sainclair's flat turned up a photo of a beautiful green-eyed girl in a pink suit, known to the police as Marie-Ange Courrier, and with an established reputation of being a real little liar.

*

As communications had been cut between Titus and Silistri, messages were passed via Gervaise. Which explains why Titus was in the know when he visited Marie-Ange in her cell that afternoon.

"I've got some bad news for you, Marie-Ange."

Inspector Titus didn't know how to broach the subject.

"I'm afraid you're going to be rather upset."

He placed a thermos flask on the fixed table.

"Hot chocolate today. The best! A bar melted down with cordon-bleu patience. With a hint of coffee, right at the end."

There were silver-gilt spoons.

"I'm back in their good books, Marie-Ange."

She stared at him intently.

"That's right. Things have turned sour between Nepos and his methodicals. So they dug me out of my hole."

He wanted to reassure her.

"But this is only a trial period! A test! I still have to get results."

To go with the chocolate, he'd brought along a collection of Flemish shortbread, as yellow as sandy beaches.

"The good point is that I can visit you for free now. I'm saving 500 francs a throw. Plus you can't chuck me out any more. Would you rather we met in the interrogation room, as stated in the rule book?"

Apparently, she didn't. With a tiny shaker, Titus was finishing off Marie-Ange's bowl.

"A touch of dark chocolate on the surface . . ."

He was serving her impeccably. He wanted her to imagine that she was on a terrace overlooking, say, the Luxembourg Gardens.

"I don't like prisons."

This was true. But it had slipped out. He decided to turn his carelessness to his advantage.

"I don't like to see you in here, instead of somebody else."

Completely off target. He would never have imagined that a woman could put so much scorn into a smile. He corrected his aim at once.

"I mean, I'd prefer to see you both in the same cell."

Marie-Ange's smile changed.

"Do you think love could stand up to that? Growing old together in the same cell?"

Marie-Ange's smile faded.

"Me and my bird couldn't, that much is for sure. Not even us! And we've been through the lot!"

Marie-Ange's smile vanished completely. Marie-Ange couldn't give a toss about Titus's love life.

"No, no, you're right. In the end, it's better for you to be inside, and him to be outside."

She took a deep breath. She was trying hard to stop herself ripping his eyes out.

"But it could be worse! Being in the can when you've done nothing, for instance . . . like that Malaussène . . . who you don't even know."

The reference to Malaussène in the can calmed her down a bit. And then she had to force herself to be patient with this Inspector Titus. After all, he'd taught her so many things. And would teach her more.

"Old Malaussène's really unlucky! He must have fallen in the shit at birth! Just imagine, you're not the only one trying to drop him in it. Another team has put him in the frame for another pile of stiffs. He's supposed to have dynamited an entire family in the Vercors, the centre of the French Resistance. And what do you know? It wasn't really him! It was them! We nicked them last week. Two men and a girl. They worked for a magazine called *Affection*. Ever heard of it?"

She was barely breathing.

"Apparently the boss was involved too. His name's Sainclair . . ."

Something inside her went tense.

"But he managed to escape."

Something inside her relaxed.

Titus looked at her over a piece of shortbread.

"Because I've obviously put two and two together. I can't believe that various people who don't know each other would all try and frame up the same butter wouldn't melt, harmless goat. That really would be too much of a coincidence. So there must be a link between the two cases. Your case, I mean, and theirs. Because they knew Malaussène only too well. Our Vercors explosives team wouldn't be friends of yours, would they, Marie-Ange? Really not? Not even vague acquaintances?"

No, no, no, not at all.

"The names of Lehmann, Dutilleul, Cazeneuve and Sainclair don't ring any bells?"

No, not a single bell.

Titus grinned with relief.

"Just as well! Because, if you want my opinion, they're a bad crowd to hang out with."

The chocolate at the bottom of the thermos was thicker. A final drop in each cup. And a final piece of shortbread, which he gave her, but which she broke into two equal parts.

"Thanks," he said.

Then:

"Anyway, I still have my problem to solve."

A pause.

"You know, the father of the sperm . . ."

He glowered.

"What's doing my head in is that I've looked everywhere and I still can't find a likely candidate. Not one."

His brows smoothed out in fury.

"I just can't get it how that bastard could have done that to Gervaise of all people! To Gervaise! Shit!"

There was a patch of chocolate in the corner of her mouth.

"Sorry. I get beside myself when I think of that egg-seeking sperm. You've got some chocolate there, in the corner of your . . ."

He reached out and wiped it away with his thumb. She didn't draw back. In all these weeks, it was the first time he'd touched her.

"I have to be going."

He stood up.

"The down side with my new position is that I have to write a report after each visit."

She helped him tidy away the dirty crockery into his wicker basket.

When the cell door opened, he added:

"Oh, I was forgetting . . . Malaussène is going to be released soon. Nepos and Képlin don't really agree yet, but we're talking them round."

Chapter 60

COUDRIER CAME AND got me out of my prison cell in person. This was an exceptional event, and the little corporal was clearly much feared and respected in this establishment, if the special treatment I started to get one week before my release is anything to go by – an individual cell, with refurbished walls, a palatial bed, cordon-bleu nosh, lots to read, vitamins galore – all in all, a real horror story for any self-respecting taxpayer. When there was a knock on my door, it was to ask if everything was to my liking. I had to put my foot down when refusing a TV, a sun-lamp and some body-building apparatus.

"If I'd known you were being pampered like this, then I would not have come out of retirement to save you," Coudrier observed, while extracting me from my cocoon.

Then, while Inspector Caregga was driving us towards freedom:

"I always thought you had friends in high places, Malaussène . . ."

The world hadn't changed much during my months of darkness. The faces of wannabe presidents were lined up on election posters, but they'd been the same ones for years. How long would I have to get before I'd find new faces on the block? Thirty years minimum? Not enough. On the other hand, I wasn't really displeased to see those mugs on their posters again. There might have been nothing in their eyes, but the sky above their heads was vast.

"Caregga and Silistri have arrested the Vercors gang," Coudrier announced in the middle of my daydream. "They were working for Sainclair."

I asked drowsily:

"Sainclair? Sainclair from the Store?"

"Yes, now Sainclair from *Affection*," Coudrier went on. "The man who got you fired from the Store a few years back, and whom you beat up a few months ago. It's almost as if the only reason Inspector Caregga joined the force was to save you from Sainclair's clutches, Malaussène. So thank him."

"Thanks, Caregga."

"Don't mention it," Caregga replied in his rear-view mirror. "You saved me from admin."

Electoral promises continued to pass by. But Paris was also celebrating the centenary of the cinematograph. The sun was sunning. The buds were budding. And, on the pavements, the pigeons were pigeoning.

Coudrier went on with his explanations:

"You were infiltrated, Malaussène. When Jeremy cast Lehmann to play his own role in that play, he let the wolf into the fold. Lehmann learnt many things about your family. In particular, that Julie was Old Job Bernardin's heiress. He found the business about The Only Begotten Film extremely interesting."

So it was time for the denouement? I suddenly felt drained. Who? Why? How? Who cares? I'd have to have a word with Jeremy on the subject. That's what I was thinking as the car drove me back home . . . I'd have to warn Jeremy about the dangers of plot foreclosure.

"It all started when your friend Suzanne, the owner of The Zebra, sent the King of the Living Dead packing; or, if you prefer, forbade him to attend the showing of The Only Begotten Film."

What strange indifference . . . I'd spent months going over and over all that injustice in the prison of my mind, and now all I wanted was to sleep. Sleep. At home. Between Julie's breasts. With the window open above the chestnut trees.

"Are you listening to me Malaussène?"

I nodded, but couldn't take my eyes off the big bad world as it sped by.

"Lehmann reckoned that there was money to be made by providing the King of the Living Dead with a private showing," Coudrier continued. "He mentioned the idea to Sainclair, who went to see the King. The King of course didn't say no. So Lehmann, Cazeneuve and Dutilleul burgled the house in the Vercors, while Old Bernardin and his son were burying Liesl in Vienna. After the King had seen the film, he wanted more. Quite simply, he wanted to buy it, but legally, with a signed contract drawn up in due form. Sainclair managed to arrange the transaction, and the King asked no questions. Shortly afterwards, the King became the owner of The Only Begotten Film, thanks to a perfectly legal purchase agreement."

Yes . . .

Yes, indeed . . .

And I'd rather not be told what Sainclair did to Old Job to make him sign.

"The rest was due to the gang's own initiative. They'd fulfilled their contract, been paid and could have gone home. Instead, they decided to stay there, just for you Malaussène! By forging Fraenkhel's letters in your own handwriting, they had cooked up a lovely motive for you. They were expecting you. They knew that you and Julie would go there to fetch The Only Begotten Film. The fax Old Job sent you in fact came from them. They also stole your truck. The student at the hotel and young Clément are down to them too. Sainclair had called for a general mobilisation against you. Cazeneuve, his right-hand man, subcontracted some of the work out to a couple of associated gangs. It's incredible how much Sainclair worships you. He wrote a long article about you called 'The Criminal Transplant'."

Without taking my eyes off Paris, I asked:

"So what's so special about this sodding film for it to have caused so many deaths?"

"If you had agreed to have a television in your cell, you would now know," Coudrier replied.

"A television? They broadcast The Only Begotten Film on the TV?"

This time I did turn around. (In a flash, I pictured the horror on the buffs' faces. The Only Begotten Film on TV . . . Old Job's film shown by the headshrinkers of the box! Poor old Suzanne, Avernon, Lekaëdec!)

Coudrier confirmed the news:

"The day before yesterday, at eight thirty in the evening, on all channels. To celebrate the centenary of the cinematograph. Apparently, what Job Bernardin wanted was to make his film a planetary event . . . a single projection, but for the entire world. The idea appealed just as much to the Americans as it did to the Japanese and the Europeans. For weeks now, it has been advertised as a symbol of universal brotherhood at the end of this murderous century."

I asked:

"And did you see it?"

"I was professionally obliged."

"And?"

"And all Paris will tell you about it, my lad. They're talking about little else."

Caregga had just parked in front of the ex-hardware store where we live. I looked at the shop window. I placed my hand on the door handle, but remained sitting beside Coudrier. Caregga was looking at me in the rear-view mirror. Coudrier leant over and opened the door for me.

"You're expected."

*

They were all expecting me. What An Angel and Verdun, Jeremy, Julius and Half Pint, Thérèse, Louna, Clara, Mum and Yasmina, there was Amar and the Ben

Tayeb tribe, there was Marty of course, there was Julie, Suzanne and Gervaise. There was someone in Gervaise's belly and there was champagne.

I stayed standing in the doorway.

I just said:

"I want to sleep. Can I?"

*

I'd been crying for ages when I woke up.

"It's nothing, Benjamin," Julie whispered into my ear. "You're just a bit depressed."

I was sobbing my eyes out in Julie's embrace.

"And you've had loads of good reasons to be depressed."

She was rocking me.

"Like passing from prison to happiness, for instance."

She explained the phenomenon.

"It's called *pororoca*, Benjamin. The meeting between the River Amazon and the Atlantic Ocean, the collision of sentiments . . . a terrible tidal wave, and an incredible din!"

I was desperately clinging on to her.

"Shall I tell you about my finest depression?"

I drifted back to sleep while she told me about her own *pororoca*.

"It was the day after we met, Benjamin. I didn't see you again for weeks, remember? Weeks of *pororoca*. My freedom was bridling up against my happiness. I cried a lot, screwed around a lot, smashed things a lot, then you came for me . . . you forced your way through . . . you went to my source . . . I became . . . extremely happy . . ."

She was laughing silently. I heard her voice coming from afar.

"Extremely happy, and extremely daft . . ."

Queen Zabo would censor this Amazon metaphor if she found it in Jeremy's writings. I could just hear her voice: "This meeting of waters, my lad, don't you think it's a bit of a mixed metaphor?"

Chapter 61

I FINALLY DRIED MY tears and let the tribe revive me. There were Julie's breasts, Clara's voice, Half Pint's laughter, Jeremy's saga, Thérèse's good omens, Julius's tongue, Louna's Valium, the Ben Tayebs' Sidi-Brahim, Yasmina's couscous, Mum's compliments – "you're a good son to me, Benjamin" – loved ones' love, friends' friendship . . . (O the bill we all owe!)

My recovery was no foregone conclusion. It even provoked a difference of opinion.

"Benjamin's gotta get out more," Jeremy claimed.

"He's gorra see people," Half Pint added.

"He's gorra relax," Thérèse objected.

As for me, I'd decided to let them get on with it. (Such decisions are more easily made in prison.) If the truth were told, I'd have loved to pitch my tent around Julie, but she was watching over Gervaise's belly.

"It's better if I spend nights with Gervaise. You never know. She tires easily. She could give birth at any moment."

I now had two Julies to deal with, my one and Gervaise's one.

"She really is amazing, you know. Her Templars are at each other's throats, but she doesn't seem the slightest bit curious about who made her pregnant or how. She attends to her whores as if nothing was unusual, and her whores look back at her as though it was normal for virgins to get pregnant. She's an odd customer, Benjamin. There's something celestial about her."

Julie left me. She stood up. Straightened herself, hands on her hips, mouth twisted by a sudden jab of pain.

"See you tomorrow."

She went through the door with her belly out and feet splayed. She went downstairs cautiously and crossed the hardware store as if she was eight months carrying. No-one laughed. This was no longer the daft caricature of me in my maternal empathy, this was Julie weighed down by Gervaise's mystery.

Jeremy being Jeremy, I got taken out, so as to make me forget my stay in prison, but also to fill in Julie's absence, with dinners at Amar's, Zabo's, Marty's, Theo's, Loussa's, Gervaise's, Suzanne's and with the film buffs, I ate out with Coudrier, had a Silistrian evening, made new friends at friendly tables, received new invitations, buckets of compassion, a variety of faces, but only one subject of conversation on the menu – Old Job's film!

Coudrier had been right, Paris was talking about little else.

Which didn't surprise Jeremy.

"What do you expect them to talk about? The elections? Who on the right's going to screw up the right? Who on the left's going to screw up the left? And who in the centre will sell his soul? And which one of these conmen we're going to be stuck with for the next seven years? It's been going on for months, Ben, they bent our ears the entire time you were in the slammer! You want to know what you missed? A parade of cannibals!"

"The fact is that the film saved France from the presidential elections," Queen Zabo agreed. "Which was certainly quite an event!"

All of which was vigorously rejected by Suzanne and the buffs.

"It was the very opposite of an event!" Avernon yelled. "An event that had been utterly distorted. Whipped up by months of advertising! Since when have real events taken months to materialise, madam?"

"A happy event, then . . ."

"Every video recorder came on at the first second of your happy event," Lekaëdec remarked. "Even as we speak, Old Job's film has become an endlessly repeatable event!"

"A cultural phenomenon, at least," Queen Zabo insisted.

"Reduced to a cultural commodity," Suzanne corrected.

"Shall I tell you what the real event was, dear lady?" Avernon summed up. "*The real event is that we are the only people who haven't seen the film!*"

Sure enough, not one of them had deigned to watch it. Neither Suzanne, nor anyone of the chosen twelve. It was a question of principle. A way of remaining faithful to the memory of Liesl and Job. The film had been intended for them, they were the only viewers who'd been authorised by Old Job, and so they had closed their eyes and stopped their ears while everyone else was gobbling the film up. That evening, they had turned the TV to face the wall and had got thoroughly pissed until the city had drowsily put all those images to bed. They knew that they would spend the rest of their lives struggling against the temptation of the video, but they were ready to go through with it. Such frustration would be their final honourable combat as true film lovers. They would know nothing whatsoever about this film. They swore it!

All very well . . . but as of the next day, they were besieged by conversations. A tidal wave submerged them every time they opened a door. Exclamations of friends, comments in restaurants, chatter at work, including the opinions of their bank managers, and judgements of their hairdressers. There was a chunk of the film in every mouth they encountered. And in the press they read, there wasn't a single cinema review or arts supplement which didn't have its word to say. And not one radio show worth listening to which didn't have its comments to make. After just one showing, Old Job's film had become what he most dreaded – a subject of conversation.

*

It was Julie who told me the essential.

"All Job did was to film Matthias's entire existence."

"What do you mean, his *entire* existence?"

"Matthias's whole life. From his birth to his death. From when Liesl gave birth . . ."

"To his death? Job filmed Matthias's death?"

"Yes. And Liesl's delivery."

"Job filmed his murder?"

"Matthias wasn't murdered. He died during one of their shoots. Probably a case of Quincke's oedema. Presumably, he was already dead when Sainclair's gang showed up to steal the film."

"What did filming Matthias's entire life entail exactly?"

"Just what I said. You see the body emerge from Liesl's womb on a narrow bed, like a bunk, or a stretcher, then you see him grow up into a child, still naked, still on that simple bed, then the child becomes a teenager, the teenager an adult, still on the same bed, then the adult turns into the Matthias you knew, aged seventy-five and on the verge of extreme old age. That's all you see. There's no-one else around the bed. The film shows the development of that naked body, in one fixed shot, with no apparent cuts, just a single succession of seventy-five years of celluloid."

"The proof of what Job said when he was a child, about the cinema being able to *seize the passage of time.*"

"Exactly. To start with, he filmed the baby every day (or maybe several times a day, for just few seconds each time). Then the shoots became less frequent, but still quite regular as the body grew, they were then distanced even more at the arrival of maturity, before drawing closer together again as old age neared. A body which blooms then wilts. Seventy-five years of life reduced to a three-hour film."

"So that was The Only Begotten Film."

"That plus Liesl's commentary."

"She recorded a commentary?"

"An indirect one, in which there's never any mention of Matthias."

That was the essence. Such was the film. Liesl's voice mixed with the images of her child, telling how the world was changing, while Matthias's body altered beneath the still eye of the camera.

"While Matthias was growing up, she visited battlefields and salons. She recorded everything. It isn't just her voice. The whole world talks over Matthias during the three hours of the film."

"For instance?"

"For instance, there's the fury of the German crowd on the second of April 1920 during the occupation of Düsseldorf by our Senegalese troops, their screams as our forces disarmed their policemen, the death of Georges Feydeau on the fifth of June 1921 in Rueil (Feydeau who introduced Liesl to the tape recorder, as you may remember), an interview with a certain Adolf Hitler on the twenty-seventh of January 1923 during the first National Socialist Party congress in Munich, Einstein's pacifist declaration on the twenty-third of July of the same year, the burial of Lenin on January twenty-fourth, a few words from André Breton about his *Surrealist Manifesto* . . . She was everywhere, Benjamin, she captured everything that modelled the history of the twentieth century right up until Sarajevo. And there, on the afternoon she was shot, you can hear the impact of the bullets as they hit her bones, a distinct crack, a cry, then this sentence: '*Would you be so good as to turn the cassette over? It's like me, almost run to a stop . . .*' You remember that, don't you? In hospital, when Berthold the surgeon came into her room . . ."

*

Such was Liesl's and Old Job's Only Begotten Film, and it raised such varied enthusiasm that everyone went at it with their various plaudits. Theo, my Theo, in his femininely male ecstasy:

"The burgeoning of the body was just incredible, Ben, the way that flower-man blossomed and wilted before our very eyes verged on the unbearable . . . first fragility . . . tenderness . . . eroticism in that blossoming . . . then the slow descent towards the haziness at the end . . . wrinkles, old age, the image which grows more blurred as it condenses . . . and hearing his mother talking about completely different things made me cry my eyes out . . ."

Liesl's speech, which left Loussa de Casamance speechless.

"It's unbelievable how prescient that woman was! Right from the 1920s she understood how the Treaty of Versailles was pushing us all towards 1940, then grasping how the victory at Monte Cassino (where I lost my left bollock, remember that, shit-for-brains?) would lead to the Algeria crisis, and how the bombing of Haiphong would set off the slaughter at Dien Bien Phu . . . being present at the beginning and the end of all those absurdities, on the battlefield or round the negotiating table . . . Ah! those interviews with Poincaré the unbelievable dimwit! Ah! Briand's European humanity. Ah! Hitler's scream: *'Mein Vorhaben, junge Frau? Das Siegen der Rasse über die Nationen!'* ('My project, young lady? To make race triumph over nations!') . . . No, your Austrian friend was quite something . . . You say she was Karl Kraus's niece? *Die Falke* in pictures! She and her husband discovered the language of the century. There's no doubt about that!"

As for Hadouch, he was steaming.

"You rumis are completely out of your trees! Your obsession with images will be the undoing of you! You know me, Ben, I'm no fundamentalist. I drink my pastis, like all your bad Christians, but, leaving Allah's opinion out of it, to show a man's image *that much* is an offence to mankind! It's a big sloppy kiss in the mouth of death! It made my mum faint! For a mother to expose her child like that to the eye of God made my mum weep for all the children in the world . . . and you're supposed to be afraid of us? . . . You're completely nuts, the lot of you!"

Queen Zabo, whose psychiatrist had deprived her of her body for the sake of her head, was all in a tizzy too.

"The most disturbing part was the way that naked body seemed to be following what was going on in the world. The childhood illnesses, chickenpox and measles, were like cutaneous reactions to universal folly, and then his asthma, and all those allergies, those skin eruptions . . . it's impossible to disassociate the torments of history from the torture of that flesh, the mother's newsflashes from the son's rashes . . . your friend Matthias suffered a lot . . . as much as our century."

Which Professor Berthold explained in more technical terms.

"Yes indeed, you can certainly say that this patient of the century had every possible and imaginable allergic reaction from eczema to Quincke's oedema, passing by erythema, asthma, urticaria and rheumatoid arthritis. And I haven't even mentioned the trivia, such as impetigo, angular stomatitis, chapping, sties and peeling skin. He was a walking dermatological textbook!"

Florentis, with his lion's mane, agreed with the Queen.

"In my opinion, the true suffering of the century was the empty bed the camera continued filming while Matthias was in Auschwitz . . . the empty bed and Hitler's screams in Liesl's microphone: '*Ihr Sohn ist da, wo er sein muss! Er hat sich schlecht verheiratet! Ich werde nicht zulassen, dass die jüdische Pest die Rasse verseucht!*', with the translation superimposed on the empty bed: 'Your son is where he should be! He made a bad match! I will not allow the Jewish plague to poison our race!' Then the reappearance of Matthias on the bed a few minutes later . . . so thin . . . only half of Matthias, in fact . . ."

*

"It's easier to understand Barnaby now," Julie murmured in the hollow of my shoulder. "If your father's been so completely stolen by the cinema, it's certainly enough to give you a fear of images."

"And it's also easy to understand why Matthias and Sarah divorced . . ."

"True," Julie replied.

Then, like every evening at that time:

"Well, I must be off."

*

The night was falling on my empty bed and the echoes of our conversations. A memory of Matthias hovered in the darkness. I thought again about you, my little stolen one, my private wound, such a sweet person to talk to. This time, I didn't cry over your absence. Believe me, you're far better off where you are. Because . . . what's it all about, in fact? Let's both be lucid in our shared insomnia . . . What's this story all about? *It's the story of two loonies who had a child so they could make a film . . .* Who had a child *with the sole intention* of making a film. Can you imagine such a thing? I can't. And what do you suppose happens when a man and a woman procreate the subject of their film? They film it to the bitter end, that's what. And what do you suppose is the logical end of a film which begins with a birth?

. . .

That's right, a death.

. . .

So tell me, would you like to have been born into a world where fathers intend to outlive their children?

Chapter 62

POSTEL-WAGNER AIMED THE remote control at the set. Liesl's voice stopped and Matthias Fraenkhel's body froze on the screen.

"So, what would you say the cause of death was?"

Professor Marty shook his head.

"I don't think it was Quincke's oedema. It looks rather secondary to me, a sort of reaction . . ."

"To what?"

"I don't know. To a bacterial attack, perhaps."

"That's also what Postel-Wagner thinks," Chief Superintendent Coudrier butted in. "Could you show Marty the rest please, Wagner?"

"The rest?" Marty exclaimed. "Doesn't the film end with the oedema?"

"We found the rest when we searched Sainclair's flat," the Chief Superintendent explained. "The end which Sainclair couldn't, or wouldn't sell . . . it's too . . ."

What now appeared on the screen caused such a deep silence to descend on the three men that the very memory of language almost faded to extinction. Matthias Fraenkhel's body was decomposing before their very eyes. They dumbly watched this corruption of flesh, over which no voice now commented, until the screen finally went blank once more.

It was Marty who reinvented language.

"Necrotising fasciitis," he said at last.

"That was also your diagnosis, wasn't it Postel?" Coudrier asked.

"It was. The gangrene starts just above his right wrist," Postel confirmed.

"Could we see the forearm again?" Marty asked. "I seemed to notice something . . . After his stay in Auschwitz . . ."

"The tattoo? Well spotted. He came back with a number tattooed above his right wrist."

"But I don't think it was still there in the final images. Could we check that?"

They checked. They were truth in motion. They discovered that the tattoo was no longer there at the end. That it had been cut off before the victim died. That some sort of poison – streptococcus perhaps? – must have been injected into this precise point, which had then set off an immediate reaction on the inflamed skin. They now knew that this film – universally acclaimed as a tribute to memory – finished with a murder. Matthias Fraenkhel had died of the very same putrefaction that had carried off the King of the Living Dead in just one night, before the horrified gaze of his wife. Necrotising fasciitis.

As for Matthias Fraenkhel's tattoo, Coudrier confirmed that it had been found at Sainclair's place. The numbers matched.

Sainclair had finished Old Job's film in his own way.

Sainclair, who was still at large.

"Let's get a breath of fresh air," Marty begged. "Or else a breath of good Bordeaux . . ."

"Coming with us, Chief Superintendent?" Postel asked.

"No thank you, I have an appointment with Malaussène," Coudrier replied. "There are still two or three things he ought to know."

*

Even the Bordeaux didn't enable Postel-Wagner and Marty to change the subject. They both had a corpse in their minds. Their plates remained untouched.

"One thing astonishes me," Postel-Wagner murmured. "How did Fraenkhel manage to go on practising for so long while suffering like that?"

Marty answered at once.

"He didn't suffer from allergies while he was practising. Nor while he was teaching. We were his health. Parturient women meant everything to him, and he was as passionate about newly born babies as you are about stiffs."

The second bottle brought back their dear old teacher in the flesh. Once again, they pictured Fraenkhel entering the lecture halls of their youth . . . his smile as he approached the tiers of seats . . . the explosion of dishevelled hair when he whipped off his hat . . . the ethical hesitancy in his voice . . . the unshakeable enthusiasms of the shy . . . the look in his eyes, which had decided them on their careers . . .

"So you think his attacks were just reserved for his dear family?"

"And perhaps only for the film. They gave it added symbolic weight."

"I reckon the priests must love it. I can just hear them: 'His body taking on all the sins of the world, my brothers . . .' They love it when a son dies . . . except before birth."

"One hell of a film," Marty sighed. "The whole graveyard's talking about it."

"Shall we have a third bottle?" Postel suggested.

"I'd prefer a whiskey. Do you still have your hip flask of Irish?"

They had decided to knock themselves out. Even if they ended up under the table, they had to find a way out of that film. They had to get off that stretcher. They had to turn off that set. It was Postel-Wagner who found the right button.

"Talking of priests and weird pathologies . . . Do you believe in nuns getting pregnant through the agency of the Holy Ghost?"

"It depends what they put in their Communion wafers," Marty replied. "But their pope's not very inventive in that field."

Postel-Wagner's flask offered up its last drop of whiskey.

"She's a genuine saint, Marty, a whore professor who knows everything about cocks and what to do with them, but who has remained a virgin, just as others survived Stalingrad . . . but she's eight months pregnant . . . can you explain that?"

"Maybe I can, over a cognac."

"Two, then."

When their glasses returned to the table, Marty asked:

"Who is this nun of yours exactly?"

So Postel-Wagner told his friend Marty all about his friend Gervaise. When he got to the bit about Thérèse Malaussène's prediction, Marty butted in at once:

"There you are. Look no further."

"Sorry?"

"It's in Thérèse's prediction. If Thérèse predicted that Gervaise would get up the duff, then you're the only one to be surprised when she did. She was quite simply impregnated by Thérèse's prediction. That's all there is to it."

"Wrong. She was already pregnant when Thérèse read the news in her palm."

Marty searched for a diagnosis in his last drop of brandy.

"In that case, she must have got laid."

"Oh no she didn't."

They fell silent.

"One for the road?"

"I'd prefer some calvados. We're not leaving this place till we work out how your good sister got in the family way. It wasn't you, Postel? Do you swear to that?"

"On my next bottle's life!"

"OK, so tell it to me straight. From her birth to the very moment we're speaking. I want to know everything. The whole works."

Postel told him everything he knew about Gervaise, old Thian's daughter, university friend of his wife Geraldine, holy saviour of whores, baptiser of pimps, brilliant tattoo artist . . .

"A what artist?"

"Tattoo artist . . . a brilliant tattoo artist, and Coudrier's officer, on the trail of Sainclair right from the start, along with Inspectors Titus and Silistri, then hit by a car and hospitalised in Saint-Louis . . ."

"In Saint-Louis? Whose ward?"

"Berthold's."

"When?"

Postel-Wagner, who had a good head for figures, and dates of birth or death, announced the date of the accident and the exact time she was admitted . . . and Marty leapt to his feet.

"Jesus Christ!"

Postel grabbed the bottle of calvados as it tumbled over.

"Jesus fucking Christ!" Marty yelled. "What a chancer! I just can't believe it! What a dickhead! What an out-and-out plonker! I just *won't* believe it! He never misses a trick, does he! The full fucking monty! He's really done it this time!"

Then, grabbing Postel by his collar:

"What are you doing now, I mean right now, immediately? Don't answer. You're not doing anything. Your stiffs can wait. I've solved your puzzle! The diagnosis of the century! Come on, you're going to enjoy this! You're going to learn how to make nuns pregnant! Come on, I'll give you a lift on my scooter. We're going to check my diagno . . . my diagnosis!"

"Right now? On your scooter?"

Chapter 63

The evening came, the morning came, and the Great Ogre created the Organ. He saw that it was good and soaked the aisles of his cathedral with music. Mondine reckoned this onward-looking music raining down from the stained-glass windows on to her bridal train wasn't bad either. Mondine was gliding along a stream of sound, carried towards the altar by a great rush of notes. Such a river must surely flow into an ocean of happiness. Mondine and Berthold were drifting towards bliss. Mondine had hauled her professor over from tip to toe, he'd been scrubbed, perfumed and dressed up fit to kill. All pinstripes on mousy grey. And shoes that sang. The leather of his pumps squeaked with heavenly pleasure. The Great Berthold! A splendid vessel. Dignity on its way to felicity.

"You will behave yourself, won't you?"

Mondine had given him all sorts of precautionary instructions.

"You will, won't you? You're not going to kick up a stink in the Holy of Holies? A cathedral isn't a fishmonger's!"

She it was who had decided to celebrate their union beneath this divine canopy.

"I want us to get wed in Latin, with soutanes in a cathedral."

He'd resisted a bit.

"But this God business is a pile of crap, my little Pontormo. You don't believe in it any more than I do."

But her mind was made up.

"That's not the point, professor. It's His job to believe in us!"

There was no reasoning with Mondine. You married her with her reasoning.

"Just everyone will be there. So you'll have to be good. I don't want to be taken for a tramp now you're making me Madame Professor."

Just everyone watched the beautiful vessel of marriage sail past. They made a perfect pair. They were emigrating to happy-land. Just everyone was bustling about on either side of the aisle as though on the platform of last farewells. There was Gervaise, of course, there was Malaussène's woman as well, there were Titus and Silistri, with their wives between them, there was a troop of Templars, the forces of law and order, then the other side of the tracks, the forces of the street, Pescatore and his three lieutenants, Fabio, Emilio and Tristan, there were also numerous beautiful girls, colleagues from street corners, tattooed and grateful girls come to celebrate the glory of Mondine, who'd saved them from the scalpel, works of art every single one of them, with Titians in the small of their backs, Del Sartos on the curves of their bellies, Konrad Witzes on their breasts, all skimpily dressed, for this was a springtime wedding, there was the Academy, of course, all of the eminent bearers of the caduceus, patients who'd been resurrected by Berthold's magic scalpel, enough people to fill two churches at least, plus the journalists, photographers and immortalisers.

"Just everyone, which makes quite a lot," Mondine had warned him. "So no playing silly buggers, OK professor?"

For greater security, Mondine had delivered herself fully and totally four or five times that day, so Berthold was now good as gold, floating along in a dream of satiety.

And the organ piping away . . .

When happiness joins in, all sense of measure is lost, just as it is in tragedy. And how it draws people's eyes! Mondine and her professor were drifting along, alone in the world, but all that the world had eyes for was their sole togetherness. Hearts and gazes were converging. As the quantity of hankies bore witness.

So it's not surprising that no-one heard a scooter skidding to a halt on the square outside the church, nor its metallic crash and the curses of the driver and passenger, and that no-one noticed two wastrels come in beneath the musical Niagara, or their uncertain gait as they came up behind the couple, or that no-one was put out by how odd they now looked among the bridesmaids, who were clutching on to the bridal train . . . They were obviously taken for close friends, or family, who were breathlessly late. If they were staggering a bit, it was because they must have run a long way. And if their eyes were ablaze, it was presumably from emotion.

In other words, they formed a natural part of the procession. And then happiness at the front drew all their eyes again, as though these two latecomers, along with the bridesmaids, were nothing but the distant tail of a glorious comet.

Neither Berthold nor Mondine realised they were being followed. They were gazing far beyond the horizon of eternity. So it was that Berthold didn't immediately recognise the voice which was hailing him above those celestial harmonies.

"Hey! Berthold!"

The voice had to try again.

"Hey! Berthold! Have you gone deaf or are you putting it on?"

Then Berthold recognised the voice. But he'd also promised to be good.

"You weren't invited to my wedding, Marty," he said without turning round. Mondine, who'd glanced over her shoulder, encouraged him to keep going.

"Forget them. They're completely pissed. Pescatore will chuck them out."

"My friend and I want to know how you make nuns up the duff!" Marty asked.

Mum's apple duff? Mum's apple duff? Berthold was all at sea.

"How you put holy sisters in the family way!" said a second voice, which Berthold also recognised.

"And no undertakers at my wedding either, Postel. It brings bad luck. So be a nice fellow and shove off. And take the poison dwarf with you."

Was it the organist or God Almighty eavesdropping? Whatever, someone up there heard, and the pipes swelled mightily.

"What's all this about sisters?" Mondine yelled above Johann Sebastian Bach.

"I dunno," Berthold yelled, eyes straight ahead. "They're completely bollocksed. You said so yourself."

"Gervaise!" Marty yelled. "What did you do to Gervaise? Examine your conscience!"

"Gervaise!" Postel-Wagner yelled. "What did you do to Gervaise? Search your soul!"

"Gervaise?" Mondine yelled. "But you swore to me it wasn't you!"

"Gervaise?" Gervaise wondered. "Are they talking about me?"

"Ger-vaise! Ger-vaise!" Postel and Marty were now chanting, while stamping on the flagstones.

"Shut it!" Berthold boomed, suddenly spinning round.

So loudly, that the organ was silenced and the beribboned bridesmaids and pageboys flew away into the side aisles.

It took Berthold one stride to cross the four paces separating him from Marty.

"What are you doing here, Marty? What do you want? To fuck up my marriage? You've always been jealous of my skill, are you also jealous of my private life now?"

All of which was muttered man to man, from the heights of Berthold to the depths of Marty, who refused to be intimidated.

"I'm here to check a diagnosis, Berthold. And the sooner you put your cards on the table, the sooner I'll be able to go to bed. I'm completely rat-arsed, and I need to sleep off my emotions."

"We want to know why Gervaise is pregnant," Postel-Wagner explained. "After that we'll go and mourn our teacher Fraenkhel. Promise."

"Berthold, did you really do that to Gervaise?"

"Had no choice," Berthold whispered.

"What did you say?" Mondine asked. "So it was you, was it?"

(O! how fragile the barrier is between bliss and tragedy . . .)

"No! It wasn't me! I mean, it was and it wasn't. It was that wanker Malaussène's fault, as usual!"

"So that's it, was it?" Marty asked. "I was right, was I? Jesus Christ, Berthold, what's going to stop you on the highway to buggery? Do you even realise what you've done? Can you imagine how all hell will let loose when you finally cock something up?"

"What did you do? What did you do to Gervaise? Out with it, you fucking liar!"

And Mondine laid into her man, but it was suddenly as though she'd ceased to exist, as though she was beating up a mountainside, completely insensitive to her slaps, scratches and kicks. Mondine didn't know it yet, but she was now taking measure of herself as the wife of a man of science . . . and the wife weighs in for little when her genius is speaking.

And her genius was now speaking. He was even thundering:

"What would you have done in my shoes, Marty? That dickhead Malaussène packs his Julie off for me to abort her, I start the operation, and what do I find? The neck of the womb was as open as an oven door, with an embryo dashing out, dragging its placenta behind it, like Mondine with her trousseau . . . A little thing so full of life, eyes staring in horror at the terrible news in Fraenkhel's fake letter . . . Just at that moment, they bring me along Gervaise completely out of it . . . While I was giving my instructions next door, Julie Malaussène had legged it without waiting for my conclusions, and when I went back into the operating theatre, there it still was, terribly alive, a bouncing embryo, absolutely normal with it, far more normal than you are, Marty, incredibly advanced for its ten weeks of existence, and seemingly aware of its mistake, the poor thing, curled up in its umbilical cord and wanting so desperately to go back home, but its home had pissed off, Madame Malaussène had buggered off, awash on a wave of sorrow, as so often happens with the sentimental sort! So what else could I do? Pull the chain? Would you have pulled the chain, Marty?"

The organ now had a voice. But this voice wasn't floating down from the heights, it was rising up from Berthold's lungs, to fill the vault with a song to the glory of science in the service of life.

"You mad fucking bastard," Marty joined in. "That's just what I thought. You passed the baby over to Gervaise! You transplanted Julie's sprog into Gervaise's belly!"

"There was no other solution."

"But, Berthold, how did you manage to pull it off?"

"And how about you, Marty? How did you manage to come up with such a diagnosis? I thought I'd got you there. But one day I will, Marty. Believe me, one day I'll surprise you all!"

"Surprise me now, Berthold! Tell me how you managed it!"

"That, my little fellow, will be the subject of my contribution to the next Bichat Symposium. I'll send you an invitation . . . Right then, can we get married now?"

Marty smiled his sweetest smile at Mondine and gave them his blessing:

"Marry him, young lady, and you'll get the bargain of the century. He's the dimmest genius the world has ever seen! The most brilliant dickhead! Take my word for it. I've known him for pushing twenty years now! You'll need more than one lifetime to get to the bottom of him!"

"Fraenkhel would have been proud of him," Postel-Wagner blurted out, suddenly bursting into tears.

And the wedding would have resumed its normal course, hadn't Inspectors Titus and Silistri, as though waking from a double nightmare, suddenly realised that they had each been basely suspected by the other during this long gestation. Before either Julie or Gervaise could lift a finger to stop them, they were rolling among the upturned chairs, pummelling each other with their fists . . . It looked at first as if Pescatore and his men had rushed over to separate them, but they too had been mortally offended and wanted to get even. Upon which, the Templars charged in to rescue their bosses. The honour of the street is no idle term, and the tattooed ladies joined in as well. You might have been freed from your pimp, but you're not going to let him get beaten up by a gang of pigs. And, as a woman is as good as any man, Hélène and Tanita waded in to save their husbands from their claws.

Was this proof God exists? Not a single gun was drawn during the entire set-to. Was it a sign of the Church's decline? The furnishings and statues of saints didn't put up the expected resistance. Was there something aesthetic about it all? It was certainly beautiful.

Which Mondine, wrapped like a tender tendril around her genius expressed in simple terms:

"You know what, prof? This is the most beautiful wedding I've ever seen. And it's mine!"

And Julie, folding Gervaise in her gaze and arms, drew the following conclusion:

"There's no doubt about it, Gervaise. A kid capable of triggering off a civil war before it's even been born is definitely Benjamin's son."

Chapter 64

IT WAS, OF course, at that precise moment that I confessed to Coudrier what I hadn't admitted to myself:

"In the end, I'm pleased not to have reproduced in this shit-heap . . ."

Coudrier just replied:

"What a strange notion of happiness . . ."

Then he pointed at the middle of the Seine and said:

"Number three, Benjamin. Concentrate on what you're doing!"

I looked over at the third fishing rod. Yes, I definitely had a nibble. The float was bobbing up and down. Something at the bottom of the river had got tempted.

"What do I do now?"

Coudrier came over to me, while also keeping an eye on his own floats.

"Don't panic. Just wait till the fish really bites before hooking it. When the float dips, you give a good flick of the wrist, and there you are! But no histrionics, otherwise the line will break. Go on! That's it!"

Sure enough, it felt hooked. Furious life was kicking at the end of my line.

"Don't pull. Let him get angry, but don't let him go where he wants. If he needs more line, then give him more line. But no slack. It's just like police surveillance, in fact."

My reel was reeling wildly.

"Stop! Not too long. Make him do his exercises in mid-stream and see that he doesn't hide behind a stone. There we are. He's the muscles and you're the brains, Benjamin, never forget that. When he's tired enough, he'll be only too pleased to come back to you, just as a suspect is relieved when he is arrested. He's Lehmann, and you're Silistri . . ."

After a while, I saw my aquatic Lehmann's dorsal fin appear. It was stunning! A sampan sail beneath a French spring sky. It leapt . . . A streamlined glitter, as oblique and beautiful as a ray of life.

"A pike-perch," Coudrier said. "Weighing eight or ten pounds. Well done. Quite delicious when cooked in butter with a drop of Chablis. Bring him in now. Where's your landing net? Always keep your net within reach! Like policemen, anglers must remain ever optimistic!"

I brought it in slowly until, worn out by its own resistance, the pike-perch gave itself up to its doom. That's the way we all go.

"Be careful when you bring him out. It bites like a pike, not like a perch."

But I was incapable of bringing it out.

"Here, let me."

Two seconds later, the pike-perch had left its natural element. Coudrier unhooked it with relish.

"Lovely fellow, isn't he?"

Then he threw it back in.

Although apparently half dead when in his hands, the pike-perch exploded into life as soon as it hit the Seine.

"Just to teach him that God exists," Coudrier explained. "And not to fall for lures."

I pointed at the roach, gudgeon and bream and other tiddlers in our basket, along with two perches and a catfish, and asked:

"Why him and not the others?"

"That's exactly the sort of question God never asks Himself."

*

My apprenticeship had been going on for the past hour on Quai des Orfèvres, just below the windows of Chief Superintendent Coudrier's old office.

"Just because you've interrupted my retirement doesn't mean that I have to stop fishing."

Meanwhile, I could feel Nepos's eyes weighing down on our shoulders.

"You've attracted my son-in-law's hatred, Benjamin. I did warn you . . ."

But he hadn't just got me round to cock a snook at his son-in-law.

"This is the best spot for fishing I know. Plenty of fish round here. I suppose there must be plenty of corpses on the bottom."

All this said while showing me how to fix my reel so my line doesn't twist.

"I once explained exactly this very same phenomenon to Inspector Pastor. Dumping corpses right under the police's noses must be a real turn-on for hardened killers. And it was indeed what Sainclair did with Inspector Perret. Not one of those swine can resist such provocations. They want us to take them for artists . . . In the end, it's their undoing."

Two rods for the small fry, and two others for the big catches. I had to hook on live maggots. ("You stick it in at the base, then roll it over like a sock.")

"Talking of Pastor, how is your mother?"

Mum was better, as I told him. She was eating, she was dolling herself up every morning, it was a sort of resurrection. She had a fluid, almost transparent beauty, ready to take wing . . . She sometimes started talking to herself and giggling behind her hand.

"She's emerging from a long bereavement, Coudrier told me. "Pastor's dead. Did you know that?"

No, I didn't. All the family were quietly wondering what Pastor had done to her. And there we were. He was dead. And now Mum was chatting away with Inspector Pastor's ghost.

"Your mother came to see me with Pastor's will and a signed confession for the murder of Cercaria. It's thanks to this, among other things, that you're free."

Coudrier told me how Pastor had been ill for some time, and he hadn't been play-acting when he got criminals to confess by holding a gun to their heads and telling them that he, too, was a condemned man. The deal was simple – either the bugger talked, or else he, the nice guy in the baggy sweater, would blow the bugger's brains out. An effective approach, which Cercaria had been foolish enough not to credit.

"He stopped taking his medication when he left with your mother. He wanted to die 'in love', as he put it. Your mother made him live far longer than the doctors had predicted. That's all."

That's all.

"She knew right from the start of their elopement that Pastor was busy dying. He told her. And she decided to stay with him till the end, even though she didn't know if she was going to be able to bear it. She went back to you with a terrible need for silence. She's very grateful to you for leaving her in peace with her grief. People have less and less respect for intimacy these days . . ."

One of the floats bobbed.

"It's a roach. Land it and we'll use it as live bait. Now, put a grain of wheat on hook number four. We'll let it drag along the bed. Who knows? There may be some tench . . ."

Who knows indeed?

Coudrier explained the rest of the story. How he'd defused Nepos's dossiers one by one. How, for example, Gervaise and Julie had found Chabotte's old mother in a retirement home in Switzerland.

"Pickled in her hatred for her dead son. You also owe your freedom to that

397

mother's fury. Her statement was hair-raising. When Julie asked her what was keeping her alive, she said: 'I'm in no hurry to see that liar again.'"

And so on. My months in prison had been their months of investigation. Nepos had flung open the book of my past, and Coudrier had slammed it shut on his fingers. Sainclair had raised an army against me, and a secret army had risen up against his troops. The good guys had been saved, and the bad and the cretinous worsted. Sainclair's enterprise had fallen flat.

"Just imagine it. It was him behind the tattoo trade. Probably to finance his magazine, *Affection*, which had failed to win the approval of the profession. In his flat, we found a tattoo which had been removed from Matthias Fraenkhel's forearm."

Matthias, Matthias or everyman's honour.

"Sainclair is a creative soul . . . By killing Matthias Fraenkhel and filming his death throes, he gave just the right ending to Old Job's film. As for the decomposition of the body, it was the icing on the cake!"

Coudrier was reasoning clearly, his eyes staring at the Seine's opaque waters.

"I rather think that it was the final sequence which was the last straw. When he showed it to the King of the Living Dead, he scared him to death. And when the King threatened to shop him, Sainclair had to eliminate him, too. Necrotising fasciitis. Meanwhile, he had prepared a whole set of articles about this phenomenon of sudden putrefaction which so fascinated him."

Coudrier's head was bobbing up and down like a float in the water.

"An artist, and a man of science, in fact . . . You were a great inspiration to him, Benjamin . . ."

Yes, in the end, I was just one of Sainclair's numerous sources of inspiration, a sort of collaborator in fact, perhaps even a muse. I just had to be the killer in the Vercors so that his article about criminal transplants would turn out to be completely true. Hence the trap. He'd used me like plasticine in his theories . . . There was nothing particularly strange about Sainclair, when it came down to it. He was like Chief Superintendent Nepos, or Judge Képlin, or many other honest citizens: he had a driving need for coherency. He was ready to do anything to make the Great Outside look like what went on in his little inside.

"And how are things with you, my lad. Over the glooms yet?"

I told Coudrier that I was OK, that, in the end, I was pleased not to have reproduced in this shit-heap . . .

"What a strange notion of happiness . . ."

Then the pike-perch bit.

XIV
MONSIEUR MALAUSSÈNE

. . . foolhardy son of the goat and leopardess . . .

Chapter 65

W ELL, YES, OF course I'm happy! How could you suspect me of cheating on our happiness? Have you seen your mother's face? Have you seen Julie's face bent down over Gervaise's belly? What sort of monster do you think I am? Could I possibly refuse such joy? Then the look on Gervaise's face, your other mother . . . Do you know what Gervaise said when she found out you'd slipped in through her window? That she's calm like this because she's carrying you, just as old Thian once carried her. No more, no less. Thian wasn't that bothered about who the real father was. Such curiosity wasn't part of his nature. He was the stand-in kangaroo, period. (Which is just as well, because what with Big Jeanine's turnover, he'd have had to grill the entire Toulon underworld to reach Gervaise's source.) By walking you these past few months, Gervaise has quite simply carried on a family tradition. She's carted you around like Thian carted Verdun around and was delighted to do so. For her, carrying outside or in comes down to the same thing. In this way, she's like Julie – not the sort of kangaroo to make a big deal about maternity. So how could I not be happy? Proud, even! Isn't making two women happy a good enough reason to be proud for any self-respecting goat?

. . .

Am I laying it on a bit thick?

. . .

What do you mean by "yes"?

. . .

I'm not laying it on thick at all! By talking about the happiness of the women, I'm quite simply avoiding the father's legitimate worries, not the same at all! Forget happiness for a moment, because there's more to life than just happiness, there's also life itself! Anyone can be born! Even I was! But then you have to *become*! To grow up and out (without excess), increase, burgeon, blossom, moult (without mutating), mature (without dropping), evolve (without evaluating), commit yourself (without getting committed), endure (without vegetating), age (without becoming too childish) and, in the end, die without moaning . . . one hell of a programme, something to be watched over every instant . . . because, whatever your age, age always rebels against itself! And then there's more to it than just age! . . .There's also context! And when it comes to context, my poor little thing . . .

"Father, you can talk when you've been through what I've been through even before I was born."

. . .

. . .

What did you say?

. . .

. . .

"Father, you can talk when you've been through what I've been through even before I was born."

. . .

. . .

Just as I feared. I can already hear the slanging matches to come, with your catalogue of minor filial reproach: "While we're at it, tell me the truth, Daddy dear. Thanks to your planetary lucidity, you weren't exactly over the moon when I arrived to widen the family circle, isn't that right?"

With your uncles and aunts getting their oars in, of course.

JEREMY: You have to admit it Ben, you weren't exactly keen . . .

HALF PINT: It's true . . .

THÉRÈSE: I wonder how such paternal feelings can possibly be a good influence on the child's mentality . . .

CLARA: Stop teasing Benjamin . . .

YOU: Aunt Thérèse is right, Dad. My neocortical walls are still echoing with your first piece of advice: *And you, shit-for-brains, do you really think you've picked the right world, family and epoch? You're not even here yet, and you're already hanging out with the wrong crowd!*

JEREMY: Chapter and verse, Ben, absolute chapter and verse!

THÉRÈSE: What a lovely introduction to our family . . .

YOU: I even think I heard you add: *And so foolhardy son of the goat and leopardess, I really wouldn't blame you if you decided to cash in your chips before touching down.* That was your advice, wasn't it?

HALF PINT: Really? Is that really what you told him to do, Ben?

"I didn't *tell* him to do anything, it was scarcely even a vague authorisation . . ."

YOU: Well, it certainly didn't make my embryonic existence any easier.

402

THÉRÈSE: Of course it didn't!

JEREMY: Poor kid . . .

YOU (quoting me): *Leave us alone, return to the bliss of limbo . . .*

JEREMY: That's more than just vague authorisation, Ben . . .

THÉRÈSE: And I can certainly think of better welcomes.

YOU (quoting me): *Unfold your wings and ascend, no-one here will blame you if you do . . .*

THÉRÈSE: Meaning that no-one here was really hoping for him . . .

HALF PINT: That's horrible! Even Julius thinks it's horrible!

"But that's not everything I said! A future father's highly contradictory. All at sixes and sevens! You'll see when it's your turn! You think one thing then the opposite! And what about how desperate I felt when we got Matthias's fake letter, does that count for nothing?

YOU: Tell me about it! You ran like a headless chicken for the first 500 metres, accusing yourself of all the sins in the world, then, on arrival you put the blame on me.

"What? I put the blame on you?"

"Absolutely, or at least when it came to Mum's agony. I can still hear you, all of seven months ago: *Come back you little bugger! Doesn't pain like this clip your wings? What kind of a sodding angel are you?*"

JEREMY: After telling him over and again to go back to heaven? Were you trying to drive him completely bananas or what?

THÉRÈSE: No, he just wanted to make him feel guilty, as all good fathers do. I reckon we should envisage psychiatric treatment . . .

HALF PINT: We'll love him, anyway! No worries! We'll all love him! Won't we, Julius?

CLARA: Dinner's ready! Come and get it! And give Benjamin a break!

There were now two of us talking to ourselves in the house. Mum was chatting with a former living person, and me with a would-be. If we'd managed to put you and Pastor in touch, then you could have given each other some handy tips, but eternity is such that the dead and the unborn never converse. Their only communication is via the prayers of the living. The grief dug out by those who have gone creates the nest of those to come in the hearts of those who hope. Otherwise, the roundabout would have stopped turning ages ago.

Right. Let's suppose you're Pastor's substitute in the Malaussène team. You were waiting your turn on the bench and now the divine ref's whistled for the changeover. Pastor's out, and you're in. Surely no-one can blame me for explaining the rules of the game at such a vital moment? You just can't imagine how weird the rules are! It's enough to make you wonder if they even exist. You think you're leading a good life, you're following the path as indicated and, without knowing why or how, you end up getting accused of all the crimes in the world.

An example?

You want an example?

But not mine?

A different one?

Let's take a different example from mine, then.

Ronald de Florentis

Ronald de Florentis was Old Job's oldest friend. He had absolutely nothing to do with his murder or the theft of his film. He was tricked by the King of the Living Dead, who handed him a purchase agreement, duly signed and sealed. He was a solid specimen, a rock with a lion's head, equipped since his birth for cutting out for himself a slice of movie-land's territory. A producer-cum-distributor; a sower of images, such was his role. He must have trampled on a few people's heads to get to the top of this pyramid, but that's the law of the jungle and, all in all, his fellow professionals considered him to be honest.

Ronald was deeply upset when he heard that his friend Job had been murdered, and even more so when he learnt that his brother-in-arms had concealed his lifelong obsession from him – the making of The Only Begotten Film. But he consoled himself with the fact that it was a great success. He was sincerely delighted about Job's brilliance and posthumous fame. He was pleased when the Césars, Oscars, Dellucs, Berlin Bears and Venice Lions (the zoo of cinematographic honours) lay down with the Palme d'Or on Job's grave. He was a real friend. One of those genuine ones, who are pleased because we're pleased. But it was this very friend that Chief Superintendent Nepos arrested for having contracted Old Job's murder, the theft of The Only Begotten Film and its subsequent exploitation. Chief Superintendent Nepos's consuming need for coherency meant that the only question he'd asked was: Who benefited from the crime, given that it wasn't Malaussène? Answer: Florentis, the producer of course. Distributing the film had showered him with dividends, it was the crowning point of his career and had brought him international recognition . . . a crystalline motive!

Coudrier had to go and clip his son-in-law round the ear all over again to make him release his grip.

Once freed, Ronald was no longer the same lion. Because, during his questioning, he'd learnt something terrible: *Old Job hadn't wanted his Only Begotten Film to go on the distribution circuit. It had been meant for the chosen few.* Ronald hadn't known that, and so had become an unwitting traitor. An accomplice, whether he liked it or not. With no recourse to public confessions. The Ministers of the Interior and of Culture had informed him that this unfortunate scam would henceforth be a state secret – or secret of several states, for that matter! It was out of the question to reveal to Old Job's millions of admirers that The Only Begotten Film, his monument to a century of memories, was the product of extremely shady dealing. "You can't disappoint a planet just to assuage one conscience, Monsieur de Florentis! Not even in the name of transparency! The profession will not follow you! Everyone will flatly deny what you say!"

In other words: arbitrary imprisonments can happen so quickly.

The lion's mane dimmed. A stick grew from his hand. He counted his steps. For the first time, he could clearly see The End on his own personal screen.

But that wasn't all.

As you will see, when the worst is on its way, *that* is never *all*.

There's always one piece left.

At the bottom of the pan.

Baked on.

With a view to making amends, Ronald came to see Suzanne and Julie. His idea was to save The Zebra by turning it into Old Job's film institute, as had been planned. A temple to the movies, as Matthias had put it, a foundation *ad vitam aeternam*. And the money? He'd pay. Ronald had decided to sort out his business affairs before striking camp, to sell off his collection of paintings so that his heirs wouldn't rip them apart with their teeth, and to give Suzanne what she needed for a Job Bernardin Foundation. So there we were in the Grand Hotel Whatever, listening to the auctioneer's hammer tapping out its waltzing millions. We meaning Julie, Suzanne, Jeremy (who reckoned he should never miss a new experience now that Zabo had dubbed him a novelist), Clara and me. As your arrival was due any day now, Gervaise and Professor Berthold were busy checking the parcel. They told us, your mum and me, to go and play somewhere else. So we dropped off Gervaise at the hospital in your mother's yellow 4-CV then, as one family, went to see the breaking up of Florentis's eclectic collection of paintings by Vlaminck, Valadon, Seurat, Picasso, Braque, as well as Soutine, Jim Dine, Laclavetine, under the beady eyes of Paris's high society, and the calculators of Tokyo's nobs. All in all, a tidy sum.

"Which my heirs will invest in rubbish, I'm just sure of it," old Ronald grumbled between Julie and Suzanne.

The masterpieces had been exhibited then filmed, and were appearing on a screen as the bids went by. Their disappearance, when the final fall of the hammer removed them from their easels, made a strange impression. The universe had changed. Ronald's life had suddenly slunk away.

He now leant over Suzanne's shoulder.

"The next sale concerns you directly, Suzanne. It should provide ample funding for you to run your film institute."

This was confirmed by the auctioneer, who announced a collection which was "unique to the best of his knowledge", and had thus been put at an appropriate price. It came in the form of an octavo volume, bound in ancient hide, which had been placed on a lectern before the camera's eye. Binoculars braced, breath bated, hell of a suspense . . .

"Great bit of staging . . ." Jeremy whispered.

A white-gloved presenter finally opened the book. It was apparently made of old parchment, purchased by Ronald from some dealer in things medieval.

"Look carefully."

"What is it?" Julie asked.

The answer exploded on to the screen along with the auctioneer's voice: a sort of monk, in front of his writing desk, hand on his heart, was gazing up to the heavens in a determined, but at the same time beseeching, manner making him look both strong and humble.

"Botticelli's *Saint Augustine*," the auctioneer's voice announced. "A detail from the Ognissanti fresco in Florence."

And, as Julie leapt to her feet, stifling a cry, the voice went on:

"This is neither a reproduction nor one of the Florentine master's preparatory studies, as the extraordinary fidelity of the colours might make you think, but a tattoo on a woman's skin."

An exclamation from the crowd. Julie, paralysed with horror, just managed to murmur:

"Ronald, where did you get that?"

"Oh! It's a long story . . ."

Which Ronald didn't have the opportunity to tell us, because a voice he knew only too well was whispering in his ear:

"Monsieur de Florentis, you're under arrest."

Chief Superintendent Nepos and two Inspectors in their Sunday best were standing behind us. The Inspectors discreetly grabbed the old boy by his elbows.

"I'm arresting you for aiding and abetting the murder of the young women whose tattoos appear in that book."

And, while the cops were leading de Florentis away, Chief Superintendent Nepos bade me a friendly farewell:

"I am not surprised to see you here, Monsieur Malaussène, and I hope to see you again soon."

Yonder, the upmarket three-card-trick merchant, who hadn't seen or heard a thing, kept going:

"This collection of tattoos features a variety of different trade associations. You will find tattoos from the eleventh-century bakers' and glaziers' guilds, with even older trades such as prostitution, here represented by six works copied from the finest work that the Quattrocento and Flemish schools had to offer. Such as this extraordinary *Saint Augustine*."

He'd have gone on about it much longer, but Nepos told him to shut up shop because they were taking the precious volume away as evidence.

Chapter 66

So what can you say about bad luck like that? Because, of course, Ronald de Florentis was no more guilty of the tattoo murders than he was of killing Job. At least, that's what you think, I hope? Otherwise, how can you explain why a serial killer puts the tattoos he's removed from his victims up for auction?

It was at this precise moment in our internal debate, which was taking place on the way to pick up Gervaise from Saint-Louis Hospital, that your mother interrupted our secret conversation by saying:

"What was that?"

I stared at Julie. Her 4-CV is a tiny car which she drives majestically, like an ocean cruiser, giving passers-by the impression they've seen a Rolls glide by. Julie repeated:

"What was that, Benjamin? Are you talking to yourself?"

I had been down in the depths. She recalled me to her sumptuous surface.

"No, I was just saying that Ronald has obviously got nothing to do with this."

"Why 'obviously'?"

"Because the girl in the pink suit, who tried to frame me, would just have switched goats and pointed the finger at him, that's why."

"But he must have bought those tattoos from someone."

"But not from Sainclair. Maybe from someone else."

Yes, Ronald de Florentis was the last link in a chain of diminishing guilt.

"Funny business, all the same . . ." Julie mumbled.

Which was Suzanne's opinion, too. She leant forward between our two seats.

"Quite. I can't see myself financing my film institute on human flesh. The cinema may have its faults, but cannibalism isn't one of them. So far, all it's done is gobble up souls. If you believe in the soul, of course . . ."

Then Suzanne announced, without warning, that she was dropping her projected film institute, and going back to teach Latin and Greek in her native Poitou. She was leaving that evening. For good.

"I'll send you my address. You can come and see some great home movies."

"You're abandoning The Zebra?"

She gave us one more peal of her laughter.

"I've never been much of a militant. And The Zebra is being amply defended by the residents' association. Could you drop me off at Colonel-Fabien before you go to the hospital? I'll walk the rest of the way."

Suzanne got out at Place du Colonel-Fabien, walked round the car, leant into Julie's window and, as a farewell, pronounced a sentence she couldn't have used that often in her life:

"I really liked you. Both of you. Don't change."

A final flash of her Irish eyes, a little wave of the hand, then she was off at such a stride that it looked as though she was walking straight to Poitou.

God knows why but I said:

"Did you know that our Latinist is also a judo black belt?"

"And that the Queen of the Film Buffs was also a champion tennis player? Yes, I did," Julie replied as she pulled off.

*

The first person we bumped into in the entrance hall of Saint-Louis Hospital was Professor Berthold, followed by his eternal flock of white coats. He welcomed us as only Berthold knows how. From the other side of the lobby, he pointed us out to his clutch of trained ducklings and bellowed:

"Let me introduce you to the Malaussène couple, you bunch of morons! The two of them have made a considerable contribution to medical progress. You think you're dealing with a nice normal household – a bit above average on the distaff side perhaps – and you're absolutely wrong, as usual! What you've got coming towards you is an entire experimental research department! Just look at them, my morons, and be grateful, you owe it all to them, yes, even you who are supposed to usher in the medicine of tomorrow!"

Then, to us:

"Have you forgotten something? Has the little one popped out already? After all, he is in fine fettle. He's just dying to leap out into the ring!"

"Where's Gervaise?"

From the tone of Julie's voice, Berthold sensed that something was up.

"Gervaise? She left with you about three quarters of an hour ago."

"What do you mean, she left with us? We've only just got here!" I said, uttering the only words my terror still left available to me.

"Only just got here?" Berthold soldiered on. "But you called up from the cafeteria three quarters of an hour ago, and she came down to join you!"

"From the cafeteria? Who took the call? Was it you?"

"No, it was my secretary. Gervaise was getting dressed and my secretary told her that Monsieur Malaussène was waiting for her down in the cafeteria."

*

We both dashed off in different directions, Julie to Gervaise's place, and me back home. As usual, I let my terror take over my legs, and my legs lap up Belleville, with its colours and its concrete, its dead façades which are livelier than its new ones, its stalls of hardware and shop windows of ancient rags . . . As it was market night, scraps of vegetables flew up from under my feet and, as you were the only thing I had in my mind, I tried hard not to slip over, not to shake you up again now that you'd turned back into a fragile promise, such a frail hope that one step out of line, a single wrong thought might put off your birth for good, and I no longer knew what to think, I thought nothing, I ran without even taking the time to curse that dickhead of a Berthold, I ran without thinking about what I was running towards, I was running towards a hardware store behind whose door I wanted to find Gervaise cradling Verdun, I was running towards one of Gervaise's favourite pictures, a Quattrocento virgin, pregnant with a little Malaussène and surrounded by sprogs, I was running, running so fast that the door of the hardware store exploded on impact.

But instead of a plump virgin, I was welcomed by a flat vestal, as cold as a decree.

Thérèse.

Sitting alone at the dining-room table.

Handing me a small black tape recorder.

"Don't panic like that, Benjamin. It's all explained here."

Fine. An explanation. That's better than nothing.

Thérèse added:

"I always thought things would end up this way."

Even though it was the first time I'd experienced such a situation, I had the agonising feeling of having already been through it in all its ghastly details – a sort of vertigo of the memory.

"How does this thing work?"

"You press here."

I pressed.

A little cassette started turning and I started listening for an explanation.

But it wasn't Gervaise's voice. It was Mum.

"*My little ones, now that you're all out of danger . . .*"

Maternal perspicacity . . .

". . . *now that you're all out of danger . . .*"

Got it! I knew where and when I'd been through this before. In this very place! The year when Mum left us for Pastor.

The only difference being, on that occasion I wasn't listening to a tape, but reading a letter, my heart in shreds, expecting it to announce the elopement of Julie and the charming Inspector. Wrong. It was Mum. And, now, today, when I was crying out for news of Gervaise, it was Mum all over again!

"He fell in love with her when he came to drop off his first cassette, Benjamin, the one that got you off the hook, with Clément's voice on it."

I pinned the tiny machine to my ear.

"Yes, that's just what Mum's saying, thanks. I'm not deaf!"

But Thérèse's voice doggedly went on echoing Mum's explanations.

"He fell in love with her transparent nature, Benjamin!"

Which was, indeed, exactly how Mum put it:

"*Barnaby fell in love with my transparent nature.*" (*sic*!)

"He was a great support to her during her bereavement. He succeeded where we failed. He cured her, Ben! He was the one she was whispering to. He'd given her one of his little machines . . ."

". . . *a great support to me during my bereavement . . .*"

The fact is you had to listen to it at least twice to believe it. No sooner was Mum resurrected, than she'd legged it with Barnaby! After The Zebra and the Columns of Buren, Barnaby had spirited away our mother!

"And she's never even seen him, can you believe that? She doesn't even know what he looks like! Isn't that marvellous!"

Thérèse . . . O Thérèse . . . poor wallflower wilting on your stalk . . . how I love you . . . and how I could strangle you . . .

"They plan to rebuild the house in the Vercors and turn it into a temple of transparency . . . an invisible house . . . like in a fairy tale . . . it'll be Barnaby's masterpiece!"

What if I really did strangle her?

That's where my plans stood, when the door flew open to reveal Jeremy, who was bellowing:

"Is it true Mum's done a bunk with that Barnabooth?"

I handed Jeremy the little tape recorder and ran upstairs to the phone in our

411

bedroom. Julius, who woke up with a start on my arrival, sat down on his arse and awaited the result as impatiently as I did.

Engaged.

Gervaise's phone was engaged.

Good sign.

Which Julius confirmed by snapping his jaws.

Since the police force does not value the lives of its officers, I have decided to kidnap your saint. She has a higher market value. If you want her back alive, then release my little liar at once. If you doubt my intentions, go downstairs and look in the letter box. Inside, you will find proof that Sister Gervaise is indeed in my company.

When I got to Gervaise's place, Julie, Coudrier, Inspectors Titus and Silistri, Chief Superintendent Nepos and two technicians were listening to her answering machine for the umpteenth time. The proof they'd found in the letter box was lying in front of them. It was the tip of Gervaise's little finger. The tattooed little finger.

In two days' time, you will receive her arm. If the arm is not enough, I will send you the baby. I rather feel like trying my hand at a bit of midwifery.

The letter was signed "Sainclair".

Chapter 67

THAT EVENING, SHE read the sadness on Inspector Titus's face when he arrived in her cell.

"This is the last time I'll come to see you, Marie-Ange."

As on the previous occasions, he was carrying a wicker basket. She spotted the gilded neck of a champagne bottle, with a sommelier's cloth laid over it.

"Caviar," he said.

She helped him lay the table. Silver cutlery, Limoges porcelain and two wide crystal champagne glasses.

"It's absurd to shut champagne up in flute glasses. It's an airy wine."

Marie-Ange found the name on the tin of caviar perfectly satisfactory.

Inspector Titus followed her gaze.

"Every time, you look at the names on the labels to check I'm not playing the cheapskate. What do you take me for? Coppers aren't all plain boys in blue. Some of us appreciate the finer things in life . . ."

She couldn't help smiling.

He uncorked the champagne without a pop.

The song of the wine rose up from the glasses to fill the cell. Fine bubbles and slender notes.

"I've brought you back this."

It was her original pink suit. Her second skin. Freshly laundered. And, with it, the panties and bra she'd been wearing when she was arrested. She couldn't resist. She stood up, naked in front of him, her clothes scattered around her in the cell. She reached out her arms.

He looked at her, speechless. He had to summon up all of his affection for Tanita to avoid any dereliction of duty. All the same, he did remain there for a few seconds, holding the clean suit, staring at her. He said, once more:

"No, I really don't like prisons."

He noticed what looked like a white shadow on her bright flesh. He slowly followed its contours with his index finger. It spread out above her breasts, covering her left shoulder, then thinning over her throat, before widening out once more over her belly and on to her right hip. She had the ghost of a picture on her skin.

"Let me guess what was tattooed there . . ."

She didn't react to his idling finger. He sensed the fusion of life deep inside her body.

"*Melancholia*," he said at last. "But not the one by Dürer, Cranach's version."

He nodded.

"The angel's feet started on your hip, here, and its head lay just beneath your clavicle."

He handed her the clothes.

"Why did you have your tattoo removed?" he asked while she was getting dressed.

That twist of the hips when wriggling into the skirt was always a moving moment.

"Let me guess . . ."

The bra was one of the sort which shows more than it hides.

"OK, I think I've got it. You sold it to old Florentis, didn't you?"

The pink jacket bevelled out from the waist, rising up to her shoulders, as though springing up from the neck of a curvaceous vase.

"Of course! You sold it to old Florentis to finance the launch of *Affection*."

He opened the tin of caviar.

"That's how it all began, isn't it?"

She was now sitting on her chair, before a tiny mound of grey pearls which looked almost alive. He unfolded the silver foil into which Tanita had slipped the warm blinis.

As he did so, he explained. And his words were as precise as his gestures.

"I'll tell you what happened, Marie-Ange. At the time, you were working for De Florentis Productions. Your Sainclair asked you to see your boss about possible financing for *Affection*, and you decided to invest your own capital, so to speak. But Florentis didn't fall in love with you. He fell in love with the Cranach on your skin. Old Ronald was crazy about your *Melancholia*. He showed you his collection of tattoos, and it occurred to you that you could complete it. You talked up the price. When it got sufficiently astronomical, you presented him with your *Melancholy* on a plate. Is that it?"

It was. He read in her eyes that it was. And it was also precisely what de Florentis had told them.

414

"Having a tattoo removed must be painful . . . Cream?"

(To go through all that agony to finance a pile of crap like *Affection*, he thought. She really must be crazy about her pimp Sainclair.)

She held out her plate. The cream sketched out fleeting whirls on the blinis before disappearing into the depths of the buckwheat, like snow on a field.

"That's when you thought of selling him the other tattoos, isn't it? You introduced Gervaise's girls to Sainclair. Some of them agreed to exchange their pounds of flesh for a pile of money. Meanwhile, you were selling Ronald the line that, by purchasing these whores' tattoos, he was helping to put them back on the straight and narrow. The poor old boy was packing girls off to their deaths, while he imagined he was saving them from the street."

Suddenly, he asked:

"Fun, was it?"

He asked her that while peering over a full spoon, and noticed that she seemed to be having problems swallowing. He put down his own spoon without touching it.

"But maybe you didn't know that Sainclair was simply murdering your old pals."

He'd stopped repeating old Ronald's text, and was now thinking for himself.

"They vanished and you asked no questions. You were just the procurer, that's all. A go-between."

This idea had suddenly occurred to him. He was surprising himself.

"Nor did you know that he was shooting snuff movies while torturing them."

She, too, had put down her spoon.

There was a long silence.

He asked:

"When did you find out, Marie-Ange?"

She didn't reply.

"After being arrested?"

She kept mum.

"Did you already know when you made off with old Beaujeu's body?"

Not a word.

"You refused to believe it, didn't you?"

He hung on to his idea. Maybe it wasn't so far off the mark.

"What did Sainclair tell you? That the girls had started new lives? That prossies who go off the game often want to disappear like that? That they were taking a leaf out of your book?"

Then, abruptly:

"Have you ever whacked someone, Marie-Ange? I mean, killed them, intentionally, in cold blood? Have you ever got off on somebody's death throes?"

She looked tired.

"Right," he said.

They were now stuck in the same rut. He reckoned it was time to hike them out of it.

"Sainclair's an even bigger liar than you, Marie-Ange."

(The time has come, he thought, and yet he still hesitated.)

"And mad with it!"

He looked at her. He observed the twitches of doubt. (Let's go!)

"He's the father," he said.

She looked up in disbelief.

"He fathered Gervaise's kid," he confirmed.

He stammered:

"I'm . . . sorry."

He knew she wouldn't take her eyes off him, that even if he left the cell that moment, he'd have this woman's eyes stuck on his conscience for the rest of his life. He went on speaking:

"It's an old story. A passion which goes back several years before you arrived, Marie-Ange. It's completely crazy. Just as crazy as the two of them are. The devil and God Almighty. When Gervaise nearly arrested Sainclair in the cellar where Mondine was being used as bait, she was already pregnant. She'd told him. And when Sainclair tried to kill her, it wasn't so much a police officer he wanted to get rid of, as a mother. She didn't recognise him in his surgeon's mask, and later on didn't imagine that he was driving the car. Then you were arrested. And things started to speed up. We nicked Lehmann, Cazo and young Dutilleul (even today I'm not sure if you knew them or not), and Cazo came clean – with my mate Silistri's help of course. When Gervaise found out that the whole story started and finished with Sainclair, she took the blow valiantly. But then yesterday, she went off to join him."

There wasn't a trace of colour left in Marie-Ange's face.

"She now knows he tried to kill her, once in the cellar, then again at the wheel of a car. But that hasn't stopped her going to him. You know Gervaise, Marie-Ange. She must have got it into her head that she can save him . . . or something along those lines . . . all she did was leave us a message on her answering machine, but with no forwarding address, of course. So there we are. It's been weeks now that I've been struggling with this. I tried to tell you a number of times. But I couldn't. I didn't dare."

Right.

It was done.

Titus knew that they wouldn't finish the caviar or the champagne. All he could hope for now was that the rest would go as planned.

But it didn't.

Marie-Ange quite simply threw herself on to him.

"We're getting out of here. You and me. Let's go!"

She had the voice of a tomboy.

And the tomboy had grabbed Inspector Titus's service automatic, had forced him round with a twist of her arm and was holding the barrel against the side of his head.

"Now!"

Chapter 68

No, THINGS DIDN'T go exactly to plan. They'd been expecting an escape attempt, but more probably from the prison infirmary. That she'd fake having a nasty turn, then take a hostage, but not that Titus would be the hostage! A night-time breakout, something like that . . . which is what they were prepared for, which is why they'd replaced the usual wardens with WPCs. To help the loony in the pink suit to escape. To drive unmarked cars up and down in front of the prison in the hope that she'd hijack one of them. Then to follow her from a distance, thanks to the transmitter hidden in the vehicle, all the way to Sainclair's hide-out. The plan was risky and full of loopholes, but they had no other choice. To let themselves be attacked then overcome and act as her human shield to the bitter end, without ever being sure that the nutcase wouldn't finish off his hostage once she was safe.

"She's no killer," Titus had insisted.

"Of course not. Butter wouldn't melt," Chief Superintendent Nepos had sneered. "Just ask the grandmother and little boy she kept company."

"She was role-playing," Inspector Titus explained. "She was having a bit of fun. She's like that."

"It's irrelevant whether she's a killer or not."

Everyone agreed with Coudrier.

"She's the only person who knows where Sainclair's hiding. Period."

So she had to escape and lead them there before Inspector Gervaise Van Thian was sliced into all the colours of the rainbow and young Malaussène was ejected all over again. That kid meant a lot to all of them. But, more than anyone else, it mattered to Professor Berthold, whom Chief Superintendent Nepos spoke to on the phone, when he imprudently picked up Gervaise's receiver.

"You do realise *whom* you've let him kidnap, don't you, you witless swine? And I'm not talking about the container, I'm talking about the contents! Save that sprog, my good fellow, bring him back to me in good shape, or else never fall ill!

Because if you do, I'll take care of you in person! If I make giant strides in medical science, it isn't to have moronic coppers drag us all back into the stone age!"

Chief Superintendent Nepos had never conversed with Professor Berthold before.

"He's like that," Coudrier explained. "So don't fret, son-in-law, and let's get back to the point. We have to make her escape."

And she'd escaped faster than planned.

With Inspector Titus at the end of a gun.

Titus, whose car hadn't been equipped with transmitters.

Titus, who was now handcuffed on the back seat of his own car – not even his squad car – the chain of the bracelets threaded through the handle of one door, and his feet attached to the other one. Titus chained to his car. The very image of the schemer hoisted by his own petard. He was steaming. He sensed they were driving down a motorway and tried to remember where he'd fucked up. He'd taken his eyes off the beast, even though he'd known how fast and strong she was. Before being put into solitary, she'd crushed her cellmates' bones. There was also the statement of the old boy she'd whispered horror stories to, before flinging him across the lobby on the evening when old Beaujeu was kidnapped. "Never have I felt such an iron grip! And it really wasn't a man disguised as a girl?" No, it was a girl all right, and that was what had got to Titus. He had felt the strength of her muscles while tracing out the scar left by her tattoo, but her grace had triumphed, her grace and the ghost of *Melancholia*.

She started speaking to him:

"Don't blame yourself, Inspector . . ."

Yes, she was definitely speaking to him.

"I've been observing you ever since your first visit. I've been planning our little escapade for ages."

In fact, she was carrying on their conversation.

"You've employed a variety of gestures since we first met. Laying the table, clearing it, bending over, straightening up, turning round . . . I know you as well as if I dressed you every morning. You're extremely graceful. Where does your little air of being a Tartar come from?"

It was his turn to play silent movies.

"Today, you are wearing lisle-thread Loridge socks, half length, bottle green, soft to the touch. You like pricey clothes."

She added:

"And you don't have a gun strapped to your calf."

And then:

"A Kenzo shirt, but no shoulder holster. An ostrich-skin belt with your service automatic on your left buttock, beside the handcuffs and Gervaise's rosary. By the way, I put it in your hands. Can you feel it?"

Jesus, sure enough, she'd cuffed and rosaried him.

"And I've borrowed your jacket . . . Very soft . . . And then I've got your gun, here, over my heart, it's rather comforting . . ."

She was driving with her foot down. She was heading towards Sainclair hell for leather. He now had an excellent opportunity to tell all of Gervaise's aves and paters, in fact. She drove on, with these reassuring words:

"As a matter of fact, I don't believe what you told me about Sainclair and Gervaise . . . We'll find out soon enough, but I don't believe you. I didn't swallow that for a second."

She gave her tomboyish laugh.

"You really did try every means to make me talk! It was rather touching. You have a lovely voice, you know. Has anyone ever told you that you've got a smiling, rather languid voice? With a little metallic laugh, perched just below your eyebrows."

Apparently she'd been listening carefully.

"You're cute. Which is all a woman in a cell could ask for."

She'd been watching him, too.

"You gave me a lot of pleasure . . . after you'd gone!"

She laughed.

"But I won't tell Sainclair that!"

She fell silent for a while, then she repeated:

"I don't believe you about Gervaise and Sainclair. Most of what you said was spot on, about old Florentis, for example, you guessed absolutely right, I can confirm that, but as far as the story about Gervaise and Sainclair is concerned, I just don't believe you."

She hesitated.

"No . . . I really don't."

Her tendency to doubt, despite everything, had moved Titus too. Her slow journey into doubt over all those weeks. He'd been her doubt instructor.

"In the end, everyone tells lies . . ."

A pause.

"That's what makes life so exciting!"

She didn't turn round as she spoke. She didn't try to catch his eye in the rear-view mirror. Attached to the two doors, he couldn't do a thing, except follow the route between the seat's headrest and the bodywork.

"But trying to make me believe that he's the kid's father was a good idea."

Yeah, brilliant . . .

"Because it gave me the strength to jump you."

He spotted the tollbooth at the same moment she did. Plus the blue van parked to one side of it.

"Oh look, your pals in the gendarmerie are at the toll. You're now going to see if I'm a real killer or not. One false move and you'll find out."

She slipped her hand into the jacket and placed Titus's gun on to the passenger seat.

Titus made no false moves.

Nor did the gendarmes.

Once the toll had been passed, Titus sighed with relief and finally took in how mild the evening air was. A luminous night in spring. The first one for ages. He imagined Hélène and Tanita, on Nadine's terrace, in front of their glasses of port, trying not to get worried.

They'd left the motorway.

"We're nearly there."

They crossed one of those small unlit villages which are the capital's extinct satellites.

"Turn right . . ."

The car turned right.

"Then left . . ."

She was so tense that she commented on the slightest movement of the car with the forced joviality of an on-board computer.

"Here's the gate . . ."

The car turned up a gravel drive. With horse-chestnut trees on either side. Or maybe they were plane trees. And the dark depths of the forest all around them. Then, at the end, steps leading up to a door. A notable's country seat. Lights were on in the ground-floor windows. Plus one upstairs. It vaguely reminded Titus of one of Magritte's most famous paintings.

The car stopped a few yards from the front door.

Marie-Ange left the headlamps on.

She turned the engine off.

She put Titus's gun back into the inside pocket of the jacket.

Then she hooted the horn, with what must have been a pre-arranged signal: two short blasts, one long, one short again.

Titus just heard her mutter:

"Now we'll see."

A few seconds later, the front door opened and Sainclair emerged. Titus couldn't believe his eyes. He was wearing a bathrobe and was drying his hair with a towel. He looked like the notable's son who'd been caught in the shower, but who was so looking forward to this visit that if he did have to rush outside in the nude, then rush out in the nude he would. Sainclair couldn't see Marie-Ange, but he made no attempt to hide from the glare of the headlamps. He flung the towel away and came down the steps, extending his arms wide enough to embrace the car. At the same moment, his bathrobe opened. Not only was he unarmed, he was as naked as the day he was born and had a distinct erection. And yet he was supposed to be on the run, with the entire French police force after him!

"Denis."

She leapt out of the car.

"Denis!"

It was not so much a name as the outburst of the desire which had been building up during all those months behind bars. In three strides, she was with him, and so perfectly impaled that Titus wondered how such a thing was possible without months of training. Titus's jacket, Sainclair's bathrobe, the pink suit, panties and bra were lying at their feet. The headlamps framed the couple in the darkness. Marie-Ange's back arched in and out like a tidal wave. Titus could picture the wild boars gawping at the edge of the forest, and could almost hear the stags belling. "You bastard," he thought. "When I nick you, you'd better thank me for your last lay. I've been working it up for weeks!" Then he remembered that he was in no position to arrest anyone. He pulled as hard as he could on his handcuffs. Nothing doing. The door handle remained solidly in place. "Don't come too quickly, keep it back," he muttered to himself. "Wait till I've thought of something!" As though answering his prayer, they now dropped down together amid their clothes. Time now for caresses and whispered laughter. She was talking into his neck, calling him. They called out each other's names again. Then he sank his face into her breasts while she stroked his nape. Titus's feet, strapped on to the other handle, were of no more use to him than his hands. Where the hell had she learnt to tie knots like that? Inspector Titus was an inspector with neither hands nor feet. And unarmed. With a low life expectancy. The end of a short, brilliant career. On a spring night, when the sap was making the trees quiver. He looked for strength in this evocation of nature, but his mechanical problem remained. "If I get out of here alive, I'll buy a cardboard car." He yanked at his handcuffs like a fox at its trap. He considered biting through his wrists. "Jesus Christ! Jesus Christ!" he thought. "The lights are all going to come on, and there they'll all be – Silistri, Caregga and the boss, there in the undergrowth, having a good ogle with

422

the boars and the hedgehogs." But he knew that no-one could possibly have followed them. One last try, then he slumped down exhausted on to the seat, still cuffed and bound. No way out. He glanced round gloomily at the couple and, with horror, saw that their pleasure was mounting as clearly as mercury in a thermometer. Sainclair came first. The shock wave racked Marie-Ange's body, then, through the car's bodywork and four closed windows, Titus could hear her screams. "He's shot her brains out!" Birds took wing. Marie-Ange's head slumped down on to Sainclair's shoulder. Then Gervaise appeared in the doorway.

"No," thought Titus.

A perfectly spherical Gervaise, in the light of the headlamps.

"Oh no!" Titus repeated.

Gervaise placidly standing there on the steps, with what was left of her little finger in a large dressing.

"Hide Gervaise! Run for it!" he yelled.

But all he managed to do was alert Marie-Ange.

The two women were now staring at each other. Marie-Ange was cradling Sainclair's head on her shoulder. Meanwhile her other hand had slipped into the inside pocket of the jacket.

"Noooo!" Titus roared.

The door handle gave way.

He reached for his feet, but broke his nails on the knots in the rope. He managed to open the door and scramble outside.

"Stop, Marie-Ange, it isn't what you think . . ."

There were two muffled gunshots.

Gervaise didn't move.

But Sainclair's body started to slide to the ground. Marie-Ange pulled him up against her breasts.

She turned around, holding the gun, and smiled at Inspector Titus.

He was lying on the gravel, feet in the air, still tied to the door.

"You were right, Titus, such love isn't made for growing old in a cell."

Before he had time to reply, she bent down over Sainclair's body, turned the gun towards herself and a third shot was heard, even more muffled than the other two.

Chapter 69

THAT'S WHEN YOU decided to be born. You banged mightily on the door, and Gervaise collapsed. Titus's first thought was that she'd been hit by one of the bullets. He started yelling like a thing possessed, but she got to her feet again, panting for breath, gesturing to him that she was OK, and that it was you. She went to release him, after recovering the key to his handcuffs from his jacket. On the way, she covered up Sainclair's and Marie-Ange's bodies instinctively, less from prudery than because of the chill night air. They were lying in each other's arms like an allegory of love. A stream of blood was sticking them together. Titus phoned Silistri to tell him to come along with an ambulance and warn the Malaussène tribe that you were on your way. He was going to take Gervaise straight to Saint-Louis Hospital.

"No!" Gervaise called out. "To Postel-Wagner!"

A brief argument ensued.

"What? To the morgue? Jesus Christ, Gervaise, you can't give birth in a morgue!"

"Take me to Postel!" Gervaise insisted.

"OK," Titus said into the phone. "Not to Saint-Louis, then, to the morgue!"

"The morgue?" Silistri asked.

"To Postel-Wagner," Titus explained. "She wants Postel to deliver the child."

So that's where we all met up to greet you. And when I say all, I really mean all, just trust our tribal instinct for that. There were the Malaussènes and the Ben Tayebs, of course, but there was also Loussa de Casamance, and Theo, Queen Zabo, Inspector Caregga and Chief Superintendent Coudrier, Hélène and Tanita, the wives of Titus and Silistri, Marty, Berthold and Mondine, there were the living and also the dead, our dead: Thian, Stojil, Clément, Pastor, Matthias and Cissou, but also, all around us, Postel-Wagner's dead, the unknown dead lined up in their rows of eternity, all highly curious to see what was going to spring out from between Gervaise's thighs, what this new one was going to look like, whose arrival would round off their existences and ease their departure, while the living accompanied Gervaise in gestures and words, Queen Zabo, always so remarkable at such times – "Breathe in! Push! Breathe in! Push!" – leading the others like a true choirmaster, while wondering to herself, "What the hell am I doing here? Breathe in and push! What the hell am I saying?", Berthold closely observing the manoeuvre, "Watch it Postel, and don't damage him whatever you do! Wouldn't you prefer me to handle it?" and Marty as ever weighing up Berthold's suggestions, "Leave it out, Berthold, it isn't your kid, it's Malaussène's!", which Mondine confirmed in a deep purr, "Never fret, professor, you'll soon have one of your own. I'll see to that . . .", Jeremy jotting it all down on his little notebook of novelistic realism and me, of course, me with Julie's hand crushed in mine, the other hand twisting Julius's ears, me so worried about what you were going to look like after this nine-month odyssey . . . I mean you'd be right to look furious, or completely blasé, or utterly terrified, or a touch mystic, desiring immediate assumption, or else totally and irreversibly capricious, "Encore! Encore! More gunshots! More snuff movies! More shagging in the moonlight! With Uncle Titus tied to the car door! Encore!" (because the obvious tedium of what's to follow is bound to be a bit of a downer . . . you'll have to get used to things being probable now . . . and how to "participate", they all say that the main thing is to "participate"), so extremely worried then about the possible expressions on your face – all those you avoided getting – when suddenly, here, now, at four forty a.m., or twenty to five in the morning if you prefer, there was Clara's flash, and your face! immortalised at the very moment it crossed the finishing line!

Halley loo ya! Hourrah! The crowd went wild! A joyous lift-off into the city sky for Postel-Wagner's dead . . . free at last, flying away with great flaps of their wings alongside the early-morning pigeons.

And Postel presenting the champion to the crowds.

And silence coming back down below the parachute of rapture.

Your face, my little one . . .

O the delicious silence.

Not the slightest bump. Not the face of an escapee.

Nor the slightest anger.

And not frightened, either.

And not blasé at all.

With no regrets, not a nostalgic face.

And not looking skywards, not the face of an avid supporter of the Great Paranoiac.

No preconceived ideas, no shady deals, not a litigious face.

No desire to find the world that logical, and no inclination to find it that absurd either.

Mysterious, more like. Interesting, in fact.

The very face of *curiosity*!

"He's the image of both of you," Gervaise said, kissing Julie and me.

"With something of you, too, Gervaise . . ."

And Postel-Wagner showed us your left hand, wide open. The lovely range of chubby fingers. Yes, five fingers, but five fingers *minus one phalanx* – the missing tip of Gervaise's left little finger.

"A little Monsieur Malaussène, no doubt about it," Chief Superintendent Coudrier observed.

"And that's what we're going to call him," Jeremy declared.

"What, Malaussène?" Thérèse asked.

"Monsieur Malaussène," said Jeremy.

"Monsieur Malaussène?" Thérèse insisted.

"Yes, with two capitals, Monsieur Malaussène."

"Can you imagine that at school? Malaussène Monsieur . . ."

"Schools have heard worse."

"No, Monsieur Malaussène! That's impossible!"

"It isn't. He's right here in front of you. What's more, it'll make a neat title. What do you reckon, Your Majesty?"

"Monsieur Malaussène?" Queen Zabo asked.

"Monsieur Malaussène," Jeremy confirmed.

"We'll see about that," Queen Zabo said.

"We've already seen, Your Majesty."

"Monsieur Malaussène, then?"

"Monsieur Malaussène."